THE
CONTINENT

Books by Keira Drake
available from Harlequin TEEN

The Continent

KEIRA DRAKE

THE
CONTINENT

HARLEQUIN®TEEN

ISBN-13: 978-1-335-47493-3

The Continent

www.HarlequinTEEN.com

Printed in U.S.A.

For Pea.

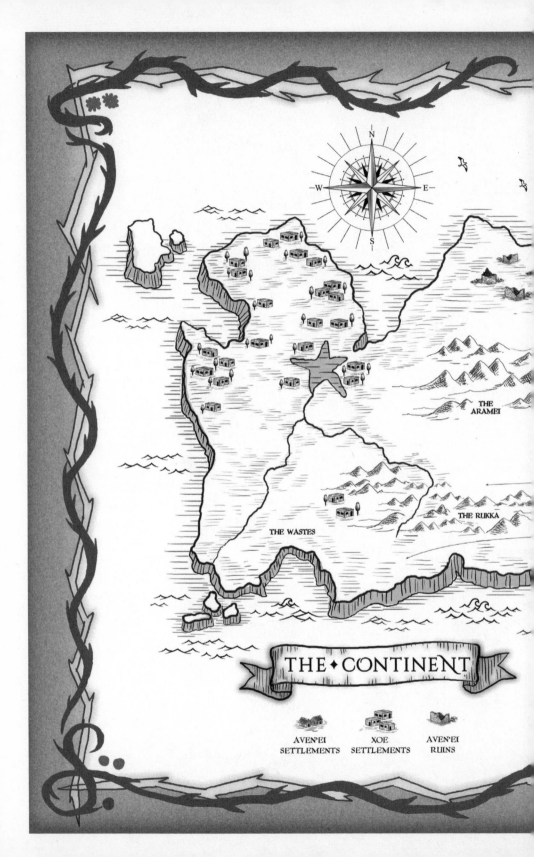

THE ✦ CONTINENT

AVEN'EI
SETTLEMENTS

XOE
SETTLEMENTS

AVEN'EI
RUINS

THE
ARAMEI

THE RUKKA

THE WASTES

CHAPTER 1

✦

THIS MUST BE THE MOST MAGNIFICENT PARTY IN the history of the Spire.

I've never felt quite like this before; my mind is awhirl, my senses dazzled, and there's a bounding joy spiraling up within me. I wonder where it's coming from, this feeling of inexhaustible delight?

Maybe it's the music, rising from the gleaming instruments of the quartet on the dais, filling the air with the cheerful sounds of the strings. Maybe it's the food and drink, the tables overflowing with dainty hors d'oeuvres, sparkling juices, and wine. Maybe it's the men and women on the dance floor, swirling by in a blur of black-and-gold finery, laughing and glittering and whispering merrily to one another. Or maybe it's just knowing that all this—this amazing affair, this wonderful gala—it's all for me. For my sixteenth birthday.

The room is filled nearly to capacity with well-wishers—people from all four corners of the Spire. I count two dozen of my friends from school, but the rest of the partygoers appear to be business associates of my father's, or society women whom my mother invites for tea at the start of every week. Now that I take a moment to look around, it seems clear that the greater portion of the Spire's nobility—as well as a sprinkling of government officials—are in attendance; even the Chancellor and his wife are here at my father's invitation.

"Vaela," calls my mother, as she approaches in a swish of cranberry chiffon, "it's time."

Her dark hair shimmers, her alabaster skin glows in the light of the chandeliers. She takes my hand and pulls me across the dance floor, smiling and nodding to the revelers as we duck through to the other side of the hall. When we're clear of the guests, she turns and gives me a long look, her eyes flickering over my face in quick assessment. Then she smiles.

"You look happy, darling. Are you pleased with the party? Is it everything you hoped it would be?"

"It's wonderful," I say. "I can't remember when I've had such a good time."

She gives my hand a little squeeze. "I can't wait to see your face when you open your gifts! You'll be absolutely astounded when you see what your father has done. There he is now—*Thomas!*"

My father stands on the dais with his back to us, arranging three crimson-wrapped packages on a small table. When he hears my mother's voice, he turns and smiles. Then he gestures for us to join him. He is grinning widely, happy, a virtual match to my mother save for his blond hair.

I follow my mother up a small stairway and we meet him at the back of the stage. He gives me a kiss on the cheek, then nods toward the packages on the table. "Are you ready to open your gifts?"

I look out on the party, at the scores of people dancing and drinking and chatting together. They are friendly, happy, many of them a bit drunk. I wasn't exaggerating when I said that people from all four corners of our great United Nation are in attendance here tonight—men and women with complexions of every shade, from darkest brown to palest white, each wearing a proud expression of cultural heritage in dress, representing all that makes the Spire such a beautiful place. Oh, how I love my homeland! I do wish for the millionth time that I could enjoy my gifts *privately*. But that is not our way, for birthday celebrations are always a big to-do, and so I give my father a smile. "Of course."

"Oh, Vaela," my mother says. "When you open the last one—that small one there at the edge of the table—you'll be the envy of everyone in the room. But I won't say another word—I don't want to spoil the surprise!"

I think she may be more excited than I am, but I must admit, my curiosity is piqued. "All right, then, I'm ready." It's a lie, but a necessary one. It's my birthday. The party is in full effect. I must play my part. I'd rather crawl under a table than make a public appearance, but I will do what I must; shyness is not a thing valued in the Spire.

The musicians play the closing notes of a lively waltz and my father signals for them to wait. Then he steps up to a small stand on the podium and taps the microphone a few times.

"Good evening," he says. "May I have your attention for just a few minutes?" The guests fall quiet as they turn toward him. Ever comfortable speaking to a room full of people, he smiles broadly and continues. "Friends and colleagues, citizens and patriots, I thank you most graciously for being here this evening. It's not every day that we have the opportunity to celebrate a milestone like this one—a sixteenth birthday, a coming of age, a step into life as a true citizen of the Spire." The guests applaud, and my father turns to me. "Vaela, your mother and I could not be more proud of the young woman you have become. I hope these three gifts will demonstrate our admiration, our respect, and most of all, our love."

He extends an arm and I step forward, trembling a bit as I realize that all eyes in the room are now on me. By *God*, by the

Maker, I am incredibly uncomfortable. My father reaches for a tiny rectangular box and places it in my hands. "Go ahead," he says.

I turn the box over and gently tear open the paper, while guests begin calling out guesses as to what might be inside.

"A bicycle!" says Evangeline Day, my closest and dearest friend, and the crowd laughs. Evangeline claps her hands demurely, but I see the giggle in her eyes. She's the picture of societal grace, but I *know* her, and she is wicked—in all the best ways, of course. She'd kiss a boy before he made any declaration of intention, and she'd tell you all about it. I adore her.

A heavyset woman at the edge of the dance floor—a friend of my mother's, I believe—says, "A great stuffed bear!" The guests titter appreciatively and the woman grins.

I smile and lift the lid from the box. Inside, suspended from a delicate golden chain, is the most spectacular ruby pendant I've ever seen; it's cut like an emerald, but mirrors the color of a deep red rose. The facets catch the light, glittering beneath the warm glow of the chandeliers. I look up at my father. "It's beautiful."

"See what's written on the back," my mother whispers.

I turn the pendant over to find a single word inscribed in tiny print: *ansana*. It's an old word, from a language now mostly lost to the Spire, but a word still known and with many meanings: *family, love, forever*. My eyes fill with tears. "Thank you," I say. "Thank you so much, both of you."

My mother takes the pendant and fixes it around my neck, and the guests applaud once again. My father hands me a second box; this one is wide and flat, and quite heavy. I set it on the table and begin to unwrap it. When I see what's inside, I draw in my breath.

It's a map of the Continent, framed in ebony wood, with a crimson mat set inside to bring out the color of the red and black pens with which the map was drawn. But it's not just any map. It's one of mine.

I drew this map over the course of a year during countless

visits to the Astor Library, which is easily the greatest source of information about the Continent in the whole of the Spire. I spent hundreds of hours poring over aerial phototypes, studying the existing cartography, and imagining the features of that vast and foreign land. This map earned me an apprenticeship with Otto Sussenfaal himself, the curator of the library and perhaps the most brilliant cartographer our Nation has borne in centuries. This map is the culmination of my study; it is my greatest achievement so far.

And now, here it is, framed like a work of art, beautiful enough to draw hushed whispers from the guests gathered around the stage. I have no words.

"This map," my father says, "was completed by Vaela herself." A surprised murmur rises from the crowd. "Her passion and her talent enabled her to create this stunning—and, I have no doubt, highly accurate—representation of the Continent. It is because of this map, because of the hours of work Vaela put into creating it, that her mother and I were inspired to choose this final gift."

He hands me the last box. It's no more than six inches wide and half an inch thick, and feels as though it contains nothing at all. I remove the paper and lift the lid; inside is a certificate of travel, embossed with the Spire's official seal and marked with my name. I look up at my father, confused.

"Turn it over," he says.

On the other side of the paper, I find the following words printed on the form:

Traveler: Vaela Sun
Depart from: Spire East
Destination: Ivanel
Tour: The Continent

My mouth falls open and I look up at him in wonder. "We're going to the Continent?"

The crowd, hearing this, erupts in thunderous applause. My father beams at me as my mother puts an arm around my shoulders. Her excitement is palpable.

"We leave in three days," she says.

A ruby pendant is the sort of gift I might have expected from my parents. A beautiful frame to display my map was an incredible, meaningful surprise. But a trip to the Continent is the most coveted privilege in the Spire—only ten tours are given each year, with a maximum of six guests per tour. Every man, woman, and child longs to see the Continent, but with more than a hundred million people across the Spire, only the very wealthy—and influential—are ever able to arrange a trip. My family is affluent, respected, and certainly very prominent in terms of society, but I still can't imagine how my father managed to secure us passage.

"What do you think?" he asks, studying my face.

This question has a thousand answers, but none seem sufficient. I throw my arms around him. "Thank you," I whisper.

The guests are delighted, stamping their feet and applauding with great enthusiasm. My father turns back to the crowd. "Dinner will be served shortly; please continue to enjoy the celebration, and thank you all for coming!"

He replaces the microphone on the stand and gives a nod to the waiting musicians, who immediately take up with an old standard.

"Are you surprised?" he asks.

"Surprised? I don't understand, I thought the wait list to tour was—"

"Endless," my mother says. "Absolutely impossible. But, as it happens, your father is working with Mr. Shaw now—you'll know the name, of course, the Director of National Affairs down at the Chancellery—and has been promoted to Trade Regulator! Overseeing the embargoes and other whatnots for the East, West, North, and South."

"Paperwork," my father says, and gives me a wink. "Mountains of it."

My mother laughs. "In any case, Mr. Shaw and your father have been getting along famously. And so the Shaws, who've had a private tour booked for absolute ages, invited us to join their family."

"What good fortune!" I say. "We shall be traveling as their guests?"

"As their companions," my father says. "Mr. Shaw was kind enough to make the arrangements, but this gift is from your mother and me alone."

"I am very grateful," I say. "To you and Mother for your generosity, and to Mr. Shaw for his graciousness. I should like to thank him properly, when we meet."

"You shall have the chance directly," says my mother, beaming. "They'll be joining us for dinner."

The Shaws, apparently, have been delayed, and so the three of us—my father, mother, and I—begin my birthday dinner at rather an empty table. A golden cloth, edged with silken tassels, is laid out before us, with a slim black runner down the center; the dishes are porcelain, the utensils silver, the glasses crystal—everything is handmade, and exceptionally fine. The decor throughout the Chancellery ballroom is striking, all in the black and gold of the Spire, according to tradition, as is the attire of our guests. Only my family is dressed in red, for as the guests of honor, we wear the crimson of the Blood Lily, the symbol of the East: the Nation we call home.

We are seated, chatting idly and awaiting the second course, when a stout, bespectacled man with smooth, light brown skin—quite rosy around the cheekbones—and a very harassed-looking woman of ruddy complexion and drawn-on eyebrows approach the table. They are accompanied by a handsome young man of about twenty; his hair is brown and slightly wavy, his eyes blue, rimmed by dark circles. He is even paler than I am, which is quite saying something.

My father rises to greet them. "Mr. and Mrs. Shaw, we're so glad you could make it! And Aaden, it's nice to see you again as well."

"It's a wonder we've made it at all," says Mrs. Shaw, "the way it's pouring rain outside. I had to change my shoes three times! Can you imagine?" She stops speaking and stares at one of the servers, who rushes forward and pulls out her chair. She sits with a huff and makes a quick inspection of the table. "We've missed the first course, have we? It's just as well. I had a late lunch."

My father smiles and settles into his chair once again. "Vaela, may I introduce Mr. and Mrs. Arthur Shaw, and their son, Aaden."

"It's a pleasure to meet you," I say.

"The pleasure is ours," says Mr. Shaw. "And happy birthday! I presume you've already had occasion to open your gifts?" He raises a brow at my father.

"Yes, sir," I say. "And I'm told it was by your invitation that we are able to see the Continent. I can't say how grateful I am."

"Not at all," he says. "It is our good fortune to have you and your family along. The more the merrier, so they say."

"I couldn't agree more," my mother says. "A journey across the sea! I can scarcely imagine how exciting it will be. Are you looking forward to the trip, Mrs. Shaw?"

Mrs. Shaw has busied herself with inspecting the silverware, but hasn't missed a word. "Oh, yes. I've been after Arthur for years to get us bumped up the wait list, but he's always too busy doing something or other for the Chancellery."

"They do keep us busy," he agrees. "As I'm sure your husband can attest, Mrs. Sun."

My mother reaches over and pats my father's hand. "It's fortunate for all of us that the government has seen fit to spare you both for a holiday."

"I've been packed and ready for two weeks," says Mrs. Shaw, adjusting her very large hat, upon which no fewer than six black ceramic birds are perched atop a spray of shining golden wheat. "No one can ever say I don't properly prepare for these events. Of course, there's always the odd thing you somehow manage to forget, isn't there?" She takes a sip of wine and smiles at me. "What a lovely pendant, Vaela. I've never been able to wear rubies—I look absolutely dreadful in red. I'd have done much better if I'd been born in the South, draped in all that luxurious purple. Haven't I always said so, Arthur? Anyhow. The color suits you very well, and that chain brings out the gold of your hair. Makes it look like—" She pauses, searching for the right word.

"Like honey," Aaden says. I glance over to find him staring at me, a contemplative expression on his face, and I quickly look away.

Mrs. Shaw considers this for a moment, then nods in agreement. "You're a lovely girl—why, you're nearly the spitting image of your mother, but with your father's hair! And what I wouldn't *give* for tresses so—heavens, Vaela, are you blushing? Oh!" She laughs. "How quaint! How *darling*! She's blushing, dear, do you see?"

I bring my glass to my lips and fix my eyes on the ice water within. My cheeks are burning, but I can think of nothing to say. My father graciously intervenes.

"Have you any thoughts, Mr. Shaw, about the Xoe and the Aven'ei? I expect we shall see a good deal of fighting during our tour."

"I favor the Xoe, myself," says Mr. Shaw, leaning forward. "I'm not as well-read as my boy Aaden here, but the Xoe seem highly skilled—masterful men- and women-at-arms, they say."

"They are a popular favorite, to be sure," my father says. "Much more formidable than the Aven'ei, or so I hear. I take no preference, myself, but I admit, it will be interesting to see them at battle."

"Thomas, really?" my mother says, a tiny crinkle appearing between her brows. "I was hoping not to see any bloodshed at all."

"Come now, madam," Aaden says, an easy smile upon his face. "Is there any other reason to go to the Continent?"

My mother is taken aback. "I'm sure there are many reasons. For my part, I have heard that the landscape is spectacular, and I shall be very glad to see it."

"Ah, yes," Aaden says. "Snow and ice, and miles and miles of treacherous wilderness." He laughs. "Let's be honest—it's not the scenery that has every citizen in the Spire clamoring to see the Continent. It's the war."

My mother smiles and sets down her fork. "I have no interest in seeing the Xoe and the Aven'ei slaughter one another."

"But that is exactly what you'll see, Mrs. Sun," Aaden says. "Surely you are prepared for it?"

"She knows perfectly well what she will and won't see," says Mrs. Shaw. "No one expects that the violence on the Continent will stop simply because we're there to observe it. The Xoe and the Aven'ei have been railing at each other for centuries. I've never understood the fascination with it, myself. I'm with you, Mrs. Sun."

"The fascination," my father says, "lies in the fact that they are at war in the first place."

"Too right," says Mr. Shaw. "We take for granted that the Spire is a place without such hostilities—that we have transcended the ways of war in favor of peace and negotiation. To see the Xoe and the Aven'ei in conflict is to look into our past—and to appreciate how far we have come."

"Did you know," my mother says, addressing the Shaws, "that Vaela and I are of Aven'ei descent?"

Aaden looks back and forth between the two of us. "Are you quite sure?" he says. "Many claim as much, but it's rarely true."

She smiles. "We can trace it all the way back to one of my ancestors, a Miss Delia Waters. She was a cultural attaché for the East—an illustrious position, all told—and spent a great deal of time on the Continent, back in that all-too-short bit of time when we had contact with those living overseas. Anyhow, we haven't *all* the details, but we know she married an Aven'ei by the name of Qia who died soon after their wedding. She returned to the Spire, kept her given name, and gave birth to a baby boy—Roderick—a man of considerable accomplishment, so the story goes."

"Qia," Aaden says, tapping his fingers upon the table. "A curious name for an Aven'ei. Typically—"

"I'm sure we don't need a lecture in linguistics, son," says Mr. Shaw, glancing sidelong at Aaden. He turns back to my mother. "What a fascinating history, Mrs. Sun. An exceedingly rare lineage among Spirians, to be sure, and one you must count with great pride."

"Absolutely," she agrees, smiling. "I have always felt part of the world at large, rather than just bound to a small space on the atlas. Does that make any sense at all?"

"I do hope you haven't inherited any violent tendencies," says Mrs. Shaw, before sticking a forkful of duck confit into her mouth, chewing it carefully, and swallowing. "I suspect that sort of thing gets passed right down through the generations. Bit of a *questionable* lineage, isn't it?"

A hush falls over the table at this remark; my mother and father shift in their chairs, and I sit quietly, poking at my entrée, my face flaming even though I am certainly not the one who should be embarrassed. Eventually, Mrs. Shaw looks round at us, her eyes wide. "What? Have I said something off?"

Mr. Shaw clears his throat. "Now, dearest," he says, "that's a rather singular way of thinking, isn't it? An *outmoded* way of thinking? Violence itself is not a thing exclusive to the Xoe and the Aven'ei. After all, before the Four Nations united to become the Spire, the people of our own lands were ever locked in some conflict or another."

My father nods. "The tour will be, as you say, like a look into our own past. But at least we can see it all from the safety of the heli-plane, yes? Not the sort of place you'd like to go tramping about on foot."

"Oh, I don't know," Aaden says, "it might be quite a thrill to see all that blood and gore up close."

"Aaden, please," says Mrs. Shaw, making a face. "We are at supper."

My mother pushes her plate away. "I think it's a dreadful shame that in all these years, the Xoe and the Aven'ei haven't been able to sort out their differences."

Mrs. Shaw rolls her eyes skyward. "I say let them kill each other. One day they'll figure out that war suits no one, or else they'll drive themselves to extinction. Either way, it makes no difference to me."

My mother, dark-haired, lovely, and generally made of warm smiles, becomes the picture of frost. "We are talking about *people*, Mrs. Shaw. Flesh and blood. Fathers, brothers, mothers, daughters."

Mrs. Shaw bristles. "People without the good sense to realize that there are ways to solve disagreements *not* involving blood or dismemberment."

"Well," says Mr. Shaw, "I believe the Xoe and the Aven'ei will work out their differences in their own time. Peace always prevails. They will find a way forward—I'd bet my hat on it." He raises a glass. "Now. Let those of us *here* be thankful that the forefathers of our great United Nation had the will and the courage to envision a world of peace for all who would choose it."

Glasses are raised all around the table.

"Hear, hear," my father says, and the whole party drinks: to peace, to hope, to the Spire. I take a small sip of champagne; from the corner of my eye, I see Aaden watching me.

I am surprised to find that I am flattered. Uneasy. But flattered.

Later that evening, when most of the guests have gone and only a few stragglers remain, my mother pulls me aside. Her brow is knit with worry.

"I never thought to ask you, Vaela, before we arranged the trip, and now I feel quite beside myself: Will you be all right seeing the Continent?"

I wave goodbye to a friend, then turn back to my mother. "But of course," I say. "Why wouldn't I be?"

She is quiet for a moment. "With the war, I mean. The things you might see."

"I suppose I haven't given it much thought," I say. "But then, I'm more interested in the topography than the Xoe and the Aven'ei. This is a dream come true for me—you know that better than anyone."

Her shoulders relax a bit. "Then you're not worried about it?"

"What is there to worry about? We'll be well out of reach of any danger, touring in the heli-plane."

"That's not what I mean."

I find a stray chair and sit down, my feet aching in my pointed shoes. "What is it, then? The violence?"

"Yes, Vaela, the violence."

I give a little shrug. "I know what to expect—we've all read the histories. The Xoe and the Aven'ei fight, and fight, and fight some more. Over land or religion or territory or whatever it is—I've never quite understood—the war goes on and on. It never changes."

"Vaela! Vaela!" Evangeline, shimmering and luminous in a gown of pale gold and black lace, flutters over and plants a kiss on my cheek. Her skin is damp with perspiration from danc-

ing, darker than deepest brown, her blue eyes bright with celebration. "Remember everything," she says breathlessly. "Draw
every single thing you see! I want to know if the Xoe are as tall
and handsome as Roslyn says they are. And the Aven'ei—do you
think they truly have grand cities surrounded by towering walls
of stone? I *know* it's true, and oh, Mrs. Sun! I—how do you do?"

"Hello, Evangeline," my mother says. "You look lovely this
evening."

"Thank you," Evangeline says, her fingers brushing the silky
fabric of her skirts. She smiles and turns back to me. "You will
come to call as soon as you return? I know my mother will want
to receive you at once. She's sick with envy, you know—she
hasn't said a word to Father all night, on account of his being
so far down the wait list."

"I'll come round as soon as we're home," I say. "I promise."

She pulls me into her arms, embraces me tightly, then steps
back and grins. "The Continent! Oh, Vaela. You'll have a spot
yet beside the scholars at the Institute. You'll be far more fa-
mous than stuffy old Sussenfaal, and lauded by your scientific
peers, and I shall tell everyone that I am practically a part of
your family."

I touch the pendant at my neck. "And so you are, forever. We
are sisters, remember?"

She giggles, and then her mother calls from the grand doors
at the entrance of the hall, an icy expression upon her perfectly
painted face. Oh, but she is a picture of discontent. Mr. Day
stands beside her, a full head shorter and twelve shades paler than
his Northern wife, looking defeated, apologetic, and miserable.
"Be well, and remember everything," Evangeline says. "I shall
miss you every moment! Goodbye, Mrs. Sun!" And with a rus-
tle of silk, she turns and hurries toward the foyer.

A glance at my mother tells me that the subject of violence
on the Continent has not been forgotten.

"The tour will be incredible," I say. "The war is tragic—of

course it is. But…perhaps we won't see any fighting at all, only the vast, sparkling beauty of the Continent! Just *imagine* the stories we shall have to tell!"

She smiles, but not with her eyes. "You're right. I'm sure it will be a lovely trip."

"It will be amazing," I say, taking her hand. Her hesitance hurts me, moves me, makes me want to comfort her. "Don't worry for even a moment. It will be the single greatest adventure of my life, I'm sure."

CHAPTER 2

✦

THE SPIRE IS A COLORFUL PLACE, AND NO CITY IS
more representative of this than Astor—the Spirian capital. Here,
citizens of all cultures, bedecked in the finery of their home
countries, come to take positions in the Chancellery: the beating heart of our Nation's government. Astor, which is but five
miles from the place I call home, is nestled firmly within the
borders of the East, though its residents maintain their original
citizenship, designated, as always, by the Nation of one's birth.

There are those of the North, most often with skin of deep
brown, eyes of pale blue—nearly white—draped in the colors
of the navy seagull that flies free upon those cold, Northern
shores. And then there are the Southern men and women, all
dressed in glorious shades of purple, their hair a frizz of blond
and brown, complexions ranging from pink to golden brown,
curls like happy tendrils falling here and there, eyes like charcoal,
or sometimes blue like stones. The Easterners are generally much
like me, pale, with eyes of every color (my mother often says
my eyes are brown, then green, then blue, and it's true—they
seem to change with the seasons), dressing formally—stiffly—
compared to every other Nation. We are certainly the most
old-fashioned of *all* the Nations, with a thousand rules of con-

duct for every behavior. And then there are those in the West—sun-kissed, tanned, with hair of every color, but auburn most commonly, with loose-fitting clothes and the most relaxed set of mores in all the Spire.

Of course, the Nations were once separate, and in the two hundred years since the borders fell, a beautiful intermingling of peoples has begun. One might now find any number of those with mixed heritage and all manner of varied features throughout the land. When the Four Nations became the Spire, the world opened up, and love spread from shore to shore. And so it is here in Astor, in the Chancellery, in this place of ultimate blending, that all come together.

The Chancellery—the place where elections are held in which officials are chosen by the people, new laws are considered and voted upon by the Heads of State, and the Astor Library houses the combined literary and scientific knowledge of the North, West, East, and South. It is also the site of the Eastern heliport—the place from which all air travel to and from the East is conducted.

Most citizens travel by train, in one of the sleek magnetic monorails that glide above and below the streets of every major city in the Spire, but my father has arranged a car for today—a special privilege indeed. It is a black limousine, its electric motor nearly silent, with plush velvet seats the color of burnished bronze. As our driver maneuvers the car to the curb in front of the Chancellery proper—a grand campus of twenty or so buildings that glimmer silver in the light of day, with arched windows winking prettily from foundation to rooftops, and slender pinnacles and steeples rising high into the sky—I begin to tremble. Today, I shall see the Continent. I will see with my own eyes the place I have imagined for so long.

My mother sets a hand on my knee for what must be the tenth time since we left the estate. "Stop jiggling your leg, dear," she says again. "It doesn't suit."

I relax my muscles, but nothing can quell the restless antici-pation I feel inside. The car rolls to a stop and a prim-looking valet hurries forward, snapping his fingers at a couple of porters waiting by the entrance. The two men rush into action, chatter-ing at one another in a familiar sort of way as they bundle our luggage out of the trunk and pile it atop shiny wheeled carts.

The valet comes round to my door and extends a hand; I smile as I step out onto the curb. The rain has stopped, and a hint of blue sky is visible beyond stern gray clouds. An important-looking woman with a National Affairs badge hurries by, a thoughtful frown on her face. From beyond the building, a heli-plane rises into the sky, the four-pointed golden star of the Spire painted boldly along its side.

This is happening. We're going to the Continent!

The porters have made quick work of the luggage; it's now stacked neatly on the brass carts and secured with sturdy straps. The valet leads us into the main building—a great towering structure of eighty floors and a hundred and sixty separate wings. We follow him through a series of short corridors while the por-ters trail behind with the trolleys.

I've been here a thousand, thousand times—the Astor Li-brary occupies floors five through ten, and I could find my way there even if I were asleep—but the rest feels like a maze. We turn down one corridor and then another, winding our way through the eastern wing at ground level. At last, we come to an immense set of double doors leading into a private hangar. As the doors open, I see our heli-plane inside, the front half lit by sunshine, its white face gleaming. The plane is larger than I thought it would be, and very beautiful in its way. The nose curves gracefully, the slender white wings stretch out like proud arms extended in triumph, each inset with a large and power-ful propeller.

The Shaws are standing near the plane with a steward who waves us over at once. He's a Westerner, by the look of him, a sweep of red-brown hair brushed back against his scalp, skin bronzed like he has spent a hundred days outdoors. His eyes are kind—they bulge out a bit beneath thick glass spectacles, which only adds to the effect of his already vivacious manner.

"Mr. and Mrs. Sun, Miss Sun," he calls as we approach. "What a pleasure to meet you. I'm Mr. Harris; I will be your steward throughout the expedition. If there is anything you need, please let me know and I shall do my utmost to accommodate you. Now if you'll just wait a few moments, we'll stow the luggage and you can board the plane directly."

"Excellent," says my father. "We can enjoy a bit of sunshine before we head into the frozen north."

The Shaws cross over to greet us, and I see that Mrs. Shaw's hat is even larger and grander than the one she wore to dinner the other night; clearly, she is not to be outdone, even by herself.

"Doesn't it just rub one the wrong way that the sun should come out the moment we're set to leave?" she says, looking insulted. "It's been raining for weeks, and now? Warm and toasty, like a tonic. I'm fit to be tied."

"Perhaps it's a sign that we shall have a safe and pleasant journey," my mother says. "A harbinger of good fortune?"

Aaden smiles, his blue eyes lit by the sun. "Whatever it means, it's delightful. I could stand here all day."

"I shouldn't like to wait too long," says Mrs. Shaw. "If we arrive in the dark, we'll miss the Continent as we fly over on our way to the island."

"Ah, yes, the island," my father says. "It's a good job we don't have to shack up on the Continent itself, now isn't it?"

"Thank the heavens," Mrs. Shaw says, and shudders. "Imagine! We'd probably be killed at once were we to set foot in *that* place. But. In any case, I've heard the facilities at Ivanel are top-of-the-line. My dearest friend—Mrs. Calista Jayne, you remember her, darling?—stayed earlier this year, and she says the staff will deliver eight kinds of coffee right to your suite. Eight kinds of coffee, on a tiny island like that!" She laughs. "Whatever will they think of next?"

Aaden takes my elbow and leads me farther into the sunlight, then leans over to whisper in my ear. "Can you imagine anything more incredible than *eight kinds of coffee*?"

I laugh. "Please, your mother is very sweet."

"Ha! She's an angel. For months, she's been rubbing this trip in the noses of all the society women who are wait-listed."

"Well...it *is* exciting, isn't it?"

He tilts his head. "Miss Vaela Sun—have you been bragging about this tour to your schoolmates?"

"No," I say, flushing. "Of course not! I only meant that I understand your mother's enthusiasm."

"Your friends were excited on your behalf, then? Not envious?"

"Thrilled for me," I say fondly. "I can't wait to tell everyone about the trip! Especially Evangeline—she's my closest friend, and a map enthusiast in her own right—though she is bound for a career in government, for that is where her talent lies."

"How nice," he says. "I haven't—well. I haven't got many companions. It's nice you have people waiting on your return."

This puzzles me; Aaden seems kind and well-spoken, and comes from a prestigious family—why should he not have an abundance of friends?

"Do you get on well with your family?" I ask, in hopes of changing the subject.

"Ah. Sadly, no. I don't quite fit the bill in terms of fatherly expectations. But you—you seem to be very close with your parents."

I smile. "Oh, yes—it's always been like that. I'm lucky, I suppose."

"We're ready to board now," calls the steward. "Please make your way through, and we'll file you up one at a time."

"That was quick," my mother says.

It's Mrs. Shaw who is quick; she's at the metal stairway in a heartbeat. Mr. Harris, the steward, gives her a friendly smile. "Let's start with you, madam. There we are, watch your step."

She clambers up the stairs, one hand on her hat and one on the railing, her shoes clacking against the grille. Then she stops and narrows her eyes. "Our luggage is all accounted for?" she asks. "There were several pieces I'm sure I didn't see on the trolley."

"Your belongings are counted and stowed, Mrs. Shaw," the steward says in a soothing tone. "The majority are in the belly of the plane, but we do have many of the smaller items in a more accessible location. Come along now."

She takes a reluctant step forward. "Oh, I do hope I haven't forgotten anything."

Her husband laughs. "My dear, if you'd brought anything more, the heli-plane might not have the strength to fly."

Aaden drops back to wait beside me as his mother and father disappear into the aircraft. "What do you think of the plane?" he says. "Ever seen one before?"

"Only in the sky," I say, and smile. "My mother prefers to travel by train, even to visit our relatives in the West. But it's very impressive—much more beautiful than I thought it would be."

"I've been to the North aboard one larger than this," he says. "It was a very nice piece of machinery. You know that's where they build them? In the North?"

"I didn't know."

My parents are at the top of the stairs now, and my mother turns back toward me. "Vaela," she calls. "It's time!"

Aaden extends an arm toward the metal stairway. "After you, Miss Sun."

As I climb toward the plane, a thrill runs through me. This is it—the first real step of the journey, the moment where everything begins. I will see the Continent before the sun sets. It is a momentous feeling indeed.

★ ★ ★

Aboard the plane, the whole group crowds into what I assume is the main cabin. We are clustered together in an open
space toward the front, facing two sections of plush seats that
are separated by a wide aisle. There are three rows in total with
two seats on each side, and six small windows punctuate the side
walls of the aircraft—something Mrs. Shaw is quick to notice.

"Is this where we're to view the Continent?" she says, a note
of surprise in her voice.

"Yes, madam," the steward says. "You will enjoy lovely views
from the window seats."

"But those are practically...portholes!" she exclaims. "Couldn't
we get a plane with proper windows, Arthur? I don't know how
we'll manage to see a thing!"

Aaden sits down in one of the front-row seats. "They're small
so the heli-plane isn't ripped apart while we're flying, Mother.
Structural integrity and all that." He taps on the thick glass and
grins at her. "Don't worry, they're big enough. I expect you
won't have any trouble watching the Xoe and the Aven'ei chop
one another to pieces."

Mrs. Shaw looks pointedly at her husband. "It was you who
gave him all those books about the Continent, and it is you who
are to blame for his vulgarity. You've stuffed his brain *chock-full*
of morbid imaginings."

"If I may," Mr. Harris says, stepping forward, looking more
than slightly uncomfortable, "I should like to familiarize each
of you with the heli-plane. You'll be spending several hours
on board each day, so I want to make sure that you're all quite
comfortable."

"Is there more to see?" Mrs. Shaw says, looking around the
small space. "I assumed this was the passenger cabin."

"So it is, madam, but we have another cabin at your disposal.
It's just aft of this one. It has no windows, and if you find your-

self overwhelmed by the scenery during any of your excursions, you might consider it a welcome retreat."

"Let's take a look," Aaden says.

One by one, we follow the steward down the aisle toward the rear of the plane and step through a narrow doorway. The aft cabin is smaller than the first, and slightly oblong in shape. There are no seats; only padded benches built into the sectioned walls.

Aaden runs a hand along one of the panels. "Are these doors?"

The steward crosses the small space. "Yes, sir, very good eye." He gives one of the panels a quick push and it springs toward him; he opens it wide to reveal several shelves stacked with luggage. "Storage, mostly. But over here, we have something much more interesting."

He closes the door and pushes on the section of wall beside it. When it opens, the group gives a collective gasp. Rather than a set of storage shelves, this panel had concealed a great glass pod, at least seven feet tall, shaped like a giant egg and standing perfectly upright. Within the pod is a padded seat with a harness attached to it.

"What in blazes is that?" says Mr. Shaw.

"It's an escape pod," the steward says, clearly delighted by our astonishment. "Ultimately, these panels were built to accommodate six pods; one for each passenger aboard the craft—six being the maximum number of passengers allowed by Spirian regulation for a plane of this size, of course. But it was an egregious waste of space, and all but this one have been removed. It's a novelty, really; it'll go on the next refit. But isn't it something?"

"Made of glass?" Aaden says. "Isn't it impossibly heavy?"

"Plasticized glass," the steward says. "Light as wind, but very strong. A marvel, truly."

I move closer and run a finger along the smooth, curved side. "The pods were meant to be used in the event of an accident, then? Is it quite safe to fly without a full complement?"

The steward laughs. "Oh, very safe indeed, Miss Sun. Do you

know, not a single pod has ever been put to use? Every heli-plane in the Spire has been equipped with them for decades, and not a one has ever been launched—save for training exercises and the like. No need for them at all. This aircraft runs smooth as a kitchen clock—our engineers and mechanics have seen to that."

I give him a smile. "If you're sure."

"Quite sure, miss," he says. "Now, if everyone would return to the passenger cabin, I can inform the pilot that we're ready to embark. We have many hundreds of miles of ocean to cross before we reach our destination, and I want you all to settle in comfortably. We'll have refreshments all around, and—"

"Just a moment," Aaden says. "What's that?" He points to a metal panel just to the right of the glass pod.

The steward blinks. "Why, those are the controls, of course." He lifts the lid of the panel to reveal two buttons: one green, one yellow. "The yellow button unlocks the pod from its casing, and the green discharges it from the plane."

"The controls are on the outside of the pod? What use is that if you're already inside?"

"The pods were not designed to be operated by passengers, Mr. Shaw. In the event of an accident, the crew would ensure that all travelers are properly secured within the pods, and eject each unit as required."

Aaden cuffs him playfully across the shoulder. "Guess we'll count on you, then, old man, should the need arise."

"Oh, trust me, sir, you'll have no need. Now then—shall we be on our way?"

"Yes, please," says Mrs. Shaw. "It's infinitely depressing back here with no windows. Although I don't suppose I could trouble you for my orchid valise? I saw it on the shelf when you opened the first door, and I wouldn't mind looking through it for a book or two."

"Now Mrs. Shaw," the steward says, "you head right back

into the main cabin and make yourself comfortable. I'll find the valise just as soon as we're on our way."

"What a dear you are," she says. "Such a help."

"Vaela, wake up. You won't believe how beautiful it is."

I open my eyes to see my mother's face. For a moment, I can't remember where I am—but the gentle hum of the heli-plane's engines brings me back to the present, and I sit up in my seat.

"How long have I been asleep?"

"Three hours or so," she says, and smiles. "Your dad's still sleeping in the back row. Look out your window."

I turn toward the porthole and draw in my breath. "Is that... are we there?"

"Yes," she says. "Isn't it magnificent?"

Magnificent seems too small a word, and yet I can't think of another that might come close to describing the incredible landscape below. Spread out beneath the crisp blue sky is the southeastern tip of the Continent, wilder and more spectacular than I ever dreamed it would be. The coastline here is marked by rocky bluffs of staggering height, with ferocious waves breaking all along the base. Broken sheets of ice dot the ocean, rising and falling atop the rolling swells of the sea. To the distant northwest are the soaring peaks of the Kinso mountain range, covered in ancient green firs that rise high into the air. And the snow—as far as the eye can see, it covers everything. This vast white world is unlike anything in the Spire—even in the North, during wintertime. The phototypes in the Astor Library did not do it justice.

"Magnificent," I say in agreement. "Those cliffs, there, along the coast—do you see them? They once boasted the tallest waterfalls ever known to exist. And that valley, a ways off to the west, that's the great Southern Vale! It's supposed to be breathtaking in the springtime, with beautiful wildflowers of red and gold—flowers quite exclusive to the Continent. Let's see, what else? Oh, I do wish I hadn't packed my maps away in the luggage! I feel so disoriented looking at everything from such a height."

My mother laughs. "Don't worry, dear—you'll have plenty of time to compare."

Mrs. Shaw, sitting in the seat in front of me, leans over and pokes her head around in the aisle. "I don't suppose you brought any extras, did you, dear? I saw the one your father framed for you—it's really quite something."

"What are you going to do with a map, Mother?" Aaden says from the seat across the aisle. "Write a shopping list on it?" He laughs and turns back to his window.

Mrs. Shaw is affronted. "I have many interests of which you are not aware, Aaden. I quite like maps, even if I never can figure out which way round they're supposed to go."

My mother gives her a kind smile. "I'm sure the steward will provide us all with reference material when we set out for a proper tour. Vaela's charts are a bit complicated for a layperson such as you or I."

"Your father tells me you're to work with Mr. Otto Sussenfaal, in the Astor Library," says Mr. Shaw. "Quite an honor, yes?"

"Very much so, sir," I say. "A dream come true."

"May I ask how you came by the apprenticeship?"

"Well…I've had special access to the library for years now, on account of my father's position at the Chancellery."

"Of course."

"There's always been something about maps that has held my fascination—the marriage of artistic expression and scientific data, it's…well, it's unlike anything else."

"She used to draw little maps of the Spire on my linen napkins," my mother says, and laughs softly. "And atlases of the world at large!"

Mr. Shaw grins. "A true calling then. And this is your ambition? To excel in this field, to make a profession of it?"

"It is all I have ever wanted," I say. "To enrich the lives of others with maps that can be admired and absorbed—to expose detail where only imagination dared previously to tread, to illuminate the world for others. I hope to achieve much with this tour."

Mr. Shaw leans toward me, his blue eyes sparkling. "I think you will succeed, my dear. I really do."

"Such approval, Father, toward an academic," Aaden says dryly. "I wonder how I might win such favor?"

"One must *do*, son, and not only *learn*."

"Oh, Arthur," Mrs. Shaw says, "he has passed his exams—"

"Now that he's taken them."

"—and has been cleared for a professorship at the Academy—the one in Astor," she adds, looking pointedly at my mother, "with all the great steeples and swirling platforms." She nods, the tiny silver chimes in her hat jangling like little bells. "It's very exciting, Arthur. Don't be such a stick in the mud."

Mr. Harris emerges from the cockpit, smiling broadly. "Hello, hello! Quite spectacular, isn't it? Well! From this point, it's just a quick flight to Ivanel, but before we turn away from the Continent and head for the island, the pilot will be taking us down to touring altitude for about ten minutes so that you may all have a closer look. At touring altitude, the plane will shift into an easy hover, and you'll be scarcely fifty feet away from the Continent itself. Today, it'll be just a quick peek, but I'm sure you'll enjoy the opportunity to see the landscape up close."

"Should we wake Father?" I say, and my mother shakes her head.

"Let him sleep—he was up so early with the porters, double-checking everything and marking off lists. I've never seen a man with so many lists. In any case, he won't mind waiting until tomorrow, and he could use the rest."

To the astonishment of his wife, Mr. Shaw gets up and moves across the aisle to the empty window seat in the front row.

"Arthur Shaw, remove yourself from that seat and come back

here at once," she says. "I didn't agree to come along on this expedition so I could sit by myself like some kind of spinster."

He doesn't budge, but crosses his arms and lifts his chin ever so slightly. "And I didn't pay a year's salary so that I could peek around that massive hat of yours at a place I've been longing to see since I was but knee-high. No, thank you, madam, I'll keep my seat."

Her mouth falls open, but my mother is quick to ease the tension. "I'd be happy to sit with you, Mrs. Shaw. Frankly, the motion of the heli-plane has made me a bit dizzy, and I'm not exactly keen on looking out the window just now."

The steward gives her a sympathetic smile. "Not to worry, Mrs. Sun, you'll get used to the movement. A day or two in the air and your constitution will be firm as a sailor's at sea."

"I'm sure you're right," she says. Now that I take a moment to look at her, she does seem a bit green about the face.

"Come right up here with me," Mrs. Shaw says. "I'll run a commentary on all the sights. You can sit back with your eyes closed, but you shan't miss a thing."

My mother, miserable as she looks, stifles a laugh. "That's very good of you, Mrs. Shaw." She gives my hand a pat and moves to the forward seat.

The heli-plane begins to descend and I feel a pressure in my ears. I look out the porthole again and watch as the scenery appears to grow larger; we're flying above a wide, flat valley that has very little vegetation. I'm wondering if it's any place of significance when Aaden gives a large whoop.

"Oh-ho-ho!" he says. "It looks like our pilot knows how to deliver; there are people down there!"

"Where?" demands Mrs. Shaw. "I can't see a thing, unless you count snow. Did you ever *imagine* there would be quite so much snow?"

"Come over to this side of the plane," Aaden says. "There

are four people hiking across the valley. Come here, Vaela, you can look out my window."

I move across the aisle to sit beside him. "Where are they, exactly?"

"Just beyond those rocks—do you see?"

It takes me a moment to spot them—four leather-clad men trudging through the heavy snow, fur collars dusted with white. "I see them!"

Mrs. Shaw gasps. "How thrilling! Are they Aven'ei, or Xoe, I wonder?"

"They're Aven'ei," Aaden says. "The Xoe don't live this far south or east. In any case, you can tell from their clothing—see how everything is sort of muted, and fitted? The Xoe are far more expressive—they wear bright colors, great painted cloaks, helmets of metal fused with bone—that sort of thing."

"Helmets adorned with bones?" says Mrs. Shaw. "How revolting."

"Human bones," Aaden adds.

"Oh, you're not serious," she says with a tinkly laugh.

"I certainly am. What better way to antagonize the Aven'ei than by flaunting the remains of their fallen companions?"

There is a pause, and then she says, "I don't think I've ever heard anything quite so ghastly."

The four Aven'ei have stopped in the snow and are looking up at the plane. Even at this distance, it is clear that they are accustomed to the sight of Spirian aircraft; they seem entirely unimpressed. We bank to the right, and the men disappear from view.

I turn to Aaden. "Your professorship…is that how you know so much about the people of the Continent? Are you an enthusiast of history?"

"Yes, actually. I am to teach a course examining the nature of conflict—covering both Spirian and Continental disputes—beginning this autumn."

"He never stops reading, not ever," says Mr. Shaw, somewhat

miserably. "Boy's spent the better part of his life with his nose stuck in a book. Athletic build like that, and he'd rather hole up in the library than spend an hour out of doors."

"Well, it's lovely to have you along, then, Aaden," says my mother. "I'm sure your insights will be most enlightening."

He smiles. "I'm at your service, Mrs. Sun."

"We don't know very much about the Xoe, do we?" says Mrs. Shaw. "Other than how vulgar and warmongering they are?"

Aaden frowns. "You make them sound like villains."

"Aren't they?"

He looks flabbergasted. "Uh, *no*?"

Mrs. Shaw adjusts her hat. "That's not what I've heard. At my Telmadge Green Flowering Bloom and Grow meetings, Mrs. Galfeather—who's been thrice to the Continent, I might add—says there's nothing to the Xoe but bloodlust. That's precisely the word she used: *bloodlust*. She says we know little else about them because there's naught else to know, and that they've bullied the Aven'ei for eons."

"That's garbage," Aaden says, turning toward her. "Absolute garbage. They're not *bullies*, for the Maker's sake. Don't you know—"

Mr. Shaw leans abruptly toward the window. "I say, what's that bit of decoration hanging from the bridge there? Some kind of flag?"

Mrs. Shaw scoots across the aisle, sits beside him, and peers over his shoulder. "I can't make it out. Just a moment—there are two of them."

I lean closer to the glass, squinting in an attempt to see what they're talking about. There's a narrow bridge a little ways off, and suspended from it are what seem to be two bright red strips of fabric. But they don't exactly look like flags; they're moving stiffly in the wind, rather than fluttering about as one might expect.

"But what kind of flags are those?" Mrs. Shaw says. "They look like—"

"They're not flags," Aaden says. "They're bodies."

One of the strips swivels on its cable, and as it turns, I see the rotted face of a Xoe warrior, mouth agape, his metal and bone helmet shattered on one side, his arms bound tightly at the wrists.

CHAPTER 3

✦

IT'S BEEN ODDLY QUIET ABOARD THE HELI-PLANE since the bodies on the bridge were spotted. Mrs. Shaw in particular has made it a point to keep herself busy, having spent the better part of half an hour focused on a book of word puzzles produced from her valise. I hadn't thought it possible for her to refrain from speaking for so long, but although she has cleared her throat several times, she has not said a word.

My father, perhaps stirred by the shift in mood, awoke to a cabin full of somber and awkward passengers. My mother gave a whispered account of what we saw.

"You all right, then, Vaela?" he said.

"We all knew that we would see unpleasant things, didn't we?" I said this, and I meant it, but I still felt sick inside.

"Knowing and seeing are two different things."

"I'm fine," I said, and I do feel a bit better, now that I've had some time to consider what I saw. This war is the stuff of legend—isn't it only natural to be curious about the morbid truth of things? Perhaps Aaden was right when he said that everyone has some interest in the conflict between the Xoe and the Aven'ei—although my mother seems to be a rare exception to this rule.

I think the lot of us were simply unprepared to see anything macabre at that moment; we were so distracted and enthralled by our first view of the landscape, marveling at the appearance of the Aven'ei, and then…the bodies. Decayed and frightening and real. Unexpected.

Now, we sit quietly, each pretending not to have been bothered by the faces of the dead warriors. I suppose it is easier to feign disinterest than to admit being disturbed. Even the steward has not spoken, although I suspect it is rather out of deference for the general mood than due to any uneasiness of his own—he must be well accustomed to the grislier sights of the Continent by now. And at length, it is he who breaks the silence by coming up the aisle and announcing our imminent arrival at Ivanel.

I hear a rustling sound and the zipping of what must be Mrs. Shaw's traveling bag. "I'm quite sure I'm ready to get off this plane," she says.

"I think we could all do with some fresh air," my mother agrees.

Mrs. Shaw turns around and looks closely at my mother, who has reclaimed her seat next to me. "You poor dear—are you feeling any better?"

"No," my mother says. "But the idea of putting my feet on solid ground has cheered me immensely."

"A good meal with a deep red wine, and you'll be ready for a new day," says Mrs. Shaw with some authority.

The aircraft tips gently to the right and then straightens out again. Aaden gives me a soft smile. "You have a map of Ivanel, I assume?"

"Oh, yes," I say. "I'm anxious to see it in person. I guess it's the closest thing to the Continent we can experience firsthand."

"Yes, and without that pesky war going on to spoil the view, am I right?"

"I—well, I hadn't thought about it that way."

He leans toward me. "You ought to. We mustn't take for

granted the security to which we are accustomed. Peace is a luxury, you know."

"We have earned it," I say, and for a split second, it occurs to me that I am reciting a thing I've read in some textbook or other. "It took ages for the Four Nations to set aside the ways of war."

He nods. "That's true. But have we really come so far, when a tour of the Continent is so desirable a thing? We've traded our swords for treaties, our daggers for promises—but our thirst for violence has never been quelled. And that's the crux of it: it can't be quelled. It's human nature."

"I have to disagree with you there, son," my father says, leaning forward from the back row. "I believe the human condition compels us to strive for the very thing we have achieved in the Spire: peace."

Aaden smiles. "Perhaps we do not all share the same nature."

"Perhaps not," my father says. "But I think curiosity is to account for any desire to see the war. Nothing more, nothing less."

"What a quaint idea," Aaden says. "I was not aware that you were a man of such philosophy, Mr. Sun."

"I have my moments. Right, Vaela?" He gives me a wink and turns his attention back to the window.

"Philosophy, war, bodies swinging dead from bridges, what more shall we discuss before we even set foot on the island?" says Mrs. Shaw. "Really, I do hope everyone is in a better mood at dinnertime. This is supposed to be a holiday!"

Mr. Shaw leans over to give her a kiss on the cheek. "We shall speak of nothing but sunshine and cheer, my darling, if that is what pleases you."

"I find that very doubtful," she says, and sniffs. "But I appreciate the sentiment."

"Tuck into your seats, now," calls the steward. "We are ready to land."

I look out the window to see a flat stretch of land rising up to greet us. The heli-plane sets down with a soft bump and my mother gives a long sigh of relief.

After a few minutes, the door is opened and we file out along the gangway. The air in the hangar is freezing; my lungs burn each time I take a breath. My father puts an arm around me and gives me a little shake.

"Cold, isn't it?" he says, the breath escaping from his lips in tiny clouds as he speaks.

The walkway leads into a large building. Mr. and Mrs. Shaw are at the front of the group with Aaden trailing behind them, and my parents and I are hurrying along at the back. I can hear Mrs. Shaw complaining about the cold from twenty feet away; I'm not at all sure why she decided a trip to the Continent would suit her.

I think we are all relieved when we reach the lobby, which is very grand and, more importantly, very warm. The room is long and wide, with a high ceiling that boasts an enormous glass dome. The whole place is filled with natural light, and the bright and spacious area is a welcome change from the small cabin aboard the plane.

Mr. Harris turns back to my father and says, "I'll just show the Shaws to their apartment and will be back for you momentarily. Please make yourself comfortable while you wait."

"I'll see you at dinner, Vaela," Aaden says, and bows before turning to head down the hallway.

I smile to myself, then wander across the foyer, admiring the tapestries along the walls.

My father puts an arm around my mother and leads her to the other side of the room. In a low voice, he says, "I'm not sure I'm fond of that young man."

From the corner of my eye, I see her lace an arm through his. "He's perfectly harmless, Thomas."

"He's awfully sure of himself for a boy his age. He thinks he has the whole world figured out."

My mother laughs. "I remember another young man who had quite the same affliction. I found it so appealing, in fact, that I married him."

"I was never *smug*," my father says.

She smiles. "True."

"He's got an eye on Vaela. Mark my words."

"That's something we can add to his list of virtues, not his faults."

My father makes a disagreeable sort of noise but doesn't pursue the subject any further. We all wait in silence until the steward returns and extends an arm toward the hallway. "Shall we?"

"This building is lovely," my mother says as we follow him down the hall. "Very warm and inviting."

"Oh yes, the facility is wonderful," he says. "Everything you'll need to enjoy yourselves has been built right into this complex. There's a dining hall, of course, and a recreation room—plenty of books and other amenities in there—an exercise facility, a fully equipped lounge…we hope to fulfill any need you could possibly have."

"I'm quite interested in the island itself," I say, "and I'd love the opportunity to take an excursion of some sort. Would that be possible?"

He stops walking. "You do know it's quite…cold? Well. Far colder out in the open than it was in the hangar."

"I understand."

He looks at me for a moment longer. "Weather permitting, I suppose something could be arranged. We do have a lovely indoor promenade, if you're merely interested in the view?"

I smile. "I'd prefer to do a bit of exploring."

He turns and continues walking. "Then I'll see to it, Miss Sun. We want your stay to be as satisfying as possible. Will Mr. and Mrs. Sun be joining you?" he adds, glancing back at my parents.

"Oh, no thank you," my mother says. "The promenade will do just fine for me."

My father shakes his head. "I have no interest in the snow, sir."

"Very well," the steward says, and then stops before a door marked B4. "Here we are—your suite." He opens the door and hands the key to my father. "Go ahead and make yourselves at home; I'll be just down the hall in the lobby if you need anything. Dinner will be in…" He pauses for a moment to check his timepiece. "…about forty minutes. I'll be along to call for you then."

"Thank you kindly," my mother says. "We'll be ready."

Mrs. Shaw was right: everything here at Ivanel seems to be of first-class quality. The accommodations are very fine; our suite is filled with elegant furniture, and possesses all of the luxury one might expect from a top-tier hotel back in the Spire. There are two bedrooms and a sitting room, all with floor-to-ceiling windows that provide extraordinary views of the island. There is also a spacious washroom that includes a sauna; the scent of warm cedar lingers like an almost tangible comfort.

By the time the steward returns to collect us for dinner, I'm famished. He is accompanied by the Shaws, who occupy the suite down the hall from our own. Aaden looks very handsome in a black suit and white bow tie, and I feel momentarily self-conscious in my simple gown of blue silk. But he smiles appreciatively when he sees me.

"You look lovely, Vaela," he says. "I don't know which suits you more: your traveling clothes, or your dinner finery."

"Why, her dinner gown, of course," says Mrs. Shaw, oblivious to the compliment behind his words. "Honestly, Aaden. It's like you have no manners at all."

As we head down the corridor to the dining hall, Mr. Harris extols the virtues of the Ivanel facility, telling us how well it functions with an incredibly small group of personnel—

between twenty and thirty workers at any given time—and how it has served as a desirable holiday spot for the Spire's most elite citizens for more than twenty-five years. No one might have asked for a finer steward for such an important trip.

Aaden peppers him with questions about the island, and the steward is only too happy to oblige. About halfway through their conversation, it occurs to me that Aaden probably knows more about Ivanel than just about anyone, and is only posing questions because the steward is so delighted to be asked. It seems a kind thing to do.

When we reach the dining hall, the steward takes his leave and we sit down to a beautiful table. The dishes are exquisite: fine cream-colored porcelain edged in gold, with gleaming flatware and cut-crystal goblets that have been polished to a shine. The servers enter without a word to set the first course on the table; it's some sort of vegetable soup with a heady aroma. Mrs. Shaw looks very pleased.

"Wonderful to have a nice meal, isn't it? After those foul refreshments on the plane." She leans over and closes her eyes, inhaling deeply, then sighs. "There's nothing like a bowl of warm soup. I believe I'm still frozen to the bone after that walk through the hangar."

"You ought to try the sauna," my father says. "I used one last year during a visit to the North. Very therapeutic."

"I believe I will," she says, with a hint of excitement in her voice. "Otherwise I shan't sleep a wink."

"How do you like the rooms?" Mr. Shaw says to my father.

"Very nice indeed. The view is exceptional."

"It's spectacular," says Mr. Shaw. "In fact, I was just suggesting to my lovely wife that she might prefer to stay at Ivanel for the duration. No sense traipsing through the hangar every day when she has a perfectly adequate view of the scenery."

"If she does stay, I might consider keeping her company," my mother says. "I'm not exactly looking forward to another ride in the heli-plane."

Mrs. Shaw wipes her mouth with a napkin and gives her husband a sour look. "I already told you, I haven't flown across a vast ocean to take in the sights of an island no bigger than a field of periwinkles. It's the Continent I've come to see, and see it I shall."

"I'm only thinking of your delicate sensibilities, darling," Mr. Shaw says. "You did seem upset by that sight on the bridge, and I simply—"

"My mind is quite made up."

Mr. Shaw hesitates, then seems to think better of pursuing the matter. He turns to my mother. "Will you be joining us on the flight tomorrow then?"

"If it's all the same to my husband and daughter, I would prefer to stay here," she replies.

"Mother, no!" I say. "You can't! We've come all this way, and I think—"

"We have nine days to tour, Vaela," she says in a soft voice. "I could use some time to recover myself after today's flight. You can tell me all about the Continent when you return to Ivanel."

I want to protest, but in truth, she still looks a bit green. "All right, then. Whatever suits you best."

"I don't mean to encroach, Miss Sun," Aaden says to me, "but I overheard the steward making inquiries as to setting up an expedition for you here on Ivanel. Are you quite serious about trekking around in the icy wilderness?"

"I just want to get a feel for the terrain," I say. "It won't help me with the maps—not strictly speaking—but I find the land-scape to be very inspiring."

"It all sounds very sensible to me," Mr. Shaw says, nodding. "You want to embrace the science of cartography, you ought to get your feet on the ground."

"Right," Aaden says, with a sidelong glance at his father

that contains more than a suggestion of sarcastic amenability. He puts down his glass and looks at me thoughtfully. "I wonder if I might join you, Vaela? I wouldn't want to impose, but it sounds like fun."

"It's no imposition at all. I'd be delighted to have you along. I'm hoping we can go the day after tomorrow—once we've had a proper tour of the Continent."

"Well," says Mrs. Shaw, "you two can tromp around in the snow all you like, but don't come complaining to me when you're both dead with cold."

"How might we complain if we're dead?" Aaden asks, his eyes wide in mock earnestness. I cover a smile with my napkin.

Mrs. Shaw ignores him and turns to her husband. "Have you no opinion about this?"

He shrugs. "At least he'll be outside."

We eat for a few minutes in silence, Mrs. Shaw picking up her fork and setting it down again with a clank after every bite. At last, the servers bring in the dessert: delectable-looking pies filled with sweet-scented berries and smothered with warm chocolate sauce.

Mr. Harris enters the room as the servers leave. "Have you all enjoyed your first meal at Ivanel?" he asks.

"Everything has been wonderful," my mother says.

"Surprisingly satisfactory," adds Mrs. Shaw. "I say, what are these berries? They're divine!"

"Those are clayberries," he says. "They're unique to this region—you can't find them anywhere in the Spire. I've developed quite a taste for them myself."

"Well, I should like to have them every evening," says Mrs. Shaw. "You'll see to it?"

"It will be my pleasure, madam," he says. "And now, I will bid you good night—I'll be by at nine a.m. to collect you all for your first real tour. Get plenty of rest—it will be a very exciting day!"

CHAPTER 4

✦

THE HELI-PLANE RUMBLES TO LIFE AND, AFTER A moment, begins to roll steadily down the runway. The steward mentioned icy conditions, so this morning's takeoff is a bit more frightening than yesterday's departure. But before I can work myself into a state of nerves, the plane lifts from the ground, smooth as silk, and rises above the island.

Mr. and Mrs. Shaw have taken the two front windows, respectively. I'm once again sitting in the middle row on the left side, and Aaden is seated across the aisle from me. My father is sitting by himself in the seat directly behind me. He was very gracious to my mother this morning and assured her that we'd be fine flying alone; her response was to plant a kiss on his cheek and promise that she will take at least one more tour before the holiday is through.

As the plane glides over the sea, the steward makes a quick announcement: today, we'll be touring the west, followed by the northeast region of the Continent—specifically, we'll ultimately be observing an area where the Aven'ei and the Xoe are often in dispute, a place that has seen some exciting skirmishes. Mr. Shaw and my father immediately strike up a robust discussion of territories, war, and other such things, while Mrs.

Shaw contents herself with sighing and clucking and otherwise affecting a generally bored disposition. Aaden is quiet, looking out the window at the icy waves below, and I busy myself with organizing my notepads and pencils.

I don't know anything about territory disputes—the histories we read in school pertained more to items of cultural interest, and did not include much detail about the reasons for conflict between the Xoe and the Aven'ei—but the northern corner of the Kinso mountain range holds a particular interest to me: it is home to the Riverbed, a great canyon carved by water and ice. I've seen one or two phototypes of it, but its depiction on maps tends to vary depending on the cartographer. The opportunity to see it for myself is a dream come true.

"All set there?" my father asks, peeking around the seat.

"Oh, yes," I say. "I only wish I had been able to requisition a camera from the Chancellery."

Ever listening, Mrs. Shaw pipes up by making a sort of snorting sound. "Technology," she says, "is best left in the hands of those who know how to use it. Look what happened when the Chancellery tried to fix up the train stations with those telly-phones—some idiot messed with all the wiring and circuit boards and whatnot, and set the whole Kinsey Metro on fire!"

"I remember that," says Mr. Shaw. "What a mess."

"Yes, and four people dead by the end of it," Mrs. Shaw replies. "No. I'm happy to call round and leave a card like a civilized person, not to ring through like an alarm bell into someone's parlor when they're least expecting it. Cameras, tele-video, computers—those are sorry things indeed, if you ask me."

"Ah, but this heli-plane," Aaden says. "This is the height of technology and engineering! Surely you can appreciate something so sophisticated?"

"I can appreciate something without wishing it to be operated outside the supervision of qualified government professionals."

My father laughs. "Well said, Mrs. Shaw. Very well said. In

any case, Vaela, that mind of yours is as good as any camera, and your sketchbook more valuable than any phototype." He gives my shoulder a pat, then disappears behind the seat.

Aaden smiles over at me. "I suppose you're interested in the Riverbed?"

I cannot hide my pleasure. "I might have guessed you would know the topography, though I must say, I'm no less impressed!"

He laughs. "I know a thing or two about the Continent itself, you know, not just the Xoe and the Aven'ei."

"Most people have never heard of the Riverbed."

"Well, I'm looking forward to seeing it. Although I must confess, its proximity to the territorial border in the north is not unwelcome."

I crinkle my nose. "You really go in for all the violence?"

He is silent for a moment. "Living in the Spire is like looking at the world from behind a veil—we don't have a true sense of what things are like. Not really. I just want to see something real."

"And bloodshed will satisfy that yearning?"

He shrugs. "It's something."

I feel disconcerted by his dark demeanor, but give him a quick smile and turn my attention back to the window, and to my sketchbook.

Mrs. Shaw begins yammering at her husband as to why he didn't suggest she bring one or two bags along for the flight, as she's dreadfully bored by all the snow and ice and sea. I hate to be unkind, but I can't help wishing that she was not along for the ride today. Her old-fashioned thinking—such as her apparent notion that the Aven'ei and the Xoe are practically less than human—her need to share an opinion at *every* opportunity, and her ridiculous, towering hats are all a bit much to take.

Shortly afterward, the pilot begins a slow descent, and we fly over a small Aven'ei village—a place, as described by many who have toured the Continent, with beautiful wood and stone buildings, piping chimneys, and what looks to be a bustling market square. A long, winding road can be seen stretching northward—probably connecting the little hamlet to another settlement.

"It looks like an actual *town*," Mrs. Shaw says. "Could you have imagined? It's all so civilized!"

"Mother," Aaden says, "you are truly ridiculous."

I can't help but agree.

A small group of children points up at the heli-plane and waves their mittened hands, while a woman scrambles around them and tries to corral the young ones. I know they can't see me through the tinted glass, but I give the children a little wave anyway.

Mr. Harris, all smiles, rises with a flourish from his seat at the front of the cabin. "Ladies and gentlemen, I hope you will allow me at this time to share some information about the Continent. In particular, a small geographical clarification may be of interest.

"The Continent," he continues, "all told, encompasses a total area of approximately one million square miles—much smaller, as you know, than the land mass of the Spire, which comes in at around 3.9 million square miles. Now, to put that into perspective for you, the Far Islands—where the exiles and defectors abide, quite a distance eastward of the Spire—amass a total of only thirty-two thousand square miles. So, while the Continent is neither the largest nor the smallest of the land masses on our beautiful planet, it is interesting to note that it may be the least populated of all three, although that is still a point of debate."

"How many people?" asks my father.

"Recent estimates show the Xoe at seventy-five to one hundred thousand, the Aven'ei at fifty to seventy thousand."

"How can that be correct?" I say, shocked. "The histories have those numbers far higher."

Aaden grins, and draws a finger across his neck. "Easy. They've nearly wiped each other out in the past two centuries."

The steward nods gravely. "Unfortunately, young Mr. Shaw here is correct. The population has dwindled steadily, and most sharply in the past fifty years or so as tensions between the two have escalated."

"That's awful," I say.

Mr. Shaw makes a disgruntled noise. "They won't last much longer if they can't find a way to mend fences, I suppose."

"A sad truth," says the steward.

We glide above the snowy landscape, taking in the splendor of the wilderness. Great are the wonders of the Continent, vast and beautiful as it is—and this tour is more comprehensive than I dreamed it would be. We head along the southern coast far into the west, where there is nothing but craggy rock and desolation—and two middling Xoe settlements, perched perhaps fifty miles from the cliffs at the shore, directly in the center of the Wastes.

"What is this?" Aaden says in surprise, leaning toward the window. "These are Xoe camps—what are they doing so far south?"

"Ah," says the steward, "that is a recent development, sir. Exploring a bit of their own territory, we suspect. They haven't been there long, and I doubt they are likely to stay. Northerners, the Xoe are, and the southwest has little to offer."

"It looks to be quite a large force," Aaden says.

Mr. Harris laughs. "Not at all, sir, not really. The majority are much farther north, settled and happy."

I make a note of the settlements in my book, but otherwise find little to see other than hard ground and rocky terrain.

Before long, the plane is headed north, and we fly over an expansive network of Xoe villages. The architecture is different from that of the Aven'ei: the buildings are small, for the most part, with long triangular rooftops dipping low toward the ground. Roads and walking paths twist here and there, looping around and about the small homes and other structures. All is sturdy and formidable in this frozen, icy territory the Xoe call home. The towns, too, while small, are much closer together than Aven'ei villages. I have the sense of greater cooperation, of community, of connection—of something like we've established in the Spire. A great lake—shaped like a five-pointed star—lies near the center of the Xoe settlements, in what looks to be the largest of all the cities.

There are villagers below, too; and quite a lot of them, with skin so white it might be made of writing paper—far paler even than those of the Spirian East. Their hair ranges from silver— not gray, *but shimmering silver*—to black and every shade in between, and most look to be very tall, even the women.

"I'm floored," Aaden says. "I mean… I've seen the photo- types, but only in black-and-white. Look at the *paint*! It must be sleet and ice nearly all year round, yet the buildings are blood- red, blue as the sea, yellow as morning light—every color in the world, represented here. It's *incredible*!"

"Looks dreary to me," says Mrs. Shaw, entirely unimpressed. "All that stone and plaster, gussied up—what a terrible, gaudy show. Most distasteful."

"The Xoe are well known for their use of color," the steward says, "whether in dress, or tattoos, or in the settlements them- selves. Most find it beautiful, madam."

"Gaudy," says Mrs. Shaw once more, and she adjusts her hat as though it were something important.

For my part, I'm enthralled. The colors below are astound- ing—it is like we are flying above cities made of rainbows. I know from what little I've learned that the Xoe are incredibly expressive and artistic. They write in runes and symbols that have never been properly decoded by Spirian scholars, they weave detailed, breathtaking patterns into the design of their clothing and weapons, all angles and twists like plaits and puz- zles, intricate and symmetrical. Even from this distance, I can see the artistry and design in every aspect of Xoe life, and I'm

mesmerized. Two men, heads shaved along the sides, with impossibly long twisted silver braids falling neatly upon their backs,
bend over a blazing fire and laugh together, joy on their faces. I
wish I could know what they are saying to one another, I wish
I could know who they are and what they enjoy and what unlikely things we might have in common. It occurs to me that
never before have I felt so isolated within my own culture; never
have I truly realized that the world has so much else to offer. It's
a lonely feeling, and fills me with yearning.

"We are heading east now," says the steward, and the Xoe
villages become increasingly scarce as we pan toward the center of the Continent. "You will see, on the port side, a number of Aven'ei ruins within the next thirty minutes of travel.
Their territory did once extend this far north and west, though
the Xoe have reclaimed it, obviously, and chosen not to in-
habit these old settlements. Not to their liking, I suppose?" He
laughs lightly, though I feel a chill at the notion of abandoned
cities—empty buildings gone to ruin, households deserted, so
many lives now forgotten.

"From what we can tell," he continues, "everything has been
left just as it was when the villages were overtaken. We've even
been able to make out dress forms and the like in store windows,
still bearing tunics and other Aven'ei garments! There are metal
pots in the bakeries, mosaics upon the walls—it is like a civilization frozen in time. We of the Spire do not land, of course, for
to do so would be to violate the Treaty—but the Chancellery
has a number of phototypes on record of these ancient Aven'ei
towns. Storefronts, armorers, residential districts, all abandoned
in the aftermath of war. Truly fascinating!"

"Grim," my father says.

"Too right," Mr. Shaw agrees.

We fly over the settlements, and grim, I think, is not the
right word. Stark...sad...overgrown, perhaps. Disintegrating
buildings of bleached white brick snaked with ivy, fields en-

croached by weeds and wildflowers peeking through the snow, pillars crumbled to half height. Children once played in the now-empty yards and meadows, men and women once worked in the buildings of industry. All has gone to rot, has been left to nature. Only the Narrow Corner—the point in the north at which the Kinso mountains recede—marks the place where the Aven'ei now begin to dwell. That small access point, north of the Kinso, wedged between mountains and northern cliffs, the Aven'ei can defend. And it is there that we are headed—but first, the Continent holds one last wonder for me.

The pilot sweeps to the south in a beautiful, graceful arc, and we come upon the thing I have most longed to see. Spreading out before me is a miracle of nature, a deep place carved into earth by water, ice, and time.

"If you'll just take a look out the window," the steward says, "you'll see that we're directly above the Riverbed—a great natural phenomenon, quite unlike anything in the Spire. Please enjoy this grand and majestic view!"

"Good grief," Mrs. Shaw says, peering out her window. "It's as though someone dug out half the earth!"

"It's amazing," I say. And it truly is: a canyon absolutely *majestic*. It is narrow in some places, impossibly wide in others, far deeper than I imagined. I find myself sketching madly as I observe—my cheeks flushed, my fingertips coated with charcoal as I draw and shade and blend. The peaks and crevasses come to life on the pages of my little book, and it occurs to me after about twenty minutes that I should like to do an extensive map of the Riverbed itself.

When the pilot finally veers away from the valley and directs the plane toward the Xoe-Aven'ei border, I feel restless and unsatisfied, like a great work has begun and must be put aside. But the steward comes down the aisle and makes a point of telling me that the pilot will return to the canyon on our way back to Ivanel—even though a second look will take us miles out of the way. I thank him profusely, and he laughs. I suppose my enthusiasm must seem strange. Most come to see the war; I have come for the beauty of the land itself. And beautiful it is, more so than I could ever have imagined.

After a while, the steward returns to the front of the plane. "We'll be approaching the border any minute," he says, "and I just want to remind you that we may see violence here today. After an advance flight this morning, the pilot did report that two parties were seen en route to this location. I should like to say at this point that although the sight of battle can be shocking—even disturbing, to some—it is a valuable thing to witness. Few Spirians ever see what battle is truly like—few have the opportunity to fully appreciate the Spire's peaceful accord." At these words I come to think, once again, of an echo in a textbook, a cheer written down in recognition of the Spire and memorized a thousand times over. "However," he continues, "if you find yourself distressed by any violence, please know that I am here to assist—and you may always retreat to the solitude of the aft cabin."

"Will we be close enough to get a good view?" Aaden says. "Will we pull in low, like yesterday?"

"Touring altitude largely depends upon the terrain, as well as the activity taking place on the ground. This part of the border sits in a wide basin, which will allow us to get quite close; these aircraft are specially equipped to hover at low altitude. The plane will stay at between forty and sixty feet—near enough so that you may see all the action taking place and enjoy a truly visceral experience. Facial expressions and the like should be very clear. Oh—there we are, the pilot is turning toward the border now. It'll be just a few minutes."

He sits on the bench opposite the passenger seats and folds his hands together. There is a quiet among us now, quite different from the awkward silence of yesterday afternoon. This is something altogether unique—it is a tension, an impatience, an uncertainty. Our curiosity is so strong, it is nearly palpable. Even I cannot take my eyes from the window.

We come upon a clearing surrounded by a wood. The quiet aboard the plane persists, and I feel my stomach twist with nerves.

"This side," Aaden says. "Come to this side."

Mrs. Shaw moves to sit beside Mr. Shaw, my father crosses to the other side of the aisle, and I sit down next to Aaden, my heart hammering in my chest.

What strikes me first of all is not the movement of the warriors—not their huge strides, not the swinging of their weapons, not the frenetic activity of the battle. What strikes me first is the blood.

It is everywhere—carved out into wild arcs, dripping from the branches of leafless bushes, coursing in rivulets along the limbs of the Xoe and the Aven'ei alike. It is bright red in the snow, spattered into patterns so delicate and graceful, they seem to have been painted there on purpose. And aside from the vibrant cloaks and vests of the Xoe, it is the only thing of color in the stark white.

Only secondarily do I become aware of the actual brutality playing out before me. It seems to register in bits and pieces, in fragments of activity. For although there is a single battle taking place, I realize that it comprises many smaller conflicts, each seeming to occur independently of the others. My eyes don't know where to look, and everywhere I cast my gaze, there is death.

An Aven'ei man is pinned to the ground, his shoulder reduced to flesh and muscle as it is struck by a Xoe hammer. Beside him, a Xoe fighter is killed by a knife driven into her chest. And on the other side of the clearing, nearest the wood, an Aven'ei archer is charged by three Xoe and decapitated before he can escape.

It goes on and on, the killing and violence and horror, while not a word is spoken aboard the plane. Finally, there are only Xoe left standing in the field—perhaps two hundred or so, while at least five hundred men and women in total lie dead around them. The field below is a mess—a terrible graveyard, an eerie panorama of bodies so unnaturally *still* that my stomach turns. The remaining Xoe scream and raise their fists to the air, drunk with victory, reveling in blood. One of them points to the heli-plane, then gestures to the fallen archer. The group laughs together, and a burly, well-muscled man darts across the clearing to retrieve the severed head.

We all watch in silence as he pushes through the snow, making his way back to the group of Xoe in the field. Another man with long silver hair—bound in golden, silken cloth, shimmering like sunlight—shouts something at the heli-plane, his face contorted with disgust. A moment later, the stocky warrior hurls the head toward us.

We're too high for it to reach, of course, but its effect is powerful nonetheless. Mrs. Shaw gets up at once and moves down the aisle toward the aft cabin; Mr. Shaw follows her directly. The steward heads forward to the cockpit, and seconds later, the plane tips gently and moves once again toward the Riverbed.

My father pulls me back to sit beside him. I stare at him, acutely aware that I am looking at him with eyes that can never unsee what has just taken place, and he looks back at me, willing me to unsee it. Then he puts his arms around me and I cry, because there is nothing else in the world to do.

CHAPTER 5

◆

THERE IS NO PART OF ME THAT CAN UNDERSTAND
how one person can harm another.

I feel like a fool, having somehow failed to ever mark the difference between *spectacle* and *death*. I take no comfort in knowing that almost every citizen in the Spire has done the same, for
their failure is just as shameful as my own. I feel this truth so
profoundly that I wonder how it never occurred to me before.
A tour of the Continent is not an exercise in education—not a
look into the past, not a reminder of how the Four Nations once
warred against one another. It is entertainment—at least, it was
meant to be—and all at the cost of countless lives. Boys who
will never see adulthood, women who will never be mothers,
men who leave children behind, orphaned, fatherless. Choose
any scenario of loss and grief: it was there, played out in full in
that icy clearing among the Xoe and the Aven'ei alike.

Even after that first flight above the Continent, after I saw
the men hanging from the bridge, I didn't fully grasp the reality of war. It took seeing with my own eyes the cleaving and
ripping of flesh. It took a severed head hurled toward us in hatred and contempt. It took *too much* to understand something
that ought to have been clear from the beginning: that war is

a thing of desperation and finality, a thing that rips one person at a time from those who love them, in accelerated motion. A man may die. A dozen may die. Hundreds may die, depending upon the battle. And each is a person, a man or woman who loves and lives. And dies.

I spent the duration of the flight in my father's arms, replaying the battle in my mind. I kept my eyes closed, terrified that I might look out the window and see anything like violence. The Continent, once a land of great fascination to me, became almost instantly a hateful arena of death and horror. I never want to go back.

The steward came round this morning, this quiet day *after*, to ask if we would be touring today. I heard my father speaking to him in hushed tones. About half an hour later, there was a second knock at the door—it was the steward again, coming to see if I would like to join Aaden on an expedition of the island. I tried to decline, but Mr. Harris implored me to consider that the fresh air—however cold—might do me some good. He left a canvas bag full of insulated clothing and said that he would be back at noon to collect me.

And so, here I sit, dressed in strange clothes that might offer protection from the frigid temperatures, waiting alone on the private indoor promenade and staring at the snow and the rocks and the sea beyond. I see now that this is what my mother feared most—that the Continent might change me. Perhaps it has. I *hope* it has.

When Aaden and Mr. Harris arrive, both seem to be in good spirits. Aaden smiles brightly when he sees me.

"All set, there?" he says, gesturing to my new attire. "I'm feeling rather outdoorsy myself today. What do you think?" He does a little spin, and despite myself, despite how morose I feel, I laugh.

"You look very fine, sir." I collect my hat and gloves, tuck a small sketchbook into the pocket of my vest, and close the door behind me. "Are you to be our escort?" I say to the steward.

"Oh, heavens, no," he says. "I try never to set foot out of doors unless I'm in the Spire. Far too cold for a Westerner like me! We're to meet your guide in the lobby—Mr. Cloud, the Director of Facilities here at Ivanel."

"Director, hmm?" says Aaden. "That sounds important."

The steward gives him a measured look. "I should say so. Mr. Cloud doesn't normally have dealings with the guests at all, but he knows more about the island than the lot of us, I'd wager. Lives here year-round, he does. It's quite a privilege, really, to have his attention."

"Well," I say, falling into step beside Aaden as we walk down the hall, "it's very kind of him to give us a tour. Is no one...is no one going to the Continent today?"

The steward's voice falls to a hush. "No, miss. Everyone required a bit of a respite, I think. It happens sometimes, after the first tour. Some folks enjoy the fighting, but others...well, you understand. It can be a bit much."

An image of snow soaked in red flashes before my eyes and I shake my head. "It was very...real," I say, looking at Aaden.

"It's miles away, now," he says lightly, too lightly. "Think no more of it." He claps his hands. "Now! Let's away, for it is very cold outside, and we gluttons for punishment must embrace it like true adventurers."

In the lobby, we are introduced to the Director. His height is astounding—he must be nearly six and a half feet tall. He has the look of a Northerner—dark, deep brown skin, blue eyes so pale they are nearly white, and a warmth and geniality about his person that is very inviting. Something in his smile, I think. I find that I like him almost at once.

"Good day," he says, with a rich rumbling voice that cannot disguise its enthusiasm. "I hear we have a couple of explorers in our group—not too common, you know." He laughs. "First time for everything, as they say."

"How do you do?" Aaden says. "I'm Aaden Shaw, and this is Miss Vaela Sun. Vaela is something of an accomplished cartographer, and she's interested in getting a feel for the island."

"So I'm told," says Mr. Cloud, looking at me with interest. "I take it you want a look up close at the terrain?"

"Very much so," I say. "It's one thing to see the landscape in phototypes, or even to view it from the plane—but I have such a yearning to feel the ground beneath my own two feet. Does that seem strange?"

"I've got the same affliction, my dear," Mr. Cloud says, "and I wouldn't call it strange. More like...irrepressible. No?"

"That's it, exactly."

He laughs. "Well, it's not too cold out today, so let's see how we do." He takes a second glance at me. "You'll want to put on that hat, miss, and those gloves. When I say it's not too cold, what I mean is that you won't get frostbite out in the open. I don't mean to say it's warm, or anything like it."

"I understand," I say, putting on my hat. Aaden does the same.

Mr. Cloud nods, grinning. "Explorers on Ivanel, I never thought I'd see the day. Whatever next? All right, then, Spirians. Off we go."

The chill cuts through me the moment we step outside. The steward was right—it is far colder out of doors than it was in the hangar. Mr. Cloud kicks aside a large clump of snow in an attempt to clear the pathway.

"All right, there? Warm enough?" he says.

I'm not sure if I can speak, so I just nod my head and attempt a smile.

He laughs and tugs my hat down around my ears. "Come along, you'll adjust to the temperature in a minute. Those clothes are plenty warm—it's just the cold on your face that's thrown you."

We follow him on a downward sloping path, and even though I find myself gasping a bit from the freezing air, I can't help but notice the pristine beauty around me. There isn't a cloud to be seen; the sky is a crisp wintry blue, the sun like a bright white stone in the sky. The Ivanel complex lies behind us, and ahead is a wide field—covered in snow, of course, with little to it other than some hardy shrubs and a few jagged boulders. Small white birds flutter here and there, pecking something or other from between the rocks; they tilt their heads and coo at us as we move along.

"Achelons," Mr. Cloud says. "Greedy little things." He produces a handful of dry bread from his pocket and tosses it onto the snow. Six or seven of the birds hop forward to snatch up the pieces.

"They're so precious," I say. "Do you feed them often?"

"I always say I won't, but then I do. Just the ones here by the facility. They've come to know me a bit, I think."

"I think so, too," I say.

As we continue on, the shore comes into view, and I'm delighted by the sight of powerful, frosty waves crashing and breaking before rolling up to kiss the rocky sand. A fishing boat floats idly in the little bay, tied to a weather-beaten post—and a great iceberg looms in the distance, shining bluish-white in the sun. I've never seen an iceberg before, and would be content to stare at it all day, but Mr. Cloud leads us away from the more accessible part of the beach toward the base of a high cliff.

I'm panting a bit by the time we reach the cliffside, as the snow is quite thick and we've been moving steadily uphill for a little ways. Mr. Cloud doesn't look as though he's exerted himself at all, but Aaden's breathing seems as labored as mine.

"I thought you might find this interesting," he says, patting a hand on the steep wall. "This cliff face is one of the tallest in the natural world, and it goes two-thirds of the way around the island."

I step back and look up, dizzied by the height. It seems impossible for anything to be so immense, so high, ripping into the sky like some ferocious force.

"Yes!" I say. "I've noticed it on some of the topographical maps—but it's quite something else to see it up close." I take another step back and shield my eyes, staring up at the immense wall before me. It's damp and glistening, with fragments of shiny rock jutting out in small clumps. "I don't suppose we can go to the top?"

He raises an eyebrow. "Are you sure you're up for that, miss? We've got steps carved into the hillside here, but it will take a bit of time and we'll be in some heavy snow by the time we get there."

"Please," I say. "If Aaden is agreeable, I should love to see the ocean from such a vantage point."

"I'm game if you are," Aaden says, with a casual shrug. "Let's do it."

By the time we reach the top, the muscles in my legs are *burning*. My whole body, in fact, is significantly warmed by the climb; the sharp breeze now feels cool and bracing against the fine layer of perspiration that has appeared on my cheeks and forehead. Mr. Cloud says it can be very dangerous to sweat in these temperatures, especially without insulated clothing. To this, I assure him that I have no intention of traipsing about on Ivanel in my dinner clothes.

The grueling climb is all but forgotten upon sight of the ocean sweeping out below us, vast and dark and beautiful, the sunlight golden upon the fragmented sea ice. The waves break against the cliff with tremendous power, creating great whorls of frothy white foam that seem to dance atop the water, ever at the mercy of the tides.

I put a hand to my breast. "Did you ever see anything so marvelous?"

"Worth every miserable step," Aaden agrees.

Mr. Cloud crosses his arms and gives a small nod, a smile at the corner of his lips. "For all the Spire's beauty, you'll never see anything quite like this." He glances back at the trees behind us. "Listen—I'd like to check a few traps while we're up here—mind if I leave you two to admire the view for a while?"

"Take your time," Aaden says, and moves to sit on a wide, flat rock. He pats the space next to him. "Sit with me, Vaela."

We rest for a few minutes, our eyes on the sea. It is quiet here atop the cliff, the stillness broken only by the trilling of the Achelons in the trees and the breaking water far below.

"Aaden?"

"Yes?" he says, his voice distant.

"Was it what you expected?"

He glances over at me, then looks back at the ocean. "Yes and no."

"Tell me what you mean."

He doesn't answer right away. When he finally speaks, it is as though he is choosing his words carefully. "It was thrilling," he says, "just as I thought it would be. There was something raw and powerful about the battle. I've never seen anything like it."

"I don't understand," I say. "When people return from the Continent, they talk about how exhilarating the battles were. They say the fighting was bloody, but they never say…they never say how *gruesome* it all is."

He tilts his head. "What did you expect, Vaela? You had to know on some level how it would be."

I pull my legs toward my chest and hug them close. "I suppose I didn't think about it at all—not in any real sense. I know how ridiculous that sounds, but it's true. I just thought it would be exciting."

"Well, it was, at that."

"It was dreadful, Aaden. The whole thing was dreadful. And to think, all those years ago, the Xoe and the Aven'ei both were offered a place as a Nation of the Spire, if only their quarrels could be set aside. But they chose dissension. They chose death and blood and perpetual hostility. Why? *Why?*"

"To be fair," Aaden says, "the Aven'ei hoped to unite with us. It was the Xoe who refused—they wanted nothing to do with our people from the very first; we were never able to establish even the simplest trade with them." He scuffs his foot along the side of the rock and shakes his head. "It was different with the Aven'ei. They traded peacefully for nearly thirty years with the North and the East—right up until the Spire was formed."

"I've always wondered about that—about the trading. What did the Aven'ei possess that the Spire could possibly want?"

He gapes at me. "You realize how that sounds?"

I flush, the heat of my cheeks in stark opposition to the chill air. "I only meant...the Aven'ei did not have nearly so many advances as did the Spire at that time."

"Not all things of value are measured in technology, Vaela," Aaden says. "The North has always taken a particular interest in societal enrichment, and its representatives were smitten by Aven'ei art and culture—smitten. You can see the influence in many Northern things even now: the clothing, the architecture— they've enfolded the Aven'ei aesthetic into the very fabric of life."

"And what did the North offer in return?"

"Medical advances. Clinical techniques. In fact, medicines were exchanged from *both* sides. It was a sharing of culture— not a measuring of one being more valuable than the other."

"I'm surprised the Aven'ei didn't ask for other things. Superior weaponry, perhaps. Something to give them an advantage over the Xoe."

"That's your own thinking, though I daresay that sort of mentality is encouraged in Spirian schools." He shakes his head, clearly disgusted. "The Aven'ei were glad to exchange with us, in measures of mutual benefit. We adopted many of their traditions, they adopted many of ours, including an exchange of languages. They were more than satisfied with their own way of life, and our own people did not dispute that, or put any pressure on them to adopt *our* ways."

"But they were at war," I insist. "Why would they not ask for an advantage, if we could provide it?"

He sighs. "When the Continent was first discovered—some...what, two hundred thirty years ago now?—the Four Nations put a treaty in place that drastically limited the divulgence of technology to the Aven'ei or the Xoe, and prohibited any disclosure of weapons schematics or combat tactics. The South, for example, had no interest in interacting with the populace of the Continent at all, but did not want to help them advance either, should they someday take their war to our land. Probably very wise."

"And the other Nations? What did they gain?"

"Now that's where it gets fun," Aaden says, turning on the rock to face me. "The West, as you know, holds the monopoly on lumber—roughly eighty-five percent of the wood in the Spire comes from the West."

Despite my mood, I can't help but smile at his enthusiasm; there is nothing so rousing as a scholar in his element. "So I've heard."

"Well. When the Continent was found, the Head of State in the East was ecstatic. Her Nation had been struggling financially for some time, and the West had cut off their lumber supply, as they had run up some bad debt. Imagine what it was like for the East to come across an entirely new land mass, covered in trees, completely uncontrolled by the West?"

"Like salvation, I suppose."

"Yes. The Aven'ei were happy to share. And in exchange, they got a significant influx of agricultural wealth—crops, farming techniques, and something the Continent had never seen before: cattle."

"No trade with the South?"

"None. They would have nothing to do with the Aven'ei at all."

I hesitate, thinking. "If all this happy trading and sharing of cultures was going on—at least with some of the Nations—why did it end when the Spire was formed?"

"You *have* read the Declaration, right, Vaela?"

I begin to recite automatically: "East, West, North, and South, these Four are now One. We come together as the Spire, as a single United Nation, as a pinnacle to those who—"

He rolls his eyes and interrupts me. "Okay, you've memorized the preamble—all of us have. But the full Declaration reads like a list of laws. Once the Nations were united as the Spire, trade with any warring country was prohibited."

"Well, then, the Aven'ei should have simply joined the Spire and left the Xoe out of it."

"Vaela…" he says, incredulous, "how could they? The only way to become a part of the Spire was to set aside the ways of war entirely. That was easily done on our piece of land, where all were in accord. But the Xoe at that time had no interest in peace; if the Aven'ei had put down their arms, they would have been massacred."

I shift on the rock, which seems to have grown colder. I have a vague recollection of learning long ago some of what Aaden has just told me—a half-remembered notion that one side or the other wanted to join with us, but had not done so. Even so, I never considered that the aggression between the Xoe and the Aven'ei might not be always mutual—that one might be trying to defend itself against the other, depending on the time period, depending on the situation. "How very sad for the Aven'ei, then."

"That's the thing about war," he says. "It's easy to avoid as long as no one is trying to break down your door."

I look down at my hands. "Will you go back for another tour?"

"I will," he says, then frowns at my astonishment. "It's important to see it, Vaela. To know the truth of it."

"I know all I need to know," I say. "I won't go back."

"You should. No—you, of all people, should. I don't have to tell you that the Continent has never been fully mapped—not in consensus, anyway. Your work is important."

"Is it?" I say. "I don't know. I don't know if it matters."

"Of course it does," he says. "And in any case, it wasn't the war that brought you here—so don't let it keep you from doing what you love."

He is right about that, but I can't say whether or not my intentions were important, not now, not after I have seen so much. "I don't know why you care," I say, looking up. "You've only just met me."

"I care because you surprise me," he says. "No one surprises me."

His eyes are like blue, blue waters, empty and full, shifting and welcoming and terrible. I cannot read him, not in this moment, not in any moment. "What do you mean?"

He casts his gaze to the sea and smiles. "You are strange, Vaela. You are beautiful and naive, but wise beyond your years. You see things that others do not." He slips a hand into mine, his gloved fingers embracing my own. "I would court you, if you wish, when we return to the Spire."

A flush comes over me, though the breeze presses a cold kiss upon my face. I am not sure at all how to react, or what to say. "I...is that what you want, Aaden?"

"Yes," he says, his breath tight, the muscles in his neck taut. "I want you to be mine. I want to discover all the things that lie deep inside you—to know what you think about, to know what you love."

"Aaden," I say, caught in the moment. An offer of courtship—my very first. Aaden's feelings are clear, but...but what about mine? He is handsome, yes. Passionate and intelligent. But—

His lips press to mine, soft and urgent, and only the wind rustling in the branches of the blackwood trees beyond is to be heard.

Mr. Cloud soon comes to collect us, and I am certain he somehow knows that Aaden has kissed me, that a declaration of courtship has been made, that my stomach is fluttering like mad. My first kiss—and from a boy I've known only a matter of days. Evangeline will want every detail—and whatever shall I say? I hardly know what to think; it was so brief, so unexpected. I liked it well enough, I suppose, but it was rather wet, sort of *unpleasantly* wet, now I come to think of it. Is that how it's supposed to be? I wish I could ask my mother, though I know she'd only ask a thousand questions in return. I feel anxious, if truth be told, and a bit sick, like I have embarked on a journey for which I am unprepared. Still...isn't that love? Is that the way it should feel?

I have no idea, and it tortures me.

My pulse races as we follow Mr. Cloud down the cliffside—no small feat, even though the trail is not terribly steep. The snow shifts and slides beneath my feet, moving in great clumps and making it impossible to stay upright. I spend half the time sliding down on my behind, feeling most undignified, but ahead of me Aaden is doing exactly the same. Only Mr. Cloud, with a practiced air, manages to stay on his feet all the way down the slope.

Back on the path, we come to the place where we first spotted the Achelons. The little birds have gone, but Mr. Cloud sprinkles a few extra crumbs for them even so. Our party has almost reached the complex when I notice a thriving berry bush a short distance away.

"Look!" I say, feeling uncomfortable about what has come to pass between me and Aaden, and eager to point out a distraction. "Clayberries—the ones we had at dinner! Shall we gather a few for your mother, Aaden?"

"No, no, miss," says Mr. Cloud. "Those are chamolines—quite poisonous."

I turn back to the plant. "Are you certain? They look exactly like the ones we've been enjoying with our meals."

Aaden steps off the path and plucks a fat, ripe berry from the branch. "They do at that," he says. "What's the difference, sir?"

"The difference is that those will kill you, and the clayberries won't," Mr. Cloud says flatly. "But if you're asking how to tell them apart, don't look at the fruit—look at the shrub. Chamoline plants have knobby branches—see those gnarls there? Clayberry branches are smooth as silk."

"I guess we oughtn't collect any then," I say, disappointed. "Mrs. Shaw would have been so delighted."

"Don't you worry," Mr. Cloud says. "The kitchen here at Ivanel is well stocked. Now, let's get you two back inside—this cold is getting sharper, and you'll probably want to rest up before dinner. After all—tomorrow is a new day, and from what I hear, the pilot has a truly fascinating trip planned for those who wish to return to the Continent. Trust me, citizens—you won't want to miss it."

CHAPTER 6

✦

THE FOLLOWING DAY, DESPITE MY PREVIOUS PRO-
testations, I find myself aboard the heli-plane once more. Aaden
was right: I didn't come for the war; why should it keep me from
doing what I came to accomplish? Cartography is the thing I
have loved more than anything in my life, and I may never
again have the chance to see the Continent with my own eyes.
I would be a fool to squander such an opportunity. The plight
of the Xoe and the Aven'ei is tragic, but what can I do about
the conflict? I am not the first to be disturbed by the violence,
the steward said as much. I am in no position to help. Not now.
But when I return to the Spire, I can make my feelings known.
Spirians have no place here, none at all.

In any case—and I know I am, in a way, turning a blind eye
to the ugly truth of the war, but honestly, I do not know what
else to do—today's tour has actually been rather pleasant. We
aboard the plane have all engaged in lively conversation from
time to time, and the general feeling of well-being among the
passengers has been one of staunch relief. Even my mother—
who came along at my request, and who, incidentally, is none
the wiser in regard to the kiss I shared with Aaden—has enjoyed the flight, having taken a remedy beforehand to alleviate

her airsickness. Mrs. Shaw is in a very happy mood because her husband was kind enough to bring along a good portion of their luggage to "keep her busy." After five hours, I've seen several geographical formations of interest—including a second tour of the southern Reaches and a flyover of the Aramaii mountains in the northwest. I've filled an entire sketchbook with illustrations and commentary, and have not set eyes upon a single Aven'ei or Xoe (Mr. Shaw apparently had a private word with the pilot before we left the island and instructed him to tour unpopulated areas whenever possible).

Aaden has been absolutely charming all day long. Throughout the afternoon, he has regaled us with fun little facts about the Continent, none related to violence. Even Mr. Shaw has been impressed by Aaden's considerable knowledge, and made a comment in passing about the prestige of his son's upcoming professorship. It has been a pleasant day indeed.

We're on our way back to the island now, and everyone has relaxed into a sort of easy quiet. My mother and father speak softly to one another in the back row, and Aaden sits beside me, looking through my drawings.

"You have quite a keen eye," he says. "I have no talent for this sort of thing."

"Cartography? It's really more of a science than anything, and with education, I think anyone could—"

"Drawing," he says with a smile. "I have no talent for drawing. I'm a mediocre artist."

"I'm sure that's not—" The heli-plane gives a sudden shudder and lurches to the side, startling me so much that I grab the seat in front of me. I look over at Aaden in wonder. "What was that, do you think?"

"What on *earth*?" exclaims Mrs. Shaw from the front row.

I lean over and peer up the aisle to see Mr. Harris smiling patiently at her. "Just a touch of turbulence, I expect. Nothing to worry about; it's quite normal."

"If I'd known we'd be in for a bumpy ride, I might have brought my adventurer's hat with me," says Mr. Shaw. "You know the one, Nora, the brown topper with the metal grommets?"

"If you'd packed that hat, I'd have stayed at home," she says, and my mother laughs. Another jolt, this one smaller than the first, rattles the heli-plane. Mrs. Shaw laughs nervously. "I wonder if I ought to have stayed at home after all? I don't go in for this turbulence one bit!"

Mr. Shaw pats her hand. "Not to worry, my dear. Remember what the steward said; these heli-planes have been fit to fly for ages. They simply do not crash. Can as much be said for automobiles, with drivers of the general public at the wheel? I think not."

The plane shudders again, dropping a few feet in the air and taking my heart with it. I close my eyes and take a deep breath.

"Don't worry, Vaela," Aaden says. "These aircraft are equipped with highly redundant systems. It would take an improbable series of malfunctions to cripple one of them, much less bring one down."

I open my eyes. "Really?"

He smiles. "Really."

Mr. Shaw stands up, steadying himself with one hand on the top of his seat, and opens his mouth to say something just as a horrible wrenching sound comes from the belly of the aircraft—something that can only be an explosion—and the whole cabin begins to shake.

"What is the meaning of this?" Mrs. Shaw says, her voice shrill. "What was that dreadful sound?"

"I'll just go and speak to the pilot," the steward says. "I'm sure we—"

"You tell him to return this plane to Ivanel *at once*."

"I'll just be a moment," he replies, and disappears behind the sliding door that leads to the forward compartment.

Mr. Shaw puts a hand on his wife's shoulder. "Let's just try to calm down and wait for Mr. Harris," he says. "I'm sure everything is under control."

He does not at all sound sure.

I glance up at the ceiling, where the light fixture is rattling in its casing. The sight of it makes me feel sick, and I look away.

The steward emerges from the cockpit, mopping his brow with a white cloth. "The pilot is going to try to land the plane," he says. "There seems to have been a mechanical failure, and if everyone will do their best to keep calm, we'll just—"

"Fire!" shrieks Mrs. Shaw. "There's a fire!"

Mr. Shaw is on his feet. "Where?"

"I don't know," she says, her voice quavering. "But *look*."

Acrid gray smoke has begun to seep through the seam of a panel in the forward part of the cabin on the right-hand side. I find myself gripping the armrest, my knuckles gleaming like pearls beneath my skin. But it is the expression on Aaden's face that brings me from nervousness to fear: gone is the easy confidence of just a moment before. Consternation and dread rule his features.

"Surely this isn't serious?" I say, my voice thick in my throat.

"The aircraft is on fire, Vaela."

I am overcome by a terrible sense of desperation. "But you... you just said the plane couldn't crash! That it couldn't fail, that there are systems in place to keep that from happening!"

"Vaela," he says quietly, "it *is* happening—though I don't understand how. It makes no sense. The—"

"The pilot will land and they'll send another heli-plane for us," I say, aware that I am beginning to sound hysterical.

"Don't you see where we are?" he says, jerking a thumb toward the window. "There's nowhere to set down. We're over the mountains south of the Riverbed."

"Please," I say, but have nothing else to add. I only want him to tell me everything will be okay. I want this plane to stop shuddering. I want to go home.

"When I kissed you," he says, "I intended to honor every implication of such a thing."

"What do you mean?"

He stands. "Excuse me, I need to pass by."

"What?" I say again, utterly confused. "Where are you going?"

He doesn't answer, but steps awkwardly into the aisle and moves forward to address the steward, who gives him a look of utter surprise before nodding emphatically. Then Aaden turns at once and stalks down the carpeted path toward the aft cabin. He does not look at me or say another word as he passes.

I turn back to my mother and father, who sit across the aisle in the row behind me. My father is looking out the window, his lips pressed into a tight line, and my mother is trembling. She reaches forward to take my hand, but says nothing.

The plane drops down, seems to rise back up for half a moment, then drops a second time. Then a third. It's shaking so violently now that my whole body is jerking back and forth.

"Put her in the escape pod," my father shouts, and in an instant, my mother is in the aisle, pulling me toward the aft end of the plane.

My father turns to the Shaws. "You two get to the rear cabin before that smoke gets any thicker."

"Wait!" wails Mrs. Shaw. "My *bags*! Arthur!"

My mother drags me along; I stumble as the floor lurches beneath my feet, but her hold on me doesn't waver. Against the cacophony of clattering metal, of Mr. Shaw and Mrs. Shaw yelling at one another, and of the steward trying to calm them down, I hear my father's voice, soft and reassuring. "It will be all right, Vaela. Don't worry. Keep moving."

I inch past my mother and step into the aft cabin. My father moves toward the panel where the escape pod is concealed; the door is ajar but not fully open, and it bangs back and forth as the heli-plane shudders in the air.

"Come along now, Vaela," my father says, holding out his right hand. "We'll put you in, just for good measure."

"Why is this panel already open?" my mother says, but as she pulls it wide, the answer becomes clear.

Staring at us from behind the thick glass of the pod, secured within the locked enclosure, is Aaden.

"Get out," my father says. "Now."

Aaden doesn't answer and makes no move to exit the pod. His blue eyes are fierce and cold; he glares at my father with a sort of hostile defiance that takes me by surprise. He does not look at me.

My father tries to open the door, but Aaden has locked it from the inside. The heli-plane drops sharply; this time, it's enough to lift my feet off the floor and send me tumbling against the op-posite wall. My mother and father have fallen, too; only Aaden, safe within the pod, remains upright.

"Coward!" my father yells, getting up and pounding on the glass door. "There are women present—have you no honor?" He turns on his heel and pushes past me, moving toward the main cabin.

My mother's eyes grow wide. "Thomas! Where are you going?" She turns back to the pod. "Aaden, please. You must let Vaela take your place."

"I don't think he can hear you," I say. "The glass is very thick."

My mother stares at him. "He knows exactly what I'm saying."

"It's all right, really. Just let him be."

"Open this door!" she says, ignoring me.

Aaden doesn't move, but his eyes dart to the cabin entrance, where my father is pushing the steward through the doorway.

"Please, sir," Mr. Harris says, "I must assist Mr. Shaw. His wife is quite upset, you see, and she doesn't wish to—"

"Open the escape pod," my father says. "I know you have a key. Open it."

The steward blinks at him before glancing at the pod. "You want me to—"

"Open it, so I can pull that miserable coward out of it," my father says. "Now!"

The steward hurries forward, flipping through a large set of brass keys. The plane lurches again, and as I steady myself, I see Aaden gripping the interior handle with both hands; there is fear in his eyes now, and he seems to be telling the steward to eject the pod.

The key clicks into place within the glass door and Mr. Harris tries to turn the handle, but Aaden is far too strong. He is no match for my father, however, who shoves the steward out of the way and yanks open the door. Aaden tries to pull it back, but my father wedges his knee into the slim opening and forces the door open. Then he punches Aaden squarely in the face and wrenches him free of the pod.

Aaden rolls forward, knocking poor Mr. Harris to the ground. Then he turns back to my father, blood dripping from his nose. "You've killed me! Do you know what you've done? You've killed me!"

My father's face is twisted with rage. "I ought to kill you, and if this heli-plane doesn't do it, I may yet finish what I've started!"

"What's going on here?" Mr. Shaw steps through the doorway, carrying a handful of baggage; Mrs. Shaw is close on his heels. "Why are you threatening my son, sir?"

"Get in the pod, Vaela," my mother says. She doesn't wait for me to answer, but takes the ring of keys from the lock and presses the cold little bundle into my hand. "Get in."

"Please, no," I say. "It's dreadfully small—I feel much safer out here. Let Aaden—"

"Get in!" she says again, the tiny muscles in her cheeks jerking sporadically.

Trembling, I step into the pod and position myself against the cushion within. "Mother, please—"

She closes the door and taps on the handle. "Lock it," she says, or at least, that's what it looks like she says; the sound of her voice is completely muted behind the thick glass. I feel as though I can't breathe, and locking the door only makes it worse.

I close my eyes, forcing myself to take long, steady breaths. When I open them, one thing becomes painfully clear: the situation in the aft cabin has devolved into chaos.

My father is shouting at a red-faced Mr. Shaw, who is shouting back and jabbing a finger into my father's chest. Mrs. Shaw is hovering over Aaden and dabbing at his bloody face with a handkerchief. The steward is moving back and forth, tucking the loose baggage into the storage bins, trying to keep his balance as the aircraft jerks and shifts. My mother stands in front of the escape pod like a sentinel, one hand on the glass door, the other balled into a fist at her side.

And then there's me. What am I doing but watching from behind the glass as everyone turns on each other? I don't even want to be here; I want to get out, I want to be with my parents.

My mother pounds her palm against the glass and I see the warning in her eyes. *Don't even think about it, Vaela.*

She knows me too well. But I can't stay in this pod any longer. I'm fumbling with the lock when a sudden silence overwhelms the heli-plane. The quiet—or rather, the lack of vibration—is so unexpected, so out of place, that I forget momentarily what I was trying to do. I look up in confusion, my fingers frozen on the handle.

It's not just me; everyone has become still. Mr. Shaw is standing with his mouth open and his finger pointed in the air; the steward is bent in mid-crouch, a look of bewilderment on his face. And then I realize what has happened.

The engines have stopped.

Thousands of feet above the Continent, the heli-plane's engines have gone silent. And as suddenly as the calm and stillness overtook us all, so quickly does panic set in as the aircraft tilts sharply to one side and begins to glide toward the earth.

My father doesn't hesitate; he lurches toward the pod, climbing over Mrs. Shaw's endless bags and totes, and places his palm atop my mother's hand on the glass door.

Vaela, I see him say, and I wish beyond anything that I could hear his voice. *Be safe.*

My mother's face is tears and anguish. *We love you. We love you.*

Too late, I see my father's other hand moving toward the control panel. And before I can stop him—before I can open the door and escape this hateful glass prison—he is gone, and all I see before me is the gray-blue sky, peppered with wispy clouds.

He has jettisoned the pod, and I am sent soaring upward as its parachute extends. The tiny craft swings languorously from side to side; the height is dizzying. At first, I can't make out anything below except trees and a vast icy lake dotted with shadowy patches of snow. The pod continues to sway back and forth, rocking madly, and it seems an eternity before it settles into steadiness. I put both hands on the glass door, craning forward to search for the heli-plane.

And finally, I see it.

Spiraling away from me, aflame on one side, the heli-plane is plunging toward the ground. Bits of metal, cloth, paper, debris are planing away as it falls—twisting and burning and carrying my family.

I want to look away, but I can't. I have the absurd notion that I can stop it somehow—if only I keep watching, the heli-plane will float aimlessly, harmlessly through the air and never reach the earth.

But, of course, I have no such power. And in the deafening silence, I watch as it crashes into the frozen tundra below and explodes in a burst of flame.

CHAPTER 7

✦

THE POD SETS DOWN IN A THICK BANK OF SNOW. The yellow parachute follows a moment later, fluttering down atop the glass, obscuring my view of the sky. I lie still, staring up at the bright silken fabric, my muscles convulsing, my mind blank. A tiny red light at the top of the pod begins to blink. I watch it flash three times. Four. I close my eyes.

I would be content to lie here forever—locked within the pod, isolated from the truth of what has just happened—but my body has other plans. Nausea, like a swell upon a restless sea, begins to roll over me in sickening waves. I seize the door handle, release the lock, and push the glass away from me. As it springs free, I clamber over the side and fall face first into the snow. Then I vomit, my body heaving with a violence borne of shock, revulsion, pain, grief.

When there is nothing left, I curl up in the snow next to the pod. I don't feel cold or sad—merely conscious in a way that echoes something like being alive, but only in the vaguest sense of the word.

I close my eyes, but do not sleep.

After what might be five minutes or five hours, I sit up and look around. I'm in a small clearing surrounded by evergreens.

There is no sound at all—no birds, no wind, no water. There is only me, and the pod, and the snow, and the trees, and the sky.

The sky. Bright and blue, except for a plume of black smoke reaching high above the distant peaks. The thought of what is burning makes me sick again, and this time I fear it might never stop.

Some time later, I'm on my feet. I have the dim realization that I am cold, that my teeth are chattering. I look down at my garments: a long-sleeved dress of fine red silk buttoned to my waist, with layered skirts flowing behind, open at the front to reveal slim white trousers. My fingertips, in contrast, are pale and tinged with blue.

Shivering, I climb into the pod and pull the door closed. I watch the red light flash, wondering if all that has taken place might be nothing more than a terrible dream. Perhaps I am asleep, safe at home in the Spire, and any moment now I will awaken with an overwhelming sense of relief.

I want to cry, but I am empty. The yellow parachute is clear of the door now, and I have a plain view of the hideous column of smoke stretching up into the sky. I put my hand on the glass.

"Take me with you," I whisper, in a voice that doesn't sound anything like my own.

The daylight is beginning to fade now, the sky turning dusky orange as the sun sets. I try to determine how long it's been since the heli-plane went down, but it's no use—my mind refuses to organize itself. All I can conclude with any clarity is that it will be dark soon, and with the dark will come colder temperatures.

After a moment of hesitation, I push open the door and reach for the parachute. A quick tug makes it clear that the chute is caught on something; I pull harder, but it won't budge. Frustrated and tired, I slip over the side and climb around to see what's wrong. The canopy is snagged on the scraggly branches of a fallen tree; I work it free in what seems a near futile effort that takes ages, gather it together, and climb back inside the pod.

The fabric is immense, and freezing to the touch. But after folding it into many layers and curling up underneath, I do feel considerably warmer.

A heli-plane will surely arrive to collect me at any moment. The flashing red light must indicate some sort of beacon; I watch it for a few minutes, my reflection appearing in the glass each time it blinks. My face looks oddly serene, peering out of the makeshift blanket with hollow eyes and a placid expression.

I close my eyes again. This time, I sleep.

I wake suddenly in the pitch black, disoriented until the quick red flash of the pod's interior light reminds me where I am. I have no idea how long I've been asleep, but of greater concern is the fact that night has fallen and no one has come to retrieve me. Was there a second aircraft in the hangar at Ivanel? Perhaps the rescue plane must wait until morning—maybe they weren't able to organize a search before nightfall.

They will come at daybreak. Only a few more hours here alone.

Alone. I push away the image of my mother and father standing beside the pod on the heli-plane, their fingers intertwined, their eyes full of pain. I can't think of it.

The sun rises quickly, its muted yellow light bleeding across the morning sky. I've been awake for hours. The day is a welcome sight, and I half expect to hear Mrs. Shaw remarking on its having taken *forever* to show itself. But Mrs. Shaw is not here. No one is here.

I wish the heli-plane would come.

The sun is overhead now, but there is still no sign of a plane. There is no sign of anything, for that matter; the tiny clearing

is eerily quiet. The pillar of smoke is gone, the sky clear save
for a few clouds.

Why haven't they come?

As night falls once again, it occurs to me that it has been more
than twenty-four hours since the crash. Something is wrong.
Ivanel should have sent someone to search for survivors by now.
Surely the pilot would have submitted a distress call? The light
inside the pod is still flashing—calling, I hope, to my rescuers.

My stomach aches, though whether from hunger or grief I
could not say, and my throat hurts. I have eaten some snow, but
it made me feel dreadfully cold and did little to quench my thirst.
I am tired—in fact, I don't know if I have ever been so very
tired. I wish I could sleep a thousand days. I wish my mother
and father were here.

I sleep, but fitfully, and awaken again before dawn. I stare
through the glass at a breathtaking sky sparkling with stars. I
think to myself how beautiful it is, and shame washes over me.
Eight people are dead. How dare I *enjoy* anything?

I close my eyes, forbidding myself to look on the starry night.

I am hungry.

Around noon, I decide to try and melt the snow before con-
suming any more of it. I accomplish this by scooping a handful
into a small corner of the parachute, which I have determined
to be quite waterproof despite its silken texture. Then I hold
the little bag of snow against my body until it melts. This takes
longer than I anticipated, but the result is actual, liquid water,
and I'm grateful for it.

It has been two days. I am starting to doubt whether anyone is looking for me. A hundred scenarios have played out in
my mind—perhaps they came at night while I was asleep and
I didn't hear the plane. Perhaps the signal from the escape pod

isn't strong enough, and they can't find me. Perhaps there is no signal—only a maddening red light that blinks incessantly for no reason at all.

If they haven't come for me by tomorrow afternoon, I'm going to have to find some food.

Three days stranded, and no one has come. I'm sick with hunger. I feel certain that I should not leave the escape pod, but I can't wait any longer—I must find something to eat.

I step outside into a fresh dusting of powdery snow, its surface brilliant and blinding. Turning around a few times, I try to figure out which way to go. The last time I looked out the window of the heli-plane, we were above the mountains south of the Riverbed—in part of the area known as the Divide. But while the pod was in the air, it was clear that the plane had edged just past the peaks and crossed into the southeastern side of the Continent. I am in Aven'ei territory—probably less than an hour's flight from Ivanel. An hour away from a hot meal, a long bath, and a warm bed. But without a plane, I might as well be on another planet.

A breeze picks up, swirling the fallen snow into the air in feathery gusts. I shiver; though the sun burns overhead like a diamond, its warmth is entirely lost on the Continent. Clearly, I cannot venture out in search of food without a coat or something like it.

After a moment's deliberation, I reach into the pod, pull a section of the parachute toward me, and study it closely. I tug at one of the seams along the edge, trying to rip away some of the fabric, but it is far too sturdily made. It will have to be cut somehow. There is nothing in the pod that might help me; I searched it extensively on my first morning here, but the only thing inside was the loop of small brass keys that belonged to the steward, and they are too dull to be useful.

A few minutes of exploration in the little glade uncovers no sharp stone or other debris—but a frozen branch might do the trick. I drag the corner of the chute over to the fallen tree and rub the fabric back and forth, attempting to saw through the heavy weave. It does not work. Frustrated, I lean against the pod, thinking. There must be a way to pierce the cloth. To *pierce* it. I turn back to the jagged branch, lift the chute high above my head, and jam it down with all my strength. A gnarled finger of frozen wood breaks through, making a hole at least four inches wide. Once punctured, the chute rips easily in a long straight line. I repeat the process a few times to punch out a lengthy rectangle of warm cloth.

With a furtive glance into the trees, I slip off my dress and wrap the heavy fabric around my torso. When it's tied off, I pull my gown back on—in itself it provides little warmth, but it's better than nothing. I can only hope I won't draw the attention of anyone who might be about. I curse myself for not having worn white.

I shield my eyes and look toward the sun; it's slipping down to my left, moving in a lazy arc toward the trees. My stomach twinges, and I head east. At least my boots are warm, and waterproof; thank heavens for Evangeline, who thought to make my birthday gift at least slightly practical, should I step foot out of doors on Ivanel. I must thank her when I return home. And I *will* make my way home.

I have found nothing. After what must have been two hours of trudging through the trees and snow and slush, I have found nothing to eat. There are rabbits hopping about everywhere, but I have no way to catch one, and I'm not even sure I would know how to kill an animal if it came to that. Thoughts of the silver tureens back at Ivanel, steaming with fresh vegetable soup, bring me almost to my knees.

The sky has become white overhead, obscuring the sun behind a thick haze of cloud cover. Soft, heavy snowflakes drift down before me, and I watch as two or three fall silently into my palm and dissolve into icy puddles. Defeated, I turn back toward the pod—if I venture any farther, this new snowfall might conceal my footprints and leave me lost in the wood. I can stand the hunger, but I doubt I could survive the cold.

I've covered about half a mile when something catches my eye: a whisper of red, twenty feet away. I stop for a moment, my eyes fixed on the unexpected burst of color. Berries.

I dash toward the bush and fall to my knees, only vaguely aware of anything but the gnawing hunger in my belly. I yank on one of the smooth branches and several berries come free. The beautiful, ruby-red marbles roll into my open palms, a few of them spilling onto the snow. I lift a handful to my lips, overcome by joy and relief—until I realize that I'm not at all sure which type of berries these might be.

I lower my hands and look closely at the tiny fruit in my palm. Are they clayberries, or chamolines? What did Mr. Cloud say about how to tell the difference? One of the bushes has knobby branches, and the other smooth. But which has which kind?

My eyes dart to the bush—the branches are slick, without gnarls or knots. Clayberry, or chamoline? My mind is in a fog, driven to distraction by cold and hunger and desperation. I take a deep breath and close my eyes.

Think, Vaela. Which berries are these? What did he say? I saw the poisonous bush myself back on Ivanel. Was it knobby? Sleek?

It's no use. May the Maker take me, curse me, punish me forever, but I *cannot* remember.

And for the first time since the crash, I cry.

I cry for myself, because I am hungry and tired and cold, and because I fear I will die in this hateful place. I cry for my mother and father. I cry for Mr. and Mrs. Shaw, and for Aaden—Aaden, who kissed me, who spoke of a future together, who might have been here instead of me if not for my father. I cry for the steward, for the pilot and the co-pilot, whom I never even met. I cry until my grief becomes quiet, and then I sit silently against the tree, too exhausted to move.

But I hear something—far off, to be sure, yet distinctive—a rhythmic hum, a steady whirring that I would recognize any-where. There's no mistaking it.

It's a heli-plane.

CHAPTER 8

✦

I'M ON MY FEET IN AN INSTANT. THE FOREST IS dense here, and the tiny patch of sky visible through the treetops reveals nothing, but I can hear the heli-plane. I stand perfectly still and listen.

The sound is coming from north of where I am now, I'm almost sure of it.

I sprint through the woods, conifer branches scratching at my hands and face as I force my way through the trees. A furious hope burns in my breast, a need to escape this place, to go home. I feel fresh tears on my face, hot and desperate.

Please, please, let them see me. Please let them take me away from here.

In the distance, the woods give way at last to a vast white field—I should be able to see the plane from there. I push through the deepening snow, my feet like blocks of stone caught in the soft white powder. I'm moving as quickly as I can, but my pace is maddeningly slow. By the time I reach the clearing, I'm gasping for breath, my sides aching from exertion. The chalky white sky is in plain view now. I can still hear the whir of the engines—closer now than before—but the plane is nowhere in

sight. Confused, breathless, I lean against the trunk of a bris-
tly evergreen and try to orient myself. Where is the heli-plane?

A few feet into the clearing, just ahead of me, an Achelon is
perched on a snow-dusted log; he tilts his head and sings his little birdsong: *to-whill, to-whill*. His eyes, black and shiny against
his soft white face, are fixed on mine as he sings.

I turn back to the sky, searching. With the steep face of the
mountains bordering the opposite side of the clearing, the sound
of the plane seems at once near and distant. I'm disoriented, and
the Achelon's endless song is not helping.

"Hush!" I say irritably. "I can't hear over your noise."

As if in answer, the bird bobs his head a few times and sings
another chorus. I glare at him, and almost incidentally, my gaze
is drawn to a dark shape beyond his snowy perch—to a subtle
hint of movement where there ought to be none.

I catch my breath, too frightened even to exhale.

Not a hundred yards away, at the far edge of the field, is a
Xoe warrior.

The man is crouched in the snow, his body angled away from
me, the back of his dark coat sprinkled with snow. A steel hatchet
lies beside him, along with a blue satchel and two or three dead
animals—squirrels, I think. I cannot see what the Xoe is doing,
but his head is bent in concentration and he appears singularly
focused on whatever silent task is at hand.

He stiffens and turns to look beyond his right shoulder, a deep
frown cast over his features; I stand frozen to the spot, certain
that he has somehow sensed my presence. But it is not I that has
drawn his attention—it is the heli-plane, cresting the mountains
and moving gracefully into the sky above the valley.

My heart lurches at the sight of it. The four-pointed star of
the Spire, painted in gold on the side of the fuselage, seems like
something from a dream. The Xoe watches the plane for a mo-

ment before resuming his previous position, his face once again turned toward the ground in front of him.

I hesitate, unsure what to do. If I run into the open, I might be able to attract the attention of those aboard the heli-plane. But if the Xoe sees me first, I may not live long enough to be rescued. Perhaps I should quietly pick my way back to the escape pod—if it's emitting a signal, they should find me quite readily, and at least then I could hide myself among the trees. But what if there is no signal? What if the light truly does indicate something else? And what if the plane has already flown over the pod—or worse, flown over and retrieved it, leaving me with no shelter whatsoever?

I wish my father were here. He would know what to do. He always knew exactly what to do.

The plane circles back, making another pass over the valley. It's relatively close now; I can plainly see the tinted windows along the port side. I cannot wait. This could be my only chance to escape the Continent.

Shaking, I move away from the concealment of the trees and swing my arms wide, crisscrossing them again and again in a furious attempt to draw the attention of my would-be rescuers. After a long moment, the plane turns toward me, and I am filled with a hope so desperate I can hardly breathe. Emboldened, I move farther into the clearing, flailing my arms wildly, willing someone to see me.

And someone does. As the plane glides past, I look across the clearing to see a second Xoe watching me intently from the rocks at the base of the mountain. He is impossibly tall, with broad shoulders and slashes of red and yellow on his face, angling from one side to the other. Behind his right shoulder is a quiver full of darkly feathered arrows. The man's expression is not fierce as I might have expected, but curious—almost amused. For a moment, neither of us moves—we just stand there, locked at an impasse. His eyes dart toward the sky; I imagine he can still see the heli-plane from his vantage point, although the trees behind me have obscured it from my view. He drops his gaze back to my face.

I take a step backward, my limbs rigid with fear. He watches me, but does not move, nor does his countenance change. For one ridiculous moment, I wonder if he has no more interest in me than a shark might have for a tiny fish in the sea—perhaps I am too small, too insignificant for concern. But then his voice booms out across the vale, a deep, heavy sound, as he calls to the warrior in the clearing. *"Ama-shiha! Laza ma ona!"*

The first man looks up in surprise and turns toward me.

There is no more indecision. I turn at once and flee.

I race through the trees, panic fueling my starving body. The skirts of my dress fly out behind me, snagging and tearing on the spindly tree branches that seem to reach for me with grasping fingers. The men are shouting, getting closer with every step. The snow is thin here, and slippery, but I manage to keep my footing as I race through the wood. I'm veering to the south-west, toward the escape pod, toward my last hope of rescue.

An arrow zips past my left shoulder and sticks firmly in one of the trees ahead of me, its shaft quivering. Terrified, I cut to my right and then again to my left, trying to become as elusive a target as possible. One of the Xoe calls out, his voice like thunder in the dense thicket; he is much closer now. Foolishly, I look over my shoulder to see how much space lies between us, and as I do, the uneven terrain rises before me. I slip and go sprawling forward, the frozen ground scraping my arms as I try to stop myself.

The Xoe is on me in an instant. He puts one hand on my head, crushing the right side of my face against the snow. There is a terrible pressure between my shoulder blades—his knee, I think. I struggle to free myself, and the force at my back increases. He must weigh twice, maybe three times, as much as I do. When at last I relax and let my body go limp, the man binds my hands together with a rough length of rope and rolls me over.

I look up at him, the edges of my vision dark with fear. It's the tall man who spotted me across the clearing, the archer with the brilliantly colored tattoos. Beneath the splashes of ink, his skin is pale, almost translucent, his veins visible like a network of twisting roads. His face is broad with hard angles and myriad scars, handsome, frightening, intimidating. A lock of silver hair has come loose from the braid at his back and hangs in a graceful curve before one of his stone-blue eyes. He stares down at me, his mouth slightly open, the curious expression returned.

"Ama-zi?" he says.

I shake my head. "I don't understand."

He bends down, crouching, his face so close to mine that I can smell his breath—it reeks of fish. *"Ama-zi?"* he repeats, more forcefully this time. He shakes me roughly by the shoulders, rattling the arrows in his quiver as he moves. *"Mo zazo. Mo zazo!"*

"Please, I don't understand," I say, tears springing to my eyes. My vision doubles, and there are two of him for a moment. "I don't know what you're saying!"

He stares at me. I lie on the ground, my hands burning with cold in the snow. The man reaches toward my face and I flinch, but he merely lifts a lock of my hair and rubs it between his fingers. *"Ama shai maza-an Aven'ei."*

Aven'ei. This word I know.

"No," I say quickly. "No, I'm not Aven'ei! Is that what you're asking? I'm not Aven'ei, I'm from the Spire, and—"

"Aka on-arimai!" he shouts, startling me into silence. The other warrior appears behind him, looks down at me, and frowns. He says something I can't understand, and the two men begin bickering back and forth. My shoulder aches and my hands have gone numb.

The archer yanks me to my feet. I sway for a moment, then sag against the tree behind me while the two men continue to argue. Finally, he turns to me once more, and taps roughly on his chest with his free hand.

"Ue," he says, and smacks his chest once more. *"Ue."* He tips his head toward the shorter man and says, *"Qelos. Qe-los."* Then he rattles me by the shoulders. *"Ama?"*

"You…you–we?" I stammer, the sounds of the Xoe language unfamiliar on my tongue. "Qelos? These are your names?"

He looks at me with a thin patience that I feel I must not test, and says once more, *"Ue,"* striking his chest, and then, reaching back to slap his companion's leather jerkin, *"Qelos."*

"Vaela!" I say. "My name is Vaela." Then, for good measure, I nod toward him carefully. "U-e." I shift my eyes to the man behind him and say, "Qelos."

He makes a small smile, which is slightly reassuring, if not a bit grim in its execution, so startling and powerful he seems to me.

"Keppa i ama In'dah?" he says.

I shake my head. "I'm sorry, I don't understand."

He pulls a knife from his boot and I recoil, but he merely leans forward and scratches something into the snow and muck with the short blade. The picture is shaped like a wide oval, and he scratches a few carets along the center, near to the right side of the drawing.

He taps a spot to the right of the carets. "Aven'ei," he says, and then taps a point at the top left of the circle. "Xoe." Then he points to me. *"Ama?"*

It's a map. He's drawn the Continent and outlined the territories, and I'm fairly certain he wants to know where I fit into all this. I lean forward and use my foot to draw another oval below his, then create a few squiggly waves between the two objects to denote the ocean.

"Spire," I say, tapping at my own circle with my toe.

He gestures to the sky, then holds his knife flat and pretends to fly it through the air, like a child might do with a toy airplane. *"Spi-er?"*

I nod eagerly. "Yes, that's right! I'm stranded here, you see?"

He is quiet for half a minute, his eyes on the map. Again, he exchanges words with the other man—Qelos—their voices rising, rattling my already shattered nerves. The Xoe language is utterly unlike any tongue in the Spire; the words seem to move gracefully into one another, almost like music. I listen for anything I might recognize, but they speak so quickly, it is difficult to discern one phrase from another.

At length, the man called Ue turns to me, presses his lips together, and stares at me for a long moment. And as soon as I realize it is happening, he lifts his arm and thunks me hard at the left temple with the butt of his knife.

All dissolves into darkness.

CHAPTER 9

◆

I OPEN MY EYES AND BLINK AT THE BRIGHTNESS of the white sky, its light blinding beyond the trees. I am on the ground, on my back, aching everywhere. I stare at the soft snowflakes drifting through the air, my mind as blank as a new canvas. It is the throbbing in my head that brings me back to myself. I sit up quickly—a dreadful mistake—and feel unconsciousness reaching for me once again. I close my eyes and force myself to stay alert.

When the dizziness ebbs, I take stock of my surroundings. I'm in some sort of campground; at least, that's what it looks like to me: there is a tent pitched nearby, and one of the Xoe—Qelos, the man I first saw in the clearing—is sitting on the ground beside me, sharpening the edge of his hatchet upon a chiseled rock. He grins when I look at him, displaying a mouth full of teeth blackened by whatever root he is chewing, and says something I can't understand. The other warrior is nowhere in sight.

Someone has placed a thick fur blanket over me; it has a strange smell to it, a scent I don't recognize. My hands are no longer bound, but my wrists are chafed and raw where the cord cut into my skin.

There's very little snow on the ground here, but considering how dense the trees are, I'm not surprised. The Xoe beside me doesn't seem at all worried that I might try to make a run for it; I briefly consider attempting an escape, but a vision of Qelos's hatchet sticking squarely in my back is enough to dissuade me.

He smiles again, a warm, black-toothed grin, and reaches behind him to produce a leather satchel, which he tosses into my lap.

Tentatively, I loosen the cord and peek inside. It contains several strips of salted meat; I can't be sure, but it smells like venison. Only for the briefest moment do I consider refusing the food. Thoughts of poison, of improper storage, of filthy hands preparing the meat—these notions carry very little weight right now. I'm famished. I shove an entire piece into my mouth, and the intense shock of salty flavor amounts to pure pleasure.

Qelos laughs and throws a second bag at me; a quick look tells me it's full of either clayberries or chamolines. I have no way to determine which they are, but it doesn't seem likely that the warrior would choose to poison me in this way, with a friendly smile and all that. In any event, the berries look delicious. I stuff a handful into my mouth and am instantly rewarded with a burst of rich clayberry juice, sweet and only very slightly tart in the aftertaste.

I eat every last bit of food. When I've finished, Qelos pulls a piece of cork from a large jug and passes the vessel to me. I drink straight from it without hesitation, dimly aware that this is probably the first time since infancy I've had anything to drink without a glass, aside from melted snow. The cold water, rich and earthy in its flavor, is more satisfying than any beverage I've had in my life.

I had worried that eating so much might make me sick after three days without food, but in truth, I feel invigorated afterward, if not still a bit dizzy. I sneak a glance at the Xoe beside me, who has returned to the task of sharpening his weapon. He has a wide face and enormous blue eyes that protrude from the sockets, with lips that seem to turn up at the corners into a natural smile. His black hair is cropped short with choppy, uneven lengths sticking out in jagged wisps. He's the only Xoe I've yet seen with short hair; all the other men seem to wear it long, either in elaborate twists and plaits, or bound with cloth and colored wool. Also unlike the others, this man has no tattoos on his face, which is noticeably darker than that of most Xoe I've seen, though still relatively pale. He doesn't seem to be well outfitted. Whereas his companion was equipped with thick, fortified leather garments that were clearly designed for protection, this Xoe wears plain woolen clothes, a close-fitting leather jerkin, and a long, faded green coat that has obviously been patched many times.

He looks at me and smiles again, but doesn't speak. His expression is kind—genuinely friendly. Perhaps the Xoe only mistook me for an Aven'ei and now, realizing that I am not an enemy, intend me no further harm. Perhaps they can even help me get home.

Home! I jerk my head skyward and strain my ears, listening for the heli-plane.

There is no sound.

Night falls, and the man called Ue—having returned some thirty minutes ago, as best as I can measure, from who knows where—builds a fire. Qelos cooks a squirrel and three small fish on a spit above the flames, and serves a generous portion to each of us; the two men share the squirrel, but I am given only fish. I have never favored seafood, but I pick at the crisp meat and force myself to swallow it down. The dull rumble in my stomach begins to quiet once again.

For the better part of the evening, the two warriors sit idly by the fire, conversing with one another in their musical language. They ignore me for the most part, content to chatter and argue and occasionally belch with great satisfaction. I sit on the opposite side of the campfire, wrapped in the fur blanket, watching the men and wondering exactly what they intend to do with me.

The Xoe seem in good spirits, though I get the impression that Ue does not much care for Qelos. An expression of disdain likely looks the same the world over, and Ue seems to wear it nearly all the time. Qelos does not seem to mind; he is definitely the cheerier of the two. I can't imagine what brought these men together as traveling companions, especially so far from their own territory.

An hour passes, perhaps an hour and a half. After a while, it becomes apparent that the Xoe are talking not of the weather or the war or any other such thing, but about *me* in particular. They speak in low tones—needlessly, as I can't understand a word they're saying—and cast glances my way more often than not. At one point, Ue offers something like a smile, but his eyes linger on my face for too long before he turns his attention back to his companion, and I feel a prickly unease in the pit of my belly.

I sit in silence, arguing with myself over whether or not I might trust these men. They have fed me and ensured that I am warm in this awful, biting cold. But I sense a restless tension, as though the air were charged with something wild and electric. I can't put my finger on what it is; I only know that it echoes *danger*.

Ue watches me, the firelight casting shadows upon his face.

"Tara," he says, gesturing for me to join him on the opposite side of the fire. *"Tara in'u ei."*

I hesitate, but get to my feet and wrap the blanket tightly about my shoulders. I move slowly, cautiously.

"Sina," he says, patting the earth beside him. He gives me a smile, as though to put me at ease, but I see the lie behind it. His eyes are dark, flat—he wants something. I sit beside him, stiff and wary, fear like acid in my throat.

"Ama-zi?" he says. His voice is calm, curious, almost sooth-ing. *"Ama shai maza-an Aven'ei?"*

I shake my head. "No. Not Aven'ei. I come from the Spire. *Spire.*"

He nods. *"Ma zay, ma zay."* Another flash of a smile, of white teeth glinting. He exchanges a glance with Qelos, who, for once, looks very dour, almost nervous.

With an air of casual patience, he retrieves a short knife from a pouch in his vest. The handle is creamy white—bone, I sus-pect—and the blade is no more than two inches in length, but very wide.

I swallow involuntarily and hug the blanket against my body. We sit like this for several minutes, Ue turning the knife over and over in his hands, his eyes on me, my eyes on the short, deadly blade. After what seems an interminable silence, he asks, once more, in a friendly tone, *"Ama shai maza-an Aven'ei?"*

"No," I say, my voice clear and strong. "No."

Within a heartbeat, he closes the distance between us and grips the back of my neck, pressing the cold blade flat against my cheek. His eyes burn into mine with a scrutiny so intense, it seems a tangible thing. He is frowning, his pale, handsome fea-tures drawn tightly against the bones of his face; he is *searching* for something, for some answer as to who I am, from whence I've come, and what purpose my wandering the region south of the Kinso might serve.

A cold breeze tickles my skin, and I realize I've let go of the fur blanket; it rests on the earth in a soft pile around me.

"Please," I whisper, "I'm not Aven'ei. I promise—I *swear* to you."

He trails the knife down my cheek until it rests at my throat. The sharp point scrapes at my skin, and my trembling only makes this sensation worse. He holds it there for a moment lon-ger, then pulls away. My hand goes immediately to my neck; I touch the tiny bit of wetness I feel there, and look to see a smear of red across my fingertips.

He does not believe me, I think to myself. *He's going to kill me. Or worse.*

Panicked, I push myself from the ground in an attempt to run, but Ue catches me by the wrist with one hand and drives the knife into the muscle of my right thigh with the other. I cry out and fall to my knees, stunned, staring at the ivory handle sticking in my leg like some gruesome adornment. The pain— it's like fire, like *agony*—like nothing I've ever felt before.

Qelos calls out, disapproval in his voice, but Ue ignores him. Composed as ever, he reaches for the knife, grips the handle, and removes it with a swift jerk. Blood oozes from the tear in my trousers, spreading in a thick, dark oval across the white fabric. I press against the wound with both hands, stars pricking my vision. I squeeze my eyes together, trying to will away the pain, the pulsing, the heat, the pressure in my thigh. A strong hand grips my throat, and I open my eyes to see Ue's face just inches from my own.

The next moment is like a blur: there is a soft noise, and Ue jerks away from me. The clasp of my necklace breaks, the chain caught in his fingers as he wrenches backward. The Xoe gropes at the side of his neck, where I see—in equal parts relief, confusion, and horror—the black handle of a knife protruding outward.

Ue yanks the blade from his neck and a soft gurgling sound emerges from his throat. Half a second later there is a man beside him; tall, garbed from head to toe in black, his features cast in shadow by the dark hood about his face. The Xoe outweighs him by at least forty pounds, but is far too slow to defend himself; the man in black slips easily behind him and, in one movement, opens the Xoe's throat from left to right. Ue falls forward into the dirt, blood bubbling through his fingers as he clutches his ruined neck. There he lies, emitting horrific noises, his body twitching as the life drains out of him in a sickening black pool.

Qelos springs into motion, his eyes wide, scrambling in the dirt for his hatchet. But the hooded man does not linger. He puts a foot on Qelos's shoulders, forcing him to the ground, and thrusts a knife into his back again and again. The Xoe is dead long before his assailant has finished his work.

Through all of this—which takes place in a matter of seconds—I am still, as though rooted to the ground, watching these events unfold in a surreal state of paralyzed disbelief. Now, as the stranger completes his grisly business—he appears to be wiping clean his blade—reality clicks into place once again and I inch backward, a cold sweat trickling down the nape of my neck. *By the Maker... he's going to kill me. I'm next.*

He turns to approach, but stops to retrieve something from the dirt before the campfire. My necklace. The ruby glows in the light of the fire as he turns it in his palm, inspecting the stone. After a moment, he looks at me, his head tilted slightly.

In the light of the dwindling flames, the features of his face emerge: dark eyes, lips set firmly in an expression of concentration. His skin is smooth, bronze in the firelight, his jawline sharply defined. He is younger than I surmised—perhaps not much older than I am—and he is most certainly Aven'ei.

He crosses the campsite and moves in my direction, sliding back the cowl to reveal a shock of straight black hair falling from one side of his head across his eyes, longer in the front than it is in the back. The rest of his scalp, perhaps a third of his head on the opposite side, is shaved. Again, I move away, the pain in my leg forgotten, not sure whether I ought to flee, doubtful that it would do me any good should this man want to kill me.

He extends his hand; the ruby pendant with its broken chain rests in his palm, but I do not dare to reach out and take it. He watches me, his dark eyes steady. After a minute or so, he retracts his hand and crouches down before me.

"The inscription on this stone reads *ansana*," he says. "*Ansana* is a word of the Aven'ei, but you are not Aven'ei. Yet neither are you Xoe." He frowns. "So tell me, girl. Who are you?"

CHAPTER 10

◆

I STARE AT HIM, MY MIND WHIRLING. HIS ACCENT is unfamiliar, certainly like none in the Spire, but his words are unmistakably of the Astorian common tongue. After three days spent in silence and grief, and these last hours in the company of men whom I could not understand, the sound of my own language is like a healing ointment upon my heart.

"Who are you?" he says again.

I shake my head as tears spill onto my cheeks. Relief, terror, grief, joy—I can no longer tell the difference. A week ago, I would have thought it shameful to weep like this in front of a stranger; I mightn't even have cried in the presence of my own friends, save perhaps Evangeline. But now, I make no attempt to disguise my anguish. Salty tears mingle with mucus below my nose, and I wipe my face without care on the torn, filthy sleeve of my dress.

At length, the Aven'ei speaks again, his voice softer now. "Are you all right, girl?"

I nod and dab at my cheeks with dirty fingers. "I think so."

"Are you injured?"

"I'm all right." My wound throbs, but I bury my bloodied

trousers beneath the skirts of my dress. Admitting a physical weakness to this man does not seem prudent.

The Aven'ei is silent for a moment. "Where is your home?"

"To the south. Another…another continent. I come from a place called the Spire."

His mouth opens slightly and his dark brows rise up an inch or so. "You come from the Nations Beyond the Sea." It is not so much a question as a realization.

"You know of my people?"

"I know this name, Spire."

"We were on a tour, you see, and the heli-plane crashed, and I—"

"What is a heli-plane?"

"It's…it's an aircraft," I say. "A machine that flies through the sky."

"Ah," he says, nodding slowly. "I have seen these since I was a child. We call them *azmera*—skyships."

"That's precisely what they are," I say. "I was traveling with my family above the Continent when our heli-plane lost power. It crashed and…" I swallow. "And all were lost but me."

"I am sorry to hear this," he says. "It sounds as though you have had a great ordeal."

These few kind words bring fresh tears to my eyes. "Thank you."

A short silence passes between us, and the Aven'ei frowns. "A tour," he says. "This is the reason for the…planes?"

"Yes."

"Why?"

I hesitate, my face growing hot. "Your region is very interesting to us."

"Interesting in what way?"

"The Continent is quite different from the Spire, in terms of geography and culture."

"And so you come to watch us?"

"Yes."

"Like animals in a menagerie?" he says.

"No," I say quickly. "It's nothing like that, we simply—"

"You see the violence between my kin and the Xoe, yet you do not interfere?" He does not sound angry, only puzzled.

I swallow. "It is not our affair."

"Then why do you observe? Oughtn't you rather tend to the concerns of your own people?"

"It's difficult to explain," I say, flustered. "The Spire has transcended the ways of war. The fighting here, it is a curiosity to us."

I regret this choice of words as soon as I have spoken, and feel my cheeks burning. He stares at me, his lips pushed out slightly, the corners of his mouth turned down.

"I lost my mother to illness and my father to the Xoe," he says. "I have no brothers left out of four—all slain in battle— only my younger sister remains alive. The Aven'ei are driven back, burned alive, tortured, and dismembered. We are on the brink of annihilation. You find this curious?"

I shake my head, my voice caught in my throat. "No," I whisper. "I do not."

"Then why are you here?"

I want to explain about the maps, about my interest in the Continent itself, but I cannot pretend that the war did not hold some fascination for me. I look down at my hands. "It's complicated."

"I'm sure it is." He holds the pendant before me, dangling it by the broken chain. "Take your trinket. You can sleep where you are, or take the tent. We will leave at daylight."

I stare up at him. "Where do you intend to take me?"

He frowns. "You are not my prisoner, girl. You are free to go wherever you like. I am returning to my village, and I assumed that you would wish to accompany me. But if you would prefer to stay here—"

"No! I will go with you. I am very grateful."

He shakes the necklace impatiently, and I take it. I feel a dizzying relief at having the precious stone in my possession again. It is all I have left of my parents.

The Aven'ei stands and stretches, then gathers two logs from the small pile beside the campfire. He adds them to the dwindling flames and pokes them around a bit.

"You should sleep," he says. "I'm going to remove these bodies, lest they attract animals."

I move closer to the fire, taking the fur blanket with me. The ground is warmer here, though not by much. I lie down, my back to the flames, and watch as the Aven'ei tucks the fallen knife—the one Ue pulled from his own neck—into a sheath at his waist.

"May I ask your name?" I say quietly.

He pauses before bending down to grab Ue's wrists. "I am called Noro."

"Thank you, Noro, for saving my life."

"It is what any Aven'ei would have done," he says, and drags the warrior toward the darkness of the forest. I watch him disappear, and only after he is gone does it occur to me that he did not ask for my name in return.

"Wake up, girl."

I had been dreaming of soft things, of clouds and wisps of fabric, of rabbit furs and feather pillows. I awaken at the Aven'ei's voice to find myself stiff and aching from the hard ground, miles away from anything remotely soft or comfortable. I sit up and rub my eyes with the back of my hand.

The fire has gone out; only a few smoldering embers remain in the pit. The morning is bitterly cold. Noro sits beside me, his legs crossed, with several knives laid out before him on a leather mat. He picks up one and then another, inspecting them carefully. Without turning his head, he says, "You said you were not injured."

I look down to see that the blanket has fallen away, exposing the tear in my trousers and the dark stain of blood surrounding it. I pull the fur over it and tuck the covering beneath me. "Well…" I stop and clear my throat. "I wasn't quite sure whether I ought to tell you last night."

He continues his inspection of the blades. "Has the wound been cleaned?"

"I—no. I don't know how I would even manage it. Nothing is clean here." The word *here* seems to linger in the air like a solid thing. "I'm sorry," I say quickly. "That was unspeakably rude. I only meant—"

"Let me see it," he says, setting down one of the knives and turning toward me.

"I beg your pardon?"

"Let me see the wound, girl." He reaches for the blanket and I stand up immediately, holding the fur around my lower body. His brows rise as he looks up at my face. "What are you doing?"

I hold the blanket firmly in place. "My leg is fine. Don't trouble yourself about it."

His eyes narrow. "What is the problem here?"

"There's no problem," I say, sitting down again—out of his reach this time. "I simply do not require a medical examination."

He peers at me, the fine features of his face chiseled and striking in the pale morning light. "If the wound is not cleaned, it may fester, and your blood will poison," he says. "We must clean it properly before we go. There is much walking to be done, for it is several days' travel to my village."

"Then I shall see to it myself," I say, and gesture to the black satchel beside him. "Have you any bandages or disinfectant?"

He stares at me for a few seconds, then picks up a wooden jug. With a patronizing smile, he leans forward and sets it on the ground in front of me. "At present," he says, "I find myself in short supply of medical dressings. However, should you apply a bit of practical care to that wound of yours, I believe you may yet survive." He nods to the jug. "There's a bit of liquor in there that might serve."

Embarrassed, I take the flask and cross to the other side of the fire pit, where I sit down with my body angled away from him. I've never thought of myself as particularly squeamish, but then, I've never been witness to anything other than minor injuries—not until touring the Continent, that is. My inclination is to continue hoping that a heli-plane will appear and deliver me to a sterile, state-of-the-art medical facility where my wound might be cared for by qualified professionals. I don't want to see the gash in my leg, much less clean it. But I can't have him looking at it either.

I purse my lips and exhale deeply, watching my warm breath fan out before me in a feathery cloud. *All right. I can do this. I can clean it. It's going to be fine.*

Gingerly, carefully, I pluck at my torn trousers. The fabric sticks to my leg at first; it's encrusted with blood, a disgusting fact that I tuck away in the back of my mind before moving on to the next step. Then I spread open my ripped clothing to expose the wound, which is far worse than I feared it would be: red, swollen, gaping in one place, and seeping some sort of wretched fluid.

Noro is sitting only a few feet away, but his voice sounds tinny and distant. "How does it look?"

I shake my head, my lips pressed together. I hear him stand, dust himself off, and move up behind me. I put my hand protectively over my leg and feel a deep aching throb. "Please," I whisper, "let's just be on our way."

"We are not leaving until it's tended," he says, a note of exasperation in his voice. "Are you ill at the sight of blood? I can do it for you in a few minutes' time."

"No," I say, looking up at him. "I don't want you to touch it."

"The longer you wait, the more painful it will be."

"It's not that," I say, my voice faltering. "It's just…my physician in the Spire, she's…she's a *woman*."

He is silent for a moment. "You do not wish to be touched by a man."

My face colors, and I look away. "Among Spirians, it's not customary for a young man to lay eyes upon a woman's bare leg."

"Is it customary for young women to die of infection for the sake of propriety?"

"Of course not," I say irritably.

He crouches down beside me and I flinch, but his gaze is steady and even. "I will not hurt you," he says. "Nor will I look anywhere other than the wound itself. You have nothing to fear from me."

"It's just… I'm afraid I will vomit if I do it myself," I say. "I think it is beginning to fester."

His eyes hold mine, but he keeps his distance. "May I see to it?"

I nod, turn my face into my right shoulder, and take a deep breath.

Noro is a fast and efficient medic, as he promised he would be. I nearly faint from the pain when he breaks open the wound to clean it, but before long, his ministrations are complete.

I sit with my hands at my belly, my eyes on the clouds above, while Noro prepares bandages for my leg. The laceration, though clean, is pulsing angrily, but the crisp morning air blows across my exposed thigh and offers a mild comfort of sorts.

"It's good we took the time," Noro says, squeezing alcohol from a strip of fabric torn from the Xoe tent. "You may yet take ill, but your chances are far better than they were."

"Thank you." I glance at him—keeping my eyes raised so as to avoid accidentally seeing the wound—and watch as he tends to the bandages. "I suppose that's twice you've helped me, in the space of two days' time."

He nods almost imperceptibly, his eyes on the fabric. Satisfied that the first strip has dried, he leans over and begins to wrap it tightly around my leg. I jerk at the feel of the cold cloth, and of his smooth fingers against my skin. Our eyes meet for a brief moment; he clenches his jaw and returns his attention to the bandage.

While he dries the second strip, I turn my gaze back to the sky. "I'm sorry about what I said earlier," I say softly. "I misspoke when I suggested that nothing on the Continent is...that nothing here is clean. It was a terribly disrespectful thing to say. I know this is your home."

He shakes his head and begins to wrap the second bandage around my leg. "There is no need to apologize. You have lost much."

"That is very kind of you," I say.

He is quiet as he sets the third and final bandage aside to dry. I think suddenly of Aaden, of the horror on his face when my father pulled him from the escape pod. *He ought to be here instead of me*, I think. *What right have I to survive when so many others were lost?* How I wish I could be with my family, wherever they are now.

Noro sits back and looks at me thoughtfully, the contours of my face reflected in his eyes. "I understand your pain. As I told you, I am no stranger to loss. But you must take care, girl, for you will quickly learn that the Continent will not afford you the luxury of grief."

"What do you mean?"

He pauses. "I mean that you must reserve your pain for quiet moments. You must not let it soften you, but rather you must become sharpened by its edges, made stronger by its grip. When it claws at your heart, you must roar back. This is not a place for softness. The weak do not survive here. Do you understand?"

This is not a place for softness. An image from my dream, one of lilac-scented pillows and gossamer curtains, flits before my eyes. I look down at my hands, coated with dirt and grime, and think how very long ago it seems that I set eyes upon anything of comfort or beauty. I recall my mother's face, soft and alabaster, luminous against her dark hair. I think of our home in the Spire, of its wide rooms and corridors, its plush carpets and familiar smells. How I long to be there—to cling to the presence of my mother and father, which must surely be etched into the very walls. The mere thought is so painful that it robs me of my breath.

How can I set such grief aside? How can I do anything other than crumble to its will, and allow myself to burn away like so much wreckage? A part of me simply wants to lie down and die—to let my grief flow through me, to allow it to infect my soul the way my wound threatens to infect my body.

And yet, these urges to surrender are at war with a stubborn fury in my heart. I am in turns broken to the point of helplessness and determined to escape this place. I look up to see Noro watching me intently, and I know the conflict within me is written on my face. Lost before this stranger, this quiet warrior, I feel like a pane of glass—brittle, fragile, and wholly transparent. I close my eyes and shake my head. "I'm not sure if I'm capable of what you suggest."

"You will find your way," he says.

"And if I don't?"

"Give it time. Grief is always followed by a quiet. In that stillness, you will find that you have learned much."

I look up at him, my lashes fringed with tears. "What will I learn?"

"I could not say. That is for you to discover. But first, you must survive."

With my wound bandaged and the rip in my trousers stitched back together, Noro begins making preparations for our journey. He provides me with a thick white vest and a pair of leather gloves, both of which feel heavenly after so many days in the constant, biting cold. We sit down to a quick breakfast of stale bread, oranges (produced from a sack in the Xoe tent), and water, and then we are on our way.

My pace is slow at first due to the pain in my leg, but after an hour or two, the increased circulation seems to improve matters. Noro is kind enough to stop from time to time and let me elevate my foot. He doesn't say much over the course of the morning, but that's fine with me; my mind is on my family, on the Spire, on my home.

From the direction we are traveling, I determine that Noro's village must be northwest of Ivanel—and since we are heading toward the coast, I feel as though each step brings me closer to the island itself. I haven't yet worked out how to *reach* Ivanel, but my hope is that the Aven'ei will be able to offer some kind of assistance.

We stop at midday to eat again—another quick meal of bread and fruit—then continue on. The weather is bright and clear. Smooth blankets of snow glisten and sparkle in the sunlight, spreading out for miles along the deep southern valleys. The trek would be exhausting on fair terrain, but the snow makes the journey even more difficult. By the time the sun begins to sink below the horizon, my legs are like two spindly pieces of yarn. When Noro announces that we are to make camp, I drop to the ground in exhausted relief, certain I could not manage another step.

The site he has chosen offers more protection from the elements than the Xoe camp; we settle at the base of a small hillside, where a natural earthen cave reaches perhaps ten feet into the slope. I watch as Noro kindles a healthy fire beneath the cave's entrance.

"How is your leg?" he says, glancing up at me.

I run my palm over the top of my thigh. "It hurts, but the pain is manageable. It was far worse this morning, to tell you the truth—perhaps I am getting used to it. My feet, on the other hand…"

"Are they numb?"

"No," I say. "Just sore."

He nods and wipes the dirt from his hands. "We will clean your wound each morning, and do what we can to try to stave off infection. Now…wait here. I have traps nearby, and with any luck, we will have meat in our bellies tonight."

I sit by the fire, my body aching with exhaustion, hunger, and the shadow of a grief too great to bear. Noro is gone only twenty or thirty minutes, and returns with an armful of wood and two white hares swinging from his belt.

"We shall have a good supper tonight," he says. It is difficult to tell, but he sounds pleased.

"I'm very grateful. For the food, and…well…for what you did."

He unhooks the game and sets it beside the fire, then begins to rummage through his pack. "The people of the Spire," he says. "Do they resemble you?"

"How do you mean?"

He makes a twirling gesture toward his head. "This golden hair," he says. "Eyes like amber."

"Oh." I pause, thoughtful, caught in the memory of home, loneliness stretching into my heart. "Well, no. There are certain traits common to each country, I suppose, but the Nations are not as separate as once they were, and the open borders have allowed for a mingling of cultures. In any city nowadays, you're as likely to see a person of one aspect as you are to see another."

"It sounds like a vast place."

"It's about three times the size of the Continent, give or take," I say, "with millions and millions of people. Astor alone—that's the capital city—has three million or more people in residence. It's a magnificent place, with swirling platforms of mathematical design, architecture so elegant it can take your breath away—and all the conveniences a citizen could hope to experience. Trains, and lifts, and moving gardens. It's a beautiful place."

He retrieves his bundle of knives from the satchel. "It sounds cluttered."

"I…well, yes, I suppose so." I sit up and cross my arms over my chest. "Do you not have your own name for this place?"

He looks around the small shelter. "For…this place?"

"I'm sorry. For the Continent. I'd have thought the Aven'ei would have a grander name for it."

He sits back on his heels. "In the old words, we only ever called it *inzua*—home."

"Home," I say, and the word is like a dagger, threatening to loose all the feelings inside that I am trying so desperately to suppress. I smooth it away, erase it, push it from my mind.

"*Inzua*," he repeats. "A very old word indeed. Kastenai—the village to which we travel—is very like a capital city. It is smaller than many other settlements, but is home to some of our greatest leaders." He removes a knife from the case before him and begins to sharpen it; this one is longer than those I saw at the Xoe camp, and shaped differently, too, with a blade curving gracefully up to the tip.

"Is there something I might do?" I say. "I would like to help, if I can."

He shifts on one foot and peers over his shoulder at me. "Can you skin a hare?"

"I—well, no. I mean, it isn't that I *can't* skin an animal, it's just that I've never done it before."

He rests his knife against the half-shorn hide. "How exactly did you eat in the Spire?"

"What do you mean?"

"Did you not eat such things as hares?" he asks.

"I prefer lamb," I say. "But I did once have a lovely rabbit stew, although now that I think of it, I'm not sure if a rabbit and a hare are quite the same."

He looks at me, his mouth open slightly. "I think you misunderstand my question. I mean to ask how you procured your food."

"Oh," I say. "Well...our meals are managed and prepared by the kitchen staff, who are specially trained in culinary matters."

"These are slaves?"

"What? No! Of course not," I say, flummoxed. "They are paid quite handsomely, I assure you."

He picks up the knife and runs it smoothly beneath the animal's pelt. "Among the Aven'ei, a child of five can trap, skin, and prepare a hare for supper."

"I suppose you think me ridiculous."

He frowns. "I do not judge you for failing to learn what was never taught, girl."

"It's Vaela," I say.

"What?"

"My name. It's Vaela."

He says nothing further but turns back to his work. When he has finished, he sets the first animal aside and gestures to the second with his knife. "Come over here, and I will teach you."

"To skin the rabbit?"

"The hare," he corrects. "There is indeed a difference between the two. You see? You are learning already."

If the gnawing hunger of the past few days were not so fresh in my mind, the process of preparing dinner might have been enough to destroy my appetite. Thankfully, once cooked, the animal's flesh resembles any other kind of roasted meat. As a meal, it is chewy, stringy, and entirely different from the succulent rabbit in the stew of my memory, but it is also warm, hearty, and nutritious, so I devour my portion with grateful enthusiasm.

"You seem to wear many hats," I say, sitting back against the wall of the cave. "Warrior, hunter, woodsman, medic, chef."

I tick off the titles on my fingers. "Thank you, Noro, for everything."

"I do what must be done when it is required of me."

"I'm afraid my own abilities are rather less useful."

He looks over at me with interest. "And what skills have you?"

I hold up my hands. "None so practical as yours. I am an apprentice cartographer."

"I do not know this word."

"I'm a mapmaker."

"A tactician!" he says, impressed. "This, I would not have guessed."

"No, not a tactician," I say. "I draw maps to record the geography. To create an accurate picture of the land."

He frowns. "The maps have no strategic purpose?"

"They are educational. Informative. And quite beautiful, in their way."

He tosses a tiny rib bone into the fire. "This seems like a waste of time, to draw a map for no reason."

"It is not a waste of time at all," I say, bristling. "And you'll pardon me to say that I think your opinion is wholly influenced by the fact that you come from a nation at war. When a society has no use for such a thing, its citizens are able to indulge in more enriching pursuits."

"Of course. Like touring around in your *he-lo-planes* and watching *others* who are at war." I open my mouth, then close it. He smiles. "No argument, girl? I am surprised."

"I actually agree with you on that point," I say. "Though you are altogether wrong in your dismissal of cartography. It is an entirely worthy pursuit."

He stretches out before the fire, propping himself up on one elbow. "What makes it worthy?"

I gape at him. "It's—it's—there's an entire science devoted to mapmaking. It requires a great deal of diligence, of meticulous attention to detail—an understanding of geology and topography, of course, and there is an artistic element, to be certain—"

"But what is the point?"

"The...point?"

"Why do you do it?"

"I...I love it."

"Is this why you came? To make a map of the Continent?"

I look beyond the fire at the dark, quiet wilderness. "Yes. I've studied the charts of this place for as long as I can remember. All I ever wanted was to tour the Continent, to see it with my own eyes. The trip was a birthday gift from my parents."

The words sting as I speak them, and I'm swept away by a memory of the party, of the dancing and the music and the excitement I felt upon learning about the tour. In my mind, I see my mother and father standing on the dais beside me. I see the Shaws at the dinner table. I see Aaden watching me with whispery blue eyes.

Noro's voice pulls me back. "Both of your parents were with you, then. They perished?"

"Yes."

"I'm sorry." He is quiet for a moment, then says, "May I ask, for I have been wondering...if the *azmera* was destroyed, how is it you survived?"

"There was an escape pod, a...a lifeboat of sorts. It was ejected from the plane before the crash."

He sits up at once and leans forward. "Made of glass?"

My stomach twists. "How do you know that?"

"I saw it yesterday, many hours before I discovered you with the Xoe, though I did not know what it was at the time."

"Please," I whisper, "can you take me to it? There's a beacon inside—at least, I think there is—and if I return to it, there's a chance I could go home."

Noro shakes his head. "It is gone, girl. One of your planes

collected it. That is how I saw it—rising into the sky, suspended by a cable and pulley. The *azmera* swallowed it whole."

I think of the red light in the pod, blinking once, twice, again and again, silently beckoning the search party to its location. Had I waited only a few hours more, I might be home by now. But the plane has come and gone; there has been no sign of it since yesterday afternoon. And although I have continued to watch the skies with restless hope, I already knew in my heart what Noro has just made clear.

The search has been conducted, the escape pod collected. They are not coming back.

The Spire has abandoned me.

CHAPTER 11

✦

THREE DAYS MORE WE WALK ACROSS THE WILD southern face of the Continent. No map or tour could ever have prepared me for the sheer vastness of this place, with its great yawning valleys and glittering frozen lakes. Ice, snow, narrow passes walled in dark craggy rock, endless thickets full of pine and blackwood trees—the land stretches out before us, ever changing, ever the same. And always, I see this world laid out before me not only as a physical place, but in the delicate strokes of ink with which I might render it on paper. I long for the feel of parchment beneath my palm, for the solid fine wood of my drafting table, for a brilliant summer day in which the warmth of the sun floats in from a breeze at the window. For home. As it used to be.

Most of the time, Noro and I travel in silence. No matter the terrain, he is astoundingly surefooted, while I slip and stumble across the icy landscape. My fine leather boots were made to be fashionable; though practical enough for short-term exposure to the cold, they were not designed for tramping across country in several feet of snow. My toes are cold, always cold, but dry at least, which is more than I can say for the rest of my body.

While the days are quiet, the evenings are quite different.

Always Noro finds some unexpected shelter; always he builds a blistering fire that melts away the chill and exhaustion of the day. There is meat and fruit, and savory nuts served with steaming teas that warm me from the inside out. Noro, I find, has an easy grace about him—a stillness in his presence. I am grateful for his company, for his words that fill the space where grief longs to dwell. He tells me a little of the Aven'ei, of their villages and strongholds, of how they came to adopt the language of the Four Nations so many years ago. Every evening I find myself wishing that he would talk all the night through, for when silence falls and I close my eyes to rest, my thoughts drift to the loss I know I cannot face.

Yet somehow, I sleep, and each morning the light of day dampens my despair—or, more accurately, allows me to bury it so that I might function. I tell myself that I can survive this—all of it—and that the time for grief will come soon enough. For now, I must merely put one foot in front of the other, focusing first on my own healing and second on forging a path home. I will return to the Spire and somehow put the pieces of my life back together. And so, as we make our way ever southward, I do my best to forget that I am moving toward a future that is both invisible and frightening.

Three days into our journey, in the unexpected calm of a clear and sunny afternoon, I feel a weakness come upon me. I do my best to keep pace with Noro, but find myself falling farther and farther behind. Finally, he doubles back to investigate the delay.

"Are you well?" he says, squinting at me. "You look poorly."

I lean one hand against the trunk of a giant spruce and wipe a fine misting of sweat from my forehead. "I'm all right. I just need a moment to rest."

He stares at me for a second before retrieving the canteen from his belt. "Drink," he says, pulling out the cork and thrusting the container into my hands. I take a few sips but do not feel recovered. I am at once hot and cold, shivering and uncomfortable.

Noro steps closer, scrutinizing my face. "You are ill."

I shake my head and return the canteen. "It's just the exertion."

Noro is unconvinced. He looks toward the south, his brows furrowed. "We are nine, perhaps ten hours from my village. I had planned to make camp at dusk and complete our journey tomorrow, but now I am not sure if we should wait. It may be unwise to delay our travels."

I sag to the ground, sinking into a snowdrift at the base of the tree. "I am only tired, Noro. A moment's rest will restore me, I'm sure of it."

He looks down at me, displeasure on his face. "I have told you not to sit in the snow."

I close my eyes again. "Does it matter? I am already wet and cold."

He crouches down before me. "This is not a game, girl. You must take care of yourself. I have seen lesser wounds than yours lead first to fever, then agony and death. Do not let pride delude you into believing you are beyond danger."

"I don't believe I am beyond anything."

"Then stop being foolish," he says. He looks again into the distance, toward the southeasterly destination that is yet so far out of reach. He nods, as if coming to a decision. "I think we should continue."

"Please...let us rest tonight and carry on tomorrow. I don't know if I can press on for another ten hours, especially in the dark."

He is unmoved. "I will carry you if I must."

"A few hours of sleep may do more good than a difficult journey in the dead of night. Don't you agree?"

He considers this. The sun casts his face in hazy orange light, dissolving the shadows along the planes of his cheeks. His features look softer, his expression less severe, even in his current state of tension.

"You may be right," he says finally, straightening up and extending a hand. "Now, please, get out of the snow. There is an outcropping ahead where we will find shelter. It's not much, but it's better than nothing at all."

Noro's description of the small outcropping as "not much" was generous at best. Consisting of a rocky ledge jutting out at a sharp downward angle and a sheltered area of perhaps three to four feet of hardened earth, the tiny refuge scarcely fits the two of us. The cave from the first night seems vast in comparison, but still, this place is secluded and dry. That makes it very near to paradise in my rapidly reforming opinion of what constitutes comfort.

"You seem improved," Noro says. He's crouched at the entrance, having just returned from some errand or other.

"Actually, I do feel better. I believe it was just the exertion after all."

He ducks below the ledge and sits beside me. "Let us hope so."

"How could I not be recuperated, sitting here out of the wet?" I pat the rich brown soil beneath me. "This little spot is as nice as a fine hotel."

"What is a hotel?"

"Well…it is a place of excellent accommodations, extraordinary food, and all the niceties one requires to feel at home."

He glances around at the cramped little hollow. "Your dwellings in the Spire are impressive, are they not?"

"None so grand as this."

He frowns at me. "You are being sarcastic."

"No, I'm not! Perspective is a mighty equalizer, you know."

He regards me with a curious expression, then reaches into the pack by his side to produce a bundle of leftover meat. He taps the parcel with one finger. "I cannot claim the food at this hotel to be *extraordinary*, but I think with a little heat, we might make a meal of it."

I laugh—and immediately cover my mouth with my hands. A sickening wave of shame and guilt washes over me. Noro leans forward at once, his eyes dark with understanding.

"It is okay to laugh," he says softly. "You have done nothing wrong."

I shake my head and bury my face in my hands. My parents have been dead hardly a week—it is far too soon to revive the pleasure of laughter. I feel as though I have spit upon the graves of all who died in the heli-plane. The guilt and grief inside me expand to fill every pore, every inch of my body, until it seems there is nothing left of me at all, and I begin to weep.

Noro is silent. He makes no move to comfort me, whispers no platitudes, attempts no consolation. Yet he is there. I feel his empathy as certainly as I feel the anguish of my own heart. For a long time, we stay like this, my pain and weakness made all the clearer in the gravity of his strength.

The sun sinks below the edge of the world, and night spreads across the Continent like a bleak, stifling blanket. In the darkness, fatigue grips me, and I fall into a black sleep, Noro still at my side.

In the morning, I find myself tucked snugly beneath the fur. Noro is seated just outside the entrance to the hollow, his arms crossed over his knees, his gaze fixed on some point in the distance. The hood of his coat is up, casting a shadow along the side of his face. In profile, he is the very picture of a warrior—solemn, powerful, and focused, with a short sword strapped to his back and the belt of black knives slung about his waist. It is difficult for me to reconcile this image with the quiet soul who sat with me last night as I wept. But then, if I learned anything from my experience with Aaden, it is that people are not always what they seem; who knows what kindness, cruelty, selfishness, or heroism may be concealed beneath the surface? Only time and circumstance bring all into view.

I sit up, keeping my hands inside the warm blanket. "Don't you ever sleep, Noro?"

He glances over at me. "Of course. How are you feeling?"

My skin is warm despite the morning chill, and my body aches. I force a smile. "Very well, thank you."

"You are a terrible liar," he says, and leans over to pour me a small cup of dark, steaming liquid. "Drink this. We should leave as soon as you are able."

I take the cup and give it an exploratory sniff; the drink smells faintly sweet. "Is it a type of tea? The aroma is not like the others you've prepared."

"Whiteroot tea, and a bit of sugar."

I've never heard of whiteroot, but a small sip reveals a mild flavor reminiscent of chamomile. A larger sip is like warm honey being poured into my upper body. "It's delightful," I say. "Thank you very much."

He nods. "Tell me the truth, now, how badly are you feeling this morning?"

"I shall be very well once we are on our way," I say, but this, too, is a lie.

"That is not what I asked."

I sigh. My Spirian upbringing has brought into focus the imposition of my illness. I ought to be self-sufficient—self-reliant. Malady is best concealed, stuffed into a sickbed, kept properly away from others—not forced upon them in the middle of the wilderness with many miles yet to travel.

"I am unwell," I concede, "but please, let it rest at that. I do not wish to complain, and you will hear no more of it from me. All right?"

"Fair enough," he says. "But we have a long way to go yet; we won't reach the village until late afternoon, and that's assuming the weather will hold. You must tell me if you need help."

I hand him the empty cup. "I am sturdier than I look. Now let us be going, for we shan't make any progress sitting around like this."

★ ★ ★

By midday, my facade of hardiness and self-sufficiency has crumbled. All I want to do is lie down in the snow and sleep. A truly alarming heat is radiating from my wound, and my muscles are drained of all strength. I have lost my footing more times than I can count. The weather, as it turns out, did *not* hold; it has been snowing steadily for the past hour, and what began as a fine drizzling of soft flakes has become a miserable flurry of ice.

I do not mean to do it, but I put one knee down in the snow, and the rest of my body follows. Noro, walking at my side, immediately stops to collect me. I do not protest as he gathers me into his arms, but merely turn my face away from the driving snow and close my eyes. Somewhere in my mind, beneath the exhaustion and fever, a prim and proper Spirian voice is telling me to stop being such a burden—to get down at once and keep moving until we reach the village. But the gentle sway of Noro's footsteps lulls me into a state of quiet acquiescence, and I make no move other than to settle my head against his chest.

Minutes or hours pass by, and on we go. Noro never stops, or speaks, or even looks at me as far as I can tell. Sleep and a comfortable delirium come to me in waves, and between these moments, I catch glimpses of his face—his eyes, really, as his mouth and nose are concealed by a black cloth he has wrapped around his head. His brows are furrowed, his dark lashes dusted with ice, his eyes unwavering from the path ahead.

The day grows dim, though whether from the passage of time or a change in the weather I cannot tell. "Is it very much farther?" I say. It is the first time I have spoken since we left the hollow.

Two deep brown eyes glance down at me. "An hour at most," he says, his voice muffled behind the mask.

"Will the people of your village be very surprised to see me?"

"No more surprised than I was."

"Do you suppose they will think me strange?" I say. He does not answer, though I wait nearly a minute. "Noro?"

He makes a noise as he shifts my weight closer to his body. "Go back to sleep, girl."

I close my eyes and drift away.

The clouds have deepened to a smoky gray by the time I wake again. The snow has stopped, but the icy wind persists, and the chill is cruel. As we reach the top of a low hillside, I see the village laid out in the center of the valley below.

It is surrounded by a rectangular wall of blue-gray stone, with parapets and slender towers set at the town entrance and at each of the four corners of the wall. The village itself is clustered within; dirt roads wind through the rows of black-shingled houses and market buildings, while wispy puffs of smoke rise from chimneys scattered throughout. I would guess that a town this size could accommodate perhaps two or three thousand people; it is far more sizable than the tiny hamlet spotted during my first tour of the Continent. A sliver of the southern sea is visible from here, and beyond that vast ocean is the Spire. The thought of home fills me with renewed hope.

"You can put me down," I say. "You must be exhausted."

The scarf around his face has come loose and I see a frown on his lips, but he sets me lightly on my feet. A finger of cold slithers up my spine; I hadn't fully appreciated the warmth of Noro's body. Still, I am steady, and that is something.

"Can you walk, then?" Noro asks.

"Yes," I say, with some confidence. "I'm terribly sorry for all the trouble."

He ignores this. "We are nearly there, and I intend to take you directly to the healer."

"Oh, but you mustn't!" I say, a knot forming in my stomach. "I wish to speak with the leaders of your village as soon as possible—I must know if they will help me to return home!"

His frown grows deeper. "You require medical attention."

"Noro, please—this cannot wait," I say. My heart beats faster; I am desperate to know if the Aven'ei will help me to reach the Spire. "A few minutes won't make a difference," I add quickly. Hopefully.

"You are very stubborn," he says.

"I wouldn't ask if it weren't important. I must request assistance without any further delay."

After a moment's hesitation, he nods, and begins to move down the hillside. I follow without a word, glad to be by his side and under his protection as we head toward the Aven'ei village.

CHAPTER 12

◆

TWO LOW TOWERS FRAME THE NARROW PORT-
cullis that bars entrance to the village. A voice calls down as
soon as we approach, the sound booming in the relative quiet
of the early evening. "Who comes?"

"It is Noro, friend."

A shadow passes between the slits of the tower on the right-
hand side. "Noro Dún? You were expected three days prior."

"Open the gate, Talan. I have traveled far and am eager to
rest."

The iron gate begins to rise, the steady click of its chain in
the pulleys a welcome and reassuring sound. A moment later,
Noro's friend—a man of twenty years, perhaps, or younger—
appears at the entrance. He is a bit shorter than Noro—perhaps
just under six feet—and ruggedly handsome, with strong, arched
eyebrows and a sweep of long, dark hair swung up into a knot
atop his head, both sides of which are shaved from the tops of
his ears downward. He is bronzed, sun-kissed, like most of the
Aven'ei, much like a Westerner back home. The man's wide
grin turns to an expression of open surprise when he sees me.

"Noro?" he says, his right hand coming to rest automatically
upon the sword at his hip. "What is this?"

"Peace, Talan. Only a wounded girl in need of help."

"She's not—" Talan pauses, suspicion written on his face. "She's not *Xoe*?"

Noro spits on the trampled snow. "Of course not. Trust me, friend—all will be explained. May we pass?"

The man shakes his head, but gestures for us to come inside. "If I catch any hell for this—"

"She is no enemy."

"Find me later?"

"I will do."

As we walk away, I look back to see Talan watching us with undisguised curiosity. He is not the last to do so; as we move through the entrance and into the town proper, we draw many stares.

Most of the townspeople are dressed in plain, practical clothes of heavy wool, but a good many of the men wear the fighting garb of the Aven'ei. And while these men look as fierce and dangerous as Noro, it strikes me that none are dressed quite like him; he alone wears black from head to toe, while they are clothed in muted fur and leather. I wonder if this is significant in some way, but I do not ask.

The buildings, like the walls of the city, are made of stone, and look to have been built with great skill and care—though I notice that the walls seem to have been constructed more recently. Kastenai seems a quiet place, and one of great beauty: pots full of winter flowers are crowded onto porches, and little courtyards, with walls tangled in ivy, are set here and there for the children.

Noro and I continue down the main thoroughfare for a good while before turning onto another lane, this one apparently far less traveled, as it is covered in powdery snow. I sag against Noro, the weakness of my fever manifesting in irregular waves, my vision darkening from the mere exertion of walking. I shake the haze from my eyes. *Nearly there. Nearly there now, and soon, I shall meet with the healer. Keep moving.* Two more eventual turns bring us to a quiet residential street, lined with single-story stone cottages built quite close to one another. Each house is so near to the next that two people could not stand side by side between them. Rather than looking crowded, however, the whole scene gives an orderly and cozy sort of impression.

"Noro!" comes the cry of an excited voice behind us. I turn to see a girl of about ten years old, accompanied by an enormous gray hound, racing up the road in our direction.

Noro's face breaks into a wide smile. He extends his arms, the girl barrels into him, and the two embrace.

"Kept the place safe and sound, I see?" Noro says.

The girl grins. "I've been practicing every day with the barrels, just as you instructed. I can hit the knothole six times out of ten."

Noro's eyebrows inch upward. "A big improvement in a short time."

The dog—if one could call it that, for it is nearly as tall as a small horse—leans heavily against Noro, who pets the beast with absentminded affection.

"Sit, Joa," the girl says, and the dog obeys, though not without issuing a sharp whine of discontent. "Who is this?" the girl adds, nodding at me.

"A friend, sister. She comes from the Nations Beyond the Sea." At the word *sister*, the resemblance between the two Aven'ei becomes immediately apparent. Each has the same aquiline nose, sharp bone structure, dark eyes, and angled jawline. The girl is Noro in youthful miniature, only with a crackling ebullience that her brother does not share.

Her mouth falls open, and she stares at me. "You lie—it's impossible."

"I tell you the truth. She was lost by her people."

"Lost how?"

Noro ruffles the girl's hair, which is parted at the side and drawn up into two large knots, one on each side of her head. "All will be explained in time. Now I must assemble the council, for they will want to meet our guest. Will you wait with her, and be hospitable? She is ill, and very tired from the journey."

The girl turns at once to face me. "Kiri Dún," she says in a distinctly formal tone. "Any friend of Noro's is a friend to me as well."

I smile, despite the pain, exhaustion, grief. "My name is Vaela Sun. I am pleased to make your acquaintance."

Noro points to a cottage down the lane, on the left-hand side. "That's our place. You and Kiri can wait for me there; I shouldn't be long."

"Come, Vaela Sun," Kiri says. "I will make you some tea, if you like."

"I should like that very much."

Noro looks back and forth between the two of us. "I shall be as quick as I can," he says, then turns to head back in the direction from which we came.

I follow Kiri—and the dog, which seems to mirror his master's every move—down the road and up a stone pathway to the little house. We enter into a small sitting room, with two low sofas upholstered in deep blue, and a fire burning behind a metal grate. The warmth of the room envelops me at once.

The place is sparsely decorated, but comfortable and refined in its way. A great tapestry hangs on the wall adjacent to the fireplace, depicting a sort of picnic scene with gold-leaved trees and elegant figures in repose. Below is a bookcase carved from shining blackwood, each of its three shelves stuffed with volumes of varying sizes.

"Sit, please," Kiri says, and disappears into the next room, a small kitchen only part of which is visible from the entry. I sink onto the sofa nearest the fire and pull off my leather gloves, marveling at the relief of simply sitting on a piece of furniture. The dog is seated at the entrance to the kitchen like some kind of sentry; he stares at me with curious brown eyes, turning his head only occasionally to mark the movements of the young girl. After a few minutes, Kiri reappears and hands me a small brass cup.

"Are you really from beyond the sea?" she asks, pouring tea from a copper kettle.

"Thank you," I say. "And yes, I am."

"You are lost?"

"I'm afraid so."

Kiri pours herself a cup and sits on the rug. The hound crosses the room, its claws clicking on the wooden floor, and curls up beside her, resting its great gray head on the girl's knee. "How will you find your way home?"

I sigh, weary from asking myself the same question. "I don't know, Kiri."

"You do not look well at all," she says, though not unkindly.

"I am quite under the weather," I admit. I wipe my brow, which has grown sticky with perspiration. "But I am to meet with one of your healers as soon as I've spoken with the village council."

"It's a good thing, too. You look fit to fall right on your face." She takes a sip of tea. "Is your family waiting for you beyond the sea?"

"No," I say, grief dancing upon my heart, waiting to show itself fully. "My family was with me when I was lost here. I'm afraid they did not survive."

Her eyes narrow, and she leans forward. "Was it the Xoe?"

"No, no, not the Xoe. It was an accident."

"The Xoe killed my family," she says. "Except my mother, who took ill, and Noro, of course. Nobody can kill Noro. He's an *inanei*, you know."

"What is an in-uh…forgive me, I don't know the word."

"*Inanei*," she repeats. "An assassin."

A prickly clarity comes upon me as I recall the black-handled blade buried firmly in Ue's neck.

"He is adept in his work," I say, unsure how to compliment so violent a thing, but still possessing a quiet admiration for Noro's abilities. "He must be very well suited for the profession."

Kiri grows somber, her darkly serious expression making her appear even more like her brother. "It is nothing so small as a profession, Vaela Sun. Though the *inanei* are few, they are more important than the whole of our fighting force. They eliminate Xoe leaders. They are expert in subterfuge and misdirection. They have prevented any number of assaults upon our villages. Without the assassins, the Xoe would have wiped us from the Continent long ago."

"Forgive me," I say again. "I know very little about these things."

She leans back and grins, her natural cheer quite returned. "It's all right. You're new here."

"You're very kind," I say. "Very much like your brother."

She smiles at this. There is a pause while we drink our tea, each of us occupied with our own thoughts.

"Are you named Sun for the color of your hair?" Kiri asks.

"No," I say, "though that is an interesting question. Sun is only a surname, from my father's family. Although now I come to think of it, his side was typically quite fair, most of them blond as far as I can remember. My mother had hair much like yours." *Had*, I think. *Past tense.* My stomach tightens at the thought of this new reality.

Kiri nods. "It is a good name, I think: Sun."

The front door opens and Noro steps inside. "The council is ready for you. Shall we go?"

I turn back to Kiri. "Thank you for making me feel so very welcome. I hope I will see you again soon."

She smiles. "Good luck in your business with the council."

And then, to Noro, "Hurry back—I want to hear all about your journey, and I have much to tell you as well."

A light snow begins to fall as Noro and I make our way to see the council. We pass by the town center—a wide market square that looks to be mostly empty—and turn on the next street toward a building that Noro offhandedly refers to as the War Room. Wagons line the lane, some fitted with oxen, while lanterns along the walking path cast the night in a warm, lazy glow, calling to mind a painting I once saw of the Spire's most northern city. The cold seems more bearable in this light—less bracing, somehow.

There is an amiable quiet between us as we go. Inwardly, I am stirred by fresh optimism—I feel confident that the Aven'ei leaders will help me, certain they will wish to return me at once to the Spire. So moved am I by this spirit of hope and expectation that I feel quite able to ignore the pounding of my head, the fever raging in my body, and the throbbing of my wounded leg.

The War Room, though ominous in name, is in fact an unassuming single-story building set between two others that look exactly like it. There are no traditional windows on the facade, but rather two slim rectangles near the roof, each glowing yellow from the light within. Noro knocks twice on the door and enters without delay; I follow with butterflies in my stomach.

The room is wide, and quite austere; a great table with at least a dozen chairs lies at the center, with an overlarge fireplace directly behind. There are no other furnishings to speak of, save a few bins filled with large sheets of rolled-up parchment—maps, I imagine.

Three people are seated along the far side of the table, and they make for an intimidating lot. The two at the ends—one man and one woman—both bear the countenance of a person faced with a difficult problem; only the man at the center wears a smile. There is a distinct air of authority about him; he looks to be around sixty years of age, with salt-and-pepper hair tied into a neat knot at the back of his head. He is dressed in gray, as are the others, and a violent scar runs at an angle across his throat, slashing downward from his chin toward his left shoulder.

He stands as I enter. "Welcome to Kastenai. It is some time since we had a visitor from the Nations Beyond the Sea—coming on two hundred years, I think, or very near. The last time your countrymen set foot on the Continent, they made to disembark by ships of the sea. Now, I am told they sail *azmera* through the clouds. Much has changed in these past centuries. But I digress from my purpose—please, sit, and we may talk awhile."

"Thank you," I say, and take the chair opposite. Noro sits beside me, his hands folded atop the table.

"My name is Nadu," the man continues, "and these are Shovo and Kinza." He indicates the man and woman at his left and right. The man called Shovo looks as though he has never smiled—not ever. A black tattoo swirls across the left half of his face, and he, too, is scarred; mottled lines mar his skin from forehead to collar. The woman, Kinza, wears the left sleeve of her tunic folded neatly in two; her arm is missing from the elbow down. Her face is handsome for her years, her eyes sharp and thoughtful. "We bid you welcome," Nadu says, "although Noro tells me you find yourself here under the most unfortunate of circumstances. You have our sympathy."

"Thank you again," I say. "Your kindness means more than I can fairly express."

"And what do you call yourself?"

"Forgive me—my name is Vaela Sun."

"Noro tells me also that you are injured, and taken with fever?"

"Yes, sir."

He nods. "Then let us be brief, so that you may see the healer directly. How can we help you, Vaela Sun?"

I feel a quiver in my chin. Now that it has come to the moment of asking for help, it seems a very difficult thing to do. "Please," I say, then find I must collect myself before continuing, for I am on the point of tears. "I would ask for your assistance in returning home."

Nadu smiles, a placid, but genuine expression. "I'm afraid we are not equipped to bear you across the sea, Vaela Sun. As I understand it, your Nations are a very great distance from here, many hundreds of miles away. Our boats are small, made for fishing local waters—not for a great journey such as you would require."

I lean forward and clasp my hands together, my fingertips trembling. "I do not need passage to the Spire, sir—only to a small island perhaps thirty miles east of the coast. We have a facility there, you see. I could provide you with a precise and accurate bearing, and it would be a very quick journey indeed."

He is silent for a moment. "I'm afraid that would not be possible."

These words are wholly unexpected. "Surely...surely your vessels could travel such a distance? I would be happy to repay your trouble with gold, or perhaps supplies of some kind. I do have a small fortune to my name, and—"

"The problem, Miss Sun, is manifold. Yes, a sailboat could likely make the distance you have described. But we are amid the *kazuri ko'ra*—the 'anger of the sea.' The coastal waters are icy at this time of year—treacherous—and remain so until the winds of autumn blow the bergs to the south. We do not venture far beyond the marina until that short time between summer and winter. To do so would be to place oneself in the belly of terrible storms that do naught to ships but sink them.

"Secondly, we are at war, as you know. Even if the weather were favorable, we have endured great violence in the north this year, and ought not spare the men required to see you safely to your island." His expression is apologetic. "I sympathize with your situation, Vaela Sun. Should the tides of war turn in our favor, and should the seasons pass without incident—ensuring safer conditions—we can reevaluate your request. But for the time, as much as it pains me to decline, I must say no."

My throat clenches and I swallow involuntarily. Silence weighs upon the room, upon me, thick and palpable like a suffocating fog. I struggle to find words, but there are none within my reach.

"I can take her to the island," Noro says quietly, his eyes fixed on the table. "I do not fear the *kazuri ko'ra*."

"Mind your place, boy," growls the man called Shovo.

Noro is unmoved. "I may speak if I wish."

The man glares back at Noro. "Nadu has spoken for the village. It is not your privilege to contradict his judgment."

"I merely offered to escort the girl back to her people," Noro says. "She does not belong here."

The man called Shovo gives him a joyless smile. "Yes, she has lost her home. And would you lose yours, Noro Dún, by abandoning your village and taking to the sea—sinking like a stone in that great yawning tomb of ice and water?"

Noro clenches his teeth, the lines of his jaw tightening. Nadu places a hand on Shovo's shoulder.

"Peace, Shovo," he says. "Young Noro only wishes to do what is honorable. He is to be commended."

"I thank you," Noro says.

Nadu nods. "But Shovo is right. You are one of our most valued *inanei*. We depend upon your skill, Noro, and need you here. You have some experience with the sea, yes—but even a salt such as you must practice wisdom. I would not commit you to the deeps just yet."

Noro's expression does not change. "I am at your command, Nadu."

Nadu turns back to me. "I hope you can understand our position, Vaela Sun. It is not my wish to keep you from the Nations Beyond."

I shake my head, feeling lost and overwhelmed—and suddenly

very ill, now that the numbing barrier of hope has fallen away. "Of course not. You are kind to even consider my request."

"Good," he says. "Then I think we shall send you to the healer without further delay. See to it, Noro—and return to the council when Vaela Sun is settled. We have more to discuss."

The night no longer seems blanketed in wintry softness, but rather feels bleak and cold. The Spire will not collect me. The Aven'ei will not deliver me. The war between the nations of the Continent is unlikely to ease, and this strange and unfamiliar place—Kastenai—is to be my home for the foreseeable future.

I ought to feel grateful—grateful to have survived the plane crash, to have been freed from the Xoe, to have been treated with such hospitality by the Aven'ei, who have no obligation to me whatsoever. But I do not feel anything of the kind; I am merely angry and resentful. A black thought snakes through my mind: *I wish I had died with the others aboard the heli-plane.*

Even as I imagine the words, I am appalled by them, scalded by their reckless, roiling venom. I did not think myself capable of such depths. Could it really have been only two weeks ago, perhaps, that I was safe at home in the Spire, laughing and dancing and enjoying my party? Now I walk through the dark night in another world, thinking dreadful, shameful thoughts, indulging my own piteous state. My mother and father would be ashamed of me.

We reach our destination after a short while—a narrow house on another residential lane. Noro turns to me before knocking at the door. "For what it may be worth," he says, "I am sorry about the council's decision. I know it was not what you wished to hear."

"Yes. Well. At least I may put the matter to rest in my heart for now." As an afterthought, I add, "Please know how much I appreciate your efforts on my behalf."

He nods, and gestures toward the house. "The healer is called

Eno, and though she is mute, you will have no difficulty in communicating with her. She will take good care of you."

"I have no doubt."

He raps on the door and takes a step back. As we wait, he looks at me thoughtfully and, for the briefest moment, takes my hand in his. "Be well, girl," he says. The warmth of his fingers around mine lingers long after he lets go, and it is a surprising comfort on a night that seems otherwise void of all consolation.

CHAPTER 13

◆

FOR FORTY-ONE DAYS, I DO NOT LEAVE THE HEAL-
ing room.

The first week is quiet; I turn my face to the wall when Eno
comes to open the drapes each morning; I close the curtains
when she goes out the door. I do the exercises she prescribes,
but decline to go outside. The four walls around me become my
personal fortress; my wound heals, my heart aches, and I sleep.

But one cannot stay forever in the eclipse of denial, and
though I try to avoid both the darkness and the light, each
waits for me in turn. And so, in the quiet hours of those long,
terrible weeks, I finally begin to face without distraction the
magnitude of all I have truly lost.

When I sleep, I dream of drifting, ghostlike, through the
halls of my home in the Spire. The rooms are dim, the furniture shrouded in billowing white sheets. I cannot touch anything; my fingers pass through objects as though they were
made of nothing. I search for something, but I cannot find it,
and eventually awaken in the purple-gray hours before dawn
with my hair wet and tangled, clinging to my skin. "Mother,"
I say aloud, the word a question on my lips, the sound of my
voice lingering in the quiet night. And, of course, there is no

answer. Only grief. Only the certainty that they are gone, that everything is gone, that I am alone now, and will be always. How I ache; how I curl into a shriveled husk of myself, every moment a wash of despair and disconsolate reflection. I feel it will kill me—I am sure it will kill me. But I wake, again and again, only to relive the loss.

Eno hears me cry out sometimes, and she comes to the healing room, clad in silence, to hold my hands in hers. I clutch her wrinkled fingers with all my strength, tears streaming down my face, my heartache a physical thing. From time to time, Eno brushes away my tears, or presses her palm against my cheek, and I am quiet for a while, until sleep comes. Sometimes, when I wake again, she is still there, asleep in the chair beside my bed, her chin resting on her chest.

In my waking hours, I obsess over details. I try to remember the fine characteristics of my mother's hands: the softness of her skin, the slender length of her fingers. I close my eyes and imagine the feel of the marble banister in the courtyard of our home in the Spire—how cold it felt in wintertime, shining white and clean in the chilly air. I strain my ears, recalling the memory of my father's voice: *This has all been a terrible dream, Vaela*, he says to me. *Everything will be just fine.*

But the worst rumination is the reimagining of my birthday party—still elegant and bright, still merry and exciting—but the third gift always some insignificant, whimsical thing. A sparkling gown. A pair of summer shoes, handmade in the South by the finest artisans in the Spire. A book—a romance, a thriller, a genealogy—it makes no difference. I only want something safe.

I want anything but a ticket to the Continent.

One afternoon in the second week of my stay, the sound of laughter rumbles through the walls of the healing room. Eno cannot speak; she scarcely makes a sound save for a scraping wheeze when she exerts herself, and so I sit up to listen closely—

not out of interest, but in hopes of determining that the mysterious visitor will be leaving promptly.

Eno's familiar shuffle step sounds down the hallway, followed by a second pair of footfalls and a clicking and scuffling I can't identify. I lean back against the wooden headboard of my bed, holding my breath, waiting for the party to pass by. There is a beat of silence, and then Eno's double knock comes at the door.

"I'm not well," I say, as she peers into the room, and this is the utter truth. "I hope there's no one come to call?"

She smiles and steps aside, ignoring me in that unflappable way of hers, and a small girl pokes her head in through the door. It takes me half a second to recognize her: it's Kiri, Noro's sister. Behind her, the great dog Joa sits in the corridor, looking bored. The Aven'ei, apparently, do not present cards to announce their arrival—nor do they wait to be received.

Kiri steps in, and Joa follows. "Hello, Vaela Sun!" the girl says brightly. "I've come with gifts, so you can't send me away."

Perplexed by her presence and reluctant to spend time just yet with anyone other than Eno, I give her a tight smile and shake my head. "I'm sorry, Kiri—it's kind of you to think of visiting, but I'm not very well just now—"

"That's what Noro said you'd say," she replies, plunking down in the chair beside my bed and gesturing for the dog to sit beside her. Kiri extends a hand to me, exposing a palm full of what look to be brightly colored, polished bits of glass. "Here. These are for you."

I frown. I want her to leave, but even in my current state, I find it impossible to be rude; Spirian manners are not easily discarded, even in the face of despair. After a moment's hesitation, I cup my hands and Kiri drops the glass into my palms. There are five pieces in total; two pink, one jade, one blue, and another almost completely white. "Thank you," I say, examining each of the glossy bits in turn. "These are…they are glass?"

"Oh, yeah," she says. "I found them on the shore of a little lake in the Kinso."

"You've been to the Kinso mountains?" I say, surprised. "That's quite a distance from here."

"My battlemaster takes me every year. You'd like him, Vaela—he's nearly eighty, but can still split a Xoe from stem to stern." Kiri mimics the motion of a sword slashing upward at lightning speed, and grins.

"Oh," I say. "That's…impressive."

"He's a legend."

"Is he an *inanei* like your brother?"

Kiri laughs. "No, no, no. He's a master of weapons—sword, bow, axe—he knows them all. Old Zuka wouldn't have the patience to creep around slitting throats and blowing poison darts. No—he likes to look the Xoe in the eye when he kills them."

All this talk of death—so casual, so indifferent—makes my stomach turn. "Your dog," I say, attempting to change the subject. "He is called Joa?"

"Yes," Kiri says. "It means 'loyal,' in the old words."

"I trust he's a good companion?"

Kiri hooks an arm around Joa's middle and nuzzles his neck. She receives a slobbery lick along the side of her cheek in return. "He might stink a little, but I keep him around."

I try to muster a smile, though my muscles feel weighted down. "Kiri," I say, "I appreciate your visiting, but as I tried to tell you earlier, I'm having rather a hard time with all that's… happened. Would you be terribly offended if I asked you to go?"

She smiles. "You like the glass?"

"It was very kind of you to think of it."

"We'll be back, you know. Me and Joa."

"Please," I say, "it's probably best that I just focus on recuperating. There's no need to—"

"We'll be back," she says, and winks at me. "See you, Vaela Sun."

★ ★ ★

Kiri, true to her word, and to my private consternation, arrives with Joa at roughly the same time the following day.

"Come outside, Vaela," she says. "Winter is melting away—you need some sunshine."

"No, thank you," I say. "I'm really not inclined to—" Here, she crosses the room and swings the drapes open wide. I squint in the glare, my eyes unaccustomed to the light. "Could you close those please?"

"Can't sit in the dark all day," she says.

I am beyond irritated. I feel as though she is intruding on my grief, stepping over it as though it does not exist. I climb out of the bed and pull the curtains closed, then turn on my heel. "Kiri, I would prefer to spend my time here alone. I don't wish to hurt your feelings, but I must ask you to leave."

She sits in the wooden chair, unfazed. "Talk to me for just a minute, Vaela. Then, if you want me to go, I will."

I stare at her for a moment, fuming, but sit stiffly at the foot of the bed. "What is it?"

"I lost my parents, too. And four brothers."

I turn my head and close my eyes. "I can't talk about this."

"You don't have to talk," she says. "Just listen. You're not alone. It will get better."

"It will never get better."

"It will."

My shoulders tremble. Who is she—who is anyone—to speak of my suffering? Who can know the particulars of my grief, the searing agony of it? I glare at her, my eyes like daggers. But then… I see her pain. So small she is, bright like a flame, yet her hurt mirrors my own. And I realize that I have stupidly ignored the fact that Kiri, too, has lost her family. At ten years old, she has been through far worse than I. She has never known peace, only danger, and loss.

She understands. As much as anyone ever could.

I chew on the inside of my lip. "I don't want to talk about it."

She holds out her hands. "Me either. We can talk about other things."

"You will talk, and I will listen."

"I will come every day to see you," she says.

"Once per week."

"Every day."

I sigh. "You will stay only briefly?"

"An hour at most."

"All right, then," I say, too tired to argue. "If you insist."

I must be, at best, a dismal and taciturn companion, but Kiri does not seem to mind. She comes day after day, never staying too long, never at a loss for words. She talks and talks and *talks*, while Joa lies at her feet, furry eyebrows arching up and down from left to right—listening. The dog actually listens to her. And so do I.

She speaks at length of her desire to become an *inanei* like her brother, describing for me the arduous training that is required. She tells me that her best friend—a boy called Jeno—has a tiny trove of jewels he keeps hidden from his parents. And she regales me with stories of the Bright Days, a period of some fifty years long ago, in which the Xoe and Aven'ei each withdrew from conflict, and peace reigned like sunshine on the Continent. Bitterness resumed when a harsh winter made for famine in the north, and the Xoe pushed outward in search of food, and that was all it took to reignite the long, long war.

Kiri complains about her schoolwork, she tells me of adventuring with friends into the Southern Vale, and she brings me new bits of glass for my "collection." And I, in my black sorrow, unable to tolerate even a sunbeam from the window, see a light within Kiri, and can abide it. My father had the very same light: an effortless brilliance that could draw others to his side, dampen an argument between friends, and calm those who were beyond reason. Kiri and my father, they would have been kindred spirits.

Weeks pass, and though Kiri and Joa visit every afternoon, Noro—to my surprise and disappointment—does not come at all. I feel this keenly at first—another hurt added to the injuries of my heart. I cannot think why he would stay away, having acted such a friend in the days before my convalescence. I ask Kiri about it, but she skirts the subject, saying only that Noro has been repeatedly deployed to the mountains. I accept this, but as I delve farther into my own dark imaginings, I remember Noro's comforting presence on the journey to Kastenai and I wonder: *Why does he not come when he is home?*

In the beginning, in those first long days, I thought I would never wish to leave the healing room. I was certain that I would be content to spend the rest of my days curled up with my heartache, blanketed in my memories. But as the weeks slipped by, I realized that I could not, as Kiri had noted early on, spend all my time in the dark. Not forever. Even the most terrible agony must be diminished by time, and today—my forty-second day at Eno's—today, the grip of my grief finally lessened.

I awoke with a peculiar sense of alteration—something akin to the fresh, salted breeze that blows in from the sea after a storm has passed. Eno opened the door to collect my chamber pot and was startled to see me standing by the window, my face turned toward the sun.

"I should like to go outside today," I said, and looked back at her. "Can we do that?"

She took me by the arm, her face marked with a brilliant smile, and led me into the enclosed yard behind the house.

Now, I stand in the garden, blinking in the dazzling light of day. There's a vegetable patch here, and flowers blooming in triumph amid the melting snow, and a beautifully hewn bench cut from sand-colored stone.

I sit on the bench and run my palm over its smooth surface,

feeling the faint warmth it has stolen from the sun. It is spring now on the Continent, and while the temperature could not be described as warm, it is far more tolerable than it was just a month ago. The fresh, cool air caresses my face, and I feel a sense of normalcy returning to me with each breath. *This is what people do. They go out of doors, and they sit in the sunshine, and they breathe. I can do this.*

Eno hovers near the door for a few minutes, then returns to the house, leaving me alone in the yard.

It is quiet. I hear footsteps occasionally as someone passes by on the road beyond the fence, the chirping of birds concealed in the trees, and the distant sound of laughter, perhaps coming from one of the nearby houses. These are the sounds of life. For the first time since the heli-plane went down, I am ready to hear them.

It is a good day. I spend one more night in the healing room, and in the morning, I am ready to leave. Kiri comes to collect me, to take me to my new home, which the council has arranged for me.

At the front door, Eno embraces me, happy tears in her green eyes. I hold her tightly for a moment, thinking how strange it will be to fall asleep in a house empty of her comforting presence. I thank her for all she has done, but the words seem to fall short; she afforded me true solace, allowing me to stay long after my leg was tended so that my heart might have a chance to be restored as well. I tell her that she is a true healer, and I bid her goodbye.

It is time to begin my life anew.

CHAPTER 14

◆

"WHAT DO YOU THINK?" KIRI ASKS EXPECTANTLY as we stop before the small cottage.

I turn to my left to look at the houses on the other side of the road. "Why does this place look so familiar?"

Kiri laughs. "That house there, across the way…that's where Noro and I live. You remember it?"

"Yes," I say slowly, my mind piecing together the memory of my first night in the village. "It looks different in the daytime—and with so little snow about."

"Noro fixed things with the council so that you would be nearby," Kiri says. "On account of you not knowing anyone."

"Did he?" I say, perplexed. "I wouldn't have thought…anyway." I turn back to my own house, a stone building with a sloping black-shingled roof and a porch to the left of the front door. A high fence surrounds the property, separating it from the houses on either side. Two windows look out from the front, the glass having recently been scrubbed clean. But what truly draws my attention is another detail: someone has put a pot bearing a dilapidated white flower next to the door. I know without asking that it was Kiri, and my heart warms. For all her ferocity, she is sweet, though she might never admit it.

"The house is lovely," I say. "I particularly like the flowerpot there—do you see it?"

She hides a smile and rushes to the door. "Come on and look at the inside. Wait here, Joa."

Kiri's perpetual shadow lies down on the porch and blinks lazily. I'm quite used to him now, having seen him so many times at Eno's, and am far less intimidated by his size than I was when first I saw him. I give him a pat as I step up onto the porch, then pass through the door into my new home.

Much like in Noro's house, the entry opens into a small, cozy sitting room. There is a low sofa (also like Noro's, although this one has green fabric instead of blue), an upholstered chair, and a bookshelf, all arranged around a fireplace on the far wall. I cross to the bookshelf to peruse its contents—titles such as *Seaships and Vessels*, *The Hero of the Brightening Bay*, and, most intriguing of all, *The Nations Beyond the Sea* immediately catch my eye. Many other books appear to be far older, with titles I can't decipher, as they are written in the original Aven'ei tongue.

"That's from Noro," Kiri says, pointing to an enormous, breathtakingly beautiful work of art above the fireplace. It must be three feet across, with lovely white trees painted across its lower half, all trimmed in gold. "He said you're probably used to fine things."

Another puzzling kindness, considering Noro's conspicuous absence during my time at Eno's.

"Kiri," I say, on the point of asking again if she knows why Noro did not come to see me, but I think better of it, and simply say, "I shall be sure to thank him when I see him next."

To my left, a doorless frame opens to a small kitchen and dining area, complete with wooden table and four chairs. To the right, a narrow hallway leads to two doors: the first reveals a washroom with a basin, tub, and chamber pot, and the second a bedchamber with a near double bed, a nightstand, and a second fireplace. A handmade quilt, sewn with perfectly shaped

squares in various greens and yellows, covers the bed. I run my
hand across it, admiring the softness of the fabrics.

"Do you like it?" Kiri says from the doorway. "It's been in
our family a long time. I'm not even sure who made it...my
grandmother, maybe, or her mother."

"It's beautiful. Surely you ought to keep it, if it's an heirloom?"

She grins. "It's yours. And you'll be plenty warm when winter comes around again."

I will be home in the Spire by winter, I think to myself. I feel
tired suddenly, though it isn't even noon. "I'm so grateful for all
you and Noro have done. Kiri...would you mind if I had some
time to settle in?"

"Of course." She heads down the hallway, humming to herself. At the front door, she turns back and says, "Come by soon,
if you want to see Noro—like I told you, they've been sending him out a good deal since you arrived. But he's home for a
few days at least."

"I will. Thank you for seeing me settled. You can bring Joa
in next time, if you like. I don't mind."

She gives me a wave and bounds across the road, the dog trot-
ting along close at her heels.

Alone in the house, I feel misplaced, as though I've sneaked
into a stranger's home and suddenly decided to live there. I turn
and head back down the hall to the bedroom, curl up atop the
soft green quilt, and close my eyes. As I drift into a hazy slum-
ber, my thoughts are of Noro.

In my mind, I see his features emerging from shadow as he
stood by the fire at the Xoe camp. I see the tightness of his jaw
as he stared at the council table, offering to convey me to Ivanel. I see his eyes, dark and veiled, as he bade me farewell on
the steps at Eno's, his fingers wrapped around my own.

I felt his absence during my stay in the healing room; I feel
it now. I wonder at his distance, when I was so clearly in his

thoughts. And then these contemplations wisp into nothingness, and I sleep without dreaming.

The following day, around noon, I decide that it is time to pay Noro a visit.

I head to the bedroom and open the top drawer of the dresser. Inside is a small looking-glass, framed in silver with a long, slender handle. It's not a true mirror—more like a plate of steel that has been finely polished—but it's the only reflective surface in the cottage, and it's better than nothing. I scrutinize my reflection; I look the same as ever, I suppose—thinner, paler perhaps than I was in the Spire, but not entirely different.

I fix my hair into two loose plaits, grasp the looking-glass again, and smile experimentally. A shadow of my former self appears—a girl who looks very like the person I once was. Am I yet the same? Or am I someone different now, someone forever changed by tragedy and circumstance?

I tuck the mirror back into the drawer, wondering abstractedly if Noro will recognize me. When I saw him last, I was bedraggled, bleeding, and sick with fever. I wore a mishmash of torn and bloodied clothes, with twigs and pine needles in my matted hair. At least now I am somewhat presentable, dressed in a clean white tunic and matching bottoms that were neatly folded in the wardrobe.

Outside, I find the narrow road between the houses to be thick and muddy with the melting snow. I pick my way across, coming to Noro's cottage with reasonably dry shoes. I knock at the door and wait, my heart pounding, my hands restless at my sides.

Half a minute passes before he answers. When he opens the door, he does not seem surprised to see me; he merely rests his palm against the top of the frame and says, after a moment, "You look well, girl."

The sight of him, familiar and new all at once, plays havoc

with my nerves. He is taller than I remember, looking very lean and elegant in a fitted gray shirt and a pair of black trousers. His hair falls loosely to one side, a bit longer than it was when I saw him last.

"Yes," I say. "Eno let me stay far longer than my wounds required."

"She knows her business."

"She does."

There is an awkward pause. Noro straightens his shoulders and takes a step back. "Would you like some tea?"

"Please," I say, and follow him inside. The house is exactly as it was on my first night in Kastenai: tidy, comfortable, quiet.

In the kitchen, Noro puts on a kettle and leans against a small table. After a moment, he says, "How do you like your new home? Does it suffice?"

"It's far more than I would ever have asked of the Aven'ei."

"We have no shortage of empty dwellings," he says. "The winter was long, and the fighting regular."

I had not considered why the house might be vacant. I swallow, feeling uncomfortable. "I...I am told you made all the arrangements for me?"

His gaze shifts over to the window. "I did."

I stare across at him, my lips trembling. "I am so grateful for all you have done—truly, I am. But...why didn't you come to see me, Noro?"

His mouth opens and closes, then he frowns. "I thought it best you were left alone."

"Kiri called on me every day."

"I know. I sent her."

"I thought as much. But you just said—"

"I know what I said. I meant to say I thought it best if you were apart from me."

"But why?"

He sighs, glances down at the kettle, and folds his arms across his chest. "I would have been no comfort to you."

"I don't think you know how wrong you are about that."

His eyes meet mine for a fraction of a second, then he turns to take two small cups from a shelf above the stove. "Kiri has a way with others. It was right to send her."

"Kiri is a very special girl, I will agree with you. But I thought you and I were…were friends, of a sort."

He shakes his head, his face in profile. "You cling to our acquaintance because I freed you from the Xoe. It's not good for you."

"I value our acquaintance, Noro. I do not cling to it. You were with me quite nearly from the beginning of all this, and despite everything—despite the Xoe, the cold, the terrible fear and grief, the fever—you somehow made me feel safe. Don't you realize what that means to me?"

The kettle whistles and he turns to add the tea. "I am not your protector, girl."

I flinch, stung by his words. "That isn't what I meant at all."

He strides across the kitchen and sets the kettle and the two cups on the table, his lips pressed tightly together. Then he drops into the chair opposite, pours for each of us, and takes up his drink without a word.

I want to explain myself, to clarify what he has misunderstood. But I do not wish to argue, or to press his mood. He has made himself clear enough, in any case. I murmur my thanks and lift the cup to my lips; the tea is bitter, tasting of mint and broadleaf, very different from the sweet brew he made on the last morning of our journey. We drink in silence, neither of us looking at the other, and after a minute or two, I consider a change of subject.

"Kiri has told me a bit of the *inanei*," I say. He looks up in surprise, the hard edges of his expression dissolving at once.

The corner of his mouth twitches ever so slightly. "What?" I say. "Did I pronounce it correctly?"

"Close enough. What did she tell you?"

I set down my teacup, relieved that the tension between us seems to have lifted. "Well, she said there are very few who hold the title. She told me the *inanei* rarely marry, which is fine with her, because boys are—I quote her here—'obnoxious.' And she insists that she shall be far more skilled than even you when she finally achieves the rank."

Noro leans back, smirking. "Did she now?"

"Yes, she did. She's quite sure of herself."

Noro smiles, and the effect is like a light upon his face. "Kiri. I wish she had another ambition. She burns far too brightly to spend life in the shadows."

"She wants to be like you, Noro."

He nods. "I know."

I tap my fingers on the table, then rise. "Well...thank you for the tea. For everything, really. I'm very grateful."

"It's nothing."

He follows me through the kitchen and opens the door, and I step out onto the stone path.

"I hope to see you again soon," I say.

"Wait." I look around to see him in the doorway, one hand on the top of the frame like before, his head tilted toward the ground. "I'm sorry that I did not call on you at Eno's. I thought I was doing what was best." He looks up at me. "It seems I was mistaken."

His expression is so earnest, his humble admission so plain, I am taken aback for a moment. "It's all right, truly," I say. "I know you meant well."

He nods. "I'm leaving in two days' time. Shall I stop in before I go?"

"I'd like that," I say. "And as it happens, my social calendar is quite clear just now."

He laughs. "Don't tell Kiri as much, or she will pester you to no end."

"She is welcome, as are you," I say, smiling. "It also happens that I am new here, and can use all the friends I can muster."

"Well," he says. "Tomorrow then—I will accompany you into town. The council wants to meet with you, now that you've left Eno's."

Could Nadu have changed his mind? Might they be willing now to send me home? It's almost too much to hope for. "Do you know… do you know why they want to see me?"

Noro shrugs. "Likely they want you to choose a field."

I smile and shake my head, confused. "A field?"

"We all must work, girl, and earn our keep."

"Of course," I say. A job. Work. I'm not to be sent home, I'm to be assigned an occupation. Obviously. One cannot be a member of society without contribution. "It's just, I wonder what I might do? I did once spend half a summer giving swim lessons…although I suppose that's not very useful around here. No…swimming pools." My face grows hot.

"You said you were a mapmaker," Noro says.

"Oh—well, yes. I had earned an apprenticeship, you see, and was to begin working with a Master cartographer shortly after my return from the Continent."

He leans against the doorjamb and crosses his arms. "Do all in the Spire undergo an apprenticeship?"

"No, no. Only those with particular scientific, mechanical, or academic inclinations are offered such positions. It is a great honor."

"And what of all the rest—those without extraordinary skills? What do they do?"

"Every citizen finds work," I say. "Some lay the roads, some repair the tracks for the trains, some manufacture the goods used throughout the Spire. Others go into politics or academia. There is a place, and there is pay, for everyone."

"No poor? No hungry, or indolent?"

"Poverty or suffering among the people would never be tolerated in the Spire," I say. "It was a factor before the Nations were united, but no longer. Every citizen is entitled to food, shelter, medical treatment, and human comfort, and those who are unable to work are cared for by the government. Wealth, of course, may vary from one person to another, according to profession. As for the indolent, there is no place for laziness in the Spire," I say. "If a person is able but does not wish to work, he is invited to relocate to the Far Islands, a place removed from our own society. Some choose it freely, others are sent by decree."

He hesitates, his eyes thoughtful. "We have many here who starve, or seek alms from others," he says. "For most of these, it is because they have suffered some difficulty, and it has become a struggle to maintain a living. Others were simply born without opportunity—or were orphaned early on, with no one to help them. War is costly, and not only in terms of human life. It has broken our communities. I do what I can to help those in need, but it saddens me to think that so many rely upon the kindness and generosity of others—and do not always find it."

"You speak of children as well as adults," I say, the realization like a splash of iced water upon my heart.

"Many," he says.

Tears prick my eyes. I have never seen a person hungry or abandoned, cast aside or without opportunity—much less a child in such circumstances. I recall Aaden once saying that living in the Spire is like looking at the world from behind a veil. He was right. In the bubble of my homeland, everyone is provided with what they need to live comfortably. Yet hundreds of miles away, here on the Continent, many are starving, broken, without opportunity, and unable to provide for themselves.

Privilege is the veil Aaden spoke of. *Privilege* is what I have known my entire life. And *privilege* has a firm and deceitful way of obscuring the truth. Without it, life can become a thing of frightening and terrible injustice. A riot of emotion washes over me, with no small measure of shame and disgust at my own shortsightedness.

"You look as though a storm has come over you," Noro says. "Your eyes reveal much, girl."

"I think it is because they are open," I say. "It might have been easier to keep them closed."

CHAPTER 15

✦

EARLY THE NEXT MORNING—BEFORE I'VE EVEN
had time for breakfast—Noro arrives to escort me to the War
Room. He has with him a small leather pouch stitched in red,
which he gives to me as soon as he steps through the door.

"To get you started," he says. "Until you have a wage of your
own."

I open the bag to find a handful of coins, roughly shaped,
dull silver in color. There are three different sizes; Noro picks
one of each out of the little bag.

"This largest," he says, holding it up for me to see, "is the
unzi. Worth quite a bit—it will buy you several weeks' worth of
food, or perhaps a small weapon of your choosing." The coin,
almost oblong, is stamped with a fir tree on either side. "The
middle coin is an *oka*. This will not usually get you a weapon,
but will do well for food and luxury items, like books, or trinkets you may find appealing."

I smile at this, and note that the *oka* bears an imprint of a
face—a woman in profile, her features strong and proud.

"And this last, the small one, this is the *tuka*. Not good for
much—a sweet, a serving of tea—maybe a packet of nuts."

"Right," I say, clutching the bag as though it were a very

fragile thing. Never in my life have I worried about coin, as I could buy anything I pleased in the Spire and had only to give the shop attendant my address. "Thank you."

"Take Kiri to the market with you while I am away, if it would make you feel more comfortable—she'll see to it that you aren't swindled."

I smile but feel my pulse at my throat. I am to be self-sufficient in a way I had never before considered—I have no parents to fall back on, no vault stuffed with gleaming coins and notes of credit. Here in Kastenai I will work for my bread and meat, I will earn these precious coins, I will spend and save—I will provide myself with all I need. The notion would be amusing if I were not so intimidated by the prospect. Still, I feel a glimmer of excitement. Surely I am capable? Surely I can embrace this new life, and find a measure of joy and success?

"You are smiling," Noro says. "Did I say something out of order?"

I laugh. "I was only thinking of myself at work. I find I rather like the idea."

He nods. "We have a saying: one must toil to find the value in each day."

I envision myself hunched over a table, sorting papers, filing things away, organizing trade receipts. Yes. I do like this idea of work.

"I'm sorry," I say, looking across the table at Nadu, a manufactured smile upon my face. "Did you just say *manure*?"

"Yes," Nadu says. "Manure is vital to the farmers—it provides nutrients that allow us to sow and harvest the same soil from year to year. All deposits made by the cows must be collected daily, lest they go to waste."

I clear my throat and glance at Noro, who is openly amused. I scowl at him and turn back to Nadu. "And I am to collect the…deposits."

"You will collect the droppings and deliver them to the out-building where the manure is stored." His brows draw together; he appears confused. "Is there a problem with this vocation? You did opt for animal husbandry as opposed to sanitation?"

Sanitation was more clearly defined—tending to the privies throughout town. I had thought I was avoiding any contact with feces when I chose to work with the animals.

"There's no problem," I say. "I'm grateful for the work."

Nadu smiles and claps his hands together. "Wonderful! I've sent for Shovo Ir'us—he should be here momentarily, and you two can work out the details."

A chill creeps up my neck. I'm not likely to forget that name, for it was he who argued at the council meeting that it would be an unthinkable waste of resources to return me to the Spire.

Noro frowns. "Why should we await Shovo?" he says, but his voice trails off, and a look of understanding comes over his face. "Oh."

As if on cue, the door opens behind me and grim-faced Shovo steps through, stomping mud from his boots on the stone floor. He raises an eyebrow when he sees me, then proceeds to sit at the far end of the table.

"How can I serve, brother?" he says to Nadu. "I came as soon as I received your summons."

I can't help but notice that the room now smells like manure. And possibly cows.

Nadu smiles warmly. "Shovo is the overseer of beef produc-tion for Kastenai and a few of our neighbors. It is he who cares for the animals that provide us with meat. You will receive your wage—two *oka* per week—by working with Shovo to clear the fields of waste, tend the animals, and, when summer comes, col-lect and bale hay for winter."

Shovo goes rigid in his chair. "Now, Nadu," he says in that oily, insipid voice of his, "surely there's a better place for the girl than my farm."

"Yes," I say at once. "I'd be willing to consider another vocation if Mr. Ir'us here has no need for me."

Nadu looks at me quizzically. "You prefer an assignment in sanitation, then?"

I almost say yes. Almost. Because I can't decide which is worse: cleaning outhouses, or working with Shovo. But the idea of human excrement…my stomach rolls, and I swallow.

"No," I say, sealing my own fate. "I would prefer to work with the animals."

Shovo is not deterred. "I have use only for skilled workers, Nadu. This girl is of the Spire—pampered and privileged, not fit for hard labor. How can she tend a farm?"

"She'll be shoveling shit," Nadu says. "I'm sure she'll catch on without too much trouble."

Shovo shrinks back into his chair, a crusty old warrior in the face of defeat, and none too pleased about it. "Whatever you think is best."

"Good," Nadu says. "When should the girl begin?"

"No sense wasting time. I'll come at daybreak and show her the way."

Nadu smiles broadly. "Wonderful. I'm sure it will be beneficial for you both."

Noro bursts into laughter as we exit the War Room. "Oh… your face, girl, when Shovo said he didn't want you. So much… so much *hope*."

"Yes, it's very funny, isn't it? Well. You shan't hear me complain. If I'm to collect cow droppings for a living, I'm sure I can find some way to enjoy it."

He crosses his arms. "You will enjoy manure?"

"Well," I say, "I'll be out in the fresh air, working with the animals. Every day will be like a sort of adventure."

"You'll be under the command of Shovo Ir'us," Noro points out. "The most miserable man I've ever met."

"I have a way with people," I say, my chin lifted ever so slightly. "I made a friend of you, didn't I? And you scarcely have ten words to say in an hour."

He smiles. "I will look forward to your opinion at the end of the week."

"If you think you'll hear one word that doesn't sing of grateful service, I'm afraid you'll be sorely disappointed."

"All right," he says, but I can see that he is unconvinced. He nods toward the far end of the street. "Shall we go to the town center? You might want to do some shopping now that you have a bit of coin."

"I think I'd like to look around on my own," I say. "But could you show me the way?"

He smiles—a small thing, a thing that makes me feel proud— and gestures for me to follow.

We pass through a short maze of winding streets—an odd mixture of residential and industrial construction, houses next to leather tanners and the like—to the village square. It's a wide-open area, with wagons full of goods—vegetables, jewelry, chickens, clothing—parked in long rows. Men and women alike are hawking merchandise, calling attention to those in the marketplace. Children run underfoot, a man spits on what seems to be an eggplant and throws it to the ground, and somewhere, a baby cries, somehow louder than all else. I am assaulted by a thousand aromas: spiced meat and body odor are the most prevalent, but there is also the tang of incense, the earthy scent of animal feed, and the freshness of the damp morning air.

"This," Noro says, "is the heart of Kastenai. Here, you will find all the goods you need, and a few luxuries as well."

"What sort of luxuries?"

"Scented soaps, fine clothes…that sort of thing. Waste of *oka* if you ask me."

"Right," I say, secretly yearning for a luxury of any kind.

"Well. I'll just have a look around then. I might find something...practical."

"Remember what I told you about the coins, girl. These vendors will not hesitate to take a little extra if they can get away with it."

I smile. "I remember."

He pauses for a moment. "You know how to get home from here?"

I tap my forehead. "Always. I've got the streets mapped in my mind."

"Ah. Cartography."

"Exactly."

"All right, then. Good luck, and I will see you soon."

"Goodbye," I say, but he has already turned away, melting almost at once into the throng of market-goers.

I head down the first row of wooden carts, inspecting the goods and deciding that I need neither pig blankets nor tiny baskets of silver-green frogs (I only hope the frogs aren't meant to be eaten).

A haggard old woman behind a rickety wagon grins at me, her lips sucking inward where her bottom teeth used to be. "Hello," I say politely, trying not to look at her puckered mouth.

She nods her head. "Are you the girl from the Nations Beyond the Sea? Is it true? You're from the Nations Beyond?"

"Oh...yes," I say, surprised.

"You've got a look about you, something nice, ugly as you are."

I can't help but laugh. "My name is Vaela. What can I call you?"

"I'm Ava. You want to sell—" here, she makes a sharp whistling sound at the start of the word *sell* "—any trinkets from beyond the sea, little Nation girl? Could give you a few *oka* for any items of interest."

"I...I haven't got anything," I say. *Other than my pendant, which I wouldn't part with for all the coin in the world.*

She screws up her face, but nods. "Offer stands. Come back soon! I've got apples, too, fat as you please."

"I will," I say. "It was very nice to meet you."

I move on to the next stall: a wagon filled end to end with daggers of all kinds, each tied firmly to the long black board on which they are displayed.

The proprietor fixes me with cold eyes. "I suspect you'll want to be moving along. Nothing for you here, *senukka*."

A young woman—strikingly pretty with the straightest, loveliest black hair I've ever seen—turns from the cart beside us, both eyebrows raised.

"A filthy word for a filthy man," she says. "Why am I not surprised?"

He grins, flashing a row of crooked white teeth. "I don't need your business either, Raia Cú." He gestures to the road. "On your way."

She laughs. "I wouldn't spare even a *tuka* for one of these rattling bits of metal you call weapons."

He spits. "Might be one of those daggers will find your throat someday."

"One can only hope," she says. "At least then I shall know I am in no danger." She links an arm through mine. "Come with me. I'll steer you clear of those who behave like Xoe."

"I'll mark you said that," the vendor growls, his face dark with anger.

"Do as you please," the girl says. "It is of no concern to me."

She pulls me along the lane, away from the wagon, until we reach a crowded little walkway spread out beneath an awning of stretched silk. She turns to me, her eyes flickering over my face. "You hear that word again, outworlder, you stick a knife in the eye of the one who said it."

"Oh," I say, "I...don't have a knife."

"Get one."

Her face is heart shaped, with a delicate pointed chin and a dimple in each cheek, and her hair falls neatly to her shoulders, shining like a curtain of smooth obsidian. She wears a long, thin sword strapped at an angle across her back, the hilt visible above her right shoulder. Her eyes are steady, sparkling hazel in the sunshine. I like her at once.

"I'm Vaela Sun," I say.

"Raia Cú," she says formally. "Tanner by trade, sword-bringer in battle." She frowns. "You're much smaller than I thought you would be."

I glance down at myself. Raia is taller than I by nearly a full foot, her body long and willowy, like a dancer's. Though our garments are similar, Raia looks far more becoming in the slender tunic she wears.

"Well," I say, "I'm sorry to disappoint."

She smiles at this. "Shall I accompany you, Vaela Sun? Even those who won't insult you outright might be inclined to add an *oka* or two to any price they offer."

"So I've been told." I glance down the shaded walkway, noting more than one hard look directed my way from villagers and merchants alike. It would seem everyone knows who I am, and most are displeased to have a stranger among them. "I would be grateful for your company."

"Good. What do you need then? Food? Tools? Weapons? A dagger, certainly."

"I...perhaps some food, to refresh the pantry."

Her eyes brighten. "Do you like *anthida*? I know a man who brings it sometimes from the sea."

"*Anthida?*"

"Mmm. Sorry. Octopus," she says, a dreamy smile upon her face. "Seared in oil, drizzled with sweet sauce, tossed in herbs. Every bite is like a taste of the ocean."

My stomach turns; the idea of eating an octopus, with its wriggling tentacles and pointy beak…no. I couldn't.

"I prefer chicken, or perhaps roast duck," I say. "And soups, breads, vegetables, wine—that sort of thing."

"The simple things," she says, nodding. "You'll find plenty of that here—but look for the rarer treasures as well. The merchants come in from far along the *olielle*—the trader's road—all the way to Ciriel and beyond. Many Aven'ei are artisans in their leisure time, and we in Kastenai can find a wealth of fine goods. Yarn, silks, tapestries, furniture, kettles—our people are industrious in their free hours. The hardworking want for nothing, so long as coin continues to pass from hand to hand."

We go up and down the rows, a dizzying array of food, staples, and luxuries proffered from the various vendors. When I express interest in a bundle of spiced bread and cheese, Raia haggles the merchant from two *oka* to one, a stern expression on her face. Happily, I hand over a silver coin and take the food, now wrapped in brown paper.

"I've never bought groceries before!" I say, unable to contain my excitement.

She gives me a sidelong glance. "That seems odd. Did your husband see to your household affairs in the Nations Beyond the Sea?"

My face turns red. "I'm not married. I'm scarcely of age!"

She stops walking. "How old are you? Fifteen, sixteen, surely?"

"I'll be seventeen on my next birthday," I say. "People do not marry so young in the Spire—there must be a long courtship, and all of the social traditions must be observed, and of course, a large wedding is something everyone desires." I close my eyes for a moment, lost in reverie. "Ah, the cakes and sandwiches and wine, the bridal gowns and ribbons, and—"

"The Aven'ei marry with a word, so long as it is witnessed by others," Raia says, looking puzzled. "There is no cake."

"You just...declare that you want to marry one another?"

"Of course."

"Oh," I say. "Well. I'm sure that's quite lovely, in its way."

"I wed at fourteen, promising myself to a kind man," she says. "It was a sturdy match—he made me laugh, and often. But my husband, he took ill shortly afterward and died the following summer. Since then, I've been on my own." She leans closer to me, a hint of mischief in her eyes. "To be honest, I prefer it that way. I mourn dear Kemu, but I've no real interest in marriage." Her eyes sweep over the crowd, over the wares in the marketplace, with a calculation that reminds me of the way Noro seems to see the world.

"Ah," she says, "look here." Along the final row, we stop before a table covered in books, and she turns to me once again. "Books are my greatest pleasure, aside from swinging a sword. May I ask you a question?"

"Of course."

She takes a tattered volume, thumbs through the pages, then sets it down. "In days long ago—when your people still came to the Continent and broke bread with the Aven'ei—we are told that the Nations of your land battled fiercely."

"Yes, that is so."

"Mmm. And your leaders chose to abandon such conflicts, and this new resolve was the reason you withdrew from the Continent and isolated yourselves."

"That is also true."

She rests a palm on the table and taps her fingers on the cover of a fat volume titled *Sheep: A Treatise*. "But...have your people managed to uphold such an ideal? Do you truly come from a place of peace?"

"Yes. The Spire has not seen battle for nearly two centuries."

She smiles. "I thought it was a legend—nothing more than whispers and words. I can't begin to imagine a life without the drums of war. Tell me, what is it like?"

As I turn the question in my mind, I think for perhaps the first time on the enormity of what I have left behind, in terms of security and peace. "It is quiet," I say finally. "Not in a literal sense—how can I explain? I mean to say there is a...a tranquility in the absence of any real threat to human life."

"Quiet," she says, thoughtful. "Yes. I can imagine it, if I try. But...is there crime, at least?"

"There is certainly crime. A person can make a weapon out of anything if she likes, and there are always those who *do*...but criminals are dealt with swiftly, and the justice of the courts prevails."

"And there is no war."

"None. I wish the Aven'ei could know such peace."

She laughs, plucks a slim volume from the back of the table, and passes an *oka* to the merchant. "As long as a single Xoe lives and breathes, there will be war upon the Continent."

"But why?" I say. "Why do they seek to destroy you?"

"A debt is owed," she says. "But furthermore, the Xoe have come to understand the riches of the south. The fertility of our soil, the safety of our shores. The agriculture we have cultivated. They love the north, but desire what the north cannot deliver. And so they seek to take it from us, here in the south and east."

"Well...the Nations of the Spire eventually found a way to make a lasting accord. Perhaps someday, such an agreement might be found between the Xoe and the Aven'ei—a sharing of resources and land."

Her eyebrows rise, and she smiles. "You *believe* this—I can see it in your face!"

"With all my heart."

A sadness comes upon her lovely features, and she shakes her head. "This hope of yours, I fear it will do you no good. Set it aside, or you will not see death when it comes."

"I will never give up hope," I say, but wonder for half a second if this is true.

She shrugs. "Hope for things that are possible, then. Hope for clear skies amid the storms of summer, or for the safe return of our warriors from the battlefields at Sana-Zo and the Narrow Corner. Hope for a happy marriage and many children, if that should please you. Never hope for peace, Vaela. Not here. Not on the Continent."

"I can't help it. After all, hope is not sustained by the likeliness of a thing, but by the desire for it, and it is my dearest wish that you would know the peace I have described."

Raia smiles. "What faith you have, and what goodwill." She clasps a hand around mine. "It is good to know you, Vaela Sun."

CHAPTER 16

✦

SHOVO WASN'T KIDDING WHEN HE SAID "DAY-break." The morning light has scarcely made an appearance when he raps on the door, though I've been lying awake for some time, my stomach in a nervous knot.

I climb out of bed, already dressed—I wanted to be prepared, so I slept in my clothes—and hurry toward the door.

The old warrior gives me a look up and down as I step onto the porch, and grunts—whether in disdain or approval, I have no idea.

"This way," he says, and leads me through town toward the gate, away from the village center. Away from the comfort of my lovely green quilt, away from all things newly familiar, and into the unknown.

An adventure, I remind myself, though I feel a bit miserable. We head toward the village gates, pass through without a word, and follow a southerly path.

"It's a lovely morning," I say brightly, hoping to somehow break the ice between us. "Very cold, but I suppose that's usual."

Shovo looks over at me for half a second, but says nothing. He begins to walk a bit faster.

I hurry along beside him, trying to keep pace. "You know,"

I say, "I think perhaps we got off on the wrong foot. I really haven't meant to impose on the Aven'ei in any way, and would go home at once if I were able to do so."

Again, he does not reply, but I continue anyway. "I'm ready to work, that's for sure. To work very hard, and do everything I can to earn an honest wage. Yes, farming is a far cry from cartography—oh, that's mapmaking, did you know?—but I'm quite determined to excel. I hope to far exceed your expectations."

Shovo comes to a halt. "Stop talking. Do you hear me? Stop."

"Oh," I say. "I'm sorry."

"No, see, you're still talking. Don't apologize. Don't reply. Just stop."

"All right," I say, and put a hand over my mouth.

He stares at me for a moment, then continues on his way.

I'd be lying if I said I wasn't intimidated. Everything about Shovo makes me nervous: his battered skin, zigzagged with scar tissue; the swirling, mysterious tattoos upon his face; his husky voice. But more than anything else, it is his hostility that puts me on edge. In truth, I am not accustomed to being disliked. I can't understand why he loathes me, why the very sight of me seems to irritate him. I don't know if he hates me personally or dislikes the idea of Spirians in general. Maybe it's just my face that bothers him. I have no idea. I only wish that I could genuinely gain his favor.

It's just…even as I long to strive for his approval—an endeavor I honestly can't explain—I'm well-aware that any effort on my part will end in flat, clear rejection. But doesn't everyone want to be liked, or is this some vanity, some flaw on my own part? Plenty of Aven'ei cast nasty looks in my direction, but with Shovo, it feels more personal.

Oh, I am a ridiculous creature. No one is liked by everyone, that is a fact. And here among the Aven'ei, at the very least, no one *pretends* to like you when in truth they think you irritating, or troublesome, or any other unpleasant thing. The more

I think about the Spire—about manners, about keeping "good society"—the more I realize that a straightforward opinion is one to be cherished. By the Maker, Shovo hates me. I've got to swallow it, and stop trying so damn hard to make it otherwise.

Yet I know I won't. Count it among my flaws. I can't let it go.

It's a long walk, nearly forty minutes, before we arrive. I must say, the farm is not quite what I expected. I thought there would be acres of lush fruit trees, dozens of neatly plowed rows of soil, perhaps ten cows or so. Instead, there is a huge, rickety wooden outbuilding (to keep the cows warm when it freezes, I imagine), a smaller building in better repair, and miles and miles and miles of grass. Roughly two hundred cows—all black as night, with shaggy hair and bored brown eyes—stand within a wooden pen before us.

"There are more than I thought there would be," I say. "And how pretty they are!"

Shovo looks at me in disgust. "They are not pretty," he says. "They are cattle. Food. Heifers, cows, bulls—some for breeding, some for trade, some for meat. Don't get attached. A cow is not a pet, and the ones meant for slaughter live only a year or so."

I feel a pang of sadness, but keep it to myself. "Do they give milk as well?" I ask hopefully, picturing myself on a white stool, singing a soothing melody as milk fills a silver pail.

"These are not dairy cows. Some of them will be, when they're old enough. But the milking animals are on another farm."

"I see. And how am I to collect their…their deposits? And what do I do with the material?"

He points to a large device I cannot name. It's like a bin resting on one wheel and two sticks, with something like handles on the back.

"Wheelbarrow," he says. "You fill it, you carry it to the

building behind that one—" he points to the wide, rickety barn "—and you fill the wagons inside. The farmers and tradesmen come to take it away in the mornings, before you even wake."

"Right," I say, eyeing the wheelbarrow and trying to figure out how it works. "Shall I just go in, then?"

He retrieves a pair of filthy gloves from a pocket in his vest and tosses them to me. "This is how it works: I bring the cows from the pen to the pasture. While they're out, you clean the pen. When they go back in, you take your little shovel and move into the pasture. Do you think you can remember that?"

My blood boils with indignant fury, but I keep my temper in check. I will not give him the satisfaction.

"I can remember it."

"All right, then. Let's get started."

Manure stinks.

I may take away from this experience a lesson in the value of hard work, or a feeling of proud independence. I might even grow to love the tightness in my muscles and the aching in my back—after all, I'm working, and there's nobility in that. But I will NEVER—not ever—get used to manure.

It's in my hair. It's in my ears. Its scent is so far up my nose, it will probably stay there forever. I am a disgusting wreck, covered in feces, having been glared at and insulted by Shovo all day, and am now trudging back to the village in a cloud of filth.

Dig in with that shovel—put your back into it, you lazy girl!

Oh, for pity's sake—it's like you've never seen a wheelbarrow before.

GET OUT OF THE MUCK. GET UP. GET UP! Gods, she's an idiot.

I think perhaps I was wrong in my initial assessment of Shovo's dislike for me. Possibly, I underestimated the sheer *fervor* of it. I honestly think he enjoys hating me. I have never before felt so inept. By the end of the day, this man has me half believing that I am some sort of idiot.

All I can think about is the tub in my washroom at home, and how long it will take to fill with hot water, and how much water it will actually take to clean my body, and the fact that I have to do this again every day for the rest of the week. The saving grace in all of this is that the Aven'ei work in alternate weeks, so fourteen days of every month will not be spent in the presence of manure. I can do this. I can.

It's early afternoon, and the sun dances in pinpricks on the path, dappled beneath the leaves of the trees overhead. I look around me, at the new flowers poking through the earth, leaves and petals stretching hungrily toward the sunlight. Spring on the Continent is a beautiful thing—at least, here in the south, it is. Everything is green and fresh, and seems to smell of honeysuckle. Well. It smelled of honeysuckle this morning, before the manure.

As humbled as I am by the disgusting beginning of my new career, I do feel somewhat satisfied. I took every one of Shovo's insults without a word, and shoveled pile after pile of feces— some of it still warm, as I was to discover when I slipped and fell. I wonder what my mother and father would say, if only I could tell them that I'd spent the day moving excrement from one place to another. I can imagine my mother's astonished expression, her dark eyebrows arching in bewilderment. And my father—would he laugh? Would he congratulate me on a job well done? I can never know. But still... I hope to make them proud. I want to bring honor to the name of Sun. I'm just not entirely sure I can accomplish this by mucking about with cow patties—and so I have another idea, a grander one, a plan that will at least allow me to make use of the skills I possess: I am going to create a map for the Aven'ei. Not a topographic map, but a tactical one.

The inspiration came to me this afternoon as I sat in the grass beneath an enormous oak tree, enjoying an apple and trying to claim a few precious minutes of rest. I was thinking about the

Divide—the natural barrier formed by the Rukka and Kinso mountain ranges that effectively partitions the Continent into two separate territories. The Rukka rise up along the south, blending into the Kinso in the east; these mountains keep the Xoe and the Aven'ei apart, for the terrain is so treacherous that one group must move around the peaks rather than cross them to reach the other. This leaves two paths without obstruction: the Narrow Corner high in the northeast—the very place where I saw my first battle from the heli-plane—and the Reaches of the south, which comprise miles of rocky cliffs and culminate in the great Southern Vale, very near to where Noro found me.

The Xoe, as a rule, do not trespass into Aven'ei territory by way of the south; most contact takes place in or around the Narrow Corner, or in the Flames, a splintered segment of land that stretches into the northeastern sea. And so it occurred to me that I might create a map and mark certain places where man-made structures—watchtowers or bridges or some such thing—might complement the natural terrain and provide improved detection of any incoming parties. I am certain the Aven'ei know their own territory well—but perhaps something comprehensive might prove useful. After all, I do have the unique position of having studied the Continent in great detail, along with the advantage of seeing it firsthand from above.

The more I think about creating a map, the more excited I become. If I must wait until autumn, for the *kazuri ko'ra* to pass in order to make passage to Ivanel by ship, then surely I can fill my free hours with purpose, and perhaps even provide the Aven'ei with a resource that could turn the tide of the war. I make a mental note to purchase parchment and quills next time I am in the marketplace. I shall keep the map a secret until it is ready for submission to the council. I marvel at how thrilled I was, not so long ago, to map the Riverbed, of all things—a place of great topographical interest for a cartographer, but of zero significance in terms of the tactical goings-on of the Continent. How strange it is that my skills as a mapmaker have shifted from the scientific to the strategic. And yet…if I can help, it seems a perfectly sensible transition.

The path home winds around an apricot tree, and the village comes into view beyond the gently sloping hillside. A burst of renewed energy floods through me—*washtub, washtub, washtub*—and I walk faster; I'm nearly jogging by the time I reach the village gates. As I make my way through the quiet streets leading to my own, I think again of Noro, gone as of this morning, sent out on some assignment or other. He will kill again, and soon.

He's a murderer. The thought comes unbidden, and a chill runs down my spine. No. He's an assassin—a soldier. Isn't there a difference? He does what he must for the survival of the Aven'ei. And he saved my life. Is there no merit in that?

An image of his shadowed figure at the Xoe camp comes to my mind: the effortless sweep of Noro's knife across Ue's throat, the blood, shining black in the near darkness, the sharp scent of iron in the air.

Noro saved me from certain violence. To think of him now, composed, at ease, seemingly no different than any other villager—it is hard to believe what he has done. What he does. I recall Aaden's words: *We've traded our swords for treaties, our daggers for promises—but our thirst for violence has never been quelled. And that's the crux of it: it can't be quelled. It's human nature.*

Is it?

I brush the thought aside, disconcerted, and turn onto the little lane leading to my cottage. At the sight of my front porch, *happiness* becomes too small a word. I'm in such a hurry to get inside that I almost miss it—a small paper bundle on the porch. I pick it up; it's oblong, and heavy, like a skipping stone.

I peel away the paper to find a bar of lilac soap, its glorious scent strong and powerful even through my haze of manure. I remember Noro at the marketplace, talking about such luxury items: *Waste of oka if you ask me.*

Noro! I clutch the soap to my heart. It is the single greatest gift I have ever received.

CHAPTER 17

✦

A KNOCK AT THE FRONT DOOR AWAKENS ME ON the morning after my first full week of work. I open one eye. Dim morning light slices through the edges of the window drapery, casting stark white lines on the floor. *No.* I let my eye close.

Another knock comes, louder this time. This time, both eyes snap open. I flip my blankets to one side, swing myself out of bed, and hurry along the hallway to the door.

"Who's there?" I say.

A muffled voice filters through the door. "It's Raia Cú, come to call."

I rub the sleep from my eyes, try to shake off my drowsiness, and open the door.

There she stands, looking immaculate (and wide-awake) in an ensemble very much like mine (an outfit I discovered in the chest of drawers in the bedroom, and changed into last night): a long tunic with a fitted neck, split at the collar by a narrow notch, and dark trousers of heavy spun cotton. The tunic—cinched at the hips by a braided black belt—falls almost to midthigh; tapered, close-fitting sleeves are so long that they reach clear to the fingertips. My garments are of deep green, while Raia's are pale blue, which is striking against the inky blackness of her hair.

"I…how did you find my house?"

"I am long acquainted with Norovo Dún."

"Noro… Norovo?"

"That's his full name," she says, "but I suggest you never say it in front of him. Only his mother called him that. Anyway, I mentioned our meeting when I saw him last, and he suggested that you might need a bit of help." She looks past me to the sitting room, which is admittedly in a bit of disarray, with soiled clothes on the floor in the corner and the dustbin overflowing at the door to the kitchen. And perhaps a small pile of additional garbage that I wasn't quite sure where to put.

My face flushes red. "Well…I've never really… You see, in the Spire, my family had servants who would tend to the…to the everyday tasks. I mean—what I mean to say is—" She has both brows raised and the smallest of smiles on her face. I take a deep breath. "Honestly, Raia, I have no idea how to manage just about anything in this house."

She nods. "Can you cook?"

"No."

"What have you been eating?"

"Mostly bread and cheese."

"No meat?"

"I wasn't sure how to…well…the chickens at the market are *alive*."

She laughs, deeply. "Vaela Sun. I would think you hopeless if only you were not so earnest. Come along, let me in. I will teach you." As she steps inside, she crinkles her nose. "By the stars. Why does it smell like manure in here?"

Thus begins my training in all things domestic. If there is one thing to be learned, it is this: a job, no matter how nauseating, is an easy thing to manage. You wake up, you go to work, you return home. Easy. Keeping one's own house, however, requires far more effort and responsibility than I could ever have imagined. Not only must one perform the general maintenance and cleaning, which is more complicated than I thought it would be, but daily chores must be managed as well: cooking, composting, tending a vegetable garden, washing and mending clothes, seeing to the dishes—and my least favorite, emptying and cleaning the chamber pot.

Raia must have thought me hopeless during the first few days of her instruction, as I learned to scrub and sew and cook the most basic of meals. But her patience is eventually rewarded: by the end of the week, I am able to clean the cottage from top to bottom, bake a loaf of bread (dense and chewy, but bread nonetheless), and mend a torn garment (a particularly nice red tunic that was caught on the fence of the cattle pen). And laundry! I can now wash the stink from my clothes and present myself as a human rather than a crumpled, pathetic outworlder.

And so I work and clean, and then, in the hours before bed, I turn my attention to the map. It is a lovely thing, now that I've practiced with the quill and have learned not to dribble ink all over the paper. I am alive when I work on the map—it makes me feel as though I am connected to something greater than myself. I feel the presence of my parents, I smell the dusty scent of the old books in the Chancellery library, I hear the smooth whir of the trains as they glide over Astor. The map takes me home, where I long to be—where I yet *hope* to be, when the anger of the sea passes and I can be returned to Ivanel. In my heart, I dream that this chart will be a valuable thing for the Aven'ei—that perhaps I can contribute *something* meaningful. But for now, I keep it a secret, my secret, my wonderful, intoxicating escape. And when I grow tired, when my eyes are closing with fatigue, I roll it up and tuck it behind the log bin in the sitting room. My perfect, happy little secret.

For now.

One evening after work, I am wrestling with a wild, overgrown thornbush at the front of the house—trying to trim it, with little success—when Noro comes up the lane, returning from his most recent excursion. He's been gone only half a week, but looks as though he's spent a year in the outdoors: grime is smeared all over his face and hands, while mud coats his trousers from the knees down. Fatigue is etched into his features, but he smiles when he sees me.

"Bit of gardening on a spring night?" he says. "Oughtn't you be reclining somewhere in luxury, while servants bring you food and drink?"

"I've had to let my servants go, unfortunately. Working for Shovo does not pay as well as you might think."

He laughs. "What a shame. You have my condolences."

I pluck a thorny twig from my hair. "Come and sit for a moment—I need a break, and you look as though you've seen the wrong end of a mudslide."

We settle on the porch, our feet dangling above the grassy cobblestones of the front walk. I sigh heavily. "Whoever knew it could feel so good to just *sit*?"

Noro leans toward me and sniffs. "Not a trace of manure," he says. "Don't you work this week?"

"A nameless benefactor gifted me with the loveliest bar of soap ever made." He looks at his feet and smiles, but says nothing. "How was your...um...assignment?" I say. "It's good to see you back safe."

"Quick," he says. "Without complications."

"That's nice," I say, trying not to wonder where he has been and what he has done. *Who, when, why, how many? Did he dispatch his prey with knives, or does he kill in different ways?* It is a strange thing to sit next to an assassin, talking of soap and other trivialities. "Glad to be home?"

"Always," he says, then glances at me. "You seem well, girl. Very...accomplished."

"Yes, well, Raia Cú has seen fit to teach me many practical skills—thank you for that, by the way. She said it was your idea."

He nods. "She's an old friend. And a fearsome warrior."

A twinge of something, some strange insecure thing, flickers in my stomach. *I could be fearsome, too,* I think to myself, which is absurd. I have no interest in violence, and no aptitude besides. Still, the note of admiration in Noro's voice when he speaks of Raia's prowess leaves me in a bit of a mood.

"I wonder," I say, eager to change the subject, "if I might make a few suggestions to the council in regard to improvements for the village?"

Noro frowns. "What sort of improvements?"

"Well...technological things. There's one item in particular I would love to see the Aven'ei adopt. I thought I could explain its function, and your engineers could see to the manufacture."

"Our engineers are quite occupied in the building and maintaining of defenses," he replies. "But I'm curious—what is this thing you feel would benefit the people so much?"

"Well—it pertains to a matter of convenience, really. I suppose some might call it a luxury. But really, it's quite practical, and—"

"What is it?"

I hesitate, a bit embarrassed now that I've come to the point of explaining. "It's...it's a toilet." He shakes his head, eyes blank. "It's sort of like a chamber pot," I continue, "only it stays permanently in the washroom—you never have to empty it at all!"

"That," he says, leaning away from me slightly, "is disgusting."

"What's disgusting about it?"

"You would keep urine and excrement in the house? Permanently?"

I laugh. "No! No! That's the beauty of the toilet! It empties itself! The...everything just washes away. There's no odor, nothing to dispose of—just comfort and convenience."

He looks at me critically. "Where does the material go?"

"Down into the pipes, of course!"

"What pipes?"

I realize that I may have gotten a bit ahead of myself, having forgotten about the matter of plumbing.

"Come inside," I say. "I'll draw you a picture."

In the house, I retrieve a quill, ink pot, and a sheet of paper from the cabinet beside the sofa, and gesture for Noro to join me at the kitchen table. I position the quill, ready to illustrate—then realize I have absolutely no understanding as to the actual mechanics of the thing. Undeterred, I begin to sketch out a commode.

"There's water in the basin, you see," I say, "and a handle here—this empties the contents into the pipes below—" I draw in a vague pipe that looks to end somewhere beneath the front door "—and then the bowl fills automatically with water once again."

Noro is looking at me as though I'm insane. "Where does the water come from?"

"From additional pipes!"

"And where do the pipes get the water?"

"I—I don't really know. But I assure you, it's all very sanitary, and if we could get toilets installed, there'd never be the need to empty a pot in the cold of winter!"

He scrutinizes the drawing, then gives me a piteous sort of smile. "Well. It's very interesting."

"Do you think the council might be inclined?"

"Ah. No."

My shoulders slump. "But why ever not?"

"I'm sorry. I know you are accustomed to your…conveniences. But frankly…" He picks up the drawing and shakes his head, then looks at me directly. "A privy inside the house, girl? That is *disgusting.*"

CHAPTER 18

◆

THERE MUST BE A WAY TO PLEASE SHOVO.

This was the thought that governed my mind as I began my second month of work, as I shoveled and toiled and smiled through my own stink and sweat out in the field. *There must be a way. He is a man like any other. A person.*

Last week, I spent half an afternoon in the kitchen making an incredible sweetened pastry—a light and golden thing drizzled with honey (Raia did most of the work, but I helped). When I brought Shovo the package, he opened it and said, "No."

No.

Not *No, thank you,* or *I appreciate this kind gesture, Vaela Sun, but I prefer savory foods,* or *Aren't you a sweet girl? Perhaps I have misjudged you all along!*

Just *no.* He closed the bag, returned it, and ignored me until I left his office. My fine dessert went to waste, sitting out in the sun while I filled my wheelbarrow with manure and tried to figure out what, exactly, had gone wrong. I decided I would re-double my efforts—perhaps working longer hours would please him. It might demonstrate my commitment to the farm.

But commitment is a difficult thing to prove, and mine was *slightly* undermined when I struck a charging bull in the face with a shovel. It had loped into the pen unannounced, and got up to quite a trot once it saw me. I did not know what to do— two thousand pounds of muscle with nasty-looking horns was coming at me so quickly, and I just... I jumped out of the way and swung the shovel with all my might. I watched in horror and relief as its knees buckled—for one long, terrible moment, I feared that I had killed it—but the bull promptly got back up. I hightailed it over the fence only to run smack into Shovo and receive an earful of what I assume was a long string of Aven'ei profanity.

I stayed late into the afternoon for the next two days, lending a hand to the other workers wherever I could make myself useful. On the third day, Shovo stopped me as I was leaving.

"Don't think you're going to get any more *oka* out of me. You'll have two a week, whether you stay six hours or ten. Two *oka*, and not a *tuka* more."

"I don't expect extra pay," I said. "I just wanted to help."

"I already see your face more than I please," he said. "Next time you work, go home when you're scheduled to leave."

He is a person, I thought to myself. *A person.*

Knowing that someone resents your actual face takes some of the fun out of trying to make him happy. But, that night, my enthusiasm was renewed, for I finally discovered it: The Thing That Would Please Him.

I've learned in my time here that the Aven'ei are very fond of repurposed Xoe weaponry—that is, weapons confiscated during battle that have been remade to suit Aven'ei standards. These are a bit like trophies, I think, and many of the broadswords and other weapons I see in the village have traces of Xoe paint, or bone accoutrements, or something to signify their origin. Even the children collect them: hammers and bows and such, though adult archers won't touch a Xoe bow—the Aven'ei consider their own design to be vastly superior.

In the marketplace after work, I saw an exciting thing: a short

Xoe dagger with a wide blade and a handle of bone—and it cost only a single *oka*! I'd never seen a weapon priced so low. Noro doesn't go in for Xoe weaponry (I think he is impervious to fads of any kind), but Shovo does. Every sword I've seen him carry—and he owns several—is a remade Xoe artifact.

I didn't hesitate when I saw how inexpensive it was; I purchased it from the grinning old proprietor and took it straight home, where I set the blade on the mantel and admired it all evening.

The following morning, I made my way to the farm with a spring in my step, the little knife jostling like a stone in my pocket. I did not go straight to Shovo's office as I had with the pastry; I thought I would affect a more casual air about things, so as not to make it seem like a grand gesture. My thinking was that he would be more receptive if the gift was not given formally.

I waited until early afternoon for Shovo to emerge from his offices, and called him over.

"What is it?" he asked. "Trouble with the wheelbarrow again?"

"Oh, no, I've got that well in hand nowadays. I actually have something for you."

His eyes narrowed. "Not another sweet, I hope?"

"No, no." My heart thrummed in my chest. "But I did bring you a small token. Nothing of consequence, just something that brought you to mind when I saw it."

I produced the knife from my pocket and held it out for him. He took the dagger and inspected it carefully, turning it several times in his palm. Then he looked up at me. "How did you come to acquire this object?"

"I found it in the marketplace."

"And you purchased it?"

"It was inexpensive," I said, waving a hand. "Just a trifle, really."

"I should think so," Shovo said. "It's a fake."

My mouth fell open. "It's…what?"

He ran a finger along the haft. "This handle has been applied in many pieces. The Xoe use larger segments of bone to enforce the sturdiness of the weapon. The knife is a fake, made to look as a Xoe piece, but obviously made by Aven'ei hands— and clumsy ones, at that."

"Oh," I said, a rush of embarrassment coloring my cheeks. "Well. Oh."

"How much did you pay for this?"

"One *oka*," I admitted. Half a week's pay. "I thought it was a special bargain."

"Indeed it was," Shovo said. "All sales final, I suppose?"

I nodded. I felt like an idiot. But Shovo put the knife in the pouch at his waist and said, "Be more careful. If it seems too good a price, it probably is."

The following morning, Shovo cursed at me and flung a rock at my wheelbarrow when I stumbled in the mud. And so the week went on in its usual manner, my failed gesture of goodwill having been shoveled away like so much manure. But at the end of the week, when it was time for me to collect my pay, Shovo pushed three *oka* toward me.

"You've miscounted," I said, taking two of the coins and leaving the third on the table.

"I've miscounted nothing. I retrieved your money from the marketplace, and added it to your wages."

"You…" My eyes fell to the silver *oka* on the table—a small fortune, spent, lost, and now mine again. Gingerly, I picked it up, my heart moved by this small kindness. "That was very thoughtful, sir. I appreciate it."

Shovo, never one to miss an opportunity to blacken a moment, looked at me directly. "Mind your purchases from now on, Vaela Sun. You really are a very stupid girl."

I am not a stupid girl, I think to myself two nights later, as I host my first ever dinner party. Noro, Raia, and Talan—Noro's friend who patrols the village gate, the one who admitted us when we arrived—are gathered around my table, laughing, talking, happy. *I am not a stupid girl at all. I am a happy one. An accomplished, hardworking, self-sufficient young woman with a full month's wages in a satchel beneath my bed. I am, quite frankly, a bit amazing.*

Hmm. I may also be slightly drunk. Raia brought wine, and she has been liberal with it all evening. But the most important thing about Raia is that she does not flirt with Noro. This has endeared her to me more deeply than ever. Not that *I* wish to flirt with Noro. That would be unbecoming, and in any case, he is merely my friend. But I don't want Raia to do it either.

"More wine?" she says, grinning, her eyes bright and glassy in the lamplight. She doesn't wait for me to answer, but rather pours another measure of glimmering red liquid into my glass.

Talan's smooth, tanned cheeks are two pink roses; he's had even more to drink than I. Which means…three glasses? Four? I'm not certain. He has turned out to be a very friendly young man, now that he doesn't suspect me of being a Xoe.

"More for me, please," he says, holding his cup high in the air. "It's a long while since I've had wine this good."

Raia beams. "It's from Ciriel, up near Sana-Zo—do you know it? The vintner is incredible. He and his wife work alternate weeks to ensure that the yield is perfect every year."

Talan opens his mouth, but Raia clamps a hand over it. "Do not sing. I've heard you warbling up on the wall, friend, and I'd not like to endure it again."

His brow furrows. "How did you know I was about to—"

"You just have the look," Raia says. "So don't."

Talan turns to Noro with wide eyes. "Do you believe this girl?"

Noro gives him a faint smile. "I believe I once heard you sing, Talan, and it was not a happy experience."

Talan presses his lips together, then says to me, "I may not trill like a bird, Vaela Sun, but I have music in my heart."

"Leave it there," Raia says, and all of us laugh, including Talan.

I rub my fingertip along the rim of my glass, feeling happy, warm, and relaxed. "I'm so glad you all could come tonight. I only hope the dinner was all right."

Awkward glances are exchanged all around the table.

"Oh, no…*really?*" I say, dismayed. "Was it that bad?"

I worked so hard, even if I managed to drum up only a sad-looking salad and supplement it with toasted bread. I burned three beautiful loaves trying to measure the heat of the stove, broke a utensil, and reduced two tomatoes to pulp before figuring out how to slice them properly. I only wanted to try my hand at hosting, so that I might offer something to my new friends.

"Well," Talan says, "it was a bit…vegetarian."

"I'm sorry," I say. "I haven't got the nerve up to kill a chicken or a duck yet, and I can't eat beef now that I work with the cows. Have you ever looked into the eyes of a cow? They're *beautiful.*"

"You're drunk," Talan says. "What you need is a husband—someone to teach you how to slaughter an animal quick and clean, and have it on the table in time for supper."

Raia groans. "The last thing she needs is a husband. She's doing perfectly fine on her own."

I feel Noro's eyes on me, but when I glance at him, he looks away. I clear my throat. "Yes," I say. "I'm just fine, now that I can put a kettle on and feed myself properly."

"Oh, don't be like that," Talan says. "I'll marry you, if you can't find anyone else. I figure you might have a hard time matching up, with your hair all yellow, and your skin so pale."

I am aghast. "My *hair,*" I say, "is not *yellow.*"

He leans over and whispers to Noro, quite loudly, "Could almost pass for a Xoe, this one—looks like she's made of porcelain."

"It is not *yellow,*" I repeat, scowling. Raia tries to take my glass of wine, but I slide it out of her reach. "It is *blond*. And as a matter of fact, I happen to be of Aven'ei descent."

Noro raises a brow. "You're serious?"

"Of course I'm serious. I have an ancestor who fell in love with an Aven'ei man, all those years ago when the Four Nations came to the Continent."

"One of us then, after all!" says Talan, clearly delighted, and raises his glass. "Blood is blood. Shall we marry, then?"

"Go find a wife up north," Raia says. "Leave our sweet Vaela out of it."

"I've tried," says Talan miserably. "All the good ones are taken."

"It's not yellow," I mumble.

"It looks yellow to me," Talan says, and promptly buries his face in his arms atop the table. Half a moment later, he is snoring.

"What do you think, then?" Noro asks quietly. "Is Talan Raye what you seek?"

"I seek nothing," I say, "except manure. It is the focus of my life. I find it, I shovel it, and I have *oka* in my pocket."

"And wine in your belly!" Raia says, eyeing my glass. "Want me to take that for you?"

"I'm fine, thank you."

She sighs, then stands up and pokes Talan in the side. "Get up, get up. It's the sofa for you tonight." He lifts his head, a thin stream of drool gleaming on the left side of his chin. Raia helps him up, rolls her eyes, and walks him to the sofa. I hear them talking softly to one another as she searches through the cupboard for a blanket.

I feel suddenly uncertain of myself, left alone with Noro. My head is swimming with wine, and the only solution seems to be to drink *more*, but I know that can't be wise. But...it *seems* wise. No. I push my glass to the center of the table.

"So," I say, "Talan is a bit of a disaster."

"No wedding plans, then?" Noro says, those calm, steady

eyes of his fixed on mine. He's hardly touched his glass, which makes me feel all the more drunk and self-conscious.

I laugh. "Talan…he is very likable, but I think we would not be well suited."

"And why not?"

"He's not my type."

"Your 'type'?"

"Well, yes. You know. The sort of person I'm attracted to."

Noro's eyes are like two black flames, burning through me. "What sort of person is that?"

I hesitate, frozen, my heart inexplicably thumping in my chest. I have words, somewhere, but can't seem to conjure them—I can hardly breathe, much less speak.

Raia leans through the kitchen entrance. "The sort who knows when to go home," she says. "Off with you, Noro Dún."

He looks at me for a moment longer, and I feel a fluttering inside that I can no longer ignore. A little fluttering that's been happening for a while now, if I am honest.

Noro, it would seem, is exactly, perfectly my type.

The following morning, Talan is gone, but I find Raia curled up with a book in the sitting room. She sets it aside when she sees me, then throws her head back and laughs.

"Oh, Vaela!" she says. "You look even worse than I expected. No more wine after dinner for you."

I close my eyes and rub my temples. "If I never see another bottle, it will be too soon."

"I have the perfect remedy," she says. "Come along."

Her eyes are clear, and she seems completely unaffected by the previous night's indulgences, though I know she drank nearly twice as much as I did. I follow her into the kitchen and sit at the table while she rummages around in the pantry cupboard.

The noise of bottles and packages clinking about is terrible. I've never had more than a single glass of wine at once, though we drank it nightly in the Spire. It's meant to complement a meal; why would anyone want to make herself sick? My head is swimming.

"Vaela," Raia says, too loudly, "do you honestly not have even a pinch of salt in the house?"

I give her a queasy smile. "I'm afraid I don't care much for salt, except in preserved meats and the like."

She stares at me with her mouth open, then shuts the pantry door with a loud clack. I wince.

"Don't care much for salt…by the stars. I suppose you've never had a salted egg, then?" I shake my head. "Well. Now I've heard everything."

"Raia?"

"Yes?"

"My mouth tastes like dirty cotton."

"Yes, well, that's what happens when you drink too much wine."

"You had your share!"

"True," she says, leaning against the table, "but I am an old widow, and have far more practice than you."

"You're seventeen."

"Shush."

I draw my knees up to my chest. "I noticed Noro didn't drink much."

"Oooh," she says, and hurries to sit in the chair opposite. "I was waiting for his name to come up. You're sweet on each other, right?"

I turn to face her, my cheeks growing warm. "We're friends."

She laughs. "Right. Well, here's how it works," she says, leaning forward. "Half the girls in this village—and some of the men, too—have their sights set on Noro. But he isn't really what they want."

"He's not?"

"No. They see the handsome *inanei*, the adept warrior. Noro is

easy on the eyes and, truly, there are few more skilled than he—
but the assassins rarely wed. They are encouraged to be alone."

"But…surely not all of them…"

Raia cackles. "I had you pegged your first week in the cottage." She widens her eyes in imitation of me, and says, in a sing-
song voice, "'Raia, do you know how long Noro usually stays
away? Raia, do you have any romantic books I might borrow?
Raia, I thought we might bake a loaf of bread for the Dúns.'"

"He's my friend," I say stubbornly. "He's helping me adjust
to life in the village."

"*I'm* helping you adjust to life in the village. Noro is…what
is Noro doing?" She chews on the tip of her finger, then points
it at me. "Watch yourself, little Vaela—there are at least four
archers, a swordswoman, and one *inanei* who are after him."

I look up, my eyes wide. "You don't really think—"

Raia erupts into giggles. "You needn't lock your doors just
yet. But I can't imagine you'll be too popular if I'm right about
you and Noro."

"You're wrong about Noro," I insist, "and I'm already un-
popular. Most of the villagers look at me like I have two heads.
And two of every three traders won't sell to me."

"The Aven'ei are wary of the unknown," she says.

"I am only a girl—one who can barely use a knife on a loaf
of bread. What do they fear?"

"You are one of an entire nation of others, Vaela—the out-
worlders who sailed away and never came back. The villagers
do not trust you. They think you are a harbinger of the end."

"Oh, only that?" I say, and Raia laughs.

"You do need to get acquainted with more than a butter knife
at some point. You know this, right?"

I stiffen, and my head throbs involuntarily. "I really would
prefer not to have a weapon in the house."

"A weapon in the—" Raia gapes at me. "You need a weapon
on your *person*, Vaela Sun, at all times. Do you think you are

still in the Nations Beyond, where life is about maps and savory foods and servants to pluck the chickens?"

"The Spire was not devoid of danger. There was crime, as I told you."

"Take my point, Vaela, and do not change the subject."

"The Xoe do not venture into this region," I say. "I have heard it said many times."

"'Every day is new,'" she quotes, "'and in its corners dwell dangers yet unseen.'"

"That's very encouraging, thank you."

"Get a weapon."

"I'll think about it."

She stands, strides over to the copper basin where I clean my clothes and dishes, and begins to bang on it with a wooden spoon. "Get a weapon."

I cover my ears, the *clang clang clang* of the pot reverberating in my head. "Raia! Stop!"

"Get a weapon," she calls, over the clatter of wood and metal.

"All right, all right," I say. "I'll buy a *broadsword* if it pleases you. Only stop with the noise."

She sets the spoon back in the basin and smiles.

"You will learn, friend, that I rarely speak out of turn, and I don't waste words. When I tell you to buy a weapon, it is because that is what you must do. When I tell you that wine is not a particular friend of yours, you must believe me, and refrain from excess. And when I tell you there is something going on between you and Noro, you must remember that I have said so." She leans back and gives me a smug smile. "I am never wrong."

CHAPTER 19

✦

ONE FINE AFTERNOON IN LATE SPRING, I AM SIT-
ting in my garden with a book when Kiri—who has been rolling
marbles around in the dirt for half an hour and complaining that
she is bored—asks me to play *kiko* with her. It's a game of ring
toss, similar to horseshoes, but with a simpler scoring method:
one point for each ring to encircle the peg, two extra points if
you can land—or *kiko*—all five of your rings.

"I don't know, Kiri," I say absently, absorbed in my book,
a delightful fiction of betrayal and dastardly deeds, lent to me
by Raia, who might be the biggest bookworm in the whole of
the world.

"Come on, Vaela."

"Mmm-hmm."

Two fingers appear over the top of the page, and the book
vanishes. "Come on," Kiri says again. "It'll be fun."

"What will be fun?" asks Noro, stepping through the doorway into the courtyard. He's been back in Kastenai for a full
week now, but I suspect the council will send him out again
before too long. Normally, scouts would first be deployed to
seek out any Xoe who have crossed into the territory, and then
the *inanei* would be dispatched as required. But as of late, with

so many enemy sightings, the assassins must also play the role of scout. This is how Noro found me; he was patrolling the area south of the mountains.

"*Kiko,*" Kiri says. "But you're not invited to play." She turns to me and makes a face. "He *always* wins."

"That's all right," Noro says, sitting down beside me. "I'll just watch."

"You can go first," Kiri says. "But stay behind the line. No cheating."

I sigh and hold out my hand for the rings. "I wouldn't dream of it."

I step behind the line Kiri has drawn in the dirt and hold one of the rings close to my chest. "All right, here I go." I toss the first one, which nicks the peg, but does not encompass it.

"Not bad," Noro says.

"Shhh," Kiri says. "No talking."

I exchange a smile with Noro and turn back to the game. I concentrate this time. My second ring goes firmly round the peg, as does the third. "Look!" I say, excited, and turn to see Noro and Kiri each wearing a look of suspicion. I feel immediately deflated. "What is it? I was behind the line, I did it just as Kiri always does."

"Throw the rest of them," Kiri says, all business.

I face the *kiko* pitch, slightly insulted and more than a bit determined to put my last two rings on the peg. The first one is wide, and I feel my cheeks burning. Five minutes ago, I didn't care one whit about this game. But the fact that Noro and Kiri apparently expected me to do poorly has more than gotten my ire up. I take a deep breath, hold the ring out before me, and toss it cleanly onto the peg.

I cross my arms, a satisfied smile upon my face. "How's that then?"

Noro collects the rings and hands them back to me. "Three out of five, and a fourth nearly. Do it again, girl."

"It's Kiri's turn!" I say.

"Go again, Vaela," Kiri says.

"Oh, for heaven's sake," I say, but I move behind the line once again. This time, four out of five land neatly around the *kiko* peg. I turn back to the Dúns and raise an eyebrow.

Kiri giggles, and I laugh as well.

"That's very well done," Noro says. "Stay here."

He turns and disappears into the house, and I look at Kiri in confusion. She shrugs and gathers up the rings, ready to take a turn. She lands two of five, leaves all where they fell, and goes back to her game of marbles.

Noro returns with a wooden block under one arm and a roll of black leather under the other—I recognize the bundle immediately as the case he uses to store his knives. Understanding dawns on me and I say, "Oh, no, I'm not throwing those."

He ignores me and tosses the block to Kiri. I've seen them practice before, and it makes me uneasy whenever they do it—I haven't forgotten about the Xoe warriors killed by those same knives.

Kiri collects the rings from the dirt, then positions the block on top of a stool at the edge of the yard. Noro unrolls the bundle atop my little outdoor table and slides one of the knives from its place.

"Did you not hear me?" I say. "I don't want to throw your knives, Noro."

He sets the blade down. "Go and wait for me at home, Kiri."

I can see in Kiri's face that she wants to protest, but she rarely—if ever—disobeys her brother. She trudges into the house without a word and closes the door behind her.

Noro turns back to me. "I only want to see if you have an aptitude, girl. Let us see what you can do."

I shake my head. "The game is one thing—these are another. I know what these are meant for. And I know what they have done."

"Forget what they have done," he says, looking down at me in that clear, steady way of his, "and forget what they might do. Simply throw."

If it were anyone else, I would insist upon withdrawing to the house and taking up a more pleasant way to pass the time. But Noro has a way with me, I don't know why. Perhaps because I trust him. I can hear Raia's voice in my head: *get a weapon*. Perhaps this could be a tiny, tiny step in that direction. I take the knife from the table and move once more to the line.

I pinch the handle between my fingertips and aim for the block. "No, not like that," Noro says, and moves in to correct me. Carefully, he slides my fingers to the blade. "Hold from here, and let go as you extend your arm. Watch me."

He takes a knife for himself and stands beside me. "Like this," he says, and the blade moves from his fingers to a knothole in the block in one deft movement.

I start to protest, to explain that I can't possibly do what he has just done, but he nods toward the wooden block and extends his arm in example once more.

I hold the blade between my fingers and bend my elbow as Noro did, the haft resting against my shoulder. I exhale through pursed lips, then fling the knife forward. It misses the block completely and skitters across the paving stones. "You see?" I say, flustered.

Noro smiles. "Patience, girl. Watch." He demonstrates the correct motion again, slowly this time. Then he moves behind me and takes my wrist, bringing it back and then forward again. I feel his breath upon my neck, and I flush at his nearness. "Try again," he says, his words dancing across my skin as he places another knife in my hands. "See its path—look only at the target—and let go."

He steps back, and I try once more. The blade sticks firmly in the wood, about an inch or so from the bottom—probably six inches from the knothole, but who cares? I wheel around, my eyes wide with excitement. "Did you see?"

"I saw," he says softly. But he is not looking at the knife. His gaze is fixed on me, and something in his expression sets my heart beating faster. This is the way I *want* him to look at me.

"Noro?" I say, the knives forgotten. "What is it?"

He reaches for my hands and pulls me close. "When first we met, you were a frightened thing, robbed of all you had known and loved. You were broken, lost, then stolen by grief as you recovered in the healing room. You have come back to life, girl— I can see it in your eyes. I have watched you carve a way out of the darkness, even as the Continent thrust you into a life you did not plan, one you have embraced at each turn with courage and grace." He smiles. "And now, I see you, girl. Alive. Brave. It is a beautiful thing."

I cannot think what to say to this, but it is no matter. Half a moment later, Noro's fingers gently brush my cheek, and his lips find mine.

It is strange what becomes clear when a small thing changes us forever. What we have counted as merely ordinary takes on new meaning when viewed with the certainty of hindsight. For me, this has never been more true: with something so small as a kiss, Noro has opened my eyes.

In my grief, in my weakness, he was there from the beginning. I was drawn to his strength, but he did not want me to rely upon him—what he wanted most of all was for me to come into a strength of my own. I see this now, by his absence when I grieved at Eno's, by his friendship over the past two months, by the look in his eyes in the moment before he kissed me. There has been no grand process involving a declaration of intention, no series of parties and family gatherings—none of the stilted, regulated romantic traditions of the Spire. The path to love has been completely unfettered by formality; Noro simply waited for me to come back to myself, and when I did, he allowed himself to love me.

When he kissed me, I knew it was all the declaration that was required. My acceptance of his affection was an admission of my own feelings, my willingness to pursue a romance. I know this, I *feel* it—and it brings me joy rather than anxiety. I embrace these new feelings with what would be considered in the Spire an almost *improper* sense of excitement and anticipation.

However, if it was difficult before to see him set out on a council mission, it is agony now. I was correct when I assumed that they would be sending him away—just a few short hours after our intimate moment in the garden, he is gone. I spend most of the evening in a state of both elation and terror; my heart soars at the memory of his kiss—a thing not wet, or brief, or strange, like it was with Aaden, but powerful enough to shatter my very sensibilities—then thrums with fear at the thought of the danger before him. Every moment brings a new emotion, like I am lost at sea, my spirit at the mercy of the cresting waves.

I count the days while he is away, *three, four, five.* In my mind, the Xoe lie in wait to ambush him. I see his blood upon the mountain snow, his body defiled and left to rot. I wake in the night with dread burning in my stomach, certain that I've somehow sensed his death. My heart, still mending from the loss of my family, surely could not survive the loss of Noro as well.

Most of his trips have been relatively short—four days, six days, ten at most. By the eighth day, I crawl into bed feeling like there is a stone in my stomach, and cry myself to sleep. I curse him for kissing me, for changing things, for making this so much harder. Raia spends most of the week at my house and tries to divert my attention as best she can; she brings me new books to read, but I stare at the pages, my mind in the wilderness with Noro.

The days tick by, *nine, ten, eleven.*

Kiri is unruffled. "Noro's been away for a month before,"

she tells me. "There isn't a Xoe alive who can kill him." I want to believe this.

I do not.

On the morning marking fourteen days, I go from task to task without care or purpose. I send Raia away when she calls on me; I tell Kiri to go home when she knocks on the door. I climb into bed at the end of the day, the green quilt drawn high around my shoulders, and watch the moon rise through the window. It surely has seen Noro, and knows where he is, but it has no answers for me. It only gleams white and silent in the blackened sky.

I hear my name, whispered from far away, in a voice I have longed to hear.

Vaela, he says. *I've returned.*

Noro, I say to the voice in my dream, *I thought you were dead. The moon wouldn't tell me a thing. Are you dead?*

A gentle shake of my shoulder draws me from the thick fog of sleep, and I see Noro sitting on the edge of my bed, his face illuminated by moonlight. I sit up at once and catch my breath.

"I'm awake?" I say. I don't want to be dreaming.

"You're awake." The deep, low sound of his voice fills me with warmth.

I reach out and take his hand, my senses coming into focus. He smells of sweat and earth, and it is the sweetest scent I have ever known. He is alive. He has come back to me.

"Is it all right that I'm here?" he says. "You left a lamp in the window, which…well…to the Aven'ei, at least, is an invitation to enter. I only wanted to ensure that you were all right. I didn't want to wait until—"

I silence him with a kiss, my arms encircling his neck, pulling him close. All sense of Spirian propriety is washed away in my relief. I feel bold, independent. My lips press against his with an urgency I cannot deny; a moment later I feel his arms slide around my waist, and I am lost to the world. This kiss is nothing like the one we shared in the garden—that was a whispered question: *Could you love me, too?* This kiss, then, is the answer; it burns through us both, splitting the world into starlight. His lips taste of salt, his hands feel like fire against my skin. Never have I felt so alive. Never have I felt such boundless, rapturous joy. *I do love you, Noro. I do.* It is a truth not spontaneous, not new, but one that has been building in my heart for many, many weeks.

The kiss is endless and momentary all at once, and when at last we break apart, I rest my hand upon his chest and take in the sight of him. He is beautiful. Everything about him is beautiful. The lines of his face, strong and masculine, his lean, muscled body. His eyes, smoldering and black in the pale white light of the moon. The beating of his heart beneath my palm, the pulsing throb of the veins in his neck. *Alive. Here. With me.*

"I worried for you when I was away," he says softly, tucking a lock of hair behind my ear.

"You worried for *me*?"

"Every moment."

"Why were you gone for so long?"

His face tightens. "Let's not talk of it tonight."

"Noro, are you hurt?"

"No, *miyara*."

I do not know this word, but don't ask what it means. I hear the fatigue in his voice. "You need rest—you must sleep now," I say.

He begins to rise, but I pull him back. "Stay, Noro."

"This is not proper for you," he says. "To be alone here with me."

"According to the Aven'ei?"

"According to the Spirians, I think."

I kiss him lightly on the cheek. "Stay."

He hesitates for a moment, but moves to the spot beside me on the bed. I draw the quilt around us, turn onto my side and tuck myself into the curve of his body. I doubt that I will be able to return to sleep, but the soft, even sound of his breathing is like a lullaby, and after a few minutes, I feel myself drifting.

"Noro," I say, my voice tinged with the heaviness of impending sleep, "did you call me Vaela when you woke me?"

"Yes."

"Not 'girl'?"

"I called you Vaela, *miyara*."

My eyes flutter, the lids heavy. This word again. "What does *miyara* mean?"

His arms pull me closer and I feel his breath upon my hair. "It means 'my love,' for that is what you are, Vaela Sun."

Sleep beckons, and I go to it with a song in my heart.

CHAPTER 20

◆

NORO LEAVES BEFORE I WAKE IN THE MORNING, as I expected he would. The council always requires an immediate report upon his return, and I sensed that whatever happened during Noro's trip was of some consequence.

He knocks on the door around noon, just as I'm preparing to take a loaf of bread from the oven. My baking has improved, but I wouldn't say it's anything special just yet. Noro looks entirely different this morning; gone is the soiled, sweaty black garb of the *inanei*. Now he is scrubbed clean, wearing fresh clothes of deep brown linen. I smile at the soapy scent of him as he steps through the door.

"How did it go?" I ask, setting the bread on the table to cool. He bends over the loaf and takes a deep breath, a small smile on his face.

"You're becoming quite domestic, Vaela Sun. Is there anything left of the spoiled Spire girl I first met?"

"You'd be surprised," I say, ushering him out of the kitchen and gesturing to the sofa.

"Still on about the *toilets*?" he says.

"Don't change the subject. I want to know what happened with the council, and why you were away for two entire weeks."

He sits down with a sigh and stares ahead, his shoulders tense. The light seems to have gone out of him completely. "I should have been able to return after only six days. I tracked the men I sought to an area just south of the mountains—very near to where I found you. Perhaps fifty miles or so from the village. I accomplished what I set out to do, and I was in good spirits."

I try not to think of what he must have accomplished. "What happened?"

"I thought to go west, if only to satisfy myself that the region was clear. We do not see many Xoe there, for their settlements are far to the north. But Xoe rangings in the south have become more frequent, and I could not put the matter to rest in my mind. I truly did not expect to find anyone west of the Kinso."

My heart catches in my chest, and I stiffen. "But you did find Xoe there."

Noro turns to me, his brows drawn together. "Why do you say this with such certainty?"

My throat is dry. "Because they have settlements in that region, Noro—far to the west. I have seen them."

His eyes narrow. "That is not possible. We thoroughly scouted the area at the dawn of winter and it was wilderness, as it always is. The Xoe prefer the hard ice of the north and the protection of the mountains—they have never dwelt in the south. Not ever."

"I would not say such a thing if it were untrue."

He looks at me for a moment, and then presses the bridge of his nose with his fingertips. "This explains much."

"What happened? What did you see?"

He drops his hands to his lap. "Ordinarily, the Xoe we find in this region are here merely to keep abreast of our movements—they send scouts, like the ones you encountered. Two men, maybe three or four. They retain the bulk of their forces in the north, sending warriors to other regions as necessary."

"I have seen this, too," I say, recalling the battle to the east of the Riverbed.

"But after only two days of searching, I found a group of not two or three Xoe, but twenty-five strong. Moving along inside the Southern Vale, in the direction of the village. They turned back not fifteen miles from here."

"But...have they not invaded your settlements before?"

"Countless times," he says, "but only in the north, where they cross easily into our territory from their own. Not in the south. If they have positioned themselves as you say, it is safe to assume they intend to launch an assault into this region as well. And if that happens, we will have Xoe on all sides. There will be no retreat."

My stomach clenches. "What will you do?"

"It is not a question of what I will do, but what you will do."

"But what can I—"

"We must assemble the council and speak with Nadu at once," he says. "It is time for you to draw a map."

My eyes dart to the rolled up parchment tucked neatly behind the bin of firewood. My map. It is unfinished, but the Xoe settlements I saw from the heli-plane are clearly marked. "It is already done," I say. "Let us meet with the council at once."

An hour later in the War Room, I push the wide sheet of parchment across the table. All three members of the council—Nadu, Kinza, and Shovo—crowd together, their eyes moving rapidly over the paper. Their existing charts do not extend as far west as the one I've drawn—when I asked Noro why this was, he said there had never been a need. An inhospitable place with rocky terrain and no accessible shoreline, the southwest corner of the Continent never seemed a viable location for anyone to settle.

"It's not perfect," I say. "I've only included the most basic elements, and I—"

"Is it accurate?" Shovo asks.

I nod. "As of three months ago, it is accurate to the mile."

Nadu's expression is pained, his lips pressed into a rigid line.

He looks up from the map and frowns at Noro. "You told us that her skills as mapmaker were not tactical."

"That was my understanding," Noro says.

Nadu makes a small noise, his eyes falling back to the paper before him. "It is not your fault, young *inanei*. I should have had the foresight to press the issue when she arrived."

Kinza stares at the map, rubbing absentmindedly at the stump of her missing arm. "This...I would not have predicted."

"Xoe in the south," Shovo says. He spits into a basin beside his chair. "It is our doom."

"Do not say such things," Kinza hisses, striking the map with her palm, rattling the pots of ink at the far end of the table. "Would you bring shadows and ill fortune upon the Aven'ei?"

"Oh, shut up," Shovo says. "You're a superstitious old hag. It was not I who manufactured this turn of fate!" He angles a crooked finger in my direction. "Find blame where it truly lies."

Noro's chair scrapes across the wooden floor as he abruptly gets to his feet. "How dare you imply that Vaela is responsible for this! Have you no honor? Apologize at once."

Shovo sneers at him. "Or what, *inanei*? You will kill me when I sleep?"

"I will kill you where you stand," Noro says, his palm on the handle of the knife at his waist. "Apologize."

"Shovo," Nadu says quietly, "it is no more the girl's fault than it is your own."

"I defer to your wisdom, of course," Shovo says in a silky voice. "I only thought...well, perhaps I was mistaken."

Nadu sighs. "Speak plainly, if you will speak at all."

"Careful," Noro growls, tapping a finger on the haft of his blade.

Shovo's eyes flick down to the knife, but he continues. "Let us only consider, Nadu, why it was that the Xoe were inclined, after these many centuries, to withdraw from the north and invade our southern borders." He pauses, but Nadu says nothing. "Why, they have followed her *planes* to our very doorstep!"

"I will not warn you again, *zunupi*," Noro says in a low voice, spitting the last word in Shovo's direction. "Implicate Vaela one more time and it will be the last thing you do."

"Noro," Nadu says sharply, "there will be no violence here today. I forbid it. And Shovo—I will hear no more of this. Do you understand? The girl is not at fault."

Shovo bows his head. "Of course. I meant no disrespect."

Nadu gives him a withering glare. "You are a fool to provoke an assassin, and a coward to point your finger at a young woman who is working even now to assist our people." He turns to Kinza. "How many scouts have you who are ready to investigate these camps?"

"Nine," Kinza says. "They can leave today."

"I shall go as well," Noro says.

My heart sinks at this, but Nadu shakes his head. "No, Noro. You have only just returned. Your body and mind need restoration. And in any event, this is a matter of reconnaissance only. Notify the scouts, Kinza. All will depend upon their success."

Noro is quiet as we walk back to my cottage. The streets are bustling with people at this time of morning, most of them headed to work, or to the marketplace. The sky is pale, the clouds gray with the promise of rain. When we reach the long road that leads to our homes, I break the silence.

"I'm glad you're not leaving, Noro. It's selfish, I know, but it's how I feel."

He glances down at me, but says nothing. A moment later, his fingers encircle mine. Silence falls over us again as we walk hand in hand along the quiet lane. Then, as we come to the walk leading up to my front door, he says, "Wait here—I have something for you," before dashing across the road to his own house.

I sit on the stone steps to wait for him, Shovo's words echoing in my mind. *They have followed her* planes *to our very doorstep.*

Could it be true? Could Spirians have unwittingly changed the course of the war by touring the Continent? Or was it a natural turn of events, an alteration of strategy in the relentless Xoe drive to destroy the Aven'ei?

I sigh. I cannot know the answer, but I fear that in the weeks to come, Shovo's suggestion will bleed through the village like ink in the fibers of parchment—spreading, twisting, covering everything in its path and making an indelible mark. The villagers already look at me with suspicion. I am an outsider still, and as the news of the Xoe advancement becomes known, I wonder if others, too, will direct the blame at me.

I hear the door close across the street and see Noro heading toward me, a brown, paper-wrapped parcel in his left hand. He sits down and hands me the package; a length of twine is tied neatly around it, knotted into a bow.

"What is this?"

"A gift," he says.

"But when did you—"

"I made an order two weeks ago, just before I left." He gives me a gentle nudge with his elbow. "Open it."

I hold the package in my hands, rubbing my thumb along the scratchy twine. My throat feels tight, my cheeks warm.

Noro leans over and scrutinizes my face. "What is the matter? Have I acted improperly?"

"No. No. It's just…well, you gave me the soap after I first began working—a thing I treasured, by the way, until it was only a tiny speck. But the last time I was given a gift in this way, the box held my ticket to the Continent."

"Ah," he says. "Vaela, I apologize. I did not mean to revive such memories."

I shake my head. "No—it's all right. It is a good memory, after all, isn't it? My parents were so happy that night."

"I imagine they were, having brought such joy to you."

I wipe the moisture from my eyes and smile. "I'm sorry. This was very thoughtful of you, I don't mean to spoil it."

"You have spoiled nothing. Would you like to open it another time?"

"No," I say, and lean over to kiss his cheek. "In truth, I quite like presents."

He laughs as I untie the twine, coil it beside me, and carefully unfold the paper. There is a black leather case inside, much like the one Noro uses to transport his knives. I look up at him in confusion.

"Unroll it," he says, nodding toward the bundle.

I unfurl the case to see, as I expected, a set of knives—six of them in total. Only the handles are exposed, made of polished, gleaming blackwood. I pull one of the knives from its sheath and the blade glitters, its beveled edges glinting in the light. It is slightly smaller than one of Noro's—perhaps six inches from the butt of the handle to the tip of the blade. I am no authority when it comes to weaponry, but I can tell that these are of very fine quality.

I turn it over in my hand, admiring the craftsmanship, the smooth lines, the graceful curves of the haft. "They're beautiful," I say, surprising myself.

"They are made especially for you, *miyara*." He takes a second knife from the case and holds it before him. "The Aven'ei believe it is a sin to waste an aptitude. Where skill is recognized, it is nurtured, lest the ability dwindle from misuse or neglect. You have a gift, Vaela—a natural talent with the knives. I give these to you that you may hone your skill, and perhaps one day master the art."

"I hope your confidence is not misplaced," I say doubtfully.

"It is not. It will take much work, but I have trained many and I know what I have seen in you."

"I don't know what to say, Noro."

"Say you will let me teach you."

I look over at him and smile. "When shall we begin?"

CHAPTER 21

◆

SUMMER COMES ON LIKE A BREATH OF WIND, spreading a bloom of red and orange brush over the southeastern tip of the Continent. One by one, the scouts return from the west, the truth of the Xoe advancement confirmed. Two settlements are reported exactly where I indicated they would be, with a significant force amassed between them. Several great assemblies are held in Kastenai, and representatives from villages as far north as the Riverbed are in attendance. No consensus is reached as to the best course of action; the leaders are divided. The villagers, too, discuss the quandary. Most seem to feel that it is best to wait, to fight on familiar ground. Among all, there is a singular certainty: blood will be shed. It is not a question of if, but of when and where.

The waiting leaves time for much contemplation, and I find myself amid a storm of mixed emotions. The *kazuri ko'ra* is near its end, and I may have the opportunity to return home within the next few months. But while the thought of the Spire fills me with longing, a small part of me is quietly ignoring the fact that to go home will mean saying goodbye to Noro and all the rest. Who might have thought that I would become so attached to the Aven'ei that the thought of home itself should be bittersweet?

The Continent is truly lovely in the summertime, and the warming of the weather stirs a restlessness in me that kindles an adventurous spirit. And so, on a mild, lovely day, I find myself in the center of a vast field, a mile or so north of the village, ready to begin my training with Noro.

Talan has joined us so that he might spar with me while Noro instructs, and Raia has come along to observe. The wind ruffles the long grass as I stand uncertainly behind Talan, who is facing the distant mountains.

"Go on, Vaela," Raia says. "Give it a try. Just as Noro showed you."

I hesitate.

"What's the problem?" Noro says.

"It feels wrong," I say. "I don't want to do it."

"It's a wooden knife, Vaela," Noro says. "You can't hurt him."

"I know, but it feels wrong. Even pretending to do this."

Noro sighs. "Your throwing knives are meant to distract or disable an attacker. You must learn how to kill, and that means you have to get close. Now do it as I showed you."

The warm wood of the training dagger rubs against my sweaty palm. "Really, I just—"

"Vaela. Please."

"Fine."

I take a breath and exhale deeply. I put a tentative hand on Talan's left shoulder; he whirls to face me and shoves me backward, so hard that I fall to the ground. Stunned, I look up at Noro—but he only laughs.

"Did you think you might just give him a friendly tap to let him know you were there?"

I get to my feet. "No."

"If you don't do it quickly, you'll be the one who dies. Again—and take his jaw in your left hand this time, as you strike. Do not touch his shoulder."

Talan turns his back and begins to whistle. Determined, I rush up behind him and reach for his jaw—but he turns and pushes me again. I stumble, but don't fall this time.

"What was that for?"

Talan spits. "You made more noise than an *azmera*. Not very light-footed, this one."

"I beg your pardon!"

"Vaela," Noro says, "remember what I told you about stealth. You are small—a young woman. You will be no less capable than any other once you learn these techniques, but you cannot physically overpower a Xoe warrior—probably not even another female. They are impossibly strong."

"They hurl rocks in sport," Talan says. "My cousin has seen it done."

"Shush," Raia says. "Let him teach."

Noro continues. "You must use the element of surprise. It is the sharpest tool of any *inanei*."

"But I'm not an *inanei*. I'm just trying to learn how not to die."

He steps closer to me, and whispers in a voice only I can hear, "You are Vaela Sun, the love of my heart. You can be whatever you wish. Now do it again, and be quiet this time."

Talan gets back into position and resumes his whistling. As I approach, again he spins about and shoves me.

"Too loud," Talan says.

And again.

"You can do better than this, Vaela. Move like a quiet breeze."

Again.

"Come on, now, don't get discouraged."

And again, and again, and again.

I sit in the grass, tears in my eyes, my shoulders aching from all the pushing and shoving. "I can't do it."

"You can," Noro says, crouching down beside me. "Get up, *miyara*. You must not quit."

His eyes burn with confidence. What does he know that I don't?

I get up. I try again.

And end up on my backside.

I'm sweating by the time it finally happens. I approach Talan like a mouse; Noro gives me a nod of approval. I reach for my victim's chin, grab it, prepare to draw the wooden blade across his neck—and scream.

"He bit me!" I say, clutching my hand. "He bit my finger!"

Noro shrugs. "You put your hand over his mouth. Of course he bit you."

"Oh, for heaven's sake." I close my eyes and exhale slowly. "Turn around, Talan. We'll go again."

I give my hand a shake and slink back into position, scowling.

This time, I keep ALL of my fingers clear of his teeth, and draw the knife from left to right as Noro showed me. Talan makes a gurgling noise, grips his throat, and falls to the ground, twitching.

"That's not funny," I say, but I'm smiling, because *I did it*, and even his grim joke can't spoil my mood.

Raia gives a cheer, and Talan grins. "That was well done," he says. "She'd have had me."

"Excellent, Vaela," Noro says, and I glow with pride at his praise. "Do it again."

My smile fades. "Again?"

"We must teach your muscles to remember. Then you can do it without thinking."

I balk at this. "I don't want to kill someone without thinking."

"You may not have a choice."

"Isn't there always a choice?"

"Not if you want to live."

His words chill me, but I can't think of a retort. What am I going to say: *okay, then, maybe I don't want to live*? That would be a lie. I don't want to take a life, but I don't want to lose my own, either—and I don't want to see those I love come to any harm. Am I selfish? There never seems to be an answer to this question. I can only ever remind myself that I am not in the Spire, and the Xoe would gladly see me dead.

I sigh. "Get up, Talan. We'll go again."

After what must be twenty more successful attacks, Noro calls for a break, and the four of us settle down with jugs of cold water from the nearby stream. I'm dripping with sweat; cool rivulets run down the back of my neck, tickled by the mild breeze.

"I say you've got a good start, Vaela Sun," Talan says, and tosses me an apple from his pack. "And you're freakish strong for such a small thing, you know that? You have a nice, firm grip. Well done."

"Do you feel confident in your progress?" Noro asks.

"I think I do," I say, surprised. I wouldn't want to try my luck with a Xoe, but I know more than I did this morning. Like how to avoid getting shoved to the ground by Talan.

"Good. Now we must teach you all the ways to kill a man with a knife."

I crinkle my nose. "You have a way with words."

"There is no point in pretending about what we must do, Vaela. I do not teach you these things for sport—I hope to provide you with a way to defend yourself." He taps himself on the chest. "Would you stab me here?"

"No."

"Good. Why?"

"Your…breastbone. It's in the way."

"Excellent." He points to the spot below his ribs, on his left side. "Here?"

"Yes."

"How?"

I stare at the spot. "What do you mean, how?"

"Show me with your knife how you would do it."

I gape at him. "I'm having an apple, Noro! We're supposed to be resting!"

"All right," he says, and reclines, resting his head in his hands. "Enjoy your fruit."

"Thank you."

"If I were a Xoe, it would be your last meal."

Talan laughs. "Oh, let her eat, Noro."

"Yes, let me eat," I say, "then I'll stab you wherever you please."

I lie back on the cool grass, lost beneath a sea of billowing white clouds. "That one looks like a great fir," I say. Noro looks up, twists his head, then moves to my side, his head on the ground next to mine. On the other side of him, Talan does the same.

"A wheelbarrow," Talan says, pointing.

"Where?" I say.

"That big one above the mountain."

"How can you possibly think that looks like a wheelbarrow?" Raia asks.

Talan points again, jabbing his finger into the air. "See the handles there?" His hand makes a loop. "And the wheel. The big wheel—how do you not see it?"

Noro gives an exasperated sigh. "You do realize that where you're pointing is different from my perspective than from yours?"

Talan points again. "Right there."

"I see a sailboat," Noro says.

"Ohhh, I see a sailboat, too!" I say. "With a great tall mast!"

Raia leans forward. "I see it as well!"

Talan groans.

We are quiet for a moment. Then I start to giggle.

"What's so funny?" Noro asks.

My giggle evolves into the kind of laughter that, when you're in the midst of it, makes it hard to breathe. I roll onto my side, my shoulders shaking, but I can't stop. Noro, Talan, and Raia have no idea what I'm laughing about; even so, they join in.

I point to the cloud above us, trying desperately to speak, but this only makes me laugh harder. Finally, with tears in my eyes, I manage a few words: "That one…it…it looks…like Shovo."

Now we are all laughing together, with Talan repeating *I see it, I see it* again and again. I've never seen Noro in stitches like this before. I bury my face in his shoulder, the warm sun like a kiss on my cheek, and laugh and laugh and laugh.

The following day, the four of us hike out to the meadow once again. The clouds today are dark and heavy, burdened with rain. From time to time, I feel a drop of water on my face.

"We'll stay until it pours," Noro says. "A little water never hurt anyone."

"Tell that to my cousin," Talan says. "He once saw a thunderstorm at Sana-Zo that flooded the entire valley. People were whisked away, carried right off! Never heard from again."

Raia glances at me, then says, "Is this the same cousin who saw the Xoe hurling rocks? The one who watched them eat their dead after a battle? The cousin who lives farther south than we do, but spends more time observing the Xoe than anyone alive?"

Talan's face goes red. "They did eat their dead. He *saw* it."

"I've heard they eat babies," I say.

"Really?" Talan says, his eyes wide.

"That's what Kiri says."

Noro sighs. "Can we focus, please?"

A large raindrop splashes onto his face, right between his eyes; Talan and I both smother a laugh. Raia chuckles and plunks herself down on a flat rock nearby.

"All right, all right," I say, trying to compose myself. "Proceed, battlemaster."

"Today, you will learn another way to kill with a knife. Talan, turn around."

Talan turns to face the mountains, and Noro pokes him beneath the left shoulder blade. "This spot, this spot here, it will give you the quickest kill of all. You drive the blade upward beneath this rib—" here, he demonstrates with my wooden knife "—directly into the heart. If you cut a man's throat, he will take minutes to bleed out, and sometimes makes noise; if you pierce his heart, he will die at once."

"Why don't we just use this technique all the time?"

"Armor," Talan says over his shoulder. "If they've got thick leather on, you can't easily penetrate it. Especially when the armor is laced with metal or bone."

"Exactly," Noro says. "I want you to know this technique, to marry it to your memory, because it is quick and silent."

We practice a few times, Noro directing my blade to the proper angle and spot.

"This is how you killed the second Xoe at the camp," I say quietly.

He nods. "It was half a moment before he was dead."

I meet Noro's eyes. "He was kind to me."

His eyes grow dark, cast with the reflections of the gathering clouds overhead. "Do you grieve for the men who captured you? They would have tortured you, killed you eventually. Do you truly not yet understand what the Xoe are?"

"I do grieve for them," I whisper. "Though I am grateful every day for what you did."

His eyes narrow. "Vaela, I fear for you. You cannot look upon the Xoe as men."

"What are they, then?"

"They are the enemy."

"The enemy."

"That's right."

"That may be, Noro, but they *are* men," I say. "Fathers, brothers, sisters, sons—the Xoe are people, just like you and me. I will not harden myself to see them otherwise."

Raia bristles. "I will remember you said that, Vaela. After all, it might be you who one day is killed and dismembered, your head put on a pike and marched around the battlefield."

"The Xoe are not the only ones to flaunt the violence of this war," I say hotly. "When I first traveled over the Continent, I saw bodies—Xoe dead—strung from a bridge in the south. The Aven'ei are no strangers to brutality."

Raia's face is dark with rage. "You would compare the Xoe to the Aven'ei?"

"That isn't what I meant," I say. "I only—"

"If those *zunupi* insist on stretching their legs into our territory," Raia says, "they shall swing from the bridges in all their rotten glory. We do not bury their dead, nor send them off in fire, as is *their* custom. The Xoe can rot—and may their corpses serve as warning to their brethren."

Talan turns, his usually jovial face set now with hard lines. "Vaela Sun is sentimental."

Noro nods. "Sentiment makes for a poor weapon, and it is certainly no shield."

"You misunderstand me, Noro," Talan says. "I do not chide her for it."

"No?" Noro says. "Are you not my brother in battle, Talan Raye? Have we not fought side by side?"

Talan crosses his arms. "Vaela sees a thing that we have forgotten."

"And what is that?"

He shrugs. "The Xoe are not a faceless enemy—they have lost much as well. They mourn and grieve as we do."

"Yet still they come," Noro says, "when the Aven'ei would stay away. Still they come and find pleasure in the slaughter of our people."

Raia frowns. "Since when are you a Xoe sympathizer, Talan?"

"I'm no sympathizer," he says, and spits. "I can't acknowledge the fact that the Xoe are human without being labeled as some kind of *senukka*?"

"Watch your mouth," Noro says, glancing over at me.

"Watch your *back*," Raia says to Talan. "You know what happens to Aven'ei that go soft and sweet."

"You threaten me? You who were my childhood friend? My childhood—"

"Oh, shut up," Raia says.

"Please," I say. "Stop arguing. I understand how you feel, Raia, how much you must hate the Xoe—"

Raia fixes me with a cold glare. "You understand nothing, Vaela. You dress like an Aven'ei, you toil like an Aven'ei, you may even have Aven'ei blood running through your veins. But you did not grow up in the shadow of war. You are an outworlder, and so you will always be."

Tears prick my eyes. "I didn't mean—"

"She knows that," Noro says, scowling in Raia's direction.

She throws up her hands and stalks away, not stopping until she reaches the western bank of the stream. There, she sits, picks up a stone, and hurls it into the water.

Talan puts a hand on my shoulder. "She's got a hot temper. She didn't mean what she said."

"She's right," I say. "I've been on the Continent scarcely five months. I oughtn't say a word."

"I've heard quite enough of this," Noro says. "Vaela, I cannot change the way you see your enemy, but I will not rest until I know you can at least dispatch a man who might kill you, and without hesitation."

The truth of the war has never felt so plain, so heavy in my heart. I nod and step into the space between Noro and Talan. I place a hand on Talan's back, searching for the vulnerable spot. "Like this?" I say, pretending to drive the knife upward and inward.

"Like that," Noro says. "Exactly like that."

Lightning rips across the sky, close enough to turn our faces white in its glow.

Noro curses under his breath, his eyes on the clouds above. "We finally begin, and now we must stop." He sighs. "Let us go, then. I do not like the look of this one, and the air is foul. There is trouble on the horizon—mark my words."

CHAPTER 22

✦

FOR THREE DAYS AND NIGHTS, A STORM UNLIKE
any I have ever seen beats viciously upon the Continent. It is a
late summer tempest, one that howls angrily, whipping water
against the panes of the windows with a terrifying ferocity. I
stand at the kitchen window on the third day, my arms braced
around my waist, marveling at the violence of the rain. The
clouds rumble with an ominous black fury, their terrible gray
faces flashing to life as lightning cracks across the sky again and
again. And though it is not yet evening, it is so dark outside that
I have set every lamp in the house to burning, with a healthy
fire in the sitting room hearth besides.

Aside from the storm, it is quiet in the cottage. Noro left
early this morning on some business with Kinza and the scouts,
and Kiri disappeared after breakfast, though where she went, I
could not say. Noro and Kiri have all but abandoned their own
cottage; Kiri and Joa sleep on the sofa in my sitting room, and
Noro with me, in my bed. In the Spire, this would constitute
a scandal beyond *belief*—anyone who heard of it would assume
that Noro and I were lovers. And we are, in our way, but we
do not know each other yet in that intimate sense. Our love is

sweet, and slow, and new. It is not a thing of disgrace, and no person could ever convince me otherwise.

Another flash of lightning tears across the sky, followed by a shattering crack of thunder. Shivering, I turn back to the sitting room, feeling restless myself. Perhaps a book by the fire—there is scarce else for me to do in this weather, since all my chores have been attended.

For once, Kiri left her great shadow Joa at home; the poor hound has been restless and unhappy since the storm began. Crouched miserably beneath the entry table, he whines as I pass by. He looks up at me with a mournful expression, his eyebrows shifting up and down above woebegone brown eyes. The effect is so sweet and pathetic that I can't help laughing.

"Oh, Joa," I say, stooping to smooth the soft gray fur along his neck. "You'll be all right. The rain has to let up sometime."

A mighty thunderclap roars overhead, and I expect him to hunker down even farther, but he stiffens and stands so abruptly that the table—not nearly so tall as Joa when he's on his feet—teeters momentarily atop his back before crashing backward against the wall. He stands before the door, his head hunched low, his ears flat against his head, a deep growl slipping through his exposed teeth.

"Joa?" I say, my voice tremulous. "What's the matter?"

He paws at the door and lets out a vicious bark, a piercing sound that startles me into taking a step backward. As if in response, the gale picks up outside, the wind whistling along the sides of the cottage. The dog turns once in a circle and then backs away, his head so low it is almost level with the floor.

"Joa?" I say again.

The door bangs open and Noro steps inside amid a spray of wind and water. His hair is slicked down along one side of his head, his black hood open at his back. Joa is out the door at once, displacing the entry rug in his hurry to get outside.

Noro grips my upper arm and pulls me along the hallway

to the bedroom. "They have come, Vaela." He takes down my black case and unrolls it in one motion across the bed. "Keep your knives at the ready and do not leave this room. Do you hear me? *Do not leave this room.*" He snuffs out the lamp and moves back down the hallway. I follow him, fear like a block of ice in my belly.

"Wait," I say desperately. "You must tell me what's happening!"

He turns and points to the bedroom. "Get back in that room and do not leave until I come for you."

"But—what if I can help? You've taught me so much already, and I—"

His face is a mask of fury. "*Get back in the bedroom!* You are not a warrior, Vaela!"

Never has he raised his voice to me, and my eyes burn with tears. He registers the look on my face, exhales sharply, then pulls me into his arms. "I cannot protect you out there, *miyara*. Please wait for me here. Will you do this?"

I nod, and see relief in his eyes. "But where is Kiri?" I ask. "She left early and I don't—"

"I will find her. Do not worry."

"But Noro…if there is trouble, she will think herself able to fight." A biting dread flows through me at the thought.

"I will find her, sweet one. I must go."

He takes my face in his hands and kisses me. And then he is gone, moving down the shadowy hallway and putting out the lights one by one before disappearing into the storm. I return to the darkened bedroom, my hands shaking as I close the door behind me. I strain to hear something, anything that will tell me what is happening in the village, but I can make out nothing over the cacophony of the wind and rain. A flash of lightning casts the room in a momentary shock of pale white light; I see the knife case on the bed, hurry to collect it, then collapse onto the floor, hugging the cool bundle against my chest.

And I wait.

★ ★ ★

The minutes tick by. The rain is relentless, as are the dark imaginings of my mind. What is happening? How bad is the attack? How many have been lost? What of Noro, of sweet Kiri? My heart beats like a wounded bird inside my chest; my hands sweat and ache from clutching the leather case. Each crash of thunder is jarring, terrifying—a reminder that out there, outside these walls, there is danger. That the Xoe have come.

The waiting is agony. I feel as I did in the glass pod—trapped, helpless, a bystander unable to stop the events unfolding around me. And in truth, isn't that the way of it? Here I am, sheltered once more while those I love face imminent and terrible danger. Here I hide, trembling and afraid, my own life safely removed from peril. The walls that protect me now are stone, not glass, but there is no true difference.

I see my father, his hand outstretched atop my mother's on the door of the pod. *Vaela*, he said, *be safe*. My breath catches in my chest at the memory of his words, at the love that shone in his eyes, and at the strength of his silent plea. No—not a plea. A goodbye.

Were Noro's words tonight also a farewell? Even if he intends to return for me, I have seen what the Xoe can do. I have seen battle—I have watched men and women paint the snow with blood.

My fingers trail restlessly along the edge of the knife case. If I could kill but one Xoe, how many Aven'ei might I save? The thought sets my heart racing, for as Noro said, I am no warrior. My training has scarcely begun. If I were to try and fight, I would almost surely die.

But I might kill *one*. One Xoe whose thirst for blood cannot be quenched except in death. One Xoe who could otherwise, on this very night, send Noro to his grave.

One might be enough.

Moving as though in a dream, I get to my feet and open the

drawer in the stand beside the bed. The black leather belt that allows me to wear my knives rests inside beneath a tangle of other items; I remove it from the drawer, fix it around my waist, and methodically tuck each of my six blades into the sturdy sheaths. Then I lace up my boots and fasten a heavy woolen cloak about my shoulders.

I will not hide like a coward in the dark.

Forgive me, Noro. My life is worth no more than that of any other.

The wind whips the hood from my head the moment I step outside; the pelting rain is like a spray of icy daggers against my skin. Shielding my eyes, I make my way down the short front walk to the road, only to step back with a gasp as the branch of a white birch tree cartwheels past and crashes into a stack of crates at the end of the lane. The shriek of the wind is shrill, almost frantic—like the wail of an accursed spirit lost to some otherworldly torment. Shivering, I press forward, struggling to see in the darkness and violence of the storm. No one is in sight, and the lights are out in all of the houses in this row and the next. The sky is still as black as sin. *Maker keep me*, I pray. *And protect those I love. Please. Please.*

I head up the road and round the corner to find that an enormous cherry tree has been uprooted and deposited thirty feet from where it once grew. Everywhere, there is debris—broken pots, slate roof tiles, clothing ripped from wash lines. I hurry through the mud and pick my way up the lane in the direction of the village gates. There is a distant pounding to be heard— at first, I mistake it for the rain, but it is too rhythmic, too monotonous to be natural. It grows louder as I advance, and I stop for a moment, puzzled.

Boom. Boom. Boom-boom-BOOM. Boom. Boom. Boom-boom-BOOM.

Suddenly, I recall the words that Raia spoke to me the first time we met: *I can't begin to imagine a life without the drums of war.*

I take off running, splashing through the deep puddles and trenches wrought by the rain. The muscles in my legs burn and ache as I race toward the gates, the mud sucking at my boots with every step. As a flash of lightning sets the sky alight, the village entrance comes into view. The shock of the scene so startles me that I slip and stumble forward, my hands and knees sinking deep into the sodden earth.

Hundreds lie throughout the square, dead or dying. A great many more are locked in battle, while the village gate lies in a twisted ruin, breached by some terrible force. The few buildings that line the entranceway are bright with flames, despite the downpour.

I scramble to my feet and move quickly toward the right-hand tower, taking a circuitous route that leads me away from the heart of the fighting. When I reach the wall, I press my body flat against the stone and try to catch my breath. Several feet away, a woman—a Xoe—calls out to me; she is flat on her belly, clawing at her hair. A closer look reveals that she has been separated from her legs. She calls out once more and then becomes still, one more dark, lifeless figure claimed in the assault.

Grateful for the cover of darkness and shaking with fear and cold, I move silently along the wall until I find the stairwell leading to the walkway. Atop the rampart, there is no one left alive; I discover only the bodies of a dozen or so Aven'ei archers. I avert my gaze as I creep along, moving south toward the tower. The clash and grinding of metal becomes more pronounced as I near the village entrance. Finally, concealed behind the battlement, I peer out beyond the wall.

The fighting is concentrated just inside the gate, but dozens of smaller skirmishes continue on either side. With each burst of lightning, there are new horrors to be seen: the silhouette of a Xoe hatchet as it is drawn back, an Aven'ei swordsman cleaved nearly in two by his own confiscated weapon, a gurgling fountain of blood pulsing upward from the thigh of a man on the ground below. And as the battle rages on, I begin to wonder if I might serve any purpose here at all, or if I will merely end up dead without ever unsheathing a knife. What can I possibly do against mighty warriors such as these?

There can be but one answer: find a Xoe who is alone, and surprise him. I have not the skill or stealth of an *inanei*, but the thunder and the everlasting torrent of rain may serve to conceal me long enough. At least, that is what I hope.

I wait, watching carefully when there is enough light to see, searching along the edges of the battle for any man who may be isolated. And at long last, I find one.

The man stands alone at the edge of the wood beyond the gate. He is an archer, and wounded, his right arm bound with cloth, soaked through with the rain and bloody as all hell. I count his injury as one small advantage. The Xoe presses himself back into the trees, searching for a target that he might dispatch from the concealment of the forest.

Quickly, I map out a route that might bring me across the field without being seen, into the safety of the trees. From there, I can approach him from behind without being heard. My heart is pumping furiously, adrenaline coursing through my body. *Can I do this? Even if I make it to the wood, can I take a life? And should I succeed—and survive—can I bear the cost?*

I falter, uncertain, allayed by doubt and fear. Yet I am keenly aware that no Aven'ei would hesitate in this way; I must go, lest I lose the opportunity. I turn to move back along the length of the wall so that I might descend out of sight, but a change in the Xoe's stance gives me pause. The man stands perfectly still, his eyes fixed on something to my left. He lifts his bow, notches an arrow and pulls the cord taut; automatically, I train my eyes to where his target must be. A sickening sense of disbelief trickles through me as I see the small girl perched upon the wall on the opposite side of the gate, a large gray hound beside her.

"Kiri!" I scream, my knives stupidly forgotten, but the wind tears the word from my lips, and the archer lets the arrow fly. It strikes Kiri in the neck, knocking her backward behind the parapet. The dog launches itself over the top of the wall, skids and rolls over in the mud below, then flies across the field toward the archer. He catches the Xoe by the throat and knocks him to the ground, tearing at the man's flesh. For a moment, I am certain Joa has killed him. But the dog goes abruptly still, and half a second later, the archer scrambles backward into the wood, one hand at his throat and the other clutching a short, sharp knife.

Shaking, I clamber down the inner side of the wall as quickly as I can, without care or fear of the battle below. I no longer hear the crash of swords or the deafening rain and thunder. I only run, my feet digging into the mud, my arms pumping at my sides. Men fall and fight and die around me; I run through them, over them, past them. I leap for the wall when I reach the other side of the ruined gate; my fingers catch the lip of the wet, broken stone and cling with a strength borne purely of will. I climb upward, steadily, quickly, and pull myself over the side when I reach the top.

Kiri is there, small and broken, convulsing in the rain, the arrow driven through her throat just below the chin. Her eyes are wide with shock, hands hovering over her neck. She opens her mouth to speak, but there is no sound.

"It's going to be all right, Kiri," I say, with a certainty I do not feel. "Everything is going to be fine."

A shadow falls over her body and I freeze, fear and remorse mingling in the pit of my stomach. *I will die now. A Xoe has followed me up the wall, and I will die here, and so will Kiri. This is the end.*

But no hatchet falls, nor any sword—only the familiar deep voice of Noro cuts through the night.

"Who has done this?" he says.

I turn, relief washing over me. Noro stands rigid in the shadow of the tower wall, a short sword in his right hand and an axe in his left. There is a man with him, someone I've not seen before; he is older than Noro, and taller, dressed all in black. This, and the telltale cascade of hair angling across one side of his head, marks him clearly as an *inanei*. He is bleeding from both ears.

"Noro!" I say. "How did you—"

"Where is the archer?" he says, his voice like an icy pond.

I point a trembling finger toward the trees. "Joa went after him."

Noro exchanges a glance with the *inanei*. The man nods and says, "I will see her to Eno Zu'n."

Crouching down before Kiri, Noro whispers something I cannot hear. To me, he says nothing. An instant later, he disappears over the side of the wall in a burst of shadow.

The Xoe archer, I surmise, does not have long to live.

CHAPTER 23

✦

THE *INANEI* IS CALLED LETO, AND THOUGH HE MAY be wounded, it does not seem to impede either his strength or his speed. He plucks Kiri from the wall and moves with all haste toward Eno's home. I murmur soft words of reassurance to Kiri, keeping pace beside Leto as we pick our way through the empty streets.

The arrow is a sleek and slender thing, made monstrous by its deceptively delicate appearance. It has gone all the way through Kiri's neck; the shaft must have cracked when she fell backward, and the last four inches of the point end—including the arrowhead—protrude at a grotesque angle. I don't understand how she breathes, but I thank the Maker that she does.

Within minutes, I am pounding on Eno's door. A curtain draws back at the front window; half a second later, the door opens. She steps back and ushers us inside.

"Down the hallway," I say to Leto. "The second room on the right-hand side."

He moves quickly and sets Kiri down on the bed in the healing room while Eno brings in a large lamp.

"Now go," he says. "We will remove the arrow. You do not want to see."

I sit at the edge of the bed and take Kiri's hand in mine. "I will not leave her. Do what you must."

As they make preparations, I smooth Kiri's wet hair away from her face.

"What courage you have," I say, tears in my eyes. "And rightly so, for all will be well soon enough."

"All right," Leto says. "Step aside now."

I give Kiri's hand a squeeze and move away from the bed. The removal of the arrow is quick, but horrifying even so. Eno holds Kiri's head in place while Leto grips the arrow by the shaft and snaps off its feathered tail. Then, in one horrible moment, he draws the arrow through to the other side, out the back of Kiri's neck. Kiri, mercifully, faints.

A slow trickle of blood oozes from the entry wound; Eno wipes it away and begins to clean it at once.

"Very little blood," Leto says. "This is good."

"She will be all right?"

Leto wipes his hands on a towel. "It has missed the artery, but this is no small puncture. Yet Eno knows healing, and the girl is strong. Time will tell."

I feel as though I've taken my first breath in hours. "Thank you, Leto." I put a hand on Eno's shoulder. "And you as well, Eno."

She smiles, but her eyes are on her work. My hope is renewed as I recall the efficiency and expertise with which she healed my own wound.

Leto turns to leave, but stops at the door. "I've seen men five times her size make a bigger fuss," he says with a nod in Kiri's direction. "You tell her I said so."

"I will."

I look down at Kiri's face, so small and pale and still. My sweet Kiri, the girl who brought me bits of shining glass, the one who reminded me every day that life was waiting beyond the bitter walls of my grief.

"You stay strong," I whisper. "Stay strong for Noro. Stay strong for me. You have a long life ahead of you, Kiri Dún."

The night inches along, every hour seeming to stretch out longer than the last. Noro has not returned, and as dawn approaches, his absence becomes more acute. The storm at last has quieted, lessening to a steady fall of rain. I wait in the healing room, my feet curled beneath me in the chair beside Kiri's bed, listening to the patter of water against the window. My heart is full of worry. *Please, Noro...please be safe.*

I glance at Kiri, who sleeps soundly thanks to Eno's potent herbs. At least I have the singular comfort of knowing she is not in pain—though I have noticed during the past hour that a fine beading of sweat has appeared across her brow and upper lip. *Normal. Of course she will have a fever.*

The soft click of the door pulls me from my thoughts, and relief ripples through me as I see Noro step inside. The room is dark, but he carries a slim white candle. He sets the taper into a holder on the table beside the bed, then sits in the chair beside me. I draw in my breath when I see his face: he is bruised, streaked with blood, his lower lip split and swollen on one side.

"Noro," I whisper, "are you all right?"

"How is my sister?"

I flinch at the sharpness of his tone. "She's all right, for now. The arrow didn't pierce anything vital. We must wait and see how she fares against infection."

Noro puts a hand on Kiri's forehead, leaves it there for a moment, then leans back in the chair. He is silent.

"She was very brave," I add. "Even Leto called it to attention."

We sit in awkward silence. Noro does not look at me, nor does he speak.

"Did you find the archer?" I say at length.

"Yes."

"Did you kill him?"

"Yes."

"Good," I say quietly.

Noro leans forward, his dark eyes stormy. "What were you thinking, Vaela?"

"What do you mean?"

"I told you to stay in the cottage!"

"If I had done so, Kiri might have died up there on the wall! You only found her because you saw me in the square. Am I wrong?" He does not answer. "Noro! How can you truly be angry with me?"

"What would you have done if I hadn't seen you?" He shakes his head. "Dragged her down the side of the wall, killed her in the process? She's more than half your weight—you could not have managed it without Leto."

"I would have found a way to help," I say. Kiri shifts onto her side and whimpers, but doesn't wake. I drop my voice to a whisper. "It is not your place to tell me what I can and cannot do, Noro. I am capable of thinking for myself."

His nostrils flare, but he tempers his anger before speaking. "It is by sheer luck that you are alive. Do you even begin to understand that? If a single Xoe had pursued you as you ran across that gateway, if I had not been there—you would be dead, Vaela."

"It was a single Xoe I meant to kill," I say. "That's why I left the cottage in the first place—I thought if I could end the violence of just *one*, I might save many lives. I might save you."

"And how would you accomplish this? You would fling a knife in the dark of night and the driving rain?"

"I would open his throat, exactly as you taught me to do."

"No. You would not have stood a chance against the warriors in Kastenai tonight. If you were not killed outright, you would have been captured, raped, and beaten—kept to be used by any who wanted you." He grips my wrists, his eyes shimmering. "Do you know what the thought of this does to me? To think of you in the hands of such men? It would drive me to madness, Vaela. It is difficult enough to recall the night we met—that *zunupi* by the fire with his filthy hands on you." He curses under his breath.

"Nothing happened, Noro. I'm perfectly fine."

He laughs joylessly. "Nothing happened *today*. They sent perhaps three hundred men—a pittance compared to the forces they have in reserve. Had they not been spotted by the guard, all might have fled. Still, it is safe to assume that many escaped, and that they will return in greater numbers—I daresay it is a certainty. And what will happen when they attack Kastenai in earnest? How will I protect you? How will I protect Kiri?"

"I don't know, Noro."

He leans forward, his shoulders slumping, his head in his hands. "For the first time in my life, I feel sure that the Aven'ei will fall. We have lost the stronghold of the south, and naught but a breath of wind from the west will mark our complete destruction." He looks up at me, defeat in his eyes. "And there is nothing I can do to stop it."

For four days, Kiri burns with a fever so intense, I am afraid that every moment will be her last. But on the fifth morning, the fever breaks—her skin becomes cool, her eyes clear. She does not speak; Eno indicates that she may never do so again, so traumatic was the wound to her throat. But it is not the loss of her voice, nor the weakness of her body after the wasting fever, nor even the humiliation of falling prey to a Xoe arrow—something the old Kiri would have borne with great shame—that renders her utterly despondent. It is Joa's death.

When first she woke, she patted the coverlets with urgency. The question was clear: *Where is Joa?* Noro answered in soft words, telling her of the hound's courageous sacrifice. Kiri wept in silence, her face turned into the pillowcase, this new agony too much to bear.

Afterward, her eyes were dark and still, all of the light in her blown out as though she were a candle in a drafty hall. To see her this way is to suffer a new kind of grief, for although she is now safe from harm, she is *lost*. Joa was her companion and guardian from birth. And now Kiri is alone, or so it seems to her.

When she rises to take her first shaky steps around the yard, I watch from the window, anger growing in my heart. At ten years old, this child has seen more suffering than even the poorest and most infirm citizen of the Spire. And for what? Why do the Xoe come again and again, reveling in their senseless war? More than a hundred Aven'ei were lost in this attack. Must every last one of them be destroyed before there is peace on the Continent?

Kiri stops to rest on the sandstone bench, the same one I sat upon so many months ago. The place where I made peace with my own grief, where I chose to return to the world. What must Kiri feel, wounded and separated from her lifelong friend? What hope will make her choose to come back to us? In this moment, I see the war not as a whole, but in the broken heart of this one child. In her tears I see the blood of her kin, of the hundreds of thousands who are dead and buried. And in her suffering, I make yet another choice—one that I hope will change the fate that seems so clearly written for Kiri and all the rest.

Noro, returning from a meeting with the council, approaches the window. He crosses his arms, frowning as he watches his sister sit silent and alone in the yard.

"I need to go home, Noro," I say.

He nods. "I think the danger is past. Kiri will recover. You should return to the cottage if you like—I will stay with her until she is well enough to leave."

"I don't mean the cottage. I need to go back to the Spire."

From the corner of my eye, I see him stiffen. He turns to me and takes my hand. "Is this because of my words the other night? I am truly sorry for my anger, *miyara*. I was afraid."

I look down to see my fingers wrapped in his. "I would never leave you for so small a thing."

He takes my face in his hands, his eyes searching mine. "Then why? Do you fear the Xoe?"

"I would be a fool if I did not fear the Xoe. But that is not the reason I must go. I hope… I believe there is something that may yet turn the tide of this war."

"Explain."

"You say that the annihilation of your people is imminent— that the Aven'ei can no longer save themselves. I trust your judgment, Noro—I truly believe it is as dire as you say. If you are to survive, you must have help."

"Help," he says, incredulous. "From the Spire?"

"Yes."

"I see. It is your opinion that they will, after two centuries of indifference to the suffering on the Continent, suddenly decide to intervene? Tell me: Why, exactly, would they do this?"

"I will explain how desperate the situation has become."

His jaw clenches. "They already know, Vaela. Their planes have flown overhead for more than a quarter of a century— longer even than I have lived! They have seen it. All of it. And they have done nothing."

"No. They have seen from a distance, with eyes of curiosity and with hearts that have forgotten the true nature of war. It has been generations since blood was shed in battle between the Nations of the Spire. They do not remember. But I can make them remember. They will ally with the Aven'ei. They will."

"How?"

"I will tell them everything that has come to pass since the heli-plane crashed. I know the Chancellor personally—he is a good man, Noro. He will not turn his back. He cannot."

"And what then?"

"Perhaps the Aven'ei would be welcome in the Spire."

He laughs. "All these months in Kastenai, yet you do not see the roots that bind us here? This is our home. The Aven'ei will never leave the Continent, even if our destruction is the price."

"I thought you would say as much. If you will not be compelled to leave, then we must find another way."

"Your people have no armies. No fighting force of any kind. What other way can there be?"

"I don't know," I say, looking up at him. "But I must find out. An alliance, in a way, is a thing of peace. They must embrace it."

He gives me a sad smile. "Go then, *miyara*. But do not waste your breath in petition for the Aven'ei—and do not return here. Stay in the Spire, where you are safe. Go back and *live*."

I kiss him softly. "Oh, Noro. I would never be parted from you. I give you my word that I will return, whether there be peace on the Continent or no."

CHAPTER 24

✦

THE SILENCE IN THE WAR ROOM IS PALPABLE. There is a distinct air of dissension. Yet no one—not Nadu, Kinza, nor even Shovo—has spoken since I put forth the specifics of my plan.

At length, it is Nadu who finally responds. "We appreciate your good intentions, Vaela Sun, but the situation here in Kastenai has become dire. We need every man and woman available to us at this time—the Xoe may be on the march even now. Our scouts are vigilant, but they cannot see all. Even a Xoe horde may progress unseen for many miles."

"I understand your position," I say. "But with such a pressing threat, mightn't it be wise to seek help while you still can?"

Nadu gives me a patient smile. "If I thought the Four Nations would offer such help, I would be inclined to agree."

"I don't know," Kinza says. "I think we should consider it."

If Nadu is surprised, he does not show it. "Speak freely then, sister. Tell me why we should do this thing."

"The Xoe have pressed our backs against the sea, Nadu. It is a matter of time now—nothing more. They will not rest until every last one of us is gone."

"I do not believe it is so hopeless as that."

Kinza's jaw tightens. "Then you are unwilling to see what is plain before you."

Nadu frowns. "Do you doubt my leadership?"

"I only feel that we must decide these matters with open eyes. Vigilance and pride did not protect us against this recent attack—"

"Yet we prevailed," Nadu interjects.

"Because we had the greater numbers!" Kinza says, her face shadowed with emotion. "My scouts report that the Xoe in the southern camps are six thousand strong—six *thousand*, Nadu. A fraction of the full strength of the Aven'ei, but still, this village would crumble before such a force."

"We have gathered neighbors to our breast, Kinza. We have doubled our scouts, and we are fortifying our defenses. We communicate daily with the villages to the north and south. We do all we can."

Kinza shakes her head. "It will not be enough. Surely you must see the truth."

"I see that you are defeated," Nadu says, "before a single blow has been struck."

"Send her to the Four Nations," Kinza insists. "Let us turn over every stone, and we may yet survive."

Nadu is silent for a moment. He turns to Shovo, who sits with his arms crossed, a bored expression on his face. "What say you, Shovo? You are never without an opinion."

Shovo glances up at him. "I say we send the girl away."

"You think the Four Nations will come to our assistance?"

Shovo blinks, and then laughs so hard, and for so long, that the rest of us stare at him in awkward, bewildered silence.

"Oh," he finally says, rubbing a knuckle over each eye. "I think it more likely that the Xoe will come for tea. Come now. We've had trouble and nothing more since the girl arrived. Put the little curse in a boat and send her home—we will be well rid of her."

Nadu frowns. "You bring dishonor to yourself each time you open your mouth."

"I am entitled to my opinion, just as you are."

"What is the harm in seeking allies?" Kinza snaps. "Are you so proud that you would refuse help if it were offered?"

"And what then, sister in arms?" Shovo says, leaning forward. "If all goes according to plan—the Nations rally with the Aven'ei—what then? What will they expect in exchange for their assistance? Will they demand a role in our government? Will they move to control us? Change us? Destroy us if we do not capitulate to any terms they might set down?"

"History bears that the Four Nations have never sought to achieve any such thing."

"*Ancient* history, Kinza." He nods in my direction. "These Spirians have had two hundred years to reconsider what they might gain from the Continent."

"A valid point," Nadu says.

"The Spire would *never*—" I say, but Nadu holds up a hand.

"Two on this council are inclined to send you to the Four Nations, Vaela Sun—though for disparate reasons, to be sure." He sighs, his shoulders slumping slightly—an uncharacteristic bearing for him. "For my part, I feel the venture is not worth the risk—either to the village, or to you and Noro."

Noro leans forward. "There is little danger where we are concerned, Nadu. It will take a day to reach the coast, and we shall spend another at sea. The journey would comprise a few days' time at most."

Nadu regards him thoughtfully. "You would escort her to the island and return at once?"

"At once."

"The distance in sailing does not trouble you? Or the last breath of the *kazuri ko'ra*?"

"One mile upon the sea is much like any other, and we are near enough to autumn," Noro says. "The fishing grounds are

ten miles out—we need to travel thirty. It is not so great a distance, and the vessels are swift."

Nadu makes a small noise of assent. "It does seem less formidable a thing, when you phrase it this way." He glances back
and forth between Noro and I. "And the two of you are willing to be parted?"

Noro leans back, relaxing a bit. "I wish to put as much distance as possible between Vaela and the Continent."

Nadu smiles at this, though sadly. "Very well, then. You will
go, Vaela Sun, with my blessing and with the fastest vessel the
two of you can manage. But waste no time. You must leave tomorrow, for Noro is needed here, with those whose very lives
depend on him. In the meanwhile, Kinza and I will convene
with every strategist we might gather. We will do what we can.
I, for one, do not believe all is lost, with or without the help of
the Four Nations."

The following morning, I wait in the sitting room at Eno's
while Noro shares a private farewell with his sister. The soft
murmur of Noro's voice hums through the wall, steady and
soothing. Even so, I am restless, frustrated by the timing of all
that has come to pass. I hate to leave Kiri behind, especially so
soon after her injury, but I must take this opportunity to see if
the Spire can help. I hope she will understand.

After a few minutes, Noro appears around the corner. "She
wants to see you. But be warned—she is angry."

In the healing room, Kiri sits cross-legged on the bed, her
face turned toward the window. A clean white bandage encir-
cles her neck—a chilling reminder of how nearly we lost her.
She glances at me as I enter, hurt and frustration in her eyes. I
sit on the edge of the bed and take her hands in mine.

"I shall miss you very much," I say. "But I will return as soon
as I can, and hopefully with very good news."

She shakes her head and jerks her hands away, a tear sliding down her cheek. She wipes angrily at her face and turns away.

"Kiri…" My heart aches at her distance, at the darkness that surrounds her. If I could mend her hurts, if I could wind back the clock and prevent Joa's death, if I could take Kiri's pain as my own, I would do so without a second thought. But I can do none of these things—I cannot even stay to help her as she once helped me. I put my arms around her and pull her close. "I will come back, sweet one. I do love you so."

She leans against my shoulder, weeping freely now. I rock her in my arms, resting my cheek atop her head, shattered by her suffering. Noro calls to me from the door, but I ignore him. How can I let go? How can I let go when Kiri is so broken, and so very alone?

"Vaela," Noro says softly. "We must be on our way if we are to reach the coast by nightfall."

I kiss the top of Kiri's head and get to my feet. After a moment's thought, I unclasp the chain about my neck and place the necklace—long since repaired, and with its precious ruby pendant—in her hands. She looks at me in surprise, her face still wet with tears. She examines the stone carefully, turning it over in her palm.

"Ansana," I say. "You know this word?"

She nods, her eyes still on the pendant.

"Love, family, forever," I say. "Think of me when you feel alone, Kiri. And know that you are not."

We depart near ten o' clock, leaving through the village gates and moving back along the walls toward the coast. The air is crisp and cool, the weather fine. Soon, the leaves will turn to russet and gold, and the chill of autumn will embrace the Continent. But for now, for our journey, the last sigh of summer promises fair temperatures and quick travel.

As I follow Noro along the rocky, winding path that will

lead us to the sea, I cannot help but to reflect upon how different this journey is from our last. The landscape has changed, of course—the snow is long since melted, while the trees and flowers now bloom in great profusion. But it is more than that.

On that last terrible crossing, my every step was taken in a haze of shock and grief. And though this journey bears its own share of sadness, there is also great joy to be found. It is the small things that bring me such happiness, bittersweet though it is: taking a meal in the sunshine near the base of a roaring waterfall, rainbows sparkling in the mist and spray; a small smile from Noro as he turns back to make sure that I am near; the laughter and easy conversation we share as we walk.

A part of me wishes he could accompany me to the Spire— how lovely it would be, under different circumstances, to show him all the wonders of my former life. But of course, he cannot be spared. And as we near the great cliffs of the eastern sea, the reality of our imminent parting stabs at me with ragged strokes. This will be our last night together. Tomorrow, we shall sail to Ivanel, and Noro will return to the Continent without me. I can hardly bear the thought.

"Come, Vaela," he calls from a few feet ahead, oblivious to my meditations. "We are nearly there."

I smile and hurry along to join him. The terrain begins to slope gently uphill, giving way at last to a flat field of reddish-brown grass that leads all the way to the edge of the cliff.

I stand at the precipice, feeling as though I have discovered the end of the world itself. The sea below glimmers in the faltering sunlight, breakers rolling into the rocky shoreline in graceful, golden curves. A small harbor, dotted with gleaming white sails, is visible about a mile to the north.

Noro moves behind me, wraps his arms about my waist, and places a soft kiss on the nape of my neck. A familiar warmth spreads through me, a mixture of love, desire, and contentment.

He pulls me closer. "It is beautiful, no?"

"Yes," I say. "I only wish we could stay."

"I wish this too." He turns me around and gazes down at me, tracing my lips with his fingertip. "How I will miss you, *miyara*."

He kisses me, gently at first, and then with an urgency that makes my heart ache. Tears slip down my cheeks and I cling to him, the world dissolving into the merest, faintest memory. The sinking sun surrenders unto darkness, the waves crash upon the rocks below. Only Noro and I remain, lost to the bliss and agony of love.

CHAPTER 25

✦

A SALTED BREEZE AND A SPILL OF PALE YELLOW light announce the coming of dawn, but I have been awake for some time. I lie curled in Noro's arms beneath a heavy blanket, watching as the last few stars wink out of sight in the hazy morning sky. I would stay like this for a hundred years, if only it were possible.

But the world does not stand still for those who wish it so, and soon enough Noro begins to stir, breaking the spell. He plants a sleepy kiss on my cheek and gets up to kindle a fire, prepare our breakfast, and begin the day.

We are quiet this morning, and quick to depart. As we leave our makeshift camp, I follow Noro down a little trail that leads to a pathway carved into the cliffside. The path meanders ever downward at a gentle grade, and though it is not steep, it is treacherous. The steps and ledges are narrow at best, gapped at worst, and I hold my breath as I pick my way to the bottom.

When at last we reach the shore, my relief is almost a tangible thing—and I cannot help but to marvel at the magnificence of the beach, which is darkly beautiful with miles of glittering black sand stretching out in either direction. To the south, great jagged rocks jut out from the sea, forming a breakwater of sorts that serves to protect the small marina. Wooden docks stretch over the water, with a fleet of sailing ships moored alongside. The boats are small, sloop-rigged vessels—larger than the pleasure craft I have sailed upon, yet not nearly as big as the commercial fishing boats of the Spire.

I wait near the shore as Noro makes arrangements with a man at one of the docks. The Aven'ei looks none too pleased about sending one of his vessels to an island that, in his likely opinion, probably does not exist. He glances my way a few times, a sour expression on his face. Finally, after ten minutes or so, he points to the far end of the harbor and returns to his work.

"Is it settled then?" I ask, as Noro returns.

"Yes. Though I can't say he ever expects to see his boat again. He did indicate that the winds have been blowing strong and true these past few days—we ought to reach your island within four or five hours, I should say."

"So quickly?" I say, surprised. "I thought it would take the better part of the day."

"No—and I'm glad, for my return trip will be easier if I do not have to sail after dark. The stars are trusty, but daylight is a certain comfort."

I look out over the sea, shielding my eyes from the bright morning sun. "I know you've said the Aven'ei do not sail for pleasure—nor venture very far out to sea—but still, I can't help but wonder how no one has ever happened upon the island by chance. Particularly if your vessels are capable of such speed."

Noro shrugs. "The Aven'ei hold no love for the ocean, Vaela. We sail to fish, and our fishing grounds lie to the north. Your island is far to the south and east—we have no purpose there."

I scan the sailboats nearest the shore, feeling a twinge of nerves. "But the vessels are quite seaworthy?"

"They are the only boats on the Continent, at least to my knowledge," he replies, pragmatic as always. "But I believe they

will serve just fine. Thirty miles is not so great a distance, especially in fair weather."

I nod. "Right. Well. I suppose we ought to be on our way
then."

He looks at me curiously. "Are you having second thoughts?"

"No," I say. "Well...no." I look back at the cliffs, at the
sprawling beach, at this strange and beautiful place I have come
to love. "I just find it hard to leave, now that it comes to it."

"It is for the best," he says, and gives me a smile that does not
reach his eyes. "Now let us go, before your sweet, sentimental
heart works to change your mind."

Noro is a handy sailor, managing the sheets and sails with
very little help from me. He moves fore and aft, his eyes on the
horizon, his hands working the rigging with practiced ease.
Since he spent his first ten years in the seaside village just north
of the marina, the mechanics of sailing and navigation are as
natural to him as breathing. And though he claims not to enjoy
his time upon the sea—he insists that no Aven'ei does—I sense
a relaxation in him that I have not seen before. Out here, upon
the ocean, we are beyond reach of all the things that strive to
tear us apart. There is but wind and water, sun and sky, Noro
and myself.

As Noro predicted, we are within sight of the island in less
than five hours. I sit in the bow, kissed by the salty spray as the
sloop cuts across the water. And as the great cliffs of Ivanel loom
larger and larger, my heart grows heavier. Noro and I will soon
be parted. My throat tightens as I turn to look at him; in his
smile, I can see that his thoughts mirror my own.

When we round the island and come to the little bay at the
rear, a knot forms in my stomach. How different Ivanel appears
in the summertime; how lush and warm and inviting, and how
familiar it seems to me, though this is only the second time I've
seen the shoreline. Mr. Cloud's fishing boat is tied to a post near

the shore; it bobs to and fro in the gentle swell, and I am heart-
ened by the sight of it, remembering the Director's warm bright
eyes and his habit of carrying bread for the Achelons. I wonder
if he is here, or if he has returned to the Spire.

A momentary panic grips me—wait—what if there is no one
here? I have not seen a single heli-plane since I was captured
by the Xoe those many months ago. Why should the Spire occupy this island, if not for the purpose of facilitating the tours?

The more I think on this, the more logical it seems that we
shall find the island abandoned, and the more stupid I feel for
not having considered it earlier. What then? And *how* could this
not have occurred to me before?

Noro secures our vessel to the post and steps out into the shal-
low water. He extends a hand, gesturing for me to climb down.
"Come to me, Vaela. I will carry you ashore."

I climb into his arms, feeling like a distressed princess in one
of Raia's adventure novels. *And the gallant warrior bore the maiden
safely to the shore, where he kissed her with the passion and brilliance of
a thousand suns. From that day forward, they lived a life of love eternal
and happiness unceasing.*

I smile to myself as he carries me through the water, looking into his face as he sloshes through the soft white foam. He
glances down at me and frowns, then sets me on the wet sand
out of reach of the lapping waves.

"Do not look at me that way, *miyara*. You make this harder
than it already is."

"I can't help it."

He takes my hand. "Our parting will come soon enough. Let
us not endure it twice."

I swallow. "It's this way," I say, gesturing toward the winding path that curves away from the shore. The path where once
I walked with Aaden, when my parents still lived. How strange
it is to be here with Noro. How very much has changed since
that frosty winter day.

★ ★ ★

Standing outside the facility, it is plain to see that Noro is impressed by the size and workmanship of the building. He runs a palm along the smooth beveled glass of the entrance door, then takes a step back and cranes his neck to see the full length of the vast outer wall.

"Is it as you expected?" I ask.

"It is very…large."

I laugh. "It is, at that. And it contains many marvelous things, you know."

"Such as?"

I tick off the amenities on my fingers. "An indoor swimming pool, two racquet courts, electric heating, cedar saunas, and, of course, *toilets*."

He makes a face. "You and your *toilets*."

I push experimentally on the door handle; there is a soft click, and the door opens slightly.

"Well," I say, "it's unlocked, at least. Shall we go in?"

He follows me inside, gaping at the enormous glass dome above the lobby. "What a thing to build into a roof," he says, a note of admiration in his voice. "The craftsmen in the Spire must be very ambitious indeed."

At that moment, Mr. Cloud comes striding into the room from the far hallway; he drops a handful of papers at the sight of us, his mouth falling open in surprise.

"Hello, Mr. Cloud," I say politely, hurrying forward to help him gather his paperwork. "Might you remember me? I am Vaela Sun."

"Miss…Sun?" he says, his blue-white eyes goggling, either in disbelief or due to my changed appearance. "But how? You were lost! You were all…lost!"

"Not all," I say quietly.

"I shouldn't believe it if my own eyes didn't tell me true," he murmurs. He looks at Noro as if noticing him for the first time, and pulls himself up sharply to his full, staggering height. "And who is this? Are you held captive by this individual, Miss Sun?"

"Only in my most willing heart, Mr. Cloud. May I introduce to you Noro Dún, who rescued me from dire circumstances after the heli-plane crashed, and whose people, the Aven'ei, welcomed me with open arms and great compassion."

Mr. Cloud is astonished by this admission, his expression altering from suspicion to open curiosity almost instantaneously.

"An honored guest, then," he says, and bows. "Welcome to our facility, Noro Dún."

Noro smiles. "Are you certain that the Spire would welcome one such as me?"

"As to that, I cannot say," Mr. Cloud replies. "But we are not in the Spire, now, are we?"

"I suppose not," Noro says. "I thank you, then, for your hospitality."

"How extraordinary," Mr. Cloud says. "In my life, I never thought to meet... Surely you will stay a night or two here at Ivanel?"

"I thank you for the invitation, but I must return to the Continent."

"Are you certain?" Mr. Cloud says, clearly dismayed. "You have only just arrived! Why the hurry?"

"The urgency is mine," I say, though it pains me to think of sending Noro on his way. "I wish to return to the Spire with all haste, if it can be managed."

Mr. Cloud nods emphatically. "Of course. Of course, Miss Sun. Mr. Dún—you must at least allow us to deliver you back to your people. We can prepare the heli-plane in no time at all—"

"Thank you, no," Noro says. "I would prefer to return in my own vessel."

"Oh, but it's perfectly safe, I assure you," Mr. Cloud says, then covers his mouth with his left hand. "Oh, Miss Sun, forgive me! I don't know how I could have said such a thing!"

"Do not think of it, sir," I say. "I know you meant no offense."

"Well," Mr. Cloud says, "I will alert the other staff that you are here. Only a few of us are left now, put in charge of closing down the facility. The tours have been discontinued indefinitely, of course. Another month or so and you might have missed us entirely."

I give him a smile. "It sounds like we are most fortunate to have found you still in residence."

"All right, then," Mr. Cloud says, nodding, determination in his eyes. "I will see to the arrangements at once. It was an honor to have met you, sir—I only wish we had the luxury of time and conversation."

Mr. Cloud bows deeply, then hurries back toward the hallway from which he came.

I turn to Noro, my heart heavy in my chest.

"Not here," he says. "Let us say our goodbye out of doors, beneath the sun and sky."

In the field overlooking the sea, I sit beside Noro on a bench of stone. I know he must not linger; I know he must go while the weather is fine and the wind is strong. I know this. But I cannot bring myself to say goodbye.

"How lovely you look, sitting here in the sunshine," Noro says. He smiles, but his eyes are full of sadness. "I can never decide if you are most beautiful in the light of day, or in the starlit shadows of the night. It must simply be that you are lovelier with every passing moment."

"Noro," I say, but I can manage no other words. Tears roll down my cheeks, and I begin to sob.

"Do not cry, *miyara*. I love you—I will love you always. In the moment of my death, it will be your face that brings me peace."

"Don't speak of such things!" I say. "You will live a long life, with me beside you."

"Vaela, you must not return to the Continent."

"Noro, stop!"

"I cannot lose you to the Xoe. Promise me that you will not come back."

I wipe the tears from my eyes and shake my head. "I would never make such a promise. Oh, Noro, have you no hope at all that the Spire will choose to ally with the Aven'ei?"

He smooths a lock of hair away from my cheek, tucking it behind my ear. "I hope for you to live a long, happy life."

"Then do not forbid me from doing so."

He sighs. "I wish you would do as I ask, but I know you will not." He stands, pulling me to my feet. "I must go."

"I know." I kiss his cheek, his forehead, his lips. "Let us not say goodbye. Let us only say that we love one another, and part with words of promise and possibility."

"I love you, Vaela."

"And I love you. With every breath, in every moment. And I will see you soon."

He turns toward the bay, his fingers slipping from mine, and heads down the path. He does not look back.

CHAPTER 26

✦

MR. CLOUD IS NOTHING IF NOT EFFICIENT. BY THE time I return to the facility, he has telephoned the Chancellery with the news of my return, instructed the pilot in residence to make ready the heli-plane, and directed the kitchen to prepare a four-course meal preceding my departure. The food is lavish, all rich, sumptuous Spirian delicacies—but after my emotional farewell with Noro, it might as well be made of ash. I taste nothing, eat little, and weep alone at the table.

Poor Mr. Cloud has a thousand questions for me; I can see it in his face. But he does not ask. He is ever the picture of grace, moving quietly about his business and pretending not to notice my distress. When it is time to leave, he accompanies me through the long hallway to the hangar.

"I can come along if you like, Miss Sun," he says, as he helps me up the metal stairway and into the heli-plane. "Unless you prefer to be alone."

I look around the cabin, feeling as though I have fallen into some terrible dream. The interior is identical to the plane we took from the Spire. Echoes of the past surround me, crushing the very breath from my body—my father gazing out the window in the back row, my mother sitting beside me, squeezing my hand in excitement. Aaden calling to me from across the aisle. *Come here, Vaela. You can look out my window.*

"No," I whisper, turning back to Mr. Cloud. "I do not wish to be alone."

He shouts a word of instruction to the steward in the hangar below, steps aboard the plane, and pulls the door shut behind him.

"You make yourself comfortable, Miss Sun. I'll let the pilot know we're all set."

He disappears into the cockpit, and I turn to face the three rows of seating. Where can I sit that will not evoke some painful memory? Which of these spaces does not hold the ghost of someone I once knew, someone I once loved?

"Is everything all right?" says Mr. Cloud from behind me.

"Fine," I say, pressing forward and sitting down in the front row on the starboard side. *Mr. Shaw sat here*, I think to myself. *Dear Mr. Shaw, ever at the beck and call of his beloved wife. How lucky she was to be adored by such a man. To live and die with him. Such a disagreeable woman, yet so loved. How does that happen?*

Mr. Cloud takes his seat on the opposite side of the aisle, and a moment later, the great doors of the hangar roll open. As the heliplane moves smoothly into position to address the runway, a rush of heat flows over my skin—my face, in particular, feels practically aflame. The sensation is so unexpected—and so intense— that I somehow feel quite certain that I am about to die, or go mad, or *something*. I swallow, the taste of fear like a bitter tang in my mouth. In my panic, I find myself gasping.

"Miss Sun! Miss Sun! Are you all right?"

My vision blurred, I blink to see a double image of Mr. Cloud kneeling before me, his twin faces each a portrait of concern.

"Please," I say, grasping for his hands. "I'm afraid. Please." I don't know what I am asking for, but I feel as though my heart may beat directly out of my chest, and all I can determine is that I need help.

He moves to the seat beside me and puts his arm around my shoulder, drawing me close, just the way my father might have done. "There, there, sweet girl. You just breathe now. Breathe. Deep breaths in, deep breaths out. Everything will be all right."

The heli-plane is picking up speed, bright sunlight flickering into the cabin as we race toward takeoff. I squeeze my eyes shut, clutching Mr. Cloud's soft blue sweater so tightly that the wool is wound around my fingers. The sound of the engine fills my ears, the gentle vibration moves through every fiber of my body.

The plane takes to the sky, and I faint.

I revive a short while later, sitting up with a start when I realize where I am. Mr. Cloud is still beside me; I realize with some embarrassment that I have been resting against his shoulder for an indeterminate amount of time. My mouth is open and his sweater is wet with drool, a fact I note with supreme humiliation.

I rub my temples, my head in a fog. "How long have I been asleep?"

"Oh, not long," he says. "Twenty minutes or so. You had a bit of a shock, that's all. Are you feeling better?"

"I don't know," I say honestly.

"Well. It's all quite understandable."

I look out the window to see the deep blue sea spreading out below in all directions. "The Continent is behind us then?"

"Yes, my dear. You're on your way home."

Home. What a curious word, and a fickle one.

"Actually," I say, "I intend to return to the Continent as soon as I have met with the Chancellery and asked for their assistance."

Mr. Cloud gapes at me. "You wish to…I'm sorry, of what assistance do you speak?"

I look carefully at him. "Do I have your word, sir, that what I say will stay between us? I should not like for anything I share to be revealed before I have the opportunity to speak with the Heads of State."

"But of course, Miss Sun," he says, looking a bit wounded. "I would not betray your trust for any purpose."

I give him a smile. "I believe you. I only wanted to clarify that what I say must be held in confidence, at least for the time being."

"On my honor, I shall reveal nothing."

"Then it is well we have a long flight ahead of us, for I have much to tell you."

Mr. Cloud is a keen listener, absorbing every detail of my story with rapt attention. When I have told it all, he sits back, wonder and sadness alike mingled in his expression.

"I had no idea things were so bad on the Continent," he says. "I mean, we all knew the Xoe had become more aggressive—their movements into the south were tracked with great interest by the tour pilots. But to think that the Aven'ei are now in peril of being utterly destroyed—what a terrible predicament. What a terrible predicament indeed."

"I am relieved to hear you say so, Mr. Cloud. It gives me great hope that the Heads of State will prove to be as thoughtful and compassionate as yourself."

"Well," he says, looking uncomfortable, "I think you have a fair challenge ahead of you there."

"But I shall tell them all that I have told you—why should they respond any differently?"

He gives me an apologetic smile. "I am a man of business, of logistics, Miss Sun. I am no politician. The folks in the Chancellery—no disrespect intended—well, they tend to have a different way of seeing things than a regular fellow might do, even one in a position such as mine."

"Is there another way to see this situation? Can there be any other answer but to offer assistance?"

"If the Aven'ei will not emigrate, as you say, I don't see any way that the Spire can help."

I look out the window, squeezing my arms against my chest. "I hope you are wrong."

"And perhaps I am. What do I know of such matters?"

I turn back to him. "You are the Facilities Director of the only place in the world from which to make contact with the Continent. You likely know more about the place than anyone else. And so I ask you, Mr. Cloud: If it were in your hands, what choice would you make?"

He straightens, his chin coming up slightly. "Well, if it were up to me, I should take up a sword myself to defend those in difficulties—whether Aven'ei or Xoe. But alas, I have no influence in such matters, or skill with a weapon, nor any right to speak against the rule of the Spire."

This last point perplexes me. "Haven't you? Oughtn't we to be free to go against the Treaty, if it proves to be fallible?"

"Oh, no, miss. The Spire has kept us safe for an absolute age—not a single drop of blood shed in battle for a hundred and ninety-seven years. That's saying quite a lot, don't you think?"

"It says a great deal. I would never deny the significance of the peace we enjoy—I only question whether it is right to wrap ourselves within it and turn a blind eye to the suffering of those less fortunate."

He nods. "It is a fair question. But I, for one, would have great difficulty in putting it to those who govern."

"Well, I mean to ask, but that is all I can do. It is up to the Nations of the Spire whether or not to offer an alliance. I only hope they will listen as you have done."

CHAPTER 27

◆

THE SCENT OF URBAN LIFE ACCOSTS ME AS I STEP once more onto Spirian soil: fuel, cleaning products, asphalt wet with recent rain—things almost forgotten, but suddenly and intrusively familiar. As I look around the hangar where once I departed for the Continent with my family, I can feel grief pulling at me; my heart beats as though it is on the precipice of breaking once again. Mr. Cloud has informed me that arrangements were made so that I might spend the night in my former home. The house has been silent and empty all these months, the estate having been held in trust by the Chancellery and not yet sold. Hasty preparations were made this morning to clean the property and employ a full complement of servants before my arrival, but I wish the house were empty; I know it will be grievously difficult to face the memories within, and I am loath to be surrounded by strangers. *A while longer*, I tell myself. *Just hold on awhile longer.*

There is no one waiting to greet us; the Chancellor and the Heads of State are en route from the West and other regions, but will not arrive until tomorrow. It is just as well; I am not quite prepared to meet with them, and it has been a long, exhausting day.

After my episode of panic aboard the heli-plane, Mr. Cloud seems unwilling to leave my side. He accompanies me on the drive to the estate, chattering mildly and relating various articles of recent news. As the car winds its way along familiar streets, his voice grows distant; I watch through the window, pieces and places of my former life flickering past like fragments of a dream that has been suddenly remembered. We pass by my former school, as well as the grand, sprawling mansion of Otto Sussenfaal, the cartographer who was to be my mentor. And when we finally inch through the gates and pull into the long drive leading up to my parents' home, it is all I can do to keep my tears at bay.

The car slows to a stop and a footman opens the door, extending a hand to assist me. How strange this formality seems after so many months on the Continent—how unnecessary the proffered help for a task so trivial. Certainly I can step out of the car by myself. Yet I reach for his hand automatically, exiting the vehicle with practiced grace. Perhaps there is something left of the Spire within me after all. This idea moves against me like a rubbing, grating thing. I let go of the footman's hand and hold my fist tightly against my side.

"No luggage, miss?" he says, casting a surreptitious glance at my clothing, and at the single black satchel slung over my back. I suspect he has never seen anything quite like the garb and accoutrements of the Aven'ei.

"None at all," I say. "Thank you kindly."

Mr. Cloud, standing beside me on the cobbled drive, stares up at the house with a deep crease between his brows. "Are you quite sure you want to stay here tonight, Miss Sun? It certainly wasn't my idea, I only told them to make arrangements for you to—"

"It's fine, Mr. Cloud. I have many happy memories of this home." *And each is breaking my heart.*

"Well. I've given the staff my number—I'm stopping at the

hotel down by the Chancellery, the great tall one with all the windows—and I will be happy to see you removed from the house if you find it too…well, too painful to stay the night. I have been appointed to manage your transportation to and from the city—so let me know if you need anything at all. It is my pleasure, of course. The Chancellery would prefer you to travel by car, and stay off the trains. A driver will come round at eight o'clock sharp to collect you in the morning."

"Very well. Will you wish me luck with the officials?"

He gives me a wry grin. "Politicians don't believe in luck."

I laugh, though the sound is brittle. "Nor do I, now I come to think of it."

"Good," he says. He hesitates for a moment, then adds, "May I offer a piece of advice?"

"I welcome anything you have to say, Mr. Cloud, at any time."

"Don't let the folks in the Chancellery see you fixed up like this," he says, indicating my attire. "You want them to see you as an equal. If you stroll in dressed like an Aven'ei, those black-robed swells will think…well, they won't see you in the proper light. Prejudice has a way of digging in deep, and I daresay the Heads of State have a bit of a superiority complex."

"You've made an incisive point. I shall wear my Spirian finest, though the idea irritates me to no end. Thank you, sir. Once again, you have done me a great service."

He returns my smile, the corners of his eyes crinkling up into a crisscross of fine lines. "Whether it be worthwhile or no, I say good luck to you, Miss Sun. The sentiment, at least, has merit. Wouldn't you say?"

"It does indeed, and I thank you."

He nods. "Tell it true, and they will listen, the Maker willing."

"The Maker willing," I repeat, in the traditional Spirian ending to any number of prayers. "And may He bless the future with His infinite grace."

★ ★ ★

I close the front door behind me as I step into my childhood home. My eyes sweep over the entrance hall, so familiar and strange all at once. Everything appears exactly as it did on the day we left for the Continent. The lights are lit. The exquisite crimson rug that my mother purchased in the North stretches out along the marble floor of the foyer, not a stray piece of lint or speck of dust to be seen upon it. My father's precious ornamental vases are gleaming and immaculate upon the entry console. My map of the Continent hangs above the fireplace in the sitting room beyond.

An elderly man, looking prim and distinguished in his butler's uniform, comes through from the dining room and stops abruptly. "Miss Sun! My apologies, I ought to have been here to greet you—we weren't expecting you quite so soon. Please, may I take your..." He trails off, observing that I have neither coat nor traveling trunk. He clears his throat. "Well. Do you have a mind for a late supper, or do you wish to retire?" His eyes flick down to my tunic, then back to my face. "I can call the housemaid to run a bath, if you like."

"Thank you, no—I'm not hungry, and I wish to be alone. I shall tend to myself this evening."

He looks relieved, as though he had not been entirely sure how best to serve an eccentric mistress dressed in strange, dirty clothing. "Please ring if you need anything at all."

"I will."

He returns to the dining room; a moment later, the soft clink of porcelain is to be heard. I assume he is making sure that the breakfast dishes are properly arranged; he does seem a fastidious sort, though a bit cold for my liking. Our former butler, Mr. Kincaid, wouldn't have batted an eye had I showed up dressed like a jester all in motley, much less in the muddy, sweat-stained garments I wear now. He would merely have welcomed me and insisted I take a meal. I wonder where Mr. Kincaid is now. I wonder if he mourned for my parents, and for me.

I move to the end of the foyer, my eyes fixed on the map above the mantel. I remember so clearly the weight of it in my hands as I took it from the box at my birthday party, how silky the smooth wood felt against my fingers. What a beautiful object it was to me once—a triumph of hard work and long hours. Yet what a black thing it seems now, the mark of death woven into its very fibers. Had I never drawn it, my parents might have lived. They might have *lived*. But this is a rumination of futility. My mother and father are gone, and nothing will bring them back.

As though compelled by these morbid thoughts, I turn down the hallway to my right: the long corridor that leads to the family bedrooms. I walk slowly, absorbing each of the portraits along the walls, delicate brushstrokes long forgotten returning to my memory. I come to a halt as I reach the two doors—both closed—at the end of the hall. To the right is my own bedroom, to the left is the suite that belonged to my parents. After a moment's hesitation, I face my parents' door, take the cold knob in my hand, and turn it slowly.

The room is dark and deathly quiet. I switch on the lights and feel a stab of desolation; everything is so clean, so orderly, so normal, that I half expect my mother to enter from the washroom, absentmindedly tying the belt of her dressing gown into a delicate bow. *Why, Vaela!* she would say, looking at me in surprise. *What are you doing up so late?*

Her voice was once so clear in my mind, but the memory of it is fading with time, a thought that both pains and terrifies me. What if I should forget her? What if I should forget my father? The people we love may live on in our recollections and impressions, but so much is lost. Already, my memories are not as vibrant as once they were—how I wish I could hold each one in my heart forever, safe and perfect and true.

I cross the room and lie down on the bed. The smooth fabric of the coverlet rustles beneath me as I slide to the far side, where I reach for my mother's pillow. I clutch it to my breast and press my cheek against it, inhaling deeply, but the freshly laundered case retains no trace of the jasmine perfume she always wore. Still, the memory of the scent lingers in my mind, and I find great comfort in this.

I turn onto my back, hugging the pillow to my chest, staring up at the crimson silks draped above the bed. Tears come at last, along with the wrenching agony of grief. I bury my face in the coverlet, weeping as though all I have lost has only just been taken from me. My fingers dig into the stiff fabric of the pillow; my heart sings with torment. My pain has not been so fresh, so sharp, since those first weeks in the healing room at Eno's, but now it is as though my loss is perfectly new. I cry and cry, my face wet and flushed, and I mourn once again for my mother and father and the life I once knew.

How very, very long this day has been. Was it truly only this morning that I set sail for Ivanel with Noro? I think of the map rolled tightly in my bag—a new map, much like the one I drew for the Aven'ei council—yet far more complete. It is not delicate and detailed like the work I might have completed as an apprentice cartographer, not drawn in the Astor Library with fine, expensive ink pens, but forged in the lamplight of the Continent with a slim goose quill. It is tactical, concise, and as accurate as I could make it from memory. Everything—everything—hinges on this map.

I hope the Spire will not fail the Aven'ei.

CHAPTER 28

✦

IN THE GRAND HALL OF THE CHANCELLERY, I watch as great silvery clouds gather beyond the gilded half-dome windows. The world has gone gray, and with the turn of the weather, some measure of my hope has diminished. I find it difficult to be cheerful in the gloom; even the bulbs in the chandeliers seem to burn white and cold, casting the corners of the vast hall in stark shadows.

I am seated at a slender table opposite the four Heads of State, waiting for the Chancellor to arrive. The officials—three men and one woman—are dressed in the black robes of government office; I wear a floor-length dress of ivory silk, accented from top to bottom with translucent blue beads. An awful choice in regard to the weather, perhaps, but even the stuffy old butler at the estate seemed impressed as I swept through the foyer on my way out the door.

The officials are, from left to right: Mr. Lowe, of the North, a man with pale-blue eyes, a complexion of darkest brown, and with a crackling sort of energy about him; Mr. Wey, of the East, a scholarly fellow of advanced years who wears a pair of crusty-looking silver spectacles at the tip of his nose; Mr. Chamberlain, of the South, a pallid, sickly-looking man with a slender mustache and watery eyes; and Mrs. Pendergrast, of the West, bronzed by the sun, who might look lively except for the fact that she appears to have spent most of her life sucking on a sour candy—even the smile she mustered when I first arrived had a sort of miserable, acidic quality to it. She could be the polar opposite of the sweet-faced Mr. Lowe, and indeed, I notice that the two of them never so much as glance at one another.

A steward passing through the Hall clears his throat, and the sound seems to fill the wide, mostly empty chamber. A moment later, the entrance clock chimes nine and the Chancellor emerges from his offices at the west side of the room.

I have met him before—several times, in fact, as he worked closely with my father—and have always found him to be a warm and congenial sort of person. Today is no exception. Grief is stamped upon his face, his expression of sympathy unguarded. This renews my hope.

"How very, very sorry I am for your loss, dear Vaela," he says, approaching the table and clasping my hands in his. "No, no. May I embrace you?"

I nod, and his arms encircle me, pulling me close. Grief wells inside me, and I sink into his comfort, into the comfort of another person who knew my family. A man who spoke to my father almost daily, a man who welcomed my mother in company with smiles and warmth. For a moment, I am safe in the past.

"You know how fond I was of your parents, and of the Shaws," he says softly. He pulls away and looks me squarely in the eyes. "What a terrible tragedy this all has been. I hope we may find some way to offer recompense, inadequate as any gesture will certainly be."

"I ask nothing for myself, Chancellor."

"How terribly you must have suffered," he says, regarding me as though I were a piteous thing. He shakes his head again. "Well. Let us begin, for while this sad exchange of testimony is all too necessary, I am sure the day holds brighter things in store."

"I hope it does."

He moves around the table, nodding to Mr. Lowe, and takes a seat at the center, directly opposite me.

"Now, Vaela," the Chancellor begins, "let me tell you what we know, and then you may tell your story—from the very beginning of course, for we must hear all that has happened." I nod, and he continues. "On the fourth morning of your tour, Ivanel received a distress call from the pilot of your heli-plane. He gave his position, stated that a failure of both engines had occurred, and said that he intended to make an emergency landing. That was the last communication received."

He leans forward. "Now, let me assure you beyond any doubt that we were extremely distressed by this information, and moved at once into action. Ivanel had no secondary aircraft, so we could not attempt an immediate rescue—but two additional heli-planes were sent to the island posthaste. Due to the late hour of departure, the planes did not arrive until after night had fallen, when it was far too dark to attempt any sort of rescue—the drastic changes in the Continent's elevation would have made any such endeavor quite unsafe—and so we were forced to wait until the following day to begin our search. We deployed the planes at the break of dawn, and from morning to night, we searched without success."

"There was a light inside the pod," I say. "It was activated almost immediately. How could the search have been so difficult?"

He gives me a sad smile. "Those beacons were designed to be detected within a radius of twenty or so miles. We collected the pod more than three hundred miles from the plane's last known position, and far to the south of where we thought it might be. We were searching largely in the northeast, along the Kinso mountains. Either the pilot's bearing was incorrect—entirely possible, as forensic analysis of the debris seems to indicate more than one very serious mechanical failure—or he sent his transmission long before the plane actually crashed. Or, potentially, both things occurred."

Forensic analysis. I dare not ask. I swallow and press the issue further. "The pod was collected, though. And on the third day, I saw a heli-plane—"

"And the plane saw you, my dear. Pursued by a pair of Xoe into the woods." He opens his hands in supplication. "There was nothing to be done."

"Nothing to be done?" I echo, stupefied. "You...you knew I was in mortal danger, yet you did nothing to save me?"

"Come now, Miss Sun. Even if the plane and search party had been equipped with the tools required to rescue you—"

"Weapons, you mean."

"Yes. Even if such equipment had been available, you know the principal law of the Spire—we do not take up arms. That law is binding, inviolable, and without exception."

"But you have tranquilizing guns—and sleeping gas. I have heard of their use against criminals and the like."

He shifts uncomfortably and exchanges a glance with Mrs. Pendergrast. "As I say, we were not properly equipped."

"I see." A silence passes. "And so, the pod and the...wreckage were collected."

"That is correct."

"And I was left to die."

"Vaela, I assure you that—"

"With all due respect, Chancellor, I think I have heard quite enough of your story. Perhaps it is time that you heard mine."

To the immeasurable discomfort of the five people before me, I tell it all. I recount every terrifying moment of the heli-plane's failure. I illustrate the horror of being interrogated by the Xoe, and explain in bloody detail how Noro came to rescue me. I describe the agony of my grief and loneliness in the wake of my parents' deaths, as well as the slow process of my eventual healing. And finally, I tell of the attack on the village of Kastenai—and of the utter peril in which the Aven'ei now find themselves.

"I wonder," says Mrs. Pendergrast, the first to speak, her brow knit in tight concern, "in light of all this terrible trauma, if you might tell us something of the accident itself."

"What do you mean?"

"The malfunction," she says, "of the heli-plane. Any details you might provide could surely prove useful in the prevention of future disaster."

"Oh, of course," I say, momentarily embarrassed by the fact that this had not occurred to me at all. "There was...there was a great shuddering, and shaking."

"Of the fuselage?" she asks.

"Yes," I say. "The plane shook terribly, and then smoke was visible from the forward panels—and the craft would drop in sudden shifts and bursts." My throat goes dry in the recalling of it.

"Mmm," Mrs. Pendergrast says. "And what was your perception of this malfunction?"

"My perception?"

She smiles. "What did you think had gone wrong, dear girl?"

"I...I don't know," I say. "Aaden...he said that there were systems in place to prevent failure of the aircraft. Redundancies— I believe that was the word he used. But things went terribly wrong, and...I don't know. I don't know what happened. I am not a mechanic."

"Of course not," she says, her smile at once bright and sympathetic. "Of course you cannot be expected to understand the technological failures of such complex machinery. We only wanted to know your observations, Miss Sun."

"I'm afraid I cannot provide much more. I only know there was a shaking, and a drop in altitude, and then I saw the plane spiraling downward, once I was in the pod, a terrible, slow spiral—inconsistent, with great periods of gliding—until it crashed."

"This," the Chancellor says after a dreadfully long silence, "this is beyond anything I would have expected to hear. To know that your mother and father were aboard the plane as it... Vaela, I have no words."

Mr. Lowe, at the far left, also struggles with a response. "What you have endured is unimaginable, and you have my most abiding compassion. How inconceivably terrible to watch the fate of those aboard the plane unfold!" He shakes his head. "But I am also deeply troubled—*deeply troubled*—by what you have brought to light in relation to the war on the Continent."

"As are we all," Mrs. Pendergrast says, a politician's pity stamped on her face. "What a sad state of affairs it has all come to be. Three hundred and forty years they have raged against one another—to see it come to this is an absolute tragedy."

The finality of her tone creates a knot in my stomach. "The situation is dire, to be sure," I say. "But it is not without hope."

Mr. Chamberlain frowns, his pointed mustache angling downward like two thin spikes. "Did you not just say that the Aven'ei will surely be destroyed? That it is only a matter of time before it comes to pass?"

"Certainly it is hopeless if they are left on their own," I say. "That is why we must take action, and quickly."

"Take action?" the Chancellor says, looking genuinely perplexed. "Surely you are not serious."

"I could not be more serious, sir. The only reason I returned to the Spire is to request your assistance. The Aven'ei need allies, and they need them now."

"Miss Sun," Mrs. Pendergrast says crisply, "we have never intervened in the war between the Aven'ei and the Xoe, and we shall not do so now. It is dreadful that this fate has befallen the

Aven'ei, but—and please, forgive my bluntness—one cannot deny that they have brought it upon themselves."

I clutch the edge of the table, stunned into temporary silence. All the blood seems to have drained from my face, my fingertips, my body, and this woman—this woman with her pinched face and her plastered auburn hair—she just stares at me. "What... what a ghastly thing to say!"

She blinks in surprise and looks over at Mr. Chamberlain as though for support.

He nods, pats her hand, then turns to address me, fixing me with a rheumy stare. "Mrs. Pendergrast has only stated what the Chancellery knows to be a fact. It was the Aven'ei, Miss Sun, who began the war in the first place. In all your time on the Continent, did no one make this known?"

I sit rigid in the chair.

It cannot be.

The Aven'ei were not the initial aggressors. They simply weren't. It is the Xoe who are warmongering, it is the Xoe who have *always* been the aggressors.

Right?

"It is true," the Chancellor says, nodding gravely. "When we met with the Aven'ei—by ship, all those years ago—we asked about the particulars of the quarrel. They were most forthcoming about their role in how it all began. It was down to territorial disputes, if I remember correctly. The Aven'ei once inhabited a much larger piece of the Continent, but even so, they weren't satisfied. They pushed outward, the Xoe fought back—bitterly so. And as we have seen, the might of such an enemy can grow into a fearsome thing with the passing of the years. But it was the Aven'ei who began it. I'm sorry, my dear, I'm sorry to be the one to tell you."

I fight to regain my composure. "Well. Even so. If that is true, must those who now live pay the price for the actions of their ancestors?"

Mr. Chamberlain smiles. "To pull the tail of the cat is to invite its claws. The Aven'ei alone unleashed the fury of the Xoe; alone, they must keep the beast at bay."

"But they cannot do so, can they?" Mr. Lowe says quietly. "It has all gone far beyond their control. They must have help, and how, in good conscience, can we leave them now to die?"

Mrs. Pendergrast is thunderstruck. "But what would you have us do, Oliver?"

Mr. Lowe turns to me. "Will they relocate?"

"To the *Spire*?" Mrs. Pendergrast says in a shrill voice, putting a hand to her breast. "Surely you must be joking!"

"It is a peaceful solution, Tara," he replies.

She sniffs. "No, no, no, no, *no*. The people of the Continent are uncivilized."

"They are *not* uncivilized," I say frostily, "as you well know. As any number of tours have proven otherwise. And I will remind you, madam, that I, of the distinguished families of Waters and Sun, have an Aven'ei ancestor. When you insult the Aven'ei, you insult me."

"Your spoiled blood is not a factor in this discussion," she says.

I feel as though the breath has been knocked from my body. "Spoiled...do you hear yourself, Mrs. Pendergrast?" I look around at the table, stunned. "Do *you* hear her, Mr. Lowe? Mr. Wey? Mr. Chamberlain? *Chancellor?*"

The Chancellor opens his mouth to answer, but Mrs. Pendergrast puts words in his place. "Emigration is not an option," she insists.

It is all I can do not to slap the look off her face. I take a deep breath. "They do not wish to emigrate, madam."

"And well they shouldn't," says Mr. Chamberlain, whom I have started to suspect is rather a pet of Mrs. Pendergrast's making. "The Continent is their home, and they certainly do not belong here."

The Chancellor regards me with undisguised curiosity. "If

you do not mean to petition for their relocation, then what is it you wish to ask of us?"

Gathering my courage, I rise and move forward to the table. "I have drawn you a map," I say, "marking every key point of battle, and every settlement of which I am aware—Xoe as well as Aven'ei."

I take the parchment from my hip and roll it out on the table, pinning down the corners with my fingertips. "You are brilliant leaders—brilliant, and resourceful. In your hands, this map is but a blueprint—and you are the engineers."

The Chancellor blinks. "I'm not sure I understand."

I tap the paper. "Build towers, so that the Aven'ei might see when a Xoe force is coming. Establish plain sight of all access points. Create defenses the likes of which have never been seen on the Continent! And then, down the line, perhaps the Spire can help the Aven'ei and the Xoe to meet in the middle, to accomplish a peace of their own accord. Don't you see? You can help without ever raising so much as a single weapon. You have the power to end this. You have the power to stop *another* war."

Mr. Lowe gets out of his seat in order to take a better view of the map; Mr. Chamberlain and the still-silent Mr. Wey follow suit. Mrs. Pendergrast remains in her chair, her back straight and stiff, her eyes fixed on some point in the distance.

"The Xoe are gathering here," I say, indicating the settlements in the south. "Likely they will advance through the Vale and try to pin the Aven'ei against the sea. They could travel through the mountains, of course, the Aramaii and the southern Kinso—but this is very unlikely. It would be far easier for their numbers to pass through the Reaches."

"And will the Aven'ei retreat?" Mr. Lowe asks. "Gather with their forces in the north?"

"I do not think they will leave the south, sir. I think they will make a stand."

Mr. Lowe studies the map intently. "Defenses might be made

before the Xoe set out, and that might buy time to work toward
allowing the two nations to establish a lasting peace. It is not a
bad idea. It is not at all a bad idea."

Mrs. Pendergrast sucks in her breath, her red lips pursed like
a deathly kiss. "And who shall pay for it, Oliver? We in the
West are not so inundated with wealth and raw materials that
we should be inclined to jaunt off to the Continent and erect
towers for a bunch of strangers."

"Mrs. Pendergrast," Mr. Lowe says hotly, "you have only
just announced your plans to construct a colossal amphitheater
in the heart of your capital city. How is it that you can spare so
little when you have already amassed a store of both funds and
materials?"

"Our civic objectives are none of your concern," she replies.
"Nor is the state of our treasury. I will ask you to tend to your
own purse, and keep your nose out of mine."

The Chancellor holds up his hands. "Let us not bicker with
one another like children. Vaela has put a reasonable point before us, and I think we should give it our fair consideration."

"There is nothing to consider," Mrs. Pendergrast says flatly.
"I refuse to contribute."

"As do I," Mr. Chamberlain puts in, nodding. "We haven't
the resources."

The Chancellor turns to Mr. Lowe. "And you, sir?"

Mr. Lowe looks at me, his blue eyes burning with intensity.
"The North shall give all it can to see the Aven'ei protected. It
is the moral thing to do."

"If you want my opinion," Mrs. Pendergrast says, "that's the
most foolish thing you've said all day."

He smiles. "I most certainly do *not* want your opinion."

She makes a face, as though she has swallowed a marble but
still intends to smile.

"It is down to you, then, Mr. Wey," the Chancellor says. "We
have heard nothing from the East at all as of yet."

Mr. Wey folds his hands in his lap. "I say no."

The Chancellor does not seem surprised. "Do you wish to give a reason?"

"It is a simple matter," he says, and shrugs in resignation. "If we choose to ally with the Aven'ei, Spirians may die. Construction of any kind will take time. It is not worth the risk."

Mr. Lowe makes a derisive noise. "Are you saying that the blood of a Spirian is worth more than that of an Aven'ei?"

"Don't act the innocent, Oliver," Mr. Wey says, pointing a gnarled finger at Mr. Lowe. "You yourself toured the Continent not five years ago. You went to see the war, just as we all have done."

"And vowed never to do so again."

"So you say," Mr. Wey replies. He is quiet for a moment, then straightens in his chair and adds, "For the sake of courtesy, and in the spirit of candor, I will answer your previous question: yes. The blood of a Spirian is worth more. I say it without malice, sir. It is only what I believe to be true, for my duty lies with my own people."

Mr. Lowe looks back and forth among his fellow Heads of State. "Is that the way of it, then? This is what you choose?"

"The majority has spoken, Mr. Lowe," the Chancellor says. "The Spire must act as One."

Mr. Lowe turns to me, anger and frustration in his eyes. "I apologize on behalf of the Spire, Miss Sun. Apparently, peace is now far too priceless a commodity to share."

"Now, Mr. Lowe," the Chancellor says, frowning, "I think that's a bit unfair. Peace is not a thing to be given, but to be chosen."

"Do not speak of peace," I say quietly. "Do not. Your words are but air, as weightless and empty as the breath in your lungs. You talk of resources and coin, amphitheaters and treasuries— as though any of these things are of consequence when the lives of *thousands* are at stake."

Mrs. Pendergrast rolls her eyes. "Your naïveté does not become you, Miss Sun. Things may not be accomplished without coin and resources. That is a fact."

"The Spire is a land of plenty. It could be done, and every one of you knows it." I rise in a cold fury and fix my gaze upon the officials at the table. "Mr. Lowe alone shall sleep with the conscience of a man who understands the value of human life—and for that, I thank you, sir." He nods. "As for the rest of you: do not doubt for a moment that the blood of the Aven'ei is on your hands. Men, women, and children will be relieved of their lives. They'll be dead—corpses rotting in the sun. Stinking, rotten corpses. I hope you dream of them every night."

I burst through the doors in my rush to leave the Grand Hall, for suddenly the dark corners of the room seem to press in from all sides. I hear the Chancellor calling to me in worried tones, asking me to return. But I do not stop. I want to be free of this place, of this great Nation that will do nothing to help the people I have come to love.

At the front of the building, a hundred or so steps lead down to the main road. I pause halfway down, looking for the car sent by Mr. Cloud. A drizzle of rain—no more than a fine mist, really—dampens my skin and hair.

The Chancellor appears at my side, breathless and distressed. "Vaela, my dear girl, please—will you come back inside?"

I look up at him, angry tears burning my eyes. "They all said you would refuse, you know. The Aven'ei. Almost to a man, they said that you would turn your back." I shake my head. "But I said they were wrong, and I believed it, Chancellor! I believed in the Spire. I believed in you. And now I must go back and tell them that all of this was for *nothing*. No help is to come. Only death."

He wipes his forehead with a handkerchief, a puzzled expression on his face. "Go back? Whatever do you mean?"

"You don't think I intend to stay here, do you?"

"But of course you must stay here! You have inherited a sizable fortune, my dear, and you have your work with Mr. Sussenfaal—"

"I should stay in the Spire to draw *maps*?" I say, incredulous. "Tell me, Chancellor—what has a map ever brought to me but grief, or death, or heartache? *Piss* on your maps. I am going back to the Continent. I will have Mr. Cloud make the arrangements."

I turn away, but he catches me by the shoulder. "I don't think you quite understand me, young lady. You will not be returned to the Continent. I wouldn't send another heli-plane to that foul place for all the gold in the Chancellery."

I smile unpleasantly. "You do not have a choice, sir."

"I beg your pardon? You forget yourself, Miss Sun, and—"

"It is you who forgets, Chancellor. My parents died on the Continent. By law, I may reside for as long as I wish in the nation where they were lost—to grieve, to mourn, to spend my days in vigil if that is what I desire."

His eyes narrow. "That regulation refers to the North, South, East, and West. There are no *nations* on the Continent; only people pretending at civilization."

"I will be returned to the nation of the Aven'ei," I say. "If you refuse me, I will make it my life's purpose to visit every corner of the Spire, recounting every detail of what has taken place. I will omit nothing—and I daresay the common folk will find your decision to abandon the Aven'ei as horrifying and unpalatable as I do. You know how much your Spirians like a good cause."

His lip curls in anger. "You dare to threaten me?"

"I dare nothing, Chancellor, for I have nothing at all to lose."

He leans toward me, his face inches from my own. "You would incite a war—the very thing you claim to abhor so passionately."

"No. I would educate a people as to what their peace has truly bought: a government that amounts to no more than five people sitting at a table, deciding the fate of the world."

He gives me a sardonic smile. "A great many things are decided at tables, dear girl. The fate of the world is but *one*."

"Make your choice, sir. Shall I sing my song to the people of the Spire, or will you send me to the Continent, where I belong?"

He regards me coolly before speaking. "Have you been in contact with anyone since your arrival yesterday? Friends, family, anyone at all?"

"No. I presume you want me to keep it that way?"

He nods. "You died once, and seem intent on dying again, only with greater success this time around."

"My extended family," I say. "And my friends—my dearest friend, Evangeline Day—"

"They need never know of your survival and subsequent suicide. I shall send you back to the Continent, if that is what you truly desire. But I warn you to think carefully on this, for if you choose this path, you will never again be welcome to return. The Spire will be lost to you forever."

"Make the arrangements," I say. "I will happily leave this place behind."

CHAPTER 29

◆

AS I CLIMB INTO THE CAR SENT BY MR. CLOUD,
my shield of anger and confidence all but evaporates. I sit sobbing, crumpled against the fine leather seat, my heart aching
with the sting of lost opportunity. How truly I believed that the
Spire would rally for the Aven'ei—all those years in school, the
values of kindness and generosity so deeply encouraged, all those
years, believing that the Spire truly was a pinnacle of freedom
and hope. How desperate I was to return to the Continent with
good news. An alliance, I thought, was obvious. I am a fool.

A gentle patter of rain begins, drumming a melancholy beat
upon the roof of the car as though to commiserate with me.
The driver waits patiently on the other side of the glass parti-
tion, no doubt wondering why I have not given him an address.
But I don't care. I can't bring myself to go back to the estate just
yet. Sitting here so near the Chancellery gives me a false sense
of security, as though I could dash back up the steps, return to
the Grand Hall, and somehow convince the officials to change
their minds.

But I can't change their minds. Save for Mr. Lowe, not one of
them so much as considered my request. And why should they
listen to me? A girl of sixteen, barely a woman—one who was

left to die on the Continent, only to inconveniently survive and return to tell the tale. I suspect they would have offered me a handsome package of compensation, had I stayed to listen. As though money, opportunity, or position would somehow erase the Aven'ei from my memory, would somehow ameliorate all I have lost.

And Noro…oh, Noro. What will he say when I return? Will he truly be angry with me for coming back? Does he not understand that my fate is bound to his as surely as the sun must rise each day? For he and Kiri are my family now, all that is left to me in the world. And if they must suffer death at the hands of the Xoe, I will not stay in the Spire to survive them. All may be lost, but love remains.

A soft knock at the window startles me, and I peer out to see Mr. Cloud ducking down, a newspaper held over his head. I open the door at once and scoot away from the window.

"Mr. Cloud," I say, wiping the tears from my face. "Get in, please! You'll catch your death out there."

He bustles into the car, closing the door behind him and exhaling deeply. "What a lot of charlatans they are at the weather bureau," he says, scowling. "'Clear skies throughout the afternoon,' eh? I should think not. Anyhow, I saw the car still parked at the curb and I thought I would just check—why, Miss Sun! Whatever is the matter?"

He pulls a clean white handkerchief from his breast pocket and hands it to me; I accept and dab at my eyes, feeling all the more miserable for his kindness.

"The Spire won't help," I say. "Only the North was willing to offer any kind of assistance. The rest overruled it, and in a terrible hurry."

His face is grim. "I feared as much. There's no gain to be had in helping the Aven'ei, and if there's anything a politician cares about, it's what good a thing can do for him."

"Oh, Mr. Cloud, what am I to do?" I begin to cry again, sobbing softly into the handkerchief.

He puts a firm hand on my shoulder. "You just go about your business, and sleep well at night knowing you've done all you *could* do."

I sniff. "But I've got to go back now and tell them what has happened. Any hope they might have had for an alliance will be dashed forever. I might have made a difference, but I've failed them all, and every last one will die."

"Dearest girl," he says, "if the Aven'ei are to fall, it is because the Xoe insist on making it so. You are not responsible. And… well, I don't like to overstep, but I do wish you would not be quite so determined to go back there. Is it your heart that compels you? The young man who brought you to Ivanel?"

"It is Noro and all the rest," I say. "I do not belong in the Spire, Mr. Cloud. I feel at odds with the very air here in the East."

"Well. I can't say I'm glad to hear it. But I think I understand."

I sit quiet for a moment, my eyes fixed on the little rivers of water meandering along the windows. "I shall be dead soon," I say finally. "It's a strange thing to know."

"Is there truly no hope?"

I give him a sad smile. "Once, I would have said that hope is unceasing—that it is born of the goodness in the world, and nurtured within our hearts." My voice falters, for I am on the brink of tears once again. "But I feel no hope now, Mr. Cloud— only certainty that there is none to be had. The Xoe have seen to that. And so has the Spire."

The Chancellor, as it turns out, is in no hurry to accommodate me. For two weeks, I wait with a restlessness that borders on insanity. I pace the hallways of the estate, doing my best to avoid the sour-faced butler and the retinue of servants. Each day, I am assured by the Chancellor's secretary—an obsequious man called Mr. Vane—that my travel arrangements are well in hand, and that he will notify me as soon as the matter has been settled. And each day, no plans are announced.

When night falls, I ache for the comfort of Noro's arms. I miss the cozy security of my little cottage, and the vastness of the southern plains. I long to walk beneath the trees of the Continent with their leaves of gold and red, savoring a few moments of beauty before winter comes. Before the Xoe come. Autumn is full upon us now, and the days slip through my fingers as I wait, and wait, and wait.

I think of defying the Chancellor's order to conceal my survival. I have family on my mother's side in the West—an aunt, two uncles, and a smattering of cousins—although I've never been terribly close to any of them, save for my aunt Lydia. She's a reckless sort, the exact kind of person who would understand my current predicament. I have never truly seen an individual intoxicated, save for her. She is my mother's sister, a woman with a great tangle of haphazard blond curls—and a penchant for loosing family secrets at the *worst* possible moments. She brings a shiny bottle of golden-brown liquor to every holiday celebration, never offers so much as a drop to anyone else, and drinks until she is red-faced and jolly and quite ready to divulge any number of things to all who will listen. I secretly adore her. And I wish, wish, *wish*, that I could reach out to her, and feel her soft, thick arms around me, and know that everything will be all right.

And as for my old friends…it hurts to know that they are here, but I cannot talk to them. To all, I am merely dead: a tragic story, a girl who once was. I ache to tell them that I live, that I think of them still—especially Evangeline, sweet, lovely Evangeline, who was so excited about my grand adventure to the Continent. But as much as I hate to agree with anything uttered from the lips of the Chancellor, I know he is right: to be resurrected only to die a second time would be a cruel thing, a conscious inflicting of further grief. It is better that no one know I survived the crash.

On the fifteenth day after my meeting with the Heads of State, Mr. Vane telephones to inform me that I shall depart on the following day. I pack a few new things into my satchel— a phototype of my mother, father, and me, a sack of expensive candy for Kiri, and eight pairs of elegant silk undergarments. If all that is left of the Spire in me is the desire for pretty underthings, I can live with that. I shall take my pleasures where I can.

This indulgence includes a long, long bath in my mother's enormous tub. I soak until my fingers and toes are like soft pink raisins, and my skin smells of jasmine from head to toe. How much the citizens of the Spire take for granted. Hot running water, modern amenities, an abundance of necessities and luxuries alike. And yet, I do so miss the simplicity of life in Kastenai. I only wish I were returning with better news.

As darkness falls, I climb into my parents' bed, thinking of how many times I did so as a child. A nightmare, a shadow— the smallest thing would send me running to the safety of their bedroom. My mother always welcomed me with open arms, her voice the most comforting thing in the world. What I would give to lie beside her now and listen to her sing the sweet lullabies of my youth! What I would give for just one more day with my mother and father, for a lifetime with Noro and Kiri. A life without fear—a life of peace.

Tears stain my face, but I eventually drift to sleep, warm and safe beneath the heavy blankets. I dream of a life I shall never know.

CHAPTER 30

✦

ABOUT A MILE FROM KASTENAI, THE HELI-PLANE shifts to a hover in order to set me down. I descend the swaying metal ladder without any trepidation, my feet scarcely touching the ground before I turn and run toward the village. I am invigorated by the musty scent of damp earth and the kiss of the brisk autumn air against my cheeks. With a whisper of a breeze behind me, I race across the plains. The long grasses of the flatland—now the color of burned cinnamon—crunch noisily beneath my feet as I fly through the valley. The wind moves among the trees, rustling sparse golden leaves as though in welcome, and joy stirs within me. For no matter what the future may bring, I am *home*.

Before long, I come upon the little hilltop that looks down upon the village—the same place where Noro once set me upon my feet—and come to a breathless stop. The late-afternoon sun has cast Kastenai in amber, and long shadows stretch lazily toward the east. I pause to marvel at the loveliness before me—at the sheer beauty of the Continent—but my eye falls almost at once upon something else: a figure standing just outside the gates below. He is dressed all in black, his hair spilling into an angled strip along one side of his head, one long leg planted firmly on the ground, another foot up against the wall behind him. He does not see me—not at first. I watch him in his casual repose, his eyes scanning the hillside, his hands thrust into the pockets of his trousers.

And then he looks up.

We are still for a moment, a thousand questions passing silently between us. I feel his rapid assessment of me, sense his tension. He has worried for me—I can see it in his face—perhaps even as much as I have worried for him. And here we are now, each of us safe, each of us returned to the other.

The foot comes down from the wall and Noro thunders up the hillside toward me. I clamber down the slope at an equal pace, and when at last we meet, he lifts me fully off the ground, his lips pressing hard against mine, and I almost weep for the joy of it.

"Noro," I say, my heart nearly broken by happiness, but he only kisses me again. Beams of scattered sunlight pierce the trees above, dancing around us like twinkling stars. Words can wait. I am home.

Night falls, bringing with it a wash of silvery moonlight and a chorus of insects calling out into the darkness. Noro and I sit atop the hillside, our fingers tangled together, our words soft and whispered. We speak of many things: Kiri's recovery, the turn of the season on the Continent, the Aven'ei patrols moving in and out to monitor the activity of the Xoe. The evening slips by, yet neither of us is willing to go home just yet; in this special place, we have only to savor each other's company.

"You look tired, *miyara*," he says. "Did you not sleep well in your time away?"

"Not very well."

He gives me a nudge. "Too many fine dinners and extravagant hotels?"

"Too many politicians."

"Ah." He gestures to the valley. "And yet, the world still spins."

I laugh. "It's a wonder it does, I assure you."

"Help will not come, then?"

I look up at him, my eyes shining with regret. I have dreaded this moment.

My silence says everything, and Noro nods. There is no rebuke, no acknowledgment that this is what he said would come to pass. There is only a softness in his expression, a certain tenderness reflected in his eyes.

"It is just as well," he says. "Why should others sacrifice for our survival?"

"I did try, Noro. But…it was not to be."

"Do not blame yourself." He gives my hand a squeeze. "No one expected that the Four Nations would join with the Aven'ei. You know this."

I shake my head. "I still think it shameful. They could do so much with only a small effort. Such a small effort."

"I only wish you had stayed where you might be safe."

"Noro…"

He gets to his feet, dusts himself off, and extends a hand to me. "Come, my love. I cannot keep you all to myself. Kiri would wish to know that you are home. I expect Raia and Talan will want to see you as well."

I take his hand, wishing that I could file my sadness away in some deep corner of my heart. It is the beginning of the end now, and there is no way to pretend otherwise.

CHAPTER 31

◆

BEING HOME AGAIN MEANS GOING BACK TO WORK. One unusually warm autumn morning—hot enough that I've broken a sweat by the time I arrive at the farm—Shovo is in a devil's mood. I don't know if it's the heat that troubles him, or the fact that several of the animals have taken ill, or if he just woke up and realized he was himself, but he has spent the better part of the morning stomping all about the yard, complaining and shouting at everyone in his path. Naomi, the young woman who feeds the animals, is in tears before lunchtime, and Shovo has actually *kicked* a man called Noaz—my counterpart, who helps with the manure and usually works in my off weeks, trying to earn more *oka* for his family—at least three times.

Even as I watch, Shovo storms out of the small building where he does his record keeping and roars at one of the feral cats we often see around the farm. The poor animal, its fur sticking up on end, races away and climbs the large oak tree next to the barn. If he's smart, he'll stay up there.

Shoveling manure is distasteful on a normal day, but on a hot day, it seems to stink twice as much. Working together, Noaz and I clean the pen long before the animals are to be returned from the pasture. Together, we stand in the shade of the oak, drinking water from our jugs and making small talk. Shovo, having just flung a pail through the paned glass of his office window and exited the building in what might as well be a burst of flame, goes rigid when he sees us.

Noaz, probably quite tired of being kicked in the seat of his pants, makes off at once for the barn, where I'm sure he will find some industrious task or other to take on. Me...I am not so quick, and once Shovo sets out in my direction, I feel trapped. I'd bet an *unzi* he would chase me if I fled.

He comes down on me like an angry bear, and spits on the ground at my feet. "What have I told you about standing around?"

"I'm sorry, Shovo. I was just having a bit of water—it's so hot today."

"No. I want you to answer me: What have I told you about standing around?"

I take a deep breath. "You've told me that the farm is not a place to be idle."

"So—you know the rules then, and just choose to flaunt your indolence in front of me? In front of the other workers?"

I bristle. Shouting at me to do better is one thing—though I still hate it. Calling me lazy is another. "I am not indolent, Shovo. I work hard, every day I am here. I stay late when there is more to be done. I never shirk, or fail to come. I am one of the hardest workers in your employ."

His expression is one of stunned rage, his mouth hanging open as though he simply cannot believe what I have just said. "The hardest worker..." he repeats, and nods his head. "Yes. You work very hard. Every day, you try to make it known that you're too good for this life, so much better than all the people of the Continent."

"Is that why you hate me so much? You think I look down on you? On the Aven'ei?"

"Everyone thinks it! You go about the village like a queen on a litter—"

"I *walk*, Shovo!"

"—with your hair smelling of flowers, your fine jewel draped around your neck—"

"I gave that jewel away, and go about smelling like manure two weeks out of every month—and I have never complained about it, to you or anyone else!"

"You're an outworlder. An unwanted guest. You weren't here a season before you took up with Noro like a *tanadai*."

I don't know what this word means, but I can guess it isn't kind. "Watch your mouth," I say tightly.

His nostrils flare. "The truth hurts, doesn't it? Death trails your footsteps, Vaela Sun—where you go, people die."

"Stop it!"

"Noro will be dead soon enough—he can't evade the Xoe forever. Then what will you do? Dupe another fool into warming your bed, into keeping you safe?"

"That's not how—"

"Every last one of us will die—by your hand."

"And all will be mourned except you!" I say, hating the cruelty of my words even as I speak them.

He laughs. "None will be left to mourn! The Aven'ei will be no more."

"You're a monster," I say, my voice shaking. "It's no surprise that you're alone, that everyone despises you—all you want is for others to share your misery."

"SHUT YOUR MOUTH!" he says, and lurches toward me, his hand raised.

I drop to the ground and guard my face with both arms. "Shovo, no!" I peer up at him, my hands trembling, my elbows high in the air. "Don't! Noro will kill you."

The muscles in his face twitch, the vein at his temple pulses madly. But he lowers his hand. Through clenched teeth, he says, "Get off my farm, and don't come back. You can clean the privies for all I care. Don't ever set foot on my land again. You understand?"

"Shovo, please—can't we settle this once and for all? You wouldn't think such terrible things about me if you just—"

"GET OFF MY FARM," he bellows, "before I have a mind to beat you bloody and to hell with the consequences."

I get to my feet, my chin quivering. "I hope one day you'll see that I'm trying here, that I'm really trying."

He points to the long, winding path.

I go.

Even after the long walk back to Kastenai, I'm still shaking with anger—and with fear, for I was truly afraid that Shovo might kill me right there on the farm, in the shade of the old oak. I make my way to Raia's, for I can't bring myself to go home just yet.

"Do you think it's my fault that the Xoe have come?" I say, when she answers the door. "Will the Aven'ei die because of me?"

Raia, ever practical, ushers me into the washroom and puts water on to heat for a bath. I forget sometimes how bad I smell.

"Vaela Sun, how can you ask such a thing? What's happened?"

"Shovo," I say, and that is explanation enough.

Raia sighs. "We have been at war for a long time. You know this."

"But the heli-planes...they could have led the Xoe into the south. Shovo believes it. Others believe it. You said yourself the villagers think I'm some kind of evil harbinger."

"The Xoe have come because they wish to surround us. With their warriors in the north and with the Kinso mountains to the east of their territory, the south has always been our only retreat. It is only logical that they have come, now that our numbers have dwindled so greatly. They are on the verge of triumph."

"There won't be any more tours of the Continent," I say. "*Now* the Spire decides to withdraw."

"It wasn't the planes, Vaela."

She pours water into the washtub, canister by canister, most of it hot thanks to her massive stove, and turns away while I undress and step inside. There are flower petals floating at the surface and a bar of soap on a tray beside the basin. I begin to scrub away the heat and exhaustion. I rub the flowers against my skin, wishing I had said something kind to Shovo, rather than having allowed myself to be provoked. *Childish. Just like him. You're no better.*

Raia stirs beside me. "Do you want to tell me what happened?"

"Well, I don't have a job anymore—he told me never to come back."

"What angered him?"

I laugh. "Who knows? The sight of me, the smell of me, the very fact that I exist? I stopped for a drink of water and he just…snapped."

"He is the most ill-tempered man I've ever met."

"He called me a…a *tanadai*, Raia. What does that mean?"

She sucks in her breath, her lips pursed together. "He didn't."

"What does it mean?"

She chews on her lip for a moment. "It is…no. It is an insult, a reference only. It implies an Aven'ei who would lie with a Xoe—a wanton, promiscuous person, man or woman—who revels in the sexual company of the enemy."

"I have never… I would never! Noro and I have not even—"

"You are no such thing, and Shovo knows it well." Her eyes narrow. "Did he strike you?"

"He did not," I say. "But nearly."

Raia frowns. "Noro would see him dead for less than that."

"I will not keep this from Noro, and I will not tolerate any violence. The trouble is between Shovo and myself—it is no one else's concern."

"You would stay Noro's hand in defense of a man who knowingly slanders your honor?"

"Oh, honestly!" I say. "My honor is intact, whether Shovo slanders it or not. I don't need his good opinion to know myself. Noro and I, we love each other. Not that Shovo could ever understand such a thing."

"Oh, he understands it. He had a love of his own once, you know. He was a different man then."

"He… Shovo?"

Raia wraps a toweling cloth about my shoulders, and I rise reluctantly from the warm water in the tub. "He had a wife once," she says. "They were very happy for a time."

"And she was killed by the Xoe?"

"Oh, nothing so bearable as that," Raia says. "We expect to lose those at war; we are hardened to it, though it hurts nonetheless. But Shovo's wife, she killed herself. We guessed it was because she could not bear children, but truly, no one knows why. Shovo came home from a skirmish at Sana-Zo to find her hanging from the beams, two or three days dead."

I hear myself shouting at him on the farm: *It's no surprise that you're alone, that everyone despises you…* Oh, if I could take those words back, if I could take them all back, I surely would. But a word spoken can never be unsaid, and so I have scraped at the wound of a warrior whose scars run far deeper than his skin.

CHAPTER 32

✦

I SEE SHOVO IN THE MARKETPLACE FROM TIME TO time, but he turns his back whenever I approach, and will not acknowledge me. I stew with shame over the words I spoke, for I no longer see this man as horrible—only broken. I've even come to miss my days on the farm, as impossible as that might seem—those quiet mornings alone with my thoughts on the way to work, and the splendor of the summer sunshine on my face, turning my skin from ivory to bronze.

The council is far too busy to place me with another work assignment, so I spend my *oka* frugally, and do odd jobs for the few traders who are friendly to me. This typically involves deliveries or fetching supplies, and the pay is low, but it's better than nothing.

As ever, the threat of the Xoe hangs in the air, casting a sickly shadow over everything: every conversation, every moment of happiness, every drifting thought as one settles down to sleep. It's like a fog that no one can see, though it taints the very air we breathe. I look for hope in the faces of the villagers, but find only resignation. Kastenai is quiet, and not in a good way.

I try to enjoy the relative hush we experience now: the calm before the storm. But the Continent is a hard and merciless place, and peace in the south was not meant to last forever. Soon enough, Kinza's scouts return with news that the Xoe are making ready to march—and that their numbers are greatly increased. There is a bustle of activity as the villages rush to join together in council—sometimes in Kastenai, sometimes farther north near Ciriel and the Narrow Corner. Time runs thin, but a decision is made: the Aven'ei—*all* of the Aven'ei, save for a small contingent to be left guarding the northern border—are to advance. We will meet the Xoe in the south; we shall not live to see them burn and plunder our homes. I am afraid, but my sadness is greater than my fear.

Over the course of the next week, preparations begin in earnest for the battle to come. Night and day, smoke rises from the forges of the smiths as new weapons are made and old ones reinforced. Woodworkers produce arrows by the thousands. Food is gathered, collected, and made ready for transport. And all through the day and night, villagers from northern settlements pass through on their way to the designated point of assembly: the wide, flat hilltop that looks down into the Southern Vale, a place scarcely twenty miles west of Kastenai. Though I am no tactician, even I can see the brilliance of this plan: the Xoe will be at a distinct disadvantage as they bottleneck through the valley, the only natural place of passage practical for a large deployment. The Aven'ei shall have the high ground and will be able to rain down arrows for quite some time before the Xoe can reach the top of the valley wall.

Every able person in the south has been called to fight—only children under the age of ten are to forgo the battle; they shall flee to a huddle of southern caves with a contingent of caretakers. And I, being skilled in only the most minimal sense of the word, am considered able—and so I shall fight along with the Aven'ei when the battle comes. Yet even if I had no skill at all, still I would fight—for the Aven'ei are my people now, though the majority may yet consider me to be an outsider.

While making preparations to leave Kastenai, I pack a few items to bring along: small things, like the phototype of my mother and father and the bits of glass given to me by Kiri. The Dúns wish to bring nothing but weapons and battle gear—the Aven'ei are not given to sentimental attachments.

The day before we are to leave, Noro arrives home from a meeting with the council. He looks very grave.

"What is it?" I ask, as he removes his shoes in the entryway. "What's the matter?"

"The Xoe are on the march, and our scouts have returned with the count. The news is not good."

"How many are they?"

"Seventy-five thousand in the south. They have reinforced their legions."

Reinforced is putting it mildly. They were not nearly so many when I flew overhead in the heli-plane just half a year ago—what was the count then, six thousand? And now seventy-five? I draw in my breath. "And the Aven'ei?"

"We can gather fifty thousand at most—we cannot withdraw all of our forces from the north, lest the Xoe burn their way through and flank us."

He glances around the room, taking in the stark tidiness of the place. Everything has been cleaned and put away—there are no blankets strewn about, no clothes draped over the sofa. It almost appears as though no one lives here at all.

"Well," he says, "Kiri should be home late, she's over with Raia baking sweets or bread or some such thing for the journey."

"All right."

"Let's retire early, Vaela. I would be alone with you in our home one last time."

"Goodbye to Kastenai," I whisper, as Noro and I lie curled up on the bed, facing one another. "And what a sad goodbye it is."

"I feel the same."

"I wish—"

"I know."

We lie quietly, lost in our own thoughts. After a moment, I reach over and take his hand. "When I was in the Spire...they said it was the Aven'ei who started the war. Is it true?"

He sighs heavily. "Yes, it's true."

"Why didn't you ever tell me?"

"You did not ask."

"Tell me how it started."

He rolls onto his back and stares up at the ceiling. "It was foolishness, no more than that. Our people thought it would be an easy thing to take land from the Xoe. We did not anticipate what they would become."

"But why hasn't it ever ended? All these years, hundreds of years, and so many dead."

The muscles in his jaw become tight, and he closes his eyes. "So many, Vaela—you cannot know how many."

I watch him for a moment. "Are you thinking of your family?"

"Yes."

"Tell me about them."

He glances at me. "What can I say? They are gone, most dead at the hands of the Xoe—save for my mother, who died of illness. She was a skilled archer, she was. Fair of face, and slight, but strong—very strong. Like you, *miyara*. She would have liked you very much, I think."

This fills me with a strange sense of longing; I would have so liked to know his mother, and to have earned her love and approval. "What was her name?"

"Azu."

"And what of your brothers?"

"All were older than I. One an *inanei* who never returned from an assignment. The other three captured and hanged after the Great Battle of Sana-Zo."

I feel his sadness in my heart, and I long to ease it, but I haven't the words. "You must miss them terribly."

"I miss them always," he says. "But I cannot bring them back."

"I wish this were not the end, Noro. How I would love to spend all of my days with you and Kiri, to face the sun and the snow and the storms of the Continent with you by my side."

A faint smile appears at his lips. "It would be a beautiful thing."

"Will we be together, do you think? At the end?"

"Don't speak of it."

"Noro… I would rather be prepared—"

"Nothing could prepare you for what is to come, Vaela. Nothing on this Earth. I only hope your death is swift, and Kiri's as well."

"This is really happening." It's surreal to think that we lie together now, so serene and quiet—and within the week, we shall likely die. And though I am frightened, I feel, as ever, that it was right to come back to the Continent. That this is my place, whether I may live or not.

"Don't let yourself be taken, my love."

"I won't."

Another silence. Noro reaches for my neck, kisses me, and presses his forehead against my own. "You are the greatest thing ever to happen to me, Vaela Sun."

I close my eyes, happy in the moment, but with heaviness in my heart. "Goodbye to Kastenai," I say softly. "Goodbye to us."

CHAPTER 33

◆

NORO, KIRI, RAIA, TALAN AND I ARRIVE AT THE assembly point three nights later. I am stunned by the sheer volume of people gathered across the plain—and not all have yet arrived. The Aven'ei are huddled in groups, clustered inside makeshift tents, looking somber, dour. There is little laughter, and less joy. But even so, there is an irrepressible sense of destiny here, and I am proud to be among them. Their fate is close at hand, but they do not flee, nor do they make a show of sorrow. They face death quietly, with courage.

A recent rainfall has muddied the field, making it difficult for Noro and Kiri to pitch our tent. Raia and I offer to help, but the Dúns are determined to go it alone. Talan stands back, giving worthless instruction. When the big canvas is finally stable, the five of us crowd around a sizzling fire, scorching bits of turkey on long sticks.

"If I were going to plan a last meal," says Raia, "I don't think charred, chewy meat would top the list."

"I have to agree," Noro says.

"This isn't anyone's last meal," I say. "Not mine, anyway. I'll be having roasted lamb in mint sauce, with wine and a flute of champagne. To start, of course."

"What's champagne?" asks Talan.

"Well...it's sort of a sparkling wine, I suppose."

Kiri makes a face; she does not favor alcohol. Having been taught by Eno to spell with her fingers, she makes the letters for *venison pie*.

"Oh, yesss," Talan says. "And let us have toasted pine nuts, day-old bread, and my mother's gravy to soak it all up."

Kiri's stomach emits an emphatic growl, and we all laugh.

Raia tosses her stripped branch into the fire, and hums a little song to herself as she warms her hands.

"I know that tune," Noro says. "But I can't recall its name."

She smiles. "'The Fields of Sana-Zo.'"

"Will you sing it for me?" I ask. "I've never heard it before."

"My voice could not do it justice," she says, and laughs softly.

"You have a beautiful voice," Talan says, then goes red about the ears. "Please. We'd all love to hear some music."

"All right, then," she says, and clears her throat. "But don't say I didn't warn you."

It is a sweet, haunting tune, not like any I have heard before:

Beyond the faithful river
In the fields of Sana-Zo
Lie the graves of wintry star-blooms
Pressed beneath the fallen snow

Sana-Zo, she knows of battle
Sana-Zo, she bears great scars
Yet her mantle lies unbroken
'Neath a heaven filled with stars

She calls to those who seek her
And she holds them to her breast
If I must die, please let it be
At Sana-Zo

At Sana-Zo
At Sana-Zo, with all the rest.

Noro smiles. "You sing very well, Raia Cú."

She waves the compliment away. "It's one of my favorite songs," she says. "Sad though it may be."

"I would have expected another battle there—in the north, at Sana-Zo," Noro says. "Never did I dream our final stand would be here in the Southern Vale."

She sighs. "And when it is over, only the Xoe will be left to sing about it."

"They don't sing," Noro says. "They howl."

Kiri's shoulders rock with laughter, and I smile.

Talan stands, his jaw clenched, his right hand gripping the hilt of his sword, twisting it nervously. "I wish to say something."

Noro raises a brow, but no one speaks. The four of us wait. Eventually, Talan clears his throat, gives his sword another twist in the scabbard, and clears his throat again. His eyes are white with...is it fear?

"Whatever is it, Talan?" I say. "You look downright spooked."

"I'm not spooked," he says, but his face is pale in the fire-light. "I... Raia? Raia Cú, I wish to marry you." He nods. "I propose a marriage to you."

Raia opens her mouth, then closes it again.

Noro chuckles. "Your timing is impeccable, friend. You ask on this, what may be the eve of our doom?"

Talan gives him a determined frown. "I ask on this, the night of the rain and song, when Raia looks lovelier than ever she has, and sings more beautifully than any bird. I ask because I now fear a rebuke far less than I fear leaving this world without her."

Raia has regained her composure. "I am no wife, Talan, no thing made for bearing children and sweeping stone floors."

Talan drops to his knee. "Of course you're not. I shall sweep the floors myself! You are a warrior, Raia—brave and strong—

and I love everything about you. I see your eyes in the twinkling stars above; I hear your voice in the words of the wind. I—"

"Stop!" Raia says, making a face. "Have you forgotten that in a day or two, we die?"

"Let our blood mingle in the killing fields—"

"Ew," I say.

Talan scowls at me, then turns back to Raia. "Let us leave this life together, and spend eternity in a spiritual embrace. The gods will bless our union. I know they will."

She sighs, measuring him in that calculating way of hers. "I will lie with you," she whispers. "There's no need for all the—"

"I do not want to *lie with you*!" Talan says between his teeth. "I mean—I do want that," he continues, "but I want to wed you first."

Raia turns to me. "Did you hear that? He wants to wed me."

I smile. "I think it's sort of romantic."

"Romantic," she says. "More like ludicrous."

He takes her hands in his. "Marry me."

"You're an idiot!" she says, but her eyes are fixed on his, and they do not waver.

"I am a man with nothing to lose."

A heartbeat passes, and Raia shakes her head. But the word she speaks is… "Yes," she says, sounding far more surprised than committed. "Yes, I will marry you."

"You…will?" Talan says. An ear-to-ear grin spreads across his face. "Then let it be so! Let us take one another as husband and wife, in life and in the hereafter, before these, our friends!"

She looks down at me, a bit dazed, and I give her an encouraging nod. "Let it be so," she whispers, and the thing is done. She seems a bit queasy—a bit shaky about the knees—but her face and neck are flushed with excitement.

Noro raises a mug of tea. "To your happiness."

To your health, Kiri spells.

"To the shortest marriage in the history of the Aven'ei," Raia says. But she smiles, flashing white teeth at all of us, and clings to Talan's hand as though she's only just discovered that hands might be held.

"I will love you forever," Talan says, and kisses her full on the lips, as bold as you please. In half a moment, her arms are wrapped around his neck, and the two are entangled like flowering vines. Kiri gestures as though to make herself vomit.

"I'm with you there," Noro says quietly.

"Oh, hush," I say. "Let them be. They have each found love at last."

"At *very* last," Noro says. "And they'd best not couple with one another by the fire. No one needs to see that."

But he need not worry, for Talan and Raia have disappeared into the night.

"Come now," I say, taking Noro's hand in my left and Kiri's in my right. "Teach me the song about Sana-Zo. This time, I shall hold the words close to my heart."

On the third morning, as the Aven'ei predicted, the Xoe come.

We stand at the north end of the field—Noro, Kiri, Raia, Talan and me—looking down upon the valley. The Xoe swarm into the hollow by the hundreds, the clatter of their weapons and armor audible even from this distance. They fill the Vale from one side to the other, advancing in a slowly moving line ever reinforced by those coming behind. I pray silently to the Maker, against all reason, that the five of us should survive this day.

This is it. A war waged for three centuries has come to this: seventy-five thousand below, fifty thousand above. Nearly all who are left of the Aven'ei have come for this battle, to die with honor.

A contingent of our archers, many men and women deep, stretches across the plain nearest the slope leading into the valley. They are waiting for the Xoe to move within range, and will shift to the rear when the enemy is close. Meanwhile, the warriors on foot have gathered behind, ready to switch places with the archers when the order is given. These brave souls will die first.

A drumbeat sounds, echoing in rhythmic bursts. But save for the drums and the clamoring metal noise of the Xoe, there is an eerie hush among the Aven'ei; not a voice is to be heard.

A gust of wind rushes up over the slope, sending my hair whipping against my face. The air is chill; a shiver runs down my spine. As I watch the enemy advance, I wonder at the circumstances: how is it that people can become so full of hatred that only violence will satisfy? The Xoe will have their revenge upon the Aven'ei for sins long past, and the Aven'ei now must fight. In the face of all this, it seems that war truly is inevitable, if but a single person wishes it to be so, and can rally others to his cause.

The pounding footfalls of the Xoe grow louder, and Noro's jaw tightens. "Soon," he says.

Within thirty minutes, there is a commotion among the ranks, and the archers move in unison to ready their bows. Commands are spoken along the line, followed by a long moment of tension, then a shout—and the arrows are loosed. It's a thing of beauty, nearly, to see more than a thousand arrows, all lit with pitch and fire, arcing across the sky as though slowed by some invisible force. But deadly they are, and though the Xoe throw up shields, many fall as they approach the hillside. Hundreds cry out in pain and fury—the noise rises up like a fearsome roar. Another volley is sent, and another, and another.

The Xoe move steadily, though their progress is slowed by the muck created in the week's rain and the arrows falling from above. The warriors fill the valley now as far as the eye can see, from one edge to another. It is the most impressive, most terrifying thing I have ever seen. Fear unlike anything I've felt before rises up like bile within me. *How has it come to this? How can a person of the Spire find herself here, in the path of war, on the precipice of disaster? Will my death be bloody? Will it be quick?* I fight to suppress panic.

A series of shouts erupts behind me, and the archers begin to change places with the hand-to-hand combatants.

"It will be minutes only, now," Noro says in a tight voice. "We must go, *miyara*. We shall take to the trees with the *ina-nei*; Kiri, you will come as well. I won't have either of you out in the open."

Talan and Raia, each skilled with a sword, will stay behind. I look into Raia's eyes, wet and glistening with tears. She embraces me, trembling. "Be safe," she says to me. "Don't say goodbye. One never knows what may come to pass."

This from Raia, who once warned me not to hope. I kiss her cheek and pull away. "Be safe," I echo. "I shall—"

A confused commotion sounds as hundreds of Xoe storm over the top of the hillside, not fifteen feet from where we are standing. Noro curses and grabs me by the wrist. "We go now."

Raia turns to see the onslaught, but a Xoe hammer collides with the side of her head, producing a sickening crunch. She whirls, her eyes open but *empty*, and falls face first into the mud.

"Raia!" I move against the force of Noro's strength, my mind reeling, registering in bits and pieces the tiny details of what has just happened: the sound of the impact, the spatter of blood when the hammer struck its target, her eyes—her *eyes*. Grief bubbles up as I struggle to reach her, to touch her, to take my sweet friend where her body cannot be violated.

Talan wastes no time; he cries out as he drives his sword through the belly of the man come to retrieve the hammer. His scream is terrible, fierce, inhuman.

Noro's hands are around my waist, dragging me toward the woods. "Vaela, stop! You can't help her! Kiri—the trees. NOW!"

As I am pulled away, I see Talan, red-faced, arc his sword up-ward in a single deft stroke, sending the head of a female warrior sailing into the maelstrom of battle, her face horribly *alive* for one long second afterward. The mass of Xoe push forward; Raia is trampled underfoot.

The trees enfold me. Something like shock paints the world in swirling madness, and I am numb.

Concealed among the trees, Noro, Kiri, and I move deeper into the wood. My head feels thick, my heartbeat weak but fast, my legs like strange bending sticks that somehow continue to propel me forward.

We stop in a spot crowded thick with giant firs. "Vaela," Noro says, snapping his fingers in my face, then lifting my chin until my eyes rise to meet his own. "Vaela. Come back. Come back to me." My skin is cold; his hands are like searing coals.

I feel I do not have the energy to open my mouth, though I see him, and I hear him speaking. I rub at the annoying itch on my face, look down at my fingers to see them slick with blood. Raia's blood? I don't know. Maybe. I wipe my hands on my trousers.

"Vaela." Noro pulls me down to my knees, his hands firm on my shoulders. "I'm here. I'm here, *miyara*."

I glance over at Kiri. There are tears in her eyes; I wonder abstractedly why I have none of my own.

"Say something," Noro says, shaking me slightly. "Say something to me, Vaela."

I nod, and continue nodding. There are words somewhere inside me. I feel them, like the drifting seeds of a cottonwood tree, moving slowly, bumping into one another. Something clicks. "We are all going to die," I say, as though I have only just realized that the annihilation of the Aven'ei means the *actual* annihilation of the Aven'ei.

Noro clenches his jaw. "Not you. Not you, Vaela. I want you and Kiri to make for the sea—you remember what I told you about the boats, Vaela? A mile at sea is unlike any other. You take a boat, you head for Ivanel. Live out your days there if you must. But live. Please, *miyara*, will you do this for me?"

Kiri shakes her head, tears still streaming down her cheeks, and points to the tree line, beyond which the great battle rages. She makes a fist and taps it to her heart.

"Your courage does you credit, sister," Noro says. "But you must go with Vaela."

I stare at him. "I'm not going to turn tail and run for the sea, Noro."

"You saw what happened," he says. "This is going to be a massacre. I should have sent the two of you away weeks ago. Now listen to me, and—"

I push his hands from my shoulders. "Don't make the mistake again of asking me to flee like a coward."

Kiri nods, double tapping her heart this time.

I see the pain and sorrow in Noro's eyes, but I cannot help him. The Aven'ei must fight, and I am no exception.

He exhales slowly. "Then both of you keep this in mind: today, you must be *inanei*. If you for even a moment lose sense of your surroundings, you will die. Follow every scenario in your mind to its conclusion before you act—and as much as possible, keep out of sight. Strike from the edges of the forest, where you may remain unseen. Return to the forest, after each strike. Be smart. Stay alive."

He kneels before Kiri, who wears an incredibly brave face considering the circumstances. "I love you, sister. I shall look for you in the hereafter, knowing that you lost your earthly life with honor."

Kiri nods, her chin trembling slightly. They embrace for a long moment, and I swallow, feeling as though there is a stone in my throat.

A moment later, Kiri turns to me. She pulls a long cord from beneath her leather tunic; my ruby dangles from the end, glittering warm and red.

"Forever," I say, throwing my arms around her. "Forever and ever, my sweet girl."

"Go, sister," Noro says, and like a whisper of wind, Kiri is gone.

Noro turns to me. Now that the moment of separation is upon us—the true goodbye—it is real. Pain is written on Noro's face—pain, regret, loss—a thousand emotions I have seen before, held close to my heart. This parting could not be more cruel. Yet still I do not cry.

"I must go as well. I cannot linger any longer—I must do what I can in battle." He takes me in his arms and kisses me. For one small moment, I am his, only his; there is no war to wrench us apart, no Xoe to deliver death. "Be strong, as I know you are. I love you."

"I love you."

"Remember what I said—be careful. Please, *miyara*, be careful."

"I will," I say, and my heart aches. I want to weep for the tragedy of it, for the senselessness and absurdity and waste of it all, but I cannot. I hurt—how I hurt—but tears are lost to me now, a thing of yesterday, a thing well beyond my reach. Tears will not bring Raia back. Tears will not save me—will not save any of us. We will bleed into the fields until the mud is scarlet with death, and the Xoe raise their voices in victory.

With one last look at me—a look so wrought with emotion I feel it may kill me where I stand—Noro turns and disappears into the trees.

CHAPTER 34

✦

I STAND ALONE IN THE WOOD, QUIET. THAT IS TO
say that *I* am quiet; the clash of steel, breaking of bones, crack-
ing of shields is thunderous, though I am a full hundred and
fifty yards from the battlefield. A vision of Raia's face in the
terrible moment of her death flashes in my mind; I close my
eyes. No. Not yet.

There is a task at hand, and I must focus. The weight of my
belt—heavy with steel, burdensome—tugs at my waist. I find
myself deeply aware of it. I run my fingers across the row of
knives, the cool blackwood hafts perfectly positioned and ready.
It is time to find a vantage point—to see what, if anything, can
be done. Despite Raia, despite everything—hope still burns in
my breast, though I accept that I will likely die within minutes
of any attempt I might make.

Nonetheless, I wipe my face and start toward the battlefield.
I will do what I can. I will survive as long as I can.

As I near the perimeter of the forest, I slow my pace, then
squat behind a wide tree. Through the sparse foliage, I can see
clearly, and before me is an unholy sight: the Xoe are pushing
the Aven'ei back with incredible power. The field is blanketed

with combatants, all moving eastward in a macabre procession of blood and death and horror.

My eyes dart from one engagement to the other, my mind boggling. The sheer mass of bodies moving and clashing together is staggering; the very ground beneath my feet shakes with the fury of war. The Aven'ei fight bravely, viciously for their survival—and everywhere, I see them fall as the Xoe press forward. For my part, I am overwhelmed—I have no idea what I can possibly do. There are no stragglers here, only thousands of warriors who are bigger, stronger, and deadlier than I. Noro said the *inanei* would move from the trees. I haven't the strength to slip in quietly and drag a man out of sight, but I may be able to move in and out unnoticed.

I watch as a Xoe cleaves the arm from an Aven'ei swordsman before plunging a dagger into his temple. My stomach roils. The Xoe turns to his right and staggers backward, the lengthy shaft of an arrow having just appeared in his chest. One knee goes to the ground as he clutches at the arrow, and before I even know what I am doing, I am sprinting toward him. Just as Noro taught me, I grip the man's chin with one hand and open his neck with the other.

A wash of blood spurts forth; I let go and race back toward the trees. I'm shaking once again, my hands trembling so much that I can scarcely grip my knife—my *knife*, slippery with blood, having finally fulfilled the dark purpose for which it was made. I head farther into the trees, stumbling on legs made of jelly.

I have killed a man.

I drop to my knees, let the blade fall from my fingers, and vomit. All I can smell is blood, and the scent makes me retch harder. My muscles convulse.

I have killed a man.

Hysteria rattles my mind and body, like a frightened animal might rail against the bars of a cage. I'm sick, so sick, and the blood won't come off my fingers, it only smears across my skin, slick and warm, drying in rusty brown streaks. I lean against the base of a tree, my breath coming in ragged gasps.

I have killed a man.

I stepped on a beetle once, many years ago in the Spire. For weeks, I could feel the crunch of its body reverberate beneath my bare foot, the oozing of its insides, wet and repulsive between my toes. Even now, I can recall the sensation, and an unpleasant shiver runs down my spine.

Today, I have made a new memory, one I'm sure I will be able to recall in vivid detail for the rest of my life, if my life were not to end today: the feel of my blade piercing the Xoe's throat, plunging through the skin, sliding across the flesh. The way the knife gave a split second of resistance before slicing through the rubbery artery that, once cut, would cause the man to bleed out.

I can feel it.

And I must do it again.

War is a convoluted thing: what is right is also wrong, and the things that must be done go against the very soul. To make war against a people who would be left alone—I see with clarity that this is wrong. To defend oneself against such an enemy—to kill, lest you be killed—it seems the only answer, but no less wrong. I cannot reconcile myself to any of it. But I cannot hide in the forest and pass the time with philosophy; I must return to the fighting. Now.

I make my way back to the battlefield. A mortally wounded Xoe lies on the ground not fifteen feet from me, her intestines spread like fat blue worms across her belly. To kill her would be a mercy, whether she be an ally or an enemy. To leave her would be cruel. This time, the decision is easy.

I hurry toward her; she looks up at me with fear in her deep gray eyes, her mouth opening and closing. A person, just like any other, now afraid, now dying. I curse the war beneath my breath—not the Xoe, the *war*—and whoever is leading it.

"Shush," I say softly. "Close your eyes. Everything will be all right."

I know she can't understand me, but I hope my words can give some measure of comfort. Her hands wander over her gut as she tries to put herself back together. I cut her throat swiftly, feeling again that same *tug* of the knife through flesh. Before I am finished, her eyes are wide, staring—her life evaporated like so much water left in the sun.

I glance up to ensure that I haven't been seen, and lock eyes with a slim, muscular Xoe just a few feet away. Bile rises in my throat. The man bears tattoos of yellow and blue on his face, wears a boiled-leather jerkin open at the sides, and carries an axe—a monstrous thing of wood and steel, smeared with blood from blade to tip.

He grins and steps toward me; I move back, matching his stride as though we are engaged in a deathly sort of dance. I reach for my belt and, with trembling hands, fling one of my knives at his face. It misses by several inches, but does buy me half a second to throw a second blade, then another in quick succession.

These two reach their mark. Both pierce the man's torso—going deeper even than I'd hoped. He glances down at his chest and I turn to run. I hear nothing over the sound of battle, but I sense the warrior behind me, and before I can reach the trees he grips me by the hair and jerks my head backward, so hard that my feet momentarily leave the ground. I reach for another knife and turn toward him; he slaps my face hard enough to make my ears ring. Stunned, I stand loosely on my feet, upright only because he still holds me by the hair.

My knives protrude from his chest like two pushpins marking locations on a map. The Xoe snarls at me under his breath—then spits in my face. The spittle is warm, tinged with blood, and it slips down my cheeks as I start to *laugh*.

I laugh hysterically, crazily, because I always thought I would die as an old woman, I would die in my sleep in the midst of a lovely dream. I would die in the Spire, safe, peaceful, surrounded by friends and family.

Not so. I will die here, today, with spit on my face, in the filthy wet muck. Alone.

The Xoe releases my hair only to tuck the axe into some type of holster at his belt and wrap both of his hands around my throat. Whispering, he tightens his grip, the muscles in his face quivering with adrenaline, with fury. The pressure at my neck increases until I can no longer draw breath. The warrior bends me to the ground and shakes me like a rag doll as he squeezes the life from my body. I claw at his fingers, raking his skin with my nails, but he holds me in place as though time has been suspended, his eyes on mine, my eyes on his. The world grows dark. My hands fall away, only to graze against one of the knives still in my belt. I don't want to die like this.

I grip the knife with my fingers, though I can scarcely feel it, and plunge it into his side, once, twice, again and again. The blade turns as it glances away from his ribs, and I stab him once more. I have become only this motion, this stabbing of the knife, this last act of desperation. My muscles are weakening, but I continue until the knife slips from my fingers.

I fought. I tried.

I feel myself moving backward, my body sinking into the mud. I am a pinprick of light in a world of shadows, and time is the water in which I dance.

It is dark and quiet in the moment of my death.

In the void, in that black place where I am content to dwell, a searing pain intrudes. I try to move against it, to ignore its noisome beckoning, but it only grows stronger; I open my eyes and draw in a breath—a thing of blistering, excruciating pain. I gasp, cough, choke, taste blood in my mouth. Not dead. Perhaps I was, but no longer.

The tunnel of my vision widens and I see the Xoe, standing a few feet away, swaying on his feet, examining the ruin of
flesh at his side made by my knife. Skin and muscle have been
flayed, now hanging in jagged flaps and ribbons. How many
times did I stab him? How does he still stand?

I roll onto my stomach. I lie scraping in the dirt, saliva dripping from my mouth, creating soft puddles in the soil beneath
my chin.

The Xoe is not done with me yet.

With one foot, he nudges me onto my back and pins me there.
I struggle to move, gasping as I try to push myself up. He pulls
the axe from his belt and swings it backward as though it were a
toy, and time seems to splinter as the blade moves toward me. I
close my eyes, my fate sealed. This time, I will die, and stay dead.

But the weapon does not reach me—there is no cold blade
at my neck, only the sound of a sharp, earsplitting *clang*. I open
my eyes to see that a long spear has been thrust directly in the
axe's path, stopping it midblow.

Shovo Ir'us stands to my left, holding the spear, his tattooed
face spattered with blood. With a swift stroke, he pulls the
weapon back and jams it up and into the Xoe's torso, piercing the man's heart. He is dead before the stroke is complete.
Skewered. His axe drops to the ground with a heavy thud, and
Shovo yanks the spear backward, wrenching it free. The Xoe
falls into the mud beside me, eyes staring, blood bubbling up
out of his mouth.

"Get up," Shovo growls, gripping me under the arms and
pulling me to my feet. He thrusts a weapon that looks like a
long, flat spade into my hands, and points to my right. "Remember the bull, Vaela Sun."

I follow his finger to see a Xoe bearing down on me with
all speed, not ten feet away. Shovo is gone; I hear the clash of
metal behind me, the grunting of men locked in battle. I grip
the long handle of the spade and brace myself. The Xoe is wild-

eyed, his face alight with a smear of tattoos, his muscled body lean and taut and dripping with sweat. He holds a hatchet in his left hand—a weapon meant for my head, I am sure. Just like the bull, that day on the farm—ready to spill my blood and remove me from his territory.

"Not today," I whisper. I spring from his reach as he raises the hatchet above his head, and bring the spade full force into collision with his face. The impact knocks him off his feet, stuns him for a moment—and a moment is all I need. I drop the weapon, pull a knife from my belt, and end him.

Shovo moves beside me; we are alone now at the edge of the wood. "The Aven'ei will be extinguished," he says, and gestures to the field.

I look out across the sea of men and women: at the thousands and thousands who fill the field above the Vale, and anguish fills my heart. The Xoe are so many, the Aven'ei seem so few. I cannot make a difference in this battle, nor can the warriors who now fight so fiercely. Numbers don't lie. The Xoe will prevail.

A noise fills the air, something greater even than the cacophony of war. It's like the buzzing of a bee; a terrible humming that echoes across the plain. Instinctively, I turn my head skyward, and joy beyond reason consumes me.

There, moving swiftly into position above the battlefield, is not one heli-plane, but *twelve*.

The Spire has come.

CHAPTER 35

✦

YES—THE SPIRE. BUT SOMETHING IS AMISS. THE
four-pointed star on each plane has been removed; a dark
blue gull is now painted across the side of each fuselage. The
Seagull—the symbol of the North.

These planes are much, much larger than the small craft I
have seen before. They hover above the center of the field,
white bodies massive and intimidating, the great propellers in
the wings spinning like mad. Enormous cargo doors slide open
on each plane, one after another, to reveal men clad in heavy
armor—six to each side, all positioned behind mounted guns.
The largest craft, the one at the center of the formation, hangs
lower in the air than the others, and has no fewer than fifteen
guns on each side.

In a pocket of clear ground, a hail of bullets rains down around
the center craft. Clods of dirt and charred grass spike upward
into the sky; the power of the Spirian weapons—weapons that
make no sense to me—cannot be denied. A crackle cuts across
the field, and an amplified voice booms out a warning: "Cease
fighting. Cease this war. Stop, or you will be killed."

The warriors are distracted, yet still they attack one another.

Even the appearance of twelve massive heli-planes is not enough to impress the people of the Continent.

The message is repeated; the fighting continues.

Shots ring out above us; the noise is deafening. Four Xoe fall nearby, and two Aven'ei, and hundreds more across the plain. With few exceptions, the battle comes to an abrupt halt.

"Cease fighting," the voice calls out again; I am astonished to realize that it belongs to Mr. Lowe. "You will cease hostilities at once, or you will be killed."

The few areas where skirmishing continues are now targeted, and more fall dead. The warriors, Xoe and Aven'ei alike, howl at the heli-planes with impotent fury. Arrows fly toward the aircraft, but glance away or are deflected by the men with shields.

"This war is ended," booms Mr. Lowe. "Any further hostilities will result in violence against the perpetrators. Return to your own territories."

There is movement and general consternation among the throng of warriors. A single arrow flies toward the center plane; the man who loosed it is shot.

"Return to your territories."

Whether or not the Xoe understand the language, they have clearly received the message. The fighters step away from one another—the Xoe backing away westward, the Aven'ei moving to the east.

Maker, I pray, *let Noro, Kiri, and Talan still live. Please, let them live.*

As the men and women disperse, another message sounds from the sky: "Vaela Sun, if you live, please come to the center craft and await further instructions. Vaela Sun, please come to the center craft."

Shovo, still beside me, raises an eyebrow. "Important, are we?"

"I'm the only Spirian on the ground."

His lip curves, but the smile is kind, not cruel. "You're no Spirian, Vaela Sun."

My throat, still aching, tightens. "No. I'm not."

He gestures to the heli-plane. "Shall I escort you?"

"I would appreciate that very much—but...I must look for Noro, Kiri, and Talan first. I have to know if they are all right."

Shovo laughs and claps me on the back, as though we are old comrades in arms. "Go to the *azmera*—if they are alive, they heard the message plain as we did, and they'll be coming to see if you survived."

I consider this. Thousands lie dead or dying around us. Thousands more tend to the wounded, or mill about in groups across the battlefield. To search the throng seems an almost impossible task.

I nod. "I'll keep a lookout from the plane."

We pick our way across the field, Shovo with his weapon still at the ready, though the Xoe have largely cleared out. I think to myself that Shovo probably sleeps with a spear in his hand, one eye open, ever on the alert. I am most likely right.

As we step into the shadow of the great center craft, Mr. Lowe looks down at me from the open cargo door. He clasps his hands together, smiles brightly, and instructs one of his men to roll out a long metal ladder.

I turn to Shovo. "Thank you for saving my life."

"There is no need to offer thanks."

Shame rushes through me. "Yes, there is. I'm sorry, Shovo. For everything. And for what I said at the farm. I was wrong, so wrong."

"There is no need for that, either. Let us put away the past, in the face of new circumstances." He gestures to the ladder. "Give my gratitude to the warriors above. They have done a good thing today."

Mr. Lowe greets me aboard the heli-plane with a grin so broad it seems to stretch across his entire face. "Miss Sun, how relieved I am to find you alive!" He gives me a once-over and his expression turns to one of horrified concern. "But...are you quite all right? There's...your throat, it's badly marked—what happened?"

I know I must look a mess; blood and dirt alike seem to be crammed into my every pore. "I'm alive, sir."

He gestures to a row of plush seats along the back of the cargo area. "Come and sit."

"Might we stay here, near the open door? I am hoping a few friends might come to find me, having heard your message."

"But of course," he says, and we take a seat along the edge while a uniformed man affixes a safety harness about my shoulders. I keep a sharp watch on the battlefield below, hoping against hope that I shall see Noro, Kiri, or Talan. "All set there?" he says.

"Thank you, Mr. Lowe. I'm sure I cannot express my surprise at your interference, and my gratitude for it. I scarcely know what to say."

He smiles and pulls a sheet of folded parchment from his breast pocket. He opens the paper and places it in my hands; it is the map I drew for the officials of the Spire. The Vale—one of the very few places I mentioned by name when I spoke of the impending Xoe attack—is encircled with bright red ink. He taps the paper lightly with one finger. "You said all that needed to be said, back in the Chancellery."

"But the Spire voted to—"

"Yes," he says. "And the North has chosen to act alone."

"But...doesn't that mean—"

He nods. "Yes. Exile. I'm sorry, my dear. The Spire is dissolved—the Nations are united no more."

I feel as though I've been hit with a hammer, as though every ounce of sense has been struck from my body. "But—that can't be. Did you speak with the Chancellery before you came?"

"Of course. We petitioned the council to review and reconsider the plight of the Aven'ei. We were rebuked, and warned that to act against a majority vote is to enter into an act of war." His eyebrows draw together, and I see for the first time how tired he looks. "The North was cut off from the other Nations in the interim, pending our decision."

"But you came anyway. Knowing it would mean the dissolution of the Treaty."

"We did."

"To save the Aven'ei?"

"To stop the ceaseless bloodshed here—something I fear we ought to have done long ago. How many thousands might have been saved if only we had tried to help, tried to assist the Aven'ei and the Xoe to establish peace sooner than this? It is shameful that we stayed away. We might have helped to save so many. So many." Grief haunts the blue-white depths of his eyes; remorse marks the smooth angles of his face.

"Mr. Lowe." I almost cannot find words, I am so confused. "You in the North have a military force—how is that possible?"

He smiles, though grimly. "Every Nation in the Spire conducts a clandestine armed force, Miss Sun, and has done so for years. Each simply turns a blind eye to the other."

This is too much. I press my hands against my forehead. The world is supposed to be a peaceful place. None of the Nations of the Spire would have been preparing for war. How could it even have happened?

Would they have?

I shake my head. "I spoke with the Chancellor before I returned to the Continent," I say. "And I daresay he himself would be happy to see the Continent burn from east to west, and the Xoe and Aven'ei with it. That's a fact, is it not?"

Mr. Lowe offers an awkward smile. "The Chancellery, as a whole, was merely charged with upholding the Treaty, and that was dissolved with the Spire. We of the North are an independent Nation now, as is the East, which declared to defect along with us. The West and South have allied together—the borders are sealed."

"Mr. Lowe," I say, my throat tightening, "have I helped to end one war only to sow the seeds of another?"

"I wouldn't use that word just yet," he says. "I am hopeful that ultimately, the Four Nations may unite again. And in any case, the responsibility for what has happened does not rest on *your* shoulders—you merely asked for help when help was needed, Miss Sun.

"Our chief concern is that the violence here comes to an end, at least for now. Clearly, an emergency has been declared. The North has taken Ivanel, Vaela, and we shall maintain patrols and assist in the construction of defenses, and, ultimately, the effort for peace, as you yourself so wisely suggested. This war will *not* be renewed—we in the North will see to it. I mourn every life taken today by my soldiers. But if the deaths of a few will save the Aven'ei and Xoe from ongoing violence, I consider it a fair price for peace."

"It's a heavy cost," I say, thinking of the blood on my own hands. "Death must always be a terrible price."

"Indeed."

"With all that's happening…will you now attempt to resume relations with the Aven'ei?"

He smiles. "Miss Sun, we intend to do far more than that. We do not look merely for intervention, or conversation, or philosophical accord. It is our deepest wish that the Aven'ei should become allies to the North."

"Allies," I say, openly surprised. "Equals?"

"In all things."

"And the Xoe? Are you to reach out to them as well?"

"Ah," he says, and smiles. "That will take a bit of doing."

"But you will try?"

He laughs. "Are you an optimist, Miss Sun, or a politician?"

"A fresh start ought to be fresh for all, no?"

"Mmm," he says. "A bit of both then. Well. We shall certainly do our very best. But forgive me, I nearly forgot—we've brought a friend of yours along! He has been so hoping to see you."

"Which friend, sir?"

"Hold on there, we'll just bring him over—he's aboard another plane."

A few minutes later, the heli-plane nearest us moves out of position; another plane takes its place, and through the open cargo door I see Mr. Cloud, looking very sharp in one of the sleek navy blue uniforms of the North. He waves and claps his hands together, his warm blue eyes reflecting a lightness I have not seen in him before. An elastic platform is laid from plane to plane, and a few men work to secure it. I peer out the door to see if Noro, Kiri, or Talan have come, but the field is empty below us; my heart twists, but I hold on to hope.

Mr. Cloud trundles across the bridge and removes his hat. "Miss Sun, you're indestructible, aren't you, now?" His eyes shine as he shakes his head. "I'm so glad to see you safe, miss."

Given all that has just happened, I cannot tolerate the formality of his manner. It gives me such great joy to see him again that I throw my arms about his waist at once. "I am glad to see you, too."

It takes him a moment, but he returns my embrace. "Well, I—I don't rightly know that I deserve such affection, Miss Sun. But I do think of you as family now, just in my own way of thinking, as it were."

I step back and smile up at him. "Just so, Mr. Cloud. It is just so."

He looks abashed, but smiles all the same. "I'm now *Military* Director of Ivanel," he says.

"I wondered about the uniform," I reply, brushing a bit of lint from his shoulder. "Congratulations to you, sir—I can't think of anyone more deserving."

"I'm proud to be of the North," he says, looking out across the Vale. "Couldn't be prouder."

"And well you should be."

"So if you're to stay here on the Continent, and I'm to be nearby at Ivanel, I don't wonder if we ought to manage a visit now and then?"

"That would be lovely! I'm sure I—"

"Vaela!" comes a call from below, nearly whisked away by the noise of the engines. *"Vaela!"*

I hurry to the edge of the plane, my heart hammering in my chest. And in one instant, hope turns to joy, as I look down to see Noro and Kiri, bloodied and battered and *alive*, waving up at me from the field.

The extension is deployed and I climb down as quickly as I can. Noro pulls me off the ladder and into his arms, holding me close, so close, and the kiss he gives me is enough to set my heart on fire. We cling to one another, awash with a relief that knows no bounds, a joy tempered only by all we have lost.

When he sets me down, I drag Kiri toward me and wrap my arms around both of them. We are all in happy tears, even my beautiful, stoic Noro, my love. I look down at Kiri. "Are you hurt, sweet one?"

She lifts her arm to reveal a gruesome gash along her side. But her eyes show pride rather than pain, and I cannot help but laugh. She points to a boy nearby who looks to be about her age.

"Go," I say, but kiss her cheek before she runs off, and she, for once, allows this soft gesture of affection, holding me tightly. I turn to Noro. "And you?"

A slim wound runs along his left cheekbone; I trace a path beside it with my finger.

"I have never felt better." He takes my hand, running his thumb over my nails, the beds of which are encrusted with blood. "Are you all right?"

"I'm fine, I promise."

He touches me lightly, just above the collarbone. "Many of your knives are missing, Vaela, and there are marks upon your neck."

"I am alive, Noro."

"Did you take life today?"

"I did what any Aven'ei would have done," I say, echoing his words from the night we first met.

There is sadness in his eyes. "This is not a burden I wanted for you."

"I know."

"I will help you bear it."

"I know that, too."

He pulls me close and rests his chin atop my head. "We have lost much today."

I close my eyes and think of Raia, so strong and skilled, dead in half a second. Grief tugs at me, familiar and new, beckoning me to that dark place of loss and regret. How I long to be home in the cottage, where I might entertain my memories and cry for the empty place she has left in the world. I pull away, and Noro releases me.

"Have you seen Talan?" I ask. "Does he live?"

Noro nods. "He is alive, but none the happier for it now that Raia is gone. He is badly wounded—the healers are seeing to him now."

"Shovo lives," I say. "He saved my life."

Noro thinks on this for a moment, then gives me a small smile. "For this, I shall swear to him my everlasting friendship. No matter how much it may pain me to do so."

"People change. Just look at you: a smile on your face and hope in your heart." He kisses me, and I wrap my arms about his neck. "What do we do now?"

"Now," he says, "we bury the dead, help the wounded, and go back to life in Kastenai."

"A life without war," I say.

"We shall see."

"It is done now," I say, gesturing up at the heli-planes. "The North has come to ensure peace. You need never wear the shadow of the *inanei* again."

"Always be mine, Vaela Sun, and no shadow shall ever pass before me."

I kiss him lightly on the lips. "I am yours, Noro. Now, and always, in war and peace, on the Continent or anywhere else in the world."

A light breeze kicks up around us, swirling dust from the field into spinning cones that sweep across the plain. I look into the eyes of the man I love, and I know peace once again. For now.

Sometimes, now is enough.

★ ★ ★ ★ ★

ACKNOWLEDGMENTS

◆

THANK YOU, THANK YOU, THANK YOU TO MY best friend forever and partner in everything, Michael.

Thank you to my daughter, for whom this book was written. Pea, you are my shining star, and I love you infinity.

Thank you to my mom and dad, who instilled in me from a very young age the belief that I could accomplish anything to which I set my mind. They also suffered through years of short stories about vengeance-seeking elk and all other kinds of ridiculousness, and paid twenty-five cents to sit through theatrical reenactments of my favorite stories—including one very busy performance of *Mrs. Piggle-Wiggle*, in which I played *all* of the characters. In short, they loved me, they encouraged me, and they put up with me. They are the best.

Thank you to my agent, the amazing Jim McCarthy, for believing in *The Continent* and finding the perfect editor for my work—Natashya Wilson at Harlequin TEEN (more on Tashya in a moment). Jim is not only The Best Agent in The Entire World, but he is also my friend and my calmer-downer, and I'm grateful every day to know and have the privilege of working with such an incredible person.

Natashya Wilson (my aforementioned editor) had the insight to help me polish *The Continent* into the book it is now, and to find skilled sensitivity readers to help in the revision. I am so grateful for her guidance and understanding.

I must also thank the rest of the people at Harlequin TEEN. From Day One, their collective enthusiasm level has been nothing short of a confetti-exploding cannon. Thank you to Siena Koncsol, Bryn Collier, Loriana Sacilotto, Evan Brown, Ashley McCallan, Rebecca Snoddon, Olivia Gissing, Lauren Smulski, Shara Alexander, Margaret Marbury, Erin Craig, Kathleen Oudit, and everyone else for your hard work and faith in the book!

Thank you to Valerie Noble, who is not *my* agent but who is an absolute Agent Extraordinaire. Without Valerie, I might still be querying. She was generous to give me incisive notes that ultimately resulted in my becoming agented. Speaking of other agents, thank you to Brent Taylor, Uwe Stender, Pam Victorio, and all the rest for always being supportive and wonderful.

I'd like to include a huge shout-out to a few of my favorite video-game composers—without their music, I don't know how I would write: Nobuo Uematsu, Darren Korb, Jesper Kyd, Koji Kondo, Jeremy Soule, Inon Zur, and Yasunori Mitsuda, just to name a few.

Thank you to my primary beta, sensitivity, and proofreaders: Cidne Balzer, Amber Bird, Chantel Street, Lucille Hamilton, Rena Olsen, May Bridges, Danyelle Toval, Tonja Tomblin, Dhonielle Clayton, Tamieka Evans, Amanda Goodman, and Jeff Baumgartner. I could not have done this without your support, encouragement, and criticism. ALL THE LOVE!

And last, but not least, let me thank my friends, and all the bloggers/reviewers who have supported me. You make every day brighter, and there are too many of you to name, but I love and appreciate you all!